RUSH OF JEALOUSY

ENTICE SERIES BOOK TWO

VICTORIA DAWSON

PAPER HEART PUBLISHING LLC

Rush of Jealousy

Publisher: Paper Heart Publishing LLC

Cover Designer: Sarah Kil Creative Studio

Editing: Happily Editing Anns

ISBN (Paperback): 978-1-959364-03-0

ISBN (ebook): 978-1-959364-02-3

AUTHOR NOTE

Rush of Jealousy is the second book in the *Entice Trilogy* that follows the same two main characters throughout the entire series. It is advised to read the books in order. This series is intended for mature audiences. Sensitive topics discussed could be triggering and not meant for anyone under the age of eighteen.

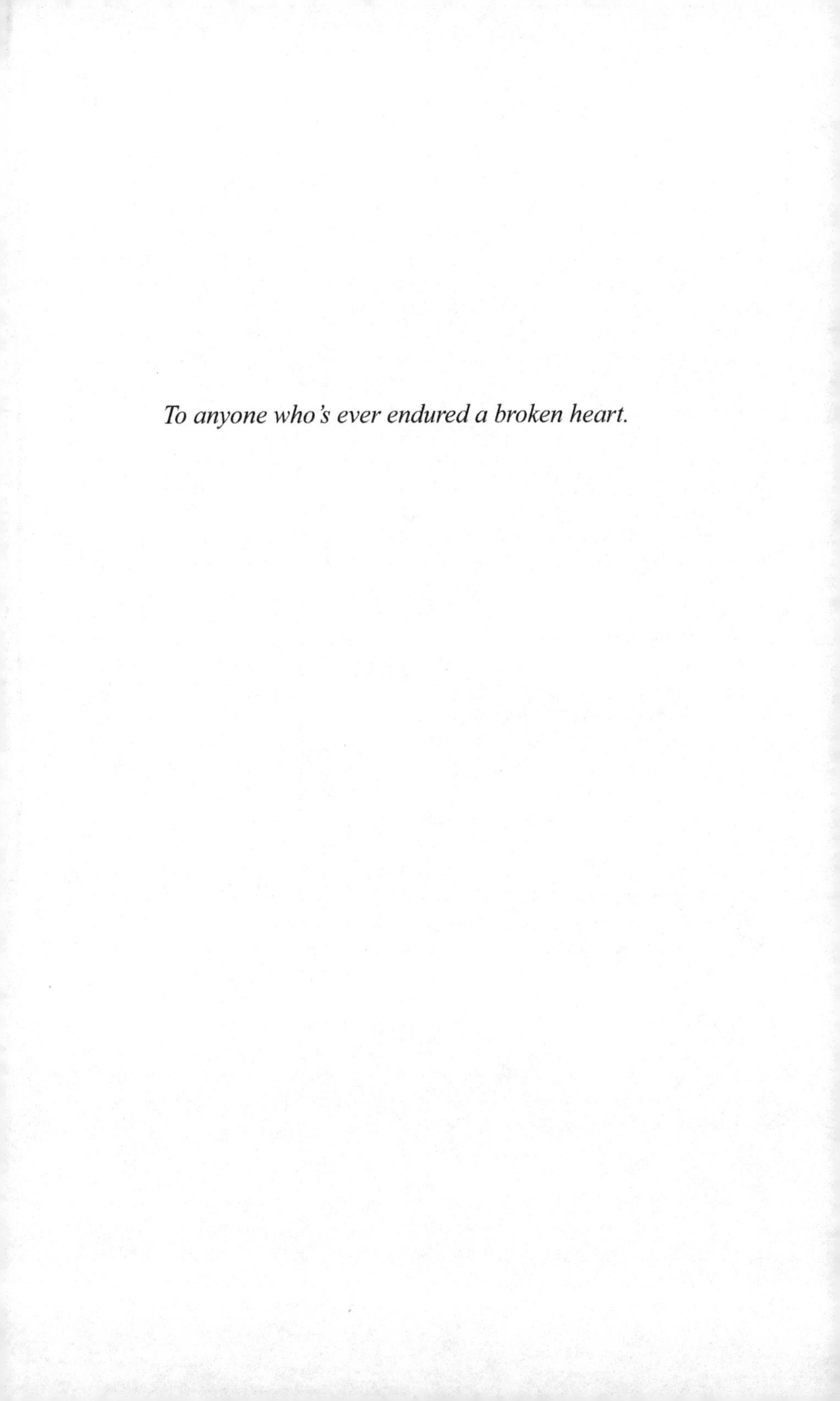

To anyone who's ever endured a broken heart.

1

When the doors open to the fifth floor, I exit and walk along a long corridor, peering inside every room. I pass six rooms and they are all deserted. The sound of a masculine timbre echoes in my ears, and it is instantly recognizable. I know the source before having the visual confirmation. It is Graham fucking Hoffman.

I tug down the flaps of my trench coat and adjust my bag's straps over my shoulder. I pick up my pace to get to the end of the hallway, adrenaline and anger spurring me on. My pulse is racing, and the air in my lungs enters and exits in a painful rhythm. I feel crazed. Like a bomb is about to go off in my soul.

I hear my phone buzz in my bag and pull it out just to see another picture appear on the screen from a mystery number. I grip my phone like a vise and run the remainder of the way to the meeting room. I slam open the door, the sound ricocheting against the walls.

Expletives explode out of the mouths of the dozen

employees who surround a long glass conference table. Several push their leather chairs back in a panic and jerk up from the table. A couple of chairs fall backward, crashing to the floor.

My eyes lock with Graham's. His hands are braced on the glass surface, leaning over it. He is at the other end of the table—in a position of power. My eyes well with tears as I hurl my phone at his head. He ducks just in time for it to graze his shoulder and fall to the ground.

"Bastard! You bastard!" I snarl.

"Angie, what the hell?" he screams, regaining his posture. He has the nerve to look astonished over my reaction, as if he didn't expect me to figure it all out.

"Don't you *what the hell* me! You have been tormenting me and lying to me for weeks!"

"Graham, do something!" a feminine voice yells. She is the only female in the room other than me.

I glance toward the melodic sound and spot the cherry-red lips before I see the dyed blonde hair. Sophia. Shocker. Nothing should surprise me anymore. I am living in some alternate reality where fact and fiction are so muddled up that it is hard to tell reality from fantasy.

I feel the air enter my coat, and I realize that the tie has come undone and my skimpy dress is now on display for every employee to see. I don't care. I can't find any fucks in me to give other than to find out why Graham has been living a double life. He owes me an explanation for the lies, the betrayal, the extortion.

"I can explain," he says calmly.

It is his quiet understated demeanor that sets me over the edge. It's as if the detonator is hit. A growl roars through my throat like a raging fire that cannot be contained. I hop up onto the table and make my way toward him.

My knees crunch on papers, and pencils break under the force. Glasses of water and mugs full of hot coffee slosh over onto folders and quarterly documents. Some fly to the floor in a sticky, broken mess.

Another male makes an announcement. I don't hear his words, just his demanding tone. The room clears out in a hurry, and Graham is left alone at the opposite end of the table, just a couple of yards away from my crawling form.

His smug face makes me want to throw up. When I reach my destination, I jump down and smack my hands at Graham's face in concentrated rage.

"Angie, stop, you are going to hurt yourself," he warns, capturing my wrists and securing them behind my back. He pins me against the table and almost looks amused. Almost.

"Bastard! Asshole!" I scream at full volume. "I hate you!"

"Good."

"Why? Why are you drugging women on campus?" I demand. "You are sick!"

Graham's flinch makes me twitch. He looks angry for the first time since I burst into his meeting.

"Why are you sending me scary text messages?" I scream. "Blackmailing me!"

"Let's talk."

"I am talking! I found all of your secrets. I found the phones and the bottles of pills and the secret clothes and IDs."

"You've been busy."

"And you own Entice? What the hell! I found it all. You've been exposed."

"It's not what you think," he mutters.

"You are deranged."

"Me? I am deranged?"

"Yes!"

"You are the one sneaking into my building, and I can only assume tricking and manipulating my employees. You are attacking *me*. On my turf, might I add. So if you think you are going to control this situation now, think again."

"Don't you dare play the victim!" I scream, pushing my bound body forward.

Graham releases my wrists.

"You need to calm down," he warns.

"Did you," I start in a shaky voice, "drug me the night at The Shack?"

"Of course not!" he snaps. "Are you out of your mind? How can you even think that? I've been spending all of my energy trying to protect you! I am in love with you and you have no freaking clue just how much. I would never hurt you."

"Love?"

"Yes, dammit." He rakes his fingers through his hair and glances away from me for just a second. "I tried to avoid it, trust me, I did. But there can be no more denying the feelings I have for you."

"You are in *love* with me?" My words come out so slow. "You have got to be joking!"

"It's true," he admits without hesitation.

"No." I shake my head adamantly. My nose runs with my watery eyes. "No, Graham. None of this"—I sweep my hands out—"is love. This is lies. Betrayal. Secrets. And even when caught, you have no concept of telling the truth. This is not love, you lunatic! This is some demented emotion you fabricated in your head that I am not interested in accepting."

"You need to calm the hell down. And then we can discuss this like adults."

"No." Minutes ago I wanted an explanation but not anymore. I won't trust whatever he has to say anyway.

"Yes, Angela." He sighs. "Let's go chat in my office where it will be more comfortable."

"No! Do you not even hear me? I do not want to listen to you spew lies and try to cover up this crap! I need to clear my head and—"

My words are halted as he grabs my elbow and guides me out of the room. Several of his employees are hovering around a coffee maker whispering what I can only assume is speculative gossip about me. Tears burn my eyes as I try to make sense of everything. Nothing adds up. But I need time to think. The only way to clear my head is to have time away from Graham.

"If you all still want to have a job after you come back from your break, then I would advise you to keep your mouths shut!" he snaps over to the snack area.

Instantly the room goes silent, and for that I'm thankful. Graham's hand still clenches my elbow, but the emotional hold on me has already been shattered. I tug my coat around me tighter, crossing my arms at my chest.

When we get to the elevator, I twist out of his hold and shove him with all of my force. He stumbles backward as I dart into the waiting car and slam my hand against the close button. Graham yells my name and hits what I assume are the metal protective doors with his fists. The echoing sound and the string of muffled curse words fill my ears. I punch the lobby button and wait for the descent.

I cannot believe I fell for the devil disguised as a white knight. Just when I think it is safe to leave my heart unprotected, it gets broken. Again. I dig through my bag for another pill to help some of the pain fade away. I look down at my wrinkled attire and try to remember this moment in time. I guess this is what rock bottom looks like. I commit it to memory, so when I feel like slipping into it again, I will know better.

The doors open, and I exit in a hurry. I hear my name being called by voices I don't recognize, but I keep walking my fast pace. I stomp past the water fountains. Then I cross in front of the section of couches. I approach the security checkpoint with determination pumping through my veins.

When I get to the metal detectors, I stumble backward, as an arm grabs at me. "Hey!" I resist and flail, only causing my body to be pulled into a wall of hard muscle and detained.

"Miss McFee," the stranger says, out of breath. "Stop fighting."

"Let me go!" I demand, spinning my body around to see a man wearing a headset and security badge that is pinned to his uniform. "Please," I beg.

"I'm not at liberty to let you leave this building, ma'am."

"Please," I plea. "Please just let me go. Tell your boss I'll text him." I try to sound convincing.

"I'm sorry," his voice cracks just enough to show a

sliver of sensitivity.

"Please," I say again. "I just need to breathe." I look toward the windows to the outside world, my freedom. "I just need some fresh air."

I wait for the sympathetic look to fill his eyes, and then I jerk to the side and run toward the emergency exit door. I am almost there when out of nowhere, Graham appears from what I assume is a stairwell door. He moves to block the exit I am on a mission to get through. As soon as my mind can catch up and I realize it is a futile attempt, I stop and hunch my shoulders in defeat.

His demeanor is angry. He looks pissed off and ready for war. He silently gives a nod to his security officer who stands on guard and ready to pounce on me if I step out of line. It is militaristic and raises every red flag I have in my arsenal.

Graham stomps toward me, and I cower back a few inches. I close my eyes in fear and open them at the tug of the tie around my waist as he conceals my outfit under the shield of my trench coat. I can only imagine how many people in this building—including those working in the security camera room—have gotten a view of my body. I guess I can add those people to the list who have seen indecent pictures of me while grinding against Graham in public places. He was in the pictures, so there is no way he could have taken them himself. My guess is that Collins is the photographer, and despite his professionalism in all things, it still will make me feel gross to be around him.

For someone who strives to avoid drama, it seems to keep finding me. The common denominator? Graham Hoffman.

Good thing for me, this all ends today.

I. Am. Done.

A string of curse words flutters out of his mouth as he rubs the sweat off his forehead. The only people here in the lobby are us and security. And I realize now that the only way for me to leave here is to have the conversation with Graham that I desperately want to avoid.

My mind spins and my head throbs from the chaos I've had to endure over the past hour. I feel on edge, as if the slightest breeze could make me crumble. I want to go home and lie down. I want to go to sleep and dream away this nightmare.

"Open up room three," Graham says in his authoritative voice to the man who stopped me just minutes ago.

"Yes, sir."

"And not a single interruption."

"Of course, sir."

"Be on standby. Call up to the CC room and figure out how to avoid this in the future."

I watch dumbly as the man scurries off to do his ordered chores.

Graham glares down at me with determined eyes and gestures toward the open door that is located back past the elevator banks.

"Walk calmly or be carried."

I shake my head at his testy directives but choose to walk just to avoid further embarrassment—even if it pisses me off beyond words. Right now, I don't have a choice. He is going to make me listen to what he has to say—whether I like it or not. And deep down, I hate him a little more for it.

When we get inside the small room that simply has a

desk, a computer, and three chairs, I take a seat at the one closest to the door we just arrived through. My sniffles are the only sound that is heard in the closed space.

Graham hands me a box of tissues, and I pull a few out. I wipe at my eyes and at my nose. Each time I wipe away moisture, more appears in its place. It's like a faucet is turned on, and I cannot stop the flow.

He leans his body up against the front of the desk and strums his fingers over the side. The pattering sound raises my anxiety.

"Please don't cry, Angie." His tone is soft and would be comforting if I wasn't so broken from what he did.

My eyes slide up his suited body until they reach his eyes. "You are the reason for the tears." I sniffle.

Graham rubs at his temple, and I wonder if he has the same splitting headache that I have. "About a year ago my sister, Penny, was drugged," he starts, "and possibly raped. At the very least, assaulted."

I swallow hard and watch as his shoulders tense. He looks exhausted. As if he has not slept in weeks. And maybe he hasn't.

"It has changed my entire family forever," he explains. "I vowed to myself that I would find out what happened to her. She remembers nothing. Has no recollection of the night or the moments leading up to being found. As I started following the trail of people she interacted with, I uncovered an escort agency she got herself wrapped up in. Penny has always been carefree and impressionable. She trusts people at face value and always tries to see the good in others. She was in college but didn't really know the direction she wanted to take for her studies. After a few modeling jobs, she started to get involved in that type of lifestyle of the elite. She encountered a few of the wrong people who wanted to use her ambition to further her portfolio against her. Anyway, after her attack and the discovery of the escort agency that she got involved with, I secretly formed a similar company so that I could"—Graham pauses as he struggles for the right words—"how do I put it?"

"Use the girls to help you get information?"

I watch as he runs his hands through his hair to the back of his neck. "Have easier access, yes."

"So you used them as bait?"

He ignores my comment. "I also have access to the men purchasing the escorts. This is invaluable to me, because then at least I have a finite list of suspects. I could also separate those who have criminal backgrounds who try to seek access and get denied. Those names are meaningful as well."

"But the girls are guinea pigs, right? Expendable?"

He lets out a sigh.

"That's messed up, Graham. And the fact that you don't understand that is the most disturbing part of all. We are all just little game pieces for your quest at revenge." I can tell I hit a nerve by the way he flinches and goes back to strumming his fingers against the side of the desk.

"The agency is a decoy, Angie. It is not my end goal or company of choice to run. I'm simply utilizing my resources. I had a suspicion that something devious was happening in the underground business world. Most cities are riddled with corruption and unsavory practices. I spent months with no real leads. Months of agony watching my little sister battle her demons in and out of psychiatric centers. She is a shell of who she used to be. Irrevocably changed forever."

"I'm sorry," I say softly.

He closes his mouth into a tight line and nods.

"How does Dominic fit in?" I ask, purely out of curiosity.

"He is, for the sake of simplicity, the second in command. However, to the outside world, he is the owner."

I think back to the few times I was in the Entice office, but specifically to Friday's mediation. No wonder it was such a circus act. The attendants probably laughed their asses off afterwards over my naivete. I imagine most were just going through the motions to make the session look believable. When in reality, there was no way for me to win all along. What a sick joke. And Dominic allowed me to hold on to hope that a happy resolution would occur. This is such a mess.

"And what am I? Just another stupid girl, that's what," I say, answering my own lame question.

"You are everything to me. Everything, Angie. During the mixer event where I saw you hanging out at the pool, I knew I was in trouble. You are the exact kind of trouble that could make men like me try to be better."

My eyes narrow at his stupid declaration. "Why is this a bad thing? Is it so wrong to want to be a decent human being, Graham?"

"Being a good guy doesn't get me justice. Being a good guy will just get me killed. Or worse, someone I love killed. So believe me when I say, I tried to steer you away from me. I knew I could not stay away from you on my own. So I tried to do the opposite."

I huff. "Well, we both know how that turned out."

"You became my obsession."

"An expensive one too," I respond bitterly over the exorbitant amount of money he threw my way.

"I never cared about the money."

"Neither did I."

"I know and that made me like you even more. Fall even harder."

I shake my head as if I'm trying to deflect the words from entering my ears. As if I can shield them from the softness of Graham's voice. He is finally opening up to me, telling me truths—if perhaps just half ones. Except it's too late. He waited too long. And deep inside I can't help but wonder what he would be sharing freely if I'd never snuck into his office.

His eyes connect with mine, studying me. "So I tried to get you to only date me. I tried to get you so pissed off that you would quit working. I tried to scare you with potential blackmail so you would—"

"Lean on you for support," I finish. "Rely only on you. Be terrified out of my mind that my life was in danger."

He gives me a shrug and crosses his ankles on the floor. I stare down at his feet, unable to lock eyes with him without wanting to gouge them out of their sockets. My anger is simmering again.

"But you are stubborn. So stubborn, Angela McFee. You just do not stop. Any sane person would have backed away. Not you. You just would not quit. You would not date solely me. You would not take the money and run. Nothing worked. Not even blackmail and a ransom."

"You can't control everything."

"Your life is still in danger, Angie. But now I have no idea whether it is in direct connection with me or by default from working in the agency."

"So why not shut everything down?"

"That would draw too much suspicion. I am working on all of this. I just need more time."

Where does Graham even draw the line on right and wrong? Are we all just puppets in his pursuit to find justice for his sister?

"You are done seeing Tanner," he bites out.

"How is Mark even involved in all of this?" I rasp, my voice strained from my mouth being parched.

"That I'm not one hundred percent sure of. But there are too many coincidences."

"Then why all the warnings about him if you have no proof? Why all the anger toward me going out on a couple of dates with him? Why any of the fuss?"

"Because you are mine!"

"Was."

"Are."

"No, Graham. Not anymore."

"Angie..."

"You tormented me by tampering with my profile. You made me have a mediation meeting where you gaslighted me. You sent me terrifying messages to convince me I was in danger, using a bunch of burner phones that could not be traced. And you had one of your worker bees snap pictures of me in compromising positions. How could you?"

"Ang—"

"Shut up! I am not done yet!" I scream at the top of my lungs. "You made me feel cheap, Graham. Used me. You think I deserved that? That you were entitled to do that to me—all for the sake of getting what you wanted? You blackmailed me into your arms. And for what? To gain me for a night just to lose me the next day?"

Graham winces at my words. He hangs his head in frustration—probably because there is no real excuse for how he behaved toward me. He could have told the truth during the weeks he has known me. He could have trusted me enough to handle the truth. But instead, he went about this entirely the wrong way. Doing the one thing that would keep me permanently away from him. He became a liar. Untrustworthy. And that is not okay with me. None of this is okay with me.

"I am sorry."

"Sorry?" I throw my hands up into the air. "That's all you have to say after all of the shit you put me through?" How traumatized in their past must someone be to believe that this is actually love?

His eyes turn desperate, and his fingers clench. "I never wanted you hurt."

"Hurt *you* caused, Graham. Take some responsibility. Your actions have consequences, despite your intentions. You did this to me! Happy now?" I ask, tears flooding out of my eyes. "You took advantage of me! You fucking took my virginity under false pretenses. If I'd known the real you, I probably wouldn't have given it up! At least not to a man like you! I deserve better than this."

He stands up from his perch, just to fall to his knees in front of me. He places his hands on my thighs, and I shove them away. The room suddenly feels claustrophobic, as if his entire existence is taking up all the available oxygen. I am unable to breathe.

"Graham," I warn.

He ignores me, as usual. He wraps his arms around my waist and rests his head in my lap. I grip the arm rests, careful not to touch him. My tears drip into his hair and onto his left cheek. He closes his eyes and squeezes them tightly shut.

"Graham," I say again. "Please. Just let me go."

"I don't know if I can."

"Well, you don't really have a choice."

"I have this strong need to protect you."

"I have a stronger need to protect myself. And right now, I need to protect my heart from further damage. But just answer me something first."

He sits back on his heels and looks up into my eyes. His are bloodshot. "Okay."

"What about Claire?"

His nose flares. "What about her?" he snarls.

"How does she fit into all of this?"

"Damn Claire for getting you involved," he says, getting up from the floor to sit across from me. "You'd be safe if it wasn't for her."

"How do you know? How do you know I wouldn't just be another number in the list of girls getting drugged anyway?"

"Because only agency girls are being drugged. That is the commonality," Graham explains. "And it's getting worse. There is no way for me to protect you if you are dating anyone from the database. No one is safe anymore."

"But Resa. I don't think she's an escort."

"She's not. But she was never drugged. Whoever was chasing her on your townhouse row must have mistaken her for someone else. Or it was related to another crime."

"But why just certain girls?"

"Probably because no one would take any girl seriously if they delve into their past. No one wants to be labeled as an escort—let alone a prostitute. Damaging someone's credibility is basically like shattering the hope in what truth will be told."

I flinch.

"And whoever is drugging these girls," he continues, "knows that holding their jobs over their heads is easy blackmail to not fight back. I'm not saying I agree with it, Angie. I, too, am just trying to understand."

This is all starting to make sense. Every piece of the puzzle is starting to fall into place, except the motive behind drugging the girls in the first place.

"Why drug anyone at all?"

"I have no idea," Graham says angrily. "It just doesn't add up. None of these girls appear to have been assaulted. I still pray that Penny was not a victim to some heinous act. But in her head, she is convinced she was raped. It is eating at her sanity. She has spent months in a rehab in Seattle trying to conquer the demons that haunt her."

"Why do you have a drawer of pill bottles?"

"Because I've been having a few of my employees collect prescription medication from various locations for testing purposes."

"Won't the missing bottles be noticed?"

"I'm taking the chance that a pill or two won't be. I also am recreating the labels on the bottles to help keep track of where the drugs have come from. I then cross reference the toxicology reports with the drugs I have in stock to see if anything aligns."

"Which employees? I am confused." Mainly because Graham has lots of employees from many different companies he apparently owns.

"My girls."

I hate that reference. Despite being utterly pissed off at him, jealousy still stabs at my heart.

"From Entice," he clarifies. "I'm having a select few take pics and confiscate a few pills for analysis. From dorm rooms. Parties. And if they get access to any client's personal residence. I am looking for trends. Any information that may lead to a supply source or a ringleader."

It's a smart approach. Except some women are being used as bait. Their lives are in greater danger if they get caught. How is he determining whether one life is better than another's?

"Do you think Mark is a ringleader?"

He shakes his head. "No. I think he's involved. I'm nearly positive he's the one who hurt Penny, but the smug bastard knows how to cover his tracks. I simply think he's taking orders from someone above him."

"So the three agency girls who got drugged are expendable?" I ask in disgust.

"No," Graham sighs. "No one is expendable, Angie. I am completely thrown off by this recent series of victims. They were found at a fraternity. This just doesn't make any sense. None of the male clients who are part of the agency database are in college."

My head spins with the overload of information being

fed to me. I guess that's why Graham went to Portland General to talk with Monica. It appears that a male client might be using a River Valley student to do some of the leg work. Mark was seen with Paul doing a handoff. I want to share this information with Graham, and under normal circumstances I probably would. However, I need to do this on my own. I may be able to interview other agency girls and see if anything unusual stands out. Graham is too emotionally driven by his sister's mental state to see clearly.

"I can see your mind is reeling," he says, studying me. "Trying to involve yourself in solving the mystery. But you're going to stay out of this, Angie. Let me handle it. Stay out of danger."

I shake my head no. "You cannot control me anymore, Graham."

"Control you? You are so fucking stubborn that the only thing my efforts did was to piss you off at me and make you not see reason!"

"I can take care of myself."

"No!" Graham snaps. "You are staying out of this."

"You do not get to boss me around. I am done with you thinking you have a say in my life."

"Consider yourself suspended then. I am your boss after all. You saw the proof firsthand when you ransacked my office. All these weeks I have been trying to get you to make good choices, and now I can with simply the truth."

My eyes glare at Graham's icy blue pair.

"What does a suspension mean?" I demand, my teeth grinding together.

"You get the benefits of being under my employment

but without the ability to actually work. Call it a paid vacation."

I stand up on wobbly legs. "We are over," I say coldly.

I leave Graham in the office and walk through the door I entered. I fish my cell phone out of my bag and dial 9-1-1 without hitting the call button. When I get to the final exit door that leads to the outside world, the security officer from before blocks my way—coming out of the shadows. Shit.

"Do not even think about stopping me," I say harshly. I am so sick of this.

"Miss McFee, I am—"

"Listen! Let me walk out of this building on my own two feet," I demand, "or I'll have the police here to file charges against you for holding me against my will." I hold up the screen of my phone to show how serious I am and hover my thumb over the call button.

With a frown, he steps off to the side, mutters something into what I am assuming is a hidden earpiece, and lets me leave.

I push the glass door open with more force than what is necessary and welcome the cool breeze that travels through my loose coat. Freedom. I look both ways along the sidewalk and decide to just turn to the right and figure it out from there. I just need to get away from this hell.

"Miss McFee."

Collins. "You have got to be kidding me!" I yell in frustration, throwing my arms up toward the sky. "Is this real life?" I ask a fluffy cloud before turning around to stare into the eyes of Graham's henchman.

"Just here to offer you a ride, ma'am."

I huff out air from my lungs. "Yeah, one back to Graham, I'm sure."

"I promise to take you wherever you want to go. I have the car parked at the curb."

I look to where Collins points and see the idling vehicle he is referencing. I look back to Hoffman Headquarters and dread fills my heart. Everything is so out of control, and it's hard to keep my emotions anchored to the ground. I just need some distance, a chance to think.

"I just want to do this on my own. Please respect that. It has nothing to do with you, Collins. You have been nothing but kind to me."

Except of course if he was the one in charge of taking compromising pictures of me. Then he can go on the two-person shit list along with Graham. Someone working for Graham was assigned that task. I can't imagine him selecting just anybody. However, that is something I do not want to address right now. Right now, I just need to distance myself from everything that reminds me of the man who shattered my heart.

Collins tips his head in understanding and steps off to the side toward the shadow of the nearby building. I feel his burning gaze on me as I walk aimlessly down the sidewalk on the busy downtown Portland street. I glance behind me and verify that I walked far enough to no longer be tracked. And for that, I am relieved.

I hear the buzz of my phone and the sound of incoming text messages. I reach into my bag and shut it off. I want to shut out the world and learn to just breathe.

2

As much as I could use Claire's company and inappropriate sense of humor right now, I'm not ready to go home. My knee-jerk reaction is to curl into a ball and go into self-preservation mode, where I just zone out all of the bad stuff and act like nothing is bothering me. I want to pretend that my heart is not shattering into a million little delicate pieces. That is what I have done in the past. The old Angie would give up and avoid feeling.

As much as my past antics are comforting in the short term, I know that everything will come back to bite me in the long term if I don't sort through my feelings now. The new and improved Angie knows that in order to move forward the fastest, I have to face the pain at full strength and not try to cope by numbing it.

So much has gone off course that it's no longer possible to see the road. Graham warned me numerous times in nonflowery language that he was dangerous. I can now see that there were no truer words. I should have listened.

Now I am standing alone on the sidewalk, walking aimlessly without a direct path. The only person who got me here is myself. I can try to place blame on others. That would be easy. I can convince myself that I was dealt a bad hand. But in truth, I have a habit of choosing wrong. It is a curse. It is the horrible flaw of trusting the wrong people.

I follow the sweet scent of chocolate and coffee to a corner café called Ground Floor. I have seen it in passing multiple times before, but today is the day I enter. Once inside the warmth, I am drawn to the unique décor of the cozy shop. All of the walls are painted with black paint, and colored chalk is available in cups on the tables where customers can write their thoughts on the makeshift blackboard. Some people draw pictures, while others write poems; some even put their email address out for anyone to see. I suppose it is a cool way to try to pick up dates. Bonding over a need for caffeine and mutual desperation.

I order the bottomless Colombian coffee and settle into a two-person rounded booth. I am completely outside of my comfort zone. Sitting alone is not one of the things I typically do—ever. I avoid it at all costs. But today may be the turning point for embracing loneliness. I scoot back into the cushioned seat and notice that underneath the cup of chalk rests a small stack of books that are available for customers to peruse. I sip my coffee and shuffle through a teenage romance book, then a nonfiction book on glassblowing, and then I find a classic. When my hands touch the battered cover of *Where the Red Fern Grows* by Wilson Rawls, I start to tremble. This was James's favorite book. I bring the book up to my nose and inhale, as if the smell alone will bring back the good memories of a time when my life was still intact. I peel back the cover and flip to where the first chapter begins and start reading.

I go through the motions without much thought or attention to details. It isn't until a worker offers me a refill that I realize I have drained my entire mug of coffee—and have finished the entire book. Granted, I skimmed some of the middle parts, but the memories that were once dormant have filtered back into the forefront of my mind.

James would beg Dad to read from this book every night, and would follow with the pleas for us to have a dog. He would even recruit me—thinking that I had the whole daddy's girl appeal going on—and make me hound and whine. He would convince me that since I was the baby, by a mere seven minutes, I had special powers that daddies couldn't resist so I had to work my magic. Through dedication to research and experimentation, I discovered that apparently my manipulation tactics worked on any male above the age of forty. It was all in the eyes. I would use a mirror and make my eyelids get as droopy as possible without cutting off all my vision. I would practice for hours and try out the cheesiest phrases in the mirror.

"*But Daddy, don't you want us to learn responsibility*?" I would try. Or, "*Please, Daddy, this would mean the world to me*." I do have to give credit to James; that boy never backed down from any kind of challenge—even if he knew the chances of success were slim.

And when Dad was just about to crack and give in, Mom was first diagnosed with cancer and everything changed. I would have given anything to keep my childhood unbroken by believing that a puppy could fix the world's problems—or just ours. But in that moment, I grew up. Fast.

And being ten was suddenly harder than anything my mind could have ever dreamed.

We never got a dog, even after mom died two years postdiagnosis. We just couldn't. When Dad suggested getting one months later, James begged for it not to happen. He actually broke down to the point of passing out from mental exhaustion. I'll never forget that day. Some memories are branded into the brain forever and scar the tissue so badly that nothing can get inside to change it.

We never read from the book ever again. It was as if all that brought us joy and comfort no longer had any appeal. In fact, it had the opposite effect. Growing up as a twelve-year-old without a mother to hold the bucket as vomit erupted, or go bra shopping with, or take embarrassing amounts of pictures at graduation was pain enough without having a puppy that would eventually grow old and die too. We most definitely didn't need a book to remind us about how life is short and how fragile the heart really is. We had our own reality as our reminder.

I stare down into the last chapter and watch as round dark spots speckle the pages. I am crying. For no other reason than for mere loneliness. I get it. I might not have gotten it as a child, but I get it now. Like animals, people, too, can die from loneliness. And I can't help but wonder if that is what is really happening to me right now. If all of the decisions I make and all of my attempts at survival are an unnecessary waste of time. If in the end, my heart will give out from the pain of being alone.

The closest thing I have felt to feeling alive was the time I spent with Graham. He turned me inside out and gave me a reason to rekindle the passion and light that was drowned with the worry of losing everything.

But where has that really gotten me in the end? I am still living a life without love. Worrying that if I give too much of my heart, I will only be worse off when they get snuffed out of my life.

I sniffle back the tears and wipe my nose that inevitably runs as soon as my eyes water. I use my hair to shield my emotions from onlookers and refill my mug with the steamy hot beverage. I add lots of cream and a little bit of sugar.

"Feel free to take the book with you, hon."

I stare up at an older woman, probably in her sixties. She has an apron on with the name Gayle embroidered in tiny print across the top and a wet rag in her hand. "They are donated from customers. Usually people exchange them, but I give you permission just to take it if you don't have anything to put back in its place."

"Oh. Ah, thanks," I whisper-cough. I watch as she walks away and moves between the tables, wiping crumbs and spills with her rag. I stare down at the beat-up cover, pieces of the corners missing and torn. I see the resemblance between the cover and my own heart. As tears continue to cascade down my cold cheeks, I hug the classic to my chest like it's my lifeline and the bridge linking my former life with my present one.

Making up my mind, I place the book into my bag and drop my empty mug into the plastic bin perched on top of the trash can. I return to my booth and grab a piece of pink chalk from the cup. On the board, I write the following piece of advice—*Enjoy everyone you love while you can.* I find another free spot and continue with—*People treat you how you allow them to treat you.*

Placing the chalk back in the holder, I retie my belt and exit out of the shop. I use my sleeve to dry my face and hold my head high. Despite being knocked down, life goes on. I can put my big girl panties on and choose to keep on keeping on.

My choices may have destroyed the visible path set out in front of me, but I have the power to form my own. I put one foot in front of the other and take off walking down the sidewalk. My fresh outlook makes me feel lighter and hopeful.

Deciding that I can no longer avoid people, I turn on my phone—but only long enough to order a taxi. The sounds of incoming texts and voice messages infiltrate my ears, but I choose to ignore everything that is nonessential.

It is time to reevaluate my priorities.

"Oh my God, Angie, is it true?" Claire asks in a panic, as soon as I turn the doorknob to enter our townhouse.

I slip off my shoes and coat. I am relieved it's just us, and I can flop onto the couch without having to worry about showing too much. I undo my confining bra, fish it out through my skimpy outfit, and toss it onto the floor.

"You kicked Graham in his balls?" she clarifies.

"First off, no, but he would have deserved it. Second off, where do you even hear these things?"

Claire frowns. "I have my sources."

"Yeah, unreliable ones," I snicker. It feels good to be

around her. I suppose rumors will start, if not already, considering Sophia witnessed some of my crazy.

"So what happened? I have been so worried about you. You haven't been answering your phone or responding to texts."

"I just needed some time to process what happened. To get my head on straight. I needed to think about what I am going to do next."

"Start from the beginning, please. And speak to me as if I am five years old."

I let out a laugh. Not because the situation is funny in any respect, but because if I didn't laugh, I would bawl my eyes out. I am going to get dehydrated if I shed another tear for a man who was overprotective with everything but my actual heart.

"Oh no," Claire says, eyeing me speculatively.

"What?" I ask dumbly.

"You did the sex, didn't you?"

I narrow my eyes at her and shake my head. And then I confirm her suspicions. "Yes, I had sex with Graham."

"Wow. I was not expecting you to lead with that."

"You are the one who blatantly asked!"

"Yeah," she agrees, "but I expected you to keep it all hush-hush."

I give a shrug. "Seems necessary to state so you can see how everything went from amazing to a shit show in a matter of days."

"Oh, good point."

"I snooped through Graham's closet and work desk and discovered that he was manipulating me by sending me creepy texts and pictures to try to convince me to quit

Entice. He is worried over my safety because his sister, Penny, was drugged a year ago, and he has made it his personal mission to try to find out how. Oh, and Dominic may be our boss for the sake of keeping things simple. However, Graham is really the owner and head of the agency. He calls the shots and uses Dominic as a cover. They are good friends."

"What? No shit."

"Yup. But it's not common knowledge nor should be. So, between the lies and the blackmail and the inability to let me live my life the way I choose to live it, I confronted the bastard. Publicly and without reservation. Oh, and there were at least a dozen witnesses."

"Oh no."

"Oh yes. I let my crazy out."

Claire makes a horrified face. "Do I need to get bail money?"

I let out a single laugh. "If Graham doesn't back off and continues to suck up all the oxygen that surrounds me…then yes."

"Well, what's next? Where do you go from here? As much as I hate Graham right now for breaking your beautiful heart, I can't help but agree with him that you are in danger. We all are. Agency girls are getting drugged, and that is terrifying."

"Well, in true asshole fashion, Graham—effective today—laid me off."

Claire groans.

"He doesn't want me involved with Mark," I explain, "nor does he want me involved in pursuing the mystery of the drugging incidents."

"I don't want you involved either, Angie."

"I've spent the last four years trying to rebuild my life from the ashes of my past. I'll not back down from this. I'm going to—"

"Let the police handle it?"

"Like they handled finding justice for James?"

"This isn't the same thing. They are not all the same. You are trying to draw a correlation between two unrelated cases."

"Fine, so be it. But I refuse to sit back and allow myself to get scared or complacent with what is going on."

"How many people do you think know Graham is the man running Entice?"

"I doubt many outsiders. I don't want you to ruin his cover. I am not looking for revenge. I just want to move on." I sigh. "But this time without him."

"He is not going to allow that, Angie. He is obsessed with you. You should have seen him at the hospital while you were there after open mic night. He went completely crazy on the entire ICU floor's staff members. It was as if I was watching a movie in 3D. And that security system that is now installed out front? That was his doing. I mean, he hired some of his men, but who do you think orchestrated it all?"

I noticed the new code box and stronger deadbolt when I came home. I just never expected Graham to go through the efforts so promptly. Does the man ever sleep? Or get tired of ordering everyone around?

"I actually thought you put it up after all the recent events happening in our area."

"Nope. It was all Graham's idea. He even had all the

locks upgraded and rekeyed. Granted, I am glad he did it. This once crime-free row of townhouses has now become the scene for vandalism and chases. Even your car was tampered with," she reminds me.

I guess she is right. Having the extra added safety features is not a bad thing. I just wish Graham would ask first. Instead, he just does what he wants, when he wants it.

"Here, give me your phone, and I can install the app that you can use to activate or deactivate the system without being home."

As Claire works on my phone, I go into the kitchen and grab a glass of ice water. My body aches from the stress of the day, and I just want to go to sleep before my dull headache turns into a throbbing migraine. I meander back into the living room and take my phone out of Claire's outstretched hand.

"I'm going upstairs, but first I need to hear how your camping trip went."

"It was one of the best trips I have been on. I really like Ethan and never expected it to happen this fast. We just stayed in and did the sex every chance we got. It was like every activity we started, ended with an excuse to get it on. We did it on the—"

"And that's my cue to leave."

I wake up to more texts, a few voice messages, and an alert that there was motion at the front door seven minutes ago. I guess the security system is doing its job. I roll out of bed and go downstairs to retrieve the huge bouquet of pink roses from the doorstep. I verify that they are for me and carry them into the house. I read the card.

One for every day I have known you. I miss you. I am sorry. -GH

It seems like ages ago that I met Graham under the stars. From that moment forward, my life has irrevocably changed. I wipe angrily at a tear that starts to fall from my eye.

"Whoa, someone doesn't understand the act of social distancing to win back a woman's heart," Claire says with a chuckle.

"Problem is, this *is* Graham distancing himself." I huff and touch the delicateness of a petal. "The man would probably camp out on the doorstep if he wasn't afraid I would flee the country."

"Hmm, that actually does sound like fun."

"Which part?"

"The fleeing the country part. We need a vacay!"

The good thing about being friends with someone like Claire is that she is always on my side—regardless of being right or wrong. I know exactly where her loyalty lies, and that is refreshing and something I never had growing up with any friends other than James. My brother was my best friend.

"I have literally missed out on being reckless and impulsive my entire college journey. Isn't this the time in our lives where we are supposed to be stupid and make mistakes and take chances?" I ask. "You know, before our prefrontal cortex completely finishes developing, and we get too old to use it as an excuse for our bad decisions?"

"Yes! Hell yes!" Claire whoops. "Let's do it. One life to live and all that, right?"

"Absolutely. And time is running out. We only have a couple of months and then it is real world time."

She gives me a smirk and then curls her lips into her mouth. "So, lucky you—"

"Oh boy, this is never good," I whine. "Please tell me you don't have a plan already."

"Hush."

I groan. "What did you do?"

"I'm already on top of this YOLO stuff after processing our conversation last night. So, you let your Fairy Godfriend Claire take over from here and make all your wishes come true." She spins around with a rose in each hand, dancing about the first floor like a sugar-infused butterfly.

I swallow. "I was kind of thinking figuratively."

"Too late. I have your week's social schedule planned."

"Claire…"

She pauses her rhythmic dance to look at me with an innocence in her eyes that contradicts everything she represents. "Yeppers?"

"How do you even know my wishes?" I ask.

Bringing the rose up to her nose, she takes a deep breath in. "Have a little faith."

"The last time I did, you almost got me arrested."

"Hold grudges much? Who would have dreamed that dancing naked on your own property is illegal?"

"Just about anyone who has ever watched *Cops*."

"Whatever." She props her hands on her hips. "You

weren't even the one who was naked, so I have no idea why you are still so huffy about it."

"Because the officer thought I was part of some weird extramarital affair with you!"

"Ugh, let's put all of that behind us and call it a learning experience and move on to bigger and brighter things. Starting at five p.m. today."

"What do you have planned?" I groan.

"Just the best stress reliever known to women. I signed you up for a workout class. And it's free!"

"Claire, first off, they are always free because you sneak me in. Second off, the last time I went, I hurt for a week."

"Okay, great." She clicks her tongue and claps her hands together in glee. "See you in a few hours."

It's as if my now freed-up time is inspiring Claire to micromanage it. At least her happiness is contagious. Maybe some good can come out of the rubble after all. At the very least, I am sure memories will be made.

Claire pulls into the parking spot, stopping just in time before she smashes into the other parked car. It's like she is playing a game of chicken where she is the only participant. She would also be the biggest loser if her car insurance gets raised.

"How are you not hitting more things?" I ask, dumbfounded.

She gives me side-eye. "I don't know but Ethan refuses to let me drive. Something about not wanting to die, yada yada."

I grumble under my breath that he is a smart man, earning some glares from Claire.

"Plus, you know I'm prone to motion sickness when I'm not in control."

"Claire, no one seems to be in control when you get behind the wheel."

"Wow." She turns in her seat and waves her hands in front of my face in a wax-on-wax-off type of move. "Erase this negativity. Be gone!"

I stick my tongue out at her, unlatch my belt, and then slide out of the car. My hair is piled messily on top of my head and I am wearing—with Claire's recommendation—a tight red tankini top and fitted black booty shorts. If it weren't for a bunch of other patrons walking into the gym wearing similar attire, I may have refused to get out of the car.

"What type of class is this? You never said."

"Cardio."

I follow her through the main entrance, where she is greeted like a celebrity. At least half a dozen people jump to say hi and ask her if she is going to add more classes to her teaching schedule. Between working here at the gym, maintaining her status at Entice, attending grad classes, and staying on top of her self-care regimen, I am amazed that Claire has time to do it all. I guess that's what happens when you are highly motivated, have unlimited energy, and barely sleep. Claire gives noncommittal answers to appease her legions of fans, introduces me to a few who linger, and then ushers me up the stairs to a large studio room.

I glance around the open space and am surprised at how dim the lights are. There is a black wooden platform at the front of the room that is surrounded by speakers. The instructor—also dressed in similar form-fitting attire—stretches and warms up. A herd of women and a few men filter into the room. I spot Blake and wave him over to us. Now I am really curious as to what type of workout class this is.

"Hey you, I didn't expect to find you here," I say, giving Blake a hug.

Claire follows suit.

"I never pass up a pilot session. They are my jam. What better way to try a variety of classes without committing," he explains. "Works for my love life too."

I scrunch up my nose. "Ew."

He bursts out laughing. "Angie McFee, you are so hopelessly monogamous."

"That she is," Claire chimes in.

I turn to Claire and snicker, "And you have room to talk." I never saw her so hung up over a man before in all the years of knowing her until she laid eyes on Ethan.

"And not anymore," I clarify. "Right now, I am *hopefully single*."

We take our stances on little black Xs marked with tape on the polished floor. We are spaced pretty far apart, so I imagine this class is going to have a lot of movement. The instructor adjusts her headset and announces, "My assistant is coming around to pass out your knee pads. Please feel free to improvise on any of the moves I show you tonight. This is your show. Be who you are. And do so unapologetically."

"Knee pads?" I whisper to Claire.

"To protect your knees."

"Well, that is obvi. But what could we be doing that would require their use?"

I am unable to hear her answer because we are each being handed a pair. I am sandwiched between Claire and Blake. Even though this is an introductory course, they seem to be well-versed on what to do. I slide my pads on and am surprised they are not more cumbersome than they initially appeared. The smooth fabric bands that stretch around the protective pads make it feel like they are a second skin. I don't mind them at all.

When Beyonce's "Crazy in Love" starts thumping through the sound system, and the instructor begins to gyrate her ass to the rhythm—making the room go wild—I know that this is not going to be a traditional workout class.

I turn to Claire who has already started to mimic the moves and is dropping to her knees and then spreading them wide to show everyone her crotch. Wonderful, just wonderful. This is so awkward.

"Claire," I hiss. Lovely, I am now the only one standing. I throw myself to the floor, thankful for the knee pads. I've been here for three minutes, and I can already appreciate their usefulness. As soon as I adjust my weight to a comfortable position so I don't pull a muscle in my groin, everyone is back to standing. Shit. "What is this, Claire?" I try again, hoisting myself up ungracefully.

"Good ol' cardio."

"My ass!"

"Oh yes, your ass," Blake chimes in, making me jerk around to glare at him.

"What is this class?" I ask again.

Claire shrugs. "Twerking. Fun, huh?" She bounces around like she is in a strip club.

"Oh, yes, like a carnival," I respond sarcastically. "I can't believe you signed me up for this. I have no freaking clue what I am supposed to do."

"Just feel the music," Blake says. "You can't mess it up. It's all free-form."

The song changes to something raunchier. I take a deep breath and let go of these high expectations I set for myself. When I do, I relax and get into the groove. It really is therapeutic, and after about thirty minutes of flaunting my ass and rolling my body, I am thankful Claire surprised me into attending. There is no other way I would have come unless she tricked me into it.

"So what did you think?" she asks, wiping sweat from her face using one of the little white gym towels.

"I'm going to be so sore tomorrow. The move where we all did the handstand booty dance against the wall was so much fun."

"Yeah, Ethan is going to enjoy that one when I replicate it later."

We all laugh and make our way out of the building. The freshness of the night's air coats my skin like the smoothest silk. I feel invigorated and recharged.

As Claire drives us back to the townhouse, I read through the messages on my phone.

Graham: What can I do to fix this mess?

Graham: I miss you baby.

Graham: I am sorry.

Graham: I know you are mad. But please just text me so I know you are okay.

I type out a quick response—*I'll never be okay*. Then I just delete it and decide that being silent is a better punishment than any words I could ever construct into thought. They might get misconstrued or taken as positive feedback. So instead, I say nothing.

I do not miss Graham. Instead, I miss the illusion of the man he created. He brought out a different side of me and helped me to start to trust again. He knocked down my walls that I built from the pain of my past. But he did this on false pretenses. It was all a lie.

Claire breaks the silence in the car ride back. "Don't make plans for tomorrow night."

I shift in my seat to look at her. "Why?"

"Just starting another chapter in the book on how Angie gets her groove back."

"Should I be worried?"

She scoffs. "We are going to go get fondue. Say around six?"

"Now that sounds like fun," I say with a smile.

"I love this new, easygoing Angie."

"Ha. I was always easygoing."

"Righhht."

3

"Hey Teach," Bryce announces, handing over my caramel macchiato. "Extra shot of espresso because it's raining."

I laugh at his justification but quickly welcome the extra jolt of caffeine.

"I have a proposition for you," he says, taking a seat beside me. "And stop looking at me with those eyes."

I frown. "What eyes?"

He points at me with the eraser tip of his pencil. "The judge-y ones. I can already tell you are rehearsing how to politely say no."

"Nothing good comes from propositions," I say flatly.

"It's not my fault your life lacked me in it prior to us meeting. Just think of how less judgmental you would have been if we met sooner."

I roll my eyes at him and groan. "Spit it out," I demand.

He digs in his backpack for a folded piece of paper. "I'll let you photocopy my class notes if you come to the frat's annual Halloween Party."

I narrow my eyes at him. "You don't even take notes."

"I will though if you agree to come." He wiggles his eyebrows. "Good notes."

From his hand, I take the homemade printed flyer that gives the location, time, and request for costume.

"You know I don't do parties, especially frat ones. Plus, aren't all the fraternity houses under an investigation after the drug incident?"

"First off, you need to have some fun in your life. You're starting to get the ol' cat lady vibe, and it's freaking me out a bit."

I shake my head at him as he rambles on.

"Teach, I can tell something is up with you. A little unwinding is always a good remedy. Second, it's still a while away. So you have time to invite your friends and make it a social outing. And third, the three girls from the weekend's supposed drugging dropped the charges, so I've heard."

Why would all three drop them? Lack of evidence? Were they intimidated or pressured to do so?

"I'll think about it," I say, taking the flyer and shoving it into my bag. Despite not being in a social mood, I need to attend this party to gather evidence. Maybe Paul will be there, and I can try to get him to talk.

"Yes!" he hoots, but quickly calms down as the professor makes her way to the front of the room to signal the start of class. "Shhh…"

"I didn't even say anything, Bryce. And why are we shushing?"

His face gets serious. "Moment of silence for the loss of the neck scarf."

I glance up at the podium and then back at him. "Oh, happy day."

"Indeed, indeed."

After class, I head over to the computer lab. Zander is working the Help Desk, and I give him a quick hello. His boss is hovering so I'm conscious not to overstay. Using the school website, I print out a map of the River Valley University dorms, apartments, and fraternity houses. I also construct a list of girls I know are part of the agency. I am going to need Claire's help if I'm going to add more names to the list. It would be easy if Graham would hand over this information; however, even if we were still together, he would be sure to sabotage my efforts and classify his actions as "protecting me."

I grab a highlighter from a supply cart and start making markings where the drugging incidents have been happening. I hand draw in a square and call it The Shack. I color it in with a highlighter, assuming I was actually drugged. I highlight the smoothie cafe and then draw rings around all of the frat houses. When weekends happen, many of the houses throw parties—not just one. So as of now, they are all under investigation.

When 5:30 p.m. approaches, I say goodbye to Zander, who looks like he wants to ask me a bunch of questions but refrains. For that, I am thankful. I head down to the main parking lot adjacent to the building to find my taxi driver waiting.

It takes about twenty minutes to get to the fondue restaurant called Double Dipper. I spot Claire dressed in a cute pink skirt and gray fitted sweater waiting by the bar. I feel slightly underdressed with my skinny jeans and lavender cashmere top. My hair is left down with a little butterfly clip pulling back some long bangs from my forehead.

"Hey you," I say and give her a hug. "You look so adorable."

She looks down at her attire and grins. "Does this scream naughty schoolgirl?"

I shake my head at her question. I don't have a clue how to answer it. "Only if you want it to."

"I do."

"Then it totally does."

"Awesome, Ethan will be so turned on."

"Eww…can we keep our minds from the gutter?"

She gives me a silly smirk. "Ready to eat?"

"Starving."

I follow her to a booth at the other end of the restaurant and am surprised to find Ethan and another guy I don't recognize already sipping on beers. Both men look up. The mystery guy gives me an approving smile, and my heart drops to the floor.

"Claire…"

She ignores me.

I grab her arm and halt her movement. "Claire!" I half yell.

She bites her bottom lip and at least has the decency to look guilty.

"What did you do?"

"Well, umm, I thought it would be fun to help you forget

about Graham if just for a couple of hours. And he sabotaged your agency job, so it's not like I could have used that avenue. And so I thought that—"

"I can't believe you are doing this." I glance over at the guy and then back at her. "And not even telling me until it is way too awkward to back out now."

"You would never have agreed," she defends.

"Damn straight I wouldn't have."

"Then this is awesome."

"Payback. That is what you are getting." I brush into her on my way over to the table, partly because I am so off balance from her subjecting me to this type of torture.

Ethan and the other man slip out of the booth to greet us. Claire gets enveloped in her man's strong arms. And I try desperately to avoid being touched.

"Hi, I'm Adam," the brown-haired man introduces. He is average in height, has strong jaw bones, and looks to utilize the gym on the regular. "Wow, you look even better than your profile picture."

I turn to Claire and silently demand clarification. She slips out of Ethan's arms and leans over to whisper in my ear. "I may have been under the influence of flavored vodka and was watching a Hallmark movie and signed you up for College Connection."

"Unfuckingbelievable," I mutter.

"But I gave you a cute profile pic. So that should count for something," she says nonchalantly.

I nervously pull out a stick of gum from my purse and fold it like an accordion in my mouth. I chomp onto it manically, making my taste buds pop with the release of flavors.

I then add two more sticks. My jaw cracks as I try to chew it all into one big ball.

I focus my attention back on Adam. He seems kind and polite—two things I should be attracted to. However, I don't feel anything other than a friend vibe from him.

Claire claps her hands together once and gains everyone's attention. "Well, this is working out better than I expected."

I narrow my eyes at her bizarre proud declaration. Adam and I basically said two sentences to each other, and she is about to do a backflip or something else equally as annoying. Claire was a cheerleader in high school, so nothing will surprise me when it comes to her.

"First and best blind date I've ever been on," Adam chimes in.

I want to smash something. We haven't done more than say hi, and quite frankly, I don't even think I actually said hi. I chomp on my gum and mumble out some excuse that I have to use the restroom, despite my body instantly going dry. Claire follows me and joins me on the sofa that is situated outside of the women's restroom door.

I spit my gum into a nearby trash can and prop one knee up onto the cushions so I can see her better. "You really think this is appropriate?" I am angry. "I went from being in a relationship with Graham for one solid freaking day"—I bite my bottom lip that seems to want to quiver—"to now being on a blind double date that I never agreed to."

"When you hurt, I hurt. When you cry, I cry. And I am trying my best, Angie, I swear. I'm trying my very best to get you to forget him. To think about anything else besides him.

He is taking up way too much real estate in your brain, and I hate him for it. I fucking hate him right now. I also hate myself and am overcome with guilt for even getting you involved in a job that could now have the potential to ruin you."

"This is not your fault, Claire."

"Yeah, it is."

I shake my head adamantly. "No. I have free will. You would never have gotten me involved if you thought it would end like this."

"You think you are holding it together, but I know you. You are strong to a fault. But any day now, you will break. You are going to fall apart. And I'm then going to go do something I may regret to that stupid man. I'll probably get arrested, or at the very least a restraining order. So right now, I'm doing everything in my power to delay that inevitable breakdown you are bound to have—at any moment of any day. I am just trying to do everything I can to keep you from crumbling."

Claire's words flood like cascading water from a waterfall, and I instantly lose the anger I had brewing inside of me. She means well. She is just trying to help. For that, I love her a bit more than I did a day ago and cut her some slack.

"Can I at least see this profile you made for me? Make sure it's accurate at least."

"Maybe later. Let's go pee."

"Claire Nettles, you show me this profile right now."

"So, I have some explanations for it."

My eyebrows rise at her sheepish look. "Oh, I'm sure you do."

I snatch her phone out of her hand and hold it hostage until she pulls up the dating site and loads my profile.

My eyes scan over the page, scrolling to view all that she uploaded. "You have got to be kidding me," I growl. "Seriously, Claire? Why did you think this was appropriate?"

"What? You look hot!"

"I look like a hooker."

In the photo, I am wearing a bikini, sipping a piña colada, and laughing at something Claire must have said. My hair is blowing in the wind on our back deck, and I can almost remember the details of the day. We were celebrating the start of summer.

"Sex sells."

"For marketing ads, sure. But for relationships that I do not want to be involved in right now, no! Might as well have signed me up for Hooked Up."

"Who knows, maybe I did that too."

"You didn't…"

"Let's pee! Peeing sounds super fun right now, yeah?"

"Do you have some sort of bladder infection? Quit trying to get me to pee. This was never about peeing. Did you sign me up for a booty-call site?"

She looks down at her twiddling fingers that cannot seem to stop moving. "Well…"

"You didn't."

"I can pause your account."

"My account?"

"Hmm?" She looks down, playing with her hair. "I'm hungry. Are you hungry?"

"My account?! Claire!" I shake her shoulders. "Have

you lost your ever-loving mind? I am not your pet project! There are real emotions involved in this! You have got to stop."

"Okay, fine. After today, I will stick to my lane."

"And what lane is that, Claire? I would love to know myself."

"The one where I stop throwing hot men your way and save them for myself in case Ethan breaks my heart."

I frown. "Why do you say that? Is something wrong?"

"No, but I just…"

"Waiting for a shoe to drop?" I finish, knowing the feeling all too well.

"Basically."

"Well, don't. That is a horrible way to live. Let my mistakes be your warning."

"Look at you, turning a page and giving me life advice."

Her words are meant to be lighthearted but still portray some truth. She is right. I have come a long way since she first met me. And over the course of those four years, we have both grown so much and learned some hard lessons from the curveballs that life throws.

"Who would have thought," I say with a chuckle. "For what it's worth, I would be reluctant about taking anything I say right now seriously. It is like I am living in a fog and can't be trusted with my own words."

"You'll get through this, Angie, I promise you. I know you're in pain right now. But you are way stronger than you give yourself credit for."

I wipe at a tear rolling down my cheek and wrap Claire into a big hug. She really is the best kind of friend. Her phone vibrates my hand with an incoming call, and I glance down to see it's Graham. I jerk my hand away as if the device is burning my skin, making it fall into my lap.

"Oh, the nerve of him," Claire snaps. She snatches the phone from my thighs and slides the bar to answer. "Listen here, you lying asshat, she is fine." There is a pause and she shifts in her seat. "Leave her alone. Leave me alone." She exhales and huffs. I can hear Graham's bellowing voice through the speaker despite being a couple of feet away from Claire. "Just enjoying a double date. Oh, and Angie's super-hot date is super-hot with hot bulging…" She looks at me, rolling her hand in a frantic circle, desperate for help completing her asinine statement. "Clavicles."

I make a face. "Clavicles?" I mouth.

"Buh-bye now," she says while hitting the end button and shutting off her device.

"Oh no. Why did you tell him that? He's going to go ballistic."

"Too late. It really did sound better in my head than actually saying it in reality."

"Don't most things?"

Claire gives a nod of her chin. "We better go back to our dates just in case Graham tracks us down and storms in before we actually eat anything."

"Shit." That is something he would do. Despite having over 600,000 people living in the metropolitan area, Portland is starting to feel claustrophobic. It is only a matter of time before I'm going to run into Graham on accident, and there is going to be a scene. And right now, I do not need any more scenes.

Claire grabs my hand and pulls me back toward the booth where the guys are chatting. Six empty beer bottles are lined up along the back edge of the table, and I wonder just how long we were gone.

"Sorry to keep you boys waiting," Claire says. "Girl talk is a religion to us."

I force a smile and slide in next to Adam. I am not in the mood for small talk, and I have no intention of getting to know him on any level. I pass the time by shoving skewers of food dipped in sauces and cheese into my mouth to avoid having to initiate conversation.

Ethan is as smitten with Claire as he ever was before. He has spent the majority of the dinner trying to get her to blush by feeding her himself. When Adam attempts to mimic the same gesture, I just grab the mini fork from his hands and shovel the food into my mouth on my own. I guess, in a way, this dinner was a success for me to go from having zero appetite to wanting to stuff my mouth with everything within an arm's radius. Silver lining, I suppose.

Ethan and Adam square away the check. When the waiter returns with the credit cards, he hands me a small black envelope. My heart drops at the sight of it, and I know instantly that he found me. But how?

"I have to take care of something. Claire, I will catch a ride back on my own. I have a feeling this is going to take a while. Ethan, good seeing you again. Adam, thanks for dinner," I say, excusing myself from the table.

"Can I call—"

"Sure, Claire can give you my number." I turn to Claire and give her a look that translates to *give the wrong one.* I am pretty sure she knows she is in the doghouse over this stunt she pulled tonight. This was definitely crossing the line.

On my way out of Double Dipper, I scan the surrounding parking lot. Is he here now? I peel back the seal on the envelope and find a little card with a handwritten note.

I would buy you an entire universe if I could...just to be sure I was a part of it.

Behind the note, there is a black credit card with my name on it. I rotate the card with my fingers and revel in how good it feels. It's like I can sense the weight of money in my hand. This small piece of plastic is not riddled with debt and hopelessness—like the one that is weighing down my own purse. As much as I would love to accept this hand-out, I would not be able to cut all of the strings that are attached to such a gift. Acceptance would imply defeat. It would give the message that I am willingly allowing Graham to control my life. That is something I'm not willing to do—especially with someone who uses lies and deceit to clear their path of success.

I climb the stairs to the townhouse and wave goodbye to the taxi driver who just dropped me off. I run up to my room and take a quick shower to decompress and ease some of the stress from my body.

When I cannot bear the weight any longer, I slip to the floor and wrap my arms around my knees. I let my tears flow freely and get absorbed by the pelting flow of the water.

Get your head on straight, Angie. You have been through worse. Quit feeling sorry for yourself.

I let my self-help thoughts enter and exit like an encouraging force.

When my skin is prune-like, I shut off the water and pull a towel down from the rack above the toilet.

I can do this.

I can find a way to move on with my life, sans Graham.

I am in control of my own destiny.

When I'm all dried off, I throw on my comfiest pajama set. I twist my hair up into a soft towel and let it take some of the dampness out naturally. I then move to my closet and pull out my old magazine bin, some scissors, and a glue stick. I find my work-in-progress dream board that Claire helped me start months ago and flop down on my bed to rework some of my goals. I flip through the magazines and try to stay open-minded to anything I see that is inspiring. Then I construct a list of my current goals.

- **Goal 1:** Work at my journalism research project.
- **Goal 2:** Secure an internship.
- **Goal 3:** Own my future.
- **Goal 4:** Stop resisting change so damn much.
- **Goal 5:** Get over Graham fucking Hoffman.

4

A week passes without much fuss. Slowly, my heart is learning to accept its broken state. When class ends, I get Claire to drop me off at the repair shop to finally pick up my car. Luckily, this was only a twelve-hundred-dollar expense versus having to find a new ride entirely. Once I hear the purr of the engine starting, I instantly relax knowing that part of my independence has been replenished. Hopefully the string of vandalizations happening on our street is all in the past.

I drive around along the waterfront and find myself heading toward Hoffman Headquarters—almost as if an undeniable force is pulling me there. This is probably an indirect violation to my Goal #5. However, this feeling of power is helping me own my future, which is Goal #3. So I guess they negate each other. I will still call it "progress" for the sake of simplicity.

I park on the street six blocks away from Graham's office, more as an excuse to work out my animosity prior to confronting him again over his lavish gift he sent to me while I was on the blind date. He is not expecting me, but I find that keeping him off guard works to my advantage. Who knows, he could be plotting my kidnapping at this very moment.

I walk past the corner coffee shop and grab a to-go cup of Americano. I didn't plan my wardrobe at the beginning of the day to accommodate another confrontation. Prior to twenty minutes ago, I wasn't even planning on going to see Graham. He very well might not even be there. Who knows what that man does on a typical day. Maybe he has left the country again.

My custom jean dress I sewed out of scraps of denim from old pairs of pants does not scream designer or power. I pretty much look like a low-budget Levi's advertisement. However, with my brown knee-high boots and my hair pulled into a high ponytail bun, at least I look sort of put together. No time to dwell on it anyway. It's not like I am trying to impress him with my looks. If anything, I just want to remind him of what he is missing out on. I am petty like that.

I window shop the rest of the way to HH and find that the little boutiques hold a lot of beauty for the business area that consists mainly of office complexes and deli-style eateries. Even the tattoo parlor has a "pretty" feel to it. I stick to the sidewalk and resist going inside to spend money I do not have. I unzip my shoulder purse and find the little black envelope inside—the one that I am only babysitting until I can give it back to its owner. While it would be nice to not have to worry about bills and growing debt, I cannot afford the hidden costs of having such a luxury.

When I arrive in front of Graham's building, I notice that even the public sidewalk is nicer to walk on. Smoother. Shinier. I guess money can buy pretty much anything. As I am about to walk through the main entrance doors, a woman swings one open and stumbles into me. A picture frame falls from the top of the box she is carrying, shattering onto the cement in hundreds of tiny pieces.

"Sorry," she sniffles, looking up into my eyes.

"Hanna?" I ask suddenly. "What's going on? Why are you crying? Can I help you with something?"

"Oh no, you have helped enough," she cries, placing her cardboard box on the ground with a thump. Her pixie brown hair blows in the wind as tears fall from her eyes.

I watch speechless as she frantically throws her loose photo into the top of the box and tries to pick up the pieces of broken frame.

I slouch to the ground to join her and retrieve the wooden back part of the frame. As soon as I rotate it in my hand, I feel a sharp pain and then watch as blood drips onto the concrete.

Blood.

It's everywhere.

Flashes of light fill my vision and I see James's swollen face.

No.

Stop.

I squeeze my eyes shut and shake my head back and forth.

My mind clears, and I open my eyes back up.

"Shit." I moan and drop the wooden piece of frame onto

the sidewalk. Blood pools in my palm, and I look up horrified into Hanna's bloodshot eyes.

My heart rate accelerates. I feel nauseous.

"Wonderful," she yells up to the sky and then turns her attention back to me, "now I am going to be out of a job *and* going to probably have to move out of state."

"What are you talking about?" I ask frantically, trying to see what I am cut on. "There is glass in my hand! Glass!"

I stare down in horror at the shiny plank that appears to grow from my bloody skin. I bite my tongue and then yank the piece out, dislodging it from its tight home. I feel bitter acid rise up in my throat. I see more blood gush out of my wound and figure the shard of glass was acting like a cork in my gashed skin. Now the flow is erupting, and I can't seem to stop it.

Hanna looks like she is going to pass out. Her once angry face is that of sympathy. Sorrow even.

"Help, please help," I beg. "I need help."

As soon as the words leave my mouth, the doors open and four security guards burst through. I am lifted up gently from the ground, and I allow myself to freak.

"Blood. Bleeding. My hand…the glass…stuck. Hanna might be hurt. Help. Ouch, how…I don't want to…"

"Calm down, Miss McFee. Someone is calling for the doctor. Let's get you inside." I have no idea who is talking to me.

Tissues are squeezed to my wound but just get saturated within seconds. I try to pull my hand away from the pain, but it is secured tightly by a man who I assume is the main guard.

I turn back to Hanna who now looks as pale as a

ghost. She is just sitting on the ground—staring at me. Her hands are over her mouth, and I can tell she is crying harder than she was when I first ran into her. “I’m sorry,” she mouths. But I cannot hear the words. There is a buzzing sound in my ear, and I struggle to stay in the present.

“This is my fault, not Hanna's,” I say to no one in particular. “I ran into her. Made her break the frame.”

Once I am in the lobby, I am pulled toward the restroom.

“Angie, what the hell?”

It’s Graham. I hear him before I see him and start to wonder if he is a figment of my imagination. My eyes blur with tears. It hurts so bad, and I just want to curl into a ball and dream away this searing pain.

“What happened to you?” he asks me, and then snaps to his employees, “What the hell happened to her? Was she attacked? Someone better talk to me!”

“We found her outside on the sidewalk with Ms. White,” the guard explains. “She appears to have cut herself on a broken picture frame while Ms. White was leaving the building.”

“Dammit,” he sneers.

I drip a trail of blood as we enter the restroom as a team.

Graham picks me up around the waist and places me on top of the long sink vanity. He turns on the faucet, and the rush of cold water feels so good that I don’t want it to stop. My blood mixes with the pooling water at the bottom of the basin and makes the white sterile sink look poisoned.

“Hey,” Graham says, cupping my chin with his free hand, pulling my attention to him. “You are going to be just fine, Angie. It’s just a cut.”

My lower lip trembles as I choke out the words, "Am I going to need stitches?"

"Hmm, I would bet yes," he says softly, still holding my gaze.

"I hate needles," I admit.

"I know, baby."

A whimper escapes my throat. "Like really hate them."

"I'll be right here with you. It's going to be okay. The doctor is on his way."

In between whispering hushed words of comfort to me, Graham barks out a few orders to his men. The contrast in his tone toward me and them is like black and white.

He looks me in the eyes and tries to calm me, but I just cannot keep them open.

"Tie it tight," Graham instructs. "It has to last until Dr. Saber can get here. He is about five minutes out."

His voice is calm and controlled. And because he is not freaking out, I try my best to just sit still and not look.

I feel the pull of the fabric over my palm and wince at the makeshift tourniquet. I hear my name chanted soothingly into my ear, but I keep my eyes sealed shut. Warm fingers graze over my clammy cheeks. I focus only on them—willing myself to ignore anything else going on around me.

I feel safe. Cared for. I want the feeling to last forever, but logically I know that it can't. Graham is incapable of bending. No matter how good his hands feel in the moment, it is just that. A moment. One speck on my timeline.

"Put your arms around my neck, sweetheart."

I do as I am told and am cradled against Graham's broad chest. I snuggle my face into his neck and revel in the feeling of being this close to him. I would be lying to myself if I pretend that I do not miss this closeness. He is everything I want and don't want wrapped up into a package of a man.

Within seconds, I am transported out of the lobby's restroom, onto an elevator, and up to Graham's main office. A female staff member gives us a nod and follows us as we travel down the hallway. I assume she's Hanna's replacement.

"Mr. Hoffman, your two o'clock—"

"Cancel it," he says sternly.

"And your two thirty ap—"

"Reschedule it," he snaps.

"Mr. Hoff—"

His body goes stiff beneath me, and I cringe over what he is going to do next. He squeezes me tighter, takes a deep breath, and then turns back to her.

"Please just clear my schedule for the rest of the day. Decide on your own what needs to be canceled versus rescheduled. When Dr. Saber arrives, please send him in right away. Afterward, take time for your lunch break. Double it."

Her shoulders slump, and she seems to let go of the breath she must have been holding. I imagine working for a hard-ass like Graham has to be stressful. All of his employees should receive hazard pay to account for his mood swings.

And then it clicks. Hanna. I instantly connect the dots between her cold words on the street and the fact she was carrying a box with what I assume were desk items.

I pull my head up to look at Graham, as he kicks the door shut to his private space—closing us in.

I have been in this office three times now, and every time I enter, I leave with more confusion than when I first arrive. I wonder if this trip will be the same.

"You fired Hanna over me?" I ask softly.

"Not your concern, Angie," he warns, placing me gently onto the couch.

"The hell it's not," I whisper yell. "You think she betrayed you in some way."

He sits down beside me, grabs my legs to drape over his lap, and holds my injured hand to examine the cloth bandage. The dark maroon blood stain makes me cringe with pain. Something about seeing blood is triggering for me.

"All my employees—even the temporary ones—need to know where their loyalties lie," he says, studying my face, "and you seem to find a way to wrap them around your fingers."

"If you are pissed off at the world, take it out on me. Not someone innocent."

"I cannot run my company and keep you safe at the same time if I have employees giving in to you every time you flash a smile."

Oh, the nerve of him! I move my legs an inch before he locks them into a grip to keep them where they are.

There is a knock at the door, and in walks a man I assume is the doctor who is going to give me stitches. Apparently being as powerful as Graham Hoffman gives you the privilege of being able to have a physician on call.

One who can come on the spur of the moment to patch up gashes.

"Good seeing you, Graham," Dr. Saber says kindly. His eyes reach mine. "And it is a pleasure to meet the woman who has finally made this man have to jump through hoops of fire."

Graham scoots me over to get up, shakes hands with the doctor, and exchanges some directive I cannot quite hear.

"Okay, Angie, my name is Dr. Saber, but please call me Mitch. I'm going to wash my hands and take a look at your cut."

Dr. Saber is about two decades older than Graham and has a bit of graying at the temples. They seem to know each other on a more personal level. I watch from the sidelines as Dr. Saber goes into what I assume is an attached bathroom and washes up. He is dressed in plain street clothes but has a big leather briefcase that contains latex gloves, a bunch of vials, needles…

And from there, I stop paying attention. Otherwise, I may faint.

Graham is at my shoulders, massaging the tension out of them, as Dr. Saber peels back the bloody cotton cloth from my right hand.

"Just close your eyes and relax, Angie," Graham instructs me. "Don't look, baby."

I inhale through my nose and exhale through my mouth. I can actually smell the rusty stench of the blood. I focus on deep rhythmic breaths. Dr. Saber works around me but doesn't tell me anything of what he is doing or is about to do. He just does it, and I'm thankful for the loss of anticipation. I sink into the couch at the feel of Graham's hands kneading into my upper shoulders. His hands come up the sides of my neck and his fingers press into the sensitive spots behind my ears. I melt at his ministrations, and he knows it because I can hear him chuckling to himself.

He is so cocky.

I hear the click of the briefcase and then Dr. Saber's voice cuts through the silence in the room.

"Okay, take a look."

I stare down at the fresh bandage wrapped around my hand.

"Angie, you are very lucky that you did not damage the nerve. You should fully heal in about seven to fourteen days —depending on how well you can follow your aftercare instructions. I need you to avoid getting your wound wet for forty-eight hours. Then, wash the site twice a day with soap and water. I'll give you some petroleum jelly and extra bandages to help with the recovery. No bathtubs, pools, or doing dishes until I tell you. I'll see you in a week's time to evaluate your progress. Please look out for signs of infection and call me immediately if you suspect you have one. On the desk over there, I have your instructions and supplies."

"Thank you, Dr. Saber. You were so gentle that I barely noticed what you were doing."

He gives me a warm smile, and I return one back.

"The joys of a little Lidocaine to numb you."

"Oh, now that makes sense. Thank you for doing that for me."

"Pretty sure I wouldn't have teeth right now if I caused you any unnecessary pain," he says, laughing and nodding to Graham.

Graham squeezes my shoulders and guides Dr. Saber out the door. I start to stand and notice the blood that is smeared all down my jean dress. I frown at the mess and flop back down into the cushions.

"I'll send it for dry cleaning, Angie. Your new outfit should be here soon."

"I, um," I start, about to argue. But then I realize that walking six blocks to my parked car looking like I currently do will be very embarrassing. "How do you even know what size to get?"

"Baby, I know a lot about you."

"Creepy."

"Practical."

"Still creepy." I stifle a giggle.

"Damn, I miss that giggle." He walks back over to me and kneels at my feet. "Please tell me what I can do to fix us."

I shake my head back and forth. "There is no us, Graham."

He lets out a sigh. "I broke us. But there most definitely was an *us*. Still is an *us*."

I start to talk but get halted by a knock at the door. Graham curses under his breath. He effortlessly gets up from the floor, saunters over to the door, and retrieves the bag out of the messenger's hands.

"I can help you get dressed, but I figure the answer is a hell no," he says sadly, handing me the bag. I recognize the store logo from the side because I just walked past the boutique on my way here from my car.

I stand up and head over to where I saw Dr. Saber disappear when he went to wash his hands. As suspected, it is a personal bathroom, except it is way bigger and nicer than even my en suite at my townhouse. I close the door and start undressing. Tucked inside the paper bag, I pull out a beautiful long-sleeved, striped wrap dress. The colors are vibrant but tasteful. Despite being a bit bold for my particular style, the dress fits wonderfully and is very flattering. I love it.

I try to secure the inside button that holds the inner panel flat; however, my bandage does not allow me to bend my fingers without causing a pulling sensation to my wound. Ouch.

"Let me just help you, baby. I hear you struggling in there."

"I'm fine."

"Please just accept help."

"I am *fine*, I said."

"No woman ever is actually fine, despite how many times she uses the word."

I giggle and continue to try to secure the button. "How are you so knowledgeable on my gender?" I call through the door.

"You ladies are the easiest species to figure out. You never mean what you say. And you never listen when you should."

"Wow. You sound bitter."

"I am."

After several minutes of failed attempts, I open the door with my left hand and lock eyes with Graham who is waiting patiently for me to come out.

"Did you plan for me to need you? Make sure your henchman finds the most difficult outfit to put on with a stitched-up hand?"

He coughs to cover a laugh. "You give me too much credit," he says softly, fastening the button and then tying the long fabric tie into a bow at my hip. His hand lingers there a little longer than necessary. He is barely touching my hip bone, and yet all my nerve endings are jolted awake. "If I wanted you to struggle, I would have gotten you an outfit with hundreds of buttons and snaps and random zippers and corset strings to lace."

I burst out laughing when his eyebrows wiggle with humor.

"Next time," I say without thinking.

His megawatt smile makes me know he caught my slipup too.

"Thanks for rescuing me today and getting a doctor to fix me up. But the reason I came here in the first place was to return your latest gift."

I search the room for my bag and see it resting on Graham's desk. I make my way over to it and notice the framed picture of us. It's the selfie we took on our first date outside of the restaurant. I look happy. Carefree almost. It hurts my heart to see something that reminds me of a time not long ago when things were still easy. Nothing is easy now. So much has happened in two months' time that has left me feeling the aftershocks of the earthquake that is Graham Hoffman.

"Angie…" Graham starts but trails off.

I pull out the little black envelope from my bag. "Here," I say softly. "Thank you for trying to take care of me, but I'm not yours to take care of. Please accept that. The more you push, the more I want to run." He doesn't reach out for the credit card, so I place it on the smooth surface of his desk.

"How am I going to make sure you are safe and healthy and have your needs met? Huh? How am I going to be able to go to bed each night without worrying the entire time over your welfare?"

"You're just going to have to trust me. Trust that I can live my life the best way I know how." I fix a stray piece of hair behind my ear with my good hand. "And do what I've been doing all these years before you crashed into it and jacked everything up."

Graham runs his hands through his hair, nods as if he is comprehending what I am trying to say, and then kisses me once on the forehead.

I want to say sorry to him. I am not even sure why I would be compelled to apologize anyway. Perhaps for shaking up his life too?

"Have dinner with me."

"I can't."

"You won't," he corrects.

"I can't."

It's the truth. I can't have dinner with him. Because dinner would lead to more. More feelings. More blurred lines. More emotional attachment.

I throw my aftercare instructions and ointment samples into my bag, along with my stained denim dress.

"Bye, Graham."

"Bye, sweetheart. Do not hesitate to contact me if you need anything."

I give him a sad smile in response and head out the door. I walk past the new assistant and make little eye contact.

The last thing I need is for her to lose her job too because I tried to be friendly. I walk into the waiting elevator, cross through the lobby without any incident, and head out the exit. All of the broken glass is cleaned up, and there is no sign of blood. The cement blocks look fresh and polished—as if nothing happened just an hour prior.

The air travels up my new dress, but it feels good. I window shop on the opposite side of the street during the six-block walk back to my car. I turn behind me and check to see if someone is following me. Although my hairs are not standing on end, I feel the presence of eyes on me. As if there is a shadow amongst the shadows. I pick up my pace and arrive at my car in half the time. The sun is about to set, and I realize just how hungry I am from skipping meals today.

I feel empty.

And there's no amount of food that will fix it.

5

"Seriously, Claire? Really?" I ask, staring down at the scraps of material that she apparently believes constitute an actual outfit—despite covering only twenty percent of my body.

"You look adorable!" she coos, clapping her hands together like she is talking to a toddler. "Super cute!"

I scrunch up my face and stick out my tongue. "Puppies and kittens and chubby babies are adorable. This"—I gesture with my hand up and down slowly in front of me—"is an outfit that usually makes a cameo appearance in the first five minutes of porn videos."

"Huh," she says examining my attire closer, "you do look like Maggy Miles a bit from the damsel in distress sex clips I have seen."

My face loses all expression, and I just stare at her with my chin dropped. "When I agreed you could pick out my Halloween costume, I did not expect you to get so—"

"Creative?"

"Diabolical."

"Inspiring?"

"Delusional."

"Innovative?"

"Unhinged."

"Wow, exaggerate much?"

"Look at me, Claire!" I shout at her. "I don't even look like a flight attendant."

"But you have cute little bags of peanuts to hand out to the crowd," she whines, thinking that her pouty face will work. I am sure it does on the opposite gender.

"I can't be handing those things out. What happens if people have allergies?"

She looks at me as if I've lost my mind. "Halloween is not the time to be realistic. It's the time to have fun!"

I shake my head at her. "Bring on the fun."

She spins around and grabs something off the floor, placing it on my head. "And your hat, don't forget your hat."

"You think it will assist in making my outfit less slutty?" I implore, furious that I even allowed her to persuade me to purchase the pre-bagged costume without first demanding a worker open it up for inspection. Apparently the outfit isn't meant for girls taller than five feet, because my five-foot-five frame looks preposterous in it.

"Add some thigh-highs and some high boots for extra coverage. Oh! And you forgot your iconic scarf and little luggage handbag."

"Gee, thanks," I grumble, slipping my feet into shoes instead. There's only so much fashion advice I can take from her before I start to question her motives.

I watch in utter silence, gaping at the flutter in front of me, as Claire sweeps up the sheer nylon white scarf and ties it around my neck. The thing only makes the bare expanse of my chest stand out more. If the short blue dress with the gold embellishments isn't enough to draw unnecessary attention to me, then the scarf will. Without any more protesting, Claire sashays about the room, picking up my handbag, a tray of peanuts, and a hat. I apparently have to wear the hat because it "*so completes the outfit*."

Claire's costume isn't conservative in any aspect either, which I guess makes this marginally better. She made something as innocent as a butterfly look downright inappropriate.

"I will wax off your eyebrows while you sleep if you post any hideous pictures online for your followers to critique."

Her mock horror makes me laugh.

"Too bad Teddy Graham can't witness your sexy self."

I choke-cough over her new nickname for him. I think back to how soothing and cuddly he was when I was getting stitched up. I guess, in a way, he was my teddy bear, so the name suits him.

"What has he been up to these days?" she asks.

"Wow, subtle transition into checking in on me to see if I'm following through with my detox and dream board goals."

"Did it work?"

I shake my head at her absurdity. She really is one of a kind. Like if Katy Perry and Jimmy Fallon made a baby…it would be Claire. It is a damn shame that her parents don't see how amazing she can be if she is allowed to fly.

"But seriously, have you talked with him?" She looks at me expectantly but continues on. "I'm surprised he hasn't sent you a million gifts during this groveling period. Or sang music from a boombox below your bedroom window."

I laugh over her usage of the word boombox. What decade is she from? "He basically sends me reminders to change my bandage, check for an infection, eat a meal, set the security system, eat another meal, and to accept a grocery delivery service that he wants to set up. And pay for, of course. He pretty much does everything in his power to treat me like an invalid. Such a turn-on."

"Oh, this could be fun if you do the latter option."

"I'm not doing any option," I remind her.

Claire's demeanor perks up. It's how she reacts when she thinks she has some amazing idea. "You could get lube and condoms and fun stuff like that delivered—just to make him squirm."

"It's not like he would have access to what I'd be ordering, Claire." As soon as I say the words, I realize how false they are.

"Yeah, right. That man makes actual stalkers look like amateurs." She grabs her detached wings, and I follow her out to her car.

I stop on the sidewalk and look back up to the house. "He didn't put any cameras inside, right?"

"Hell if I know. But I've been deliberately getting dressed in my dark closet, just in case." She laughs at my horrified expression, making me laugh in return. At least we can have fun over the circus that is known as my life.

"Maybe I should drive," I suggest calmly.

"And why is that?" She turns to me suddenly, a frown

marring her beautiful made-up face. She painted the pattern from her wings on her face with black liner and then shaded in each section with a vibrant color of makeup to look like stained glass. She looks exotic.

"Driving in that tight getup will make things challenging, right?"

"Oh hush. We are only a few miles away from the party. Plus, you need to rest your hand, and we both know how bad of a driver you are. And probably even more so now that you are handicapped."

I flip her off with my good hand and glare over her comment.

"Stop making me laugh. This underwire thingy is about to pop a boob."

She is too much sometimes. I throw my accessories into the backseat, joining her multicolored ones. I then carefully get into the passenger side and cross over with my left hand to shut the door. I cannot wait until I have full use of my right hand back.

It takes us five minutes to arrive at the frat house. It's more like a mansion. Even with the windows up, we can hear that the party is loud and already in full swing.

"Remember, if we get separated, do not accept random cups of beverages from no-names, got it?"

I nod.

"Oh, and no trying to earn wings for the Mile High Club," she says, giggling.

I roll my eyes and resist adding snark to her good-natured concern.

"But seriously, Angie, I know you are going to snoop

around here," she says. "I can already tell by the wire you stuffed into your bra and the recording device."

I feel the blood leave my face. "Shit, how did you see it?" I ask, turning in the passenger seat.

"I didn't. But you just confirmed. So yay, I win."

I feel lightheaded. "Seriously, how did you even suspect it?"

"I saw the delivery box on our front steps yesterday, and it basically told me on the outside what you ordered," she says with a shrug. "So, being super good at math, I added two and two together."

"I'm only here because I want to find out what is happening to the girls."

"And to have a tad bit of much-needed fun," she interjects.

"Hardly likely, but sure—I will try. You know these types of parties are not my thing. This is my one shot at producing something worthwhile that can land me an internship; otherwise I settle for a career I really don't want. It's like everything I've been working toward for the past four years will be a complete washout. A waste."

"Hun, you put this unreasonable amount of pressure and expectations on yourself. You need to stop doing that. There is nothing wrong with coming up with a Plan B that will also make you happy. What about all the other doors that can open?"

I shake my head sadly. "I'm okay with failing, Claire. I am not okay with failing because I gave up too soon."

"Just be careful. You've become a bit of a danger junkie."

I smirk. "Keeps life interesting."

"Okay, let's go and drink and be irresponsible. Ethan isn't here to judge my actions, so I'm a free woman tonight."

"Oh boy…" I groan.

"Oh yes," she chirps. "And I plan to send him some sexy selfies later just so he can ravish me when he is done being stuck-up."

"Drinking cheap beer and dressing in silly costumes not his scene?"

"Lame, right?"

We both slip out of the car, flashing crotches and way too much upper thigh. It is inevitable when we are both dressed like sexy sirens. The thumping of the bass is making my head throb, and I am thankful I proactively thought ahead to pop a few Motrin and a chaser pill just to help with the anxiety.

A group of guys is gathered on the front porch, blowing puffs of clouds into the air from their cigarettes—and probably a few joints. A handful have actual costumes. Some just have a scary mask or a simple printed T-shirt.

I hold my breath and follow Claire inside. The sounds of whistling and catcalls fill the air. I am sure we are above the average age in attendance—Claire working toward her master's and me taking a year off to cope after the accident—but I find their actions extra immature. Like in a couple of years, these guys might be in charge of administering medicine or verifying structural integrity or making life decisions that can affect an entire population. Yet, here they are, smoking and drinking and making lewd comments… just because they can and just because society allows "boys to be boys" no matter the outcome.

Maybe some of my jadedness is from growing up way too fast. Maybe it is from seeing the world with a new perspective. Or maybe it has always been ingrained in me to understand that people treat me how I allow them to treat me.

Despite there being at least six large couches circling a huge two-story great room, no one is sitting down. Coeds are standing in clusters, drinking and laughing and talking over each other. Orange and black Solo cups are sloshing over with mediocre beer and fruity mixed drinks.

We get greeted by a few classmates and acquaintances, but overall see no one we are mutual friends with.

"I feel like we are overdressed," Claire whisper-yells into my ear.

"Ha, that says something, considering we are barely wearing clothes."

"It's sad that society has lost the true meaning of Halloween," she says with a serious and thoughtful tone.

I laugh because I can't tell if she is being sarcastic or not.

"Let's go out back and get some liquid courage," I suggest, pointing to where the keg is set up on a couple of cinder blocks. "But one of us has to stay semisober."

"So three drink maximum?"

"Sure."

We step outside into the back courtyard, where the party comes to life. Orange outdoor lights are strung up on huge poles, lighting the entire grassy plain. The drinks station is set up in the middle of the yard, surrounded by pumpkins and fake cobwebs. Several tables feature ongoing games of beer pong. Mismatched lawn chairs line the fenced border, but no one is sitting in them. Halloween music blasts through the sound system, and drunk dancing is already in full swing. Some guests must have pregamed all day, considering the party was supposed to start just an hour ago.

Claire and I blend in better with our costumes out here, and I am finally able to relax my shoulders. Nothing looks out of place. Everyone appears to be having a good time.

"You ladies look like you both could use a drink," some dude dressed like a banana says, attempting to hand us Solo cups.

"We'll get our own, 'kay, thanks," Claire chimes in, answering for the two of us. She leans into my ear. "Not even here fifteen minutes and guys are already trying to get us drunk. Like we need assistance."

I raise my eyebrows at her. "Three drink maximum. Remember?"

She grins. "What size are the cups?"

"Normal size, Claire." I shake my head at her.

"We both know how bad my estimation on size is. Probably has to do with the male population constantly giving me false information on what eight inches means."

She grabs my good hand and pushes past Banana Boy, making a beeline for the keg. She grabs two clean cups from the middle of the stack and fills them up. I take a sip of the bitter amber liquid and am reminded why I hate cheap beer. It's gross.

"Cheers to being just the two of us," I say, smacking my cup with Claire's.

"Cheers to making horrible decisions," she says excitedly.

"Umm, no." I shake my head for added emphasis.

"Starting now"—she holds her cup up into the air—"with this awful piss potion."

"It's horrible," I agree, throwing some more down my throat, just to get it over with. It apparently is a rite of passage to drink disgusting beer at college parties. Despite having a slow start, we are checking a few items off our imaginary list tonight. I am already feeling a bit more relaxed and ready for some much-needed fun. "Let's play some pong."

"Great idea," a male voice behind us interrupts. "And you ladies sure look amazing."

I turn to see Bryce make his way over to us. He is dressed like a Twister game mat. "Hey Bryce," I say cheerily, embracing him in a hug. "Nice costume too."

"Here, take a spin," he says, showing me the spinner. "See where you land."

Upon inspection, I notice that about 90% of the spinner sections are green. When I find the only green dot on his body, it is straight over his crotch. "You are—"

"Genius, I know." He has a satisfied smirk plastered across his face. "But it does feel good to be reminded now and again."

Claire and I burst into a fit of giggles.

"You are too much."

"At least I am guaranteed a little action tonight. My poor cocktapus hasn't seen many pink clam shells these days. Probably forgets what they even look like."

I spit out my mouthful of nasty beer onto the grass below, barely missing my shoes. I try to compose myself, but Claire's laughing just makes it impossible. How Bryce can say these things with a straight face is the most intriguing part of it all.

"Selfie time," Claire announces, taking Bryce's spinner and turning it manually to green. We hover our hands over his junk as he squats down to fit in the frame. The pic is captured.

"You both are a bunch of teases," he fake whines. "Now, let's go find a fourth person so I can beat you girls at some pong."

Claire and I make our way over to an empty table and set up the cups and drinks. I drop my luggage accessory on a nearby chair. Bryce goes off in search of a partner and comes back with some dude dressed up as a skeleton. He's covered from head to toe with a spandex bodysuit; the only parts of him that are exposed are his eyes and his hands. His black and white Converse shoes even complement the color scheme.

"Guys against girls?" Skeleton Man asks.

I don't recognize his voice—which is not surprising. I can count on one hand how many campus parties I have attended in the four years here. My repertoire of men I know has only increased exponentially over the past two months. Since Bryce doesn't introduce him to us, I assume he doesn't know him personally either.

"Yup," I answer, taking my side of the table.

"Isn't that how it always is in this world?" Claire asks rhetorically, taking her stance opposite me on the other end.

Bryce wiggles his eyebrows. "Ready to lose to the stronger, more capable gender?" He knows it is a hot button topic for me.

"You are such a troll." I smack him on the arm. "And I'm even playing with my injured hand."

"Excuses," he says with a smirk.

I bounce the first ball, and it lands right into one of the cups. Claire and I jump up in unison and hoot. I quickly settle down and fix my skimpy outfit into place. Skeleton Man takes the ball out of the dirty cup, removes it from the table, and then takes a huge sip of his personal drink. We go back and forth until there is just one cup on each side left.

"What does the winning team get?" Bryce asks, now that it's even again.

"If we win," Claire starts, "we get to watch you guys dance to a Taylor Swift song. On stage." She points over to where a group of frat brothers are assembling a wooden platform stage.

Skeleton Man scowls, looking over to the setup area. "Shit, you guys are mean."

"And if we win," Bryce interjects, "we get a slow dance."

"Deal," we all agree.

Claire bounces the ball and misses. Bryce bounces and misses. I'm up. I bounce the ball and it goes right into the cup, only to hop out again.

I throw my hands up to the sky. "Are you kidding me?"

The guys laugh their asses off, doubling over like goons. Because according to their rules, it doesn't count. I glare at their obvious glee and air high fives.

"You haven't won yet," Claire reminds them.

"But we will," Skeleton Man says, sending the ball right into the cup that is a foot away from my body.

I stare at it swirling around the base until it comes to a

stop. "Shit," I mutter. I finish off my drink and feel the warm buzz that accompanies it.

It's almost as if the entire house knows what we bet, because a slow song magically comes across the sound system. It is some stalker anthem from a decade when I wasn't even born yet.

Claire and Bryce pair off because she is shorter than he is and fits better. Skeleton Man walks me to the dance area and places his hands on my hips as I reach up to drape my arms around his neck. My short mini dress pulls upward, and I just give up on trying to prevent the flashing of my backside. This is why I decided to wear the boy short panties that Graham had included in the set he gave me. They are surprisingly very comfortable, the most modest, and my new favorite style.

The whole dance is done in semisilence as neither of us have much to say, other than ask each other our majors and what year we are in school. I don't learn much, other than he is a graduate student and is studying business.

After the song ends, I decide that I need to get serious about my data collection, so I excuse myself and go back into the house. I catch Zander's roommates on the couch with a couple of girls on their laps and cross the room to chat with them. One is dressed like a lumberjack and the other is a taco. The two girls are dressed in bras, tutus, and heavy makeup. I cannot figure out if they are trying to dress differently than they typically would dress; their costumes are not recognizable.

"Nice outfit, Angie," the more extroverted one says.

"Thanks, you too." I glance around the room. "Is Z here?"

"Nah, his dad flew in for business, and they are having a late dinner out."

"Gotcha."

When the girls start revving up the PDA, I make a hasty exit and go off in search of the bathroom. I open a bunch of hallway doors, occasionally encountering a heavy petting session, until I find the one I am looking for.

I enter and lock the door, double-checking that it does in fact lock. I open the cabinet under the vanity and use my cell phone light to see if anything stands out. Just a bunch of cleaning products. Next, I check the closet and medicine cabinet. Nothing. I pull out a pair of latex gloves from my luggage and use them to rummage through the trash. Ah ha. At the very bottom, I find an empty orange pill bottle that has the entire label scratched off. Why would someone who is getting prescription medicine put so much effort into removing the pharmacy label? I throw the bottle into my bag, just in case something stands out in the future.

As I walk down the hall, I try a few more doors, finding most occupied with couples. No one even notices the sound of the doors opening. When I come to the door that has light filtering out of the bottom, I quietly open it to find someone talking. To themselves? I leave the door slightly ajar and lean against the wall to listen. The man is on his cell phone. I recognize the back of the costume as being that of Skeleton Man. He is sitting on the bed facing away from the door. His calm hushed tone has me instantly intrigued.

Despite the music blaring outside and in the great room, I am close enough to hear the entire one-sided conversation.

"I don't feel comfortable continuing on like this. She is going to catch on. You promised this would end soon. I feel

compromised. My cover is going to be blown if I get this close. She is here. Yeah, of course. Yes, I'm being careful. But she has a wire on."

Oh. Fucking. No.

I am the *she.* I feel it in my bones and the way my blood turns to ice.

How does he know? Why does he care? Who is he? Is he talking to his boss? Is Skeleton Man the one who is drugging girls? Does he think I am now a liability?

He turns and looks at the open door, and I move just in time. He yells "dammit" into the speaker. I turn my body more and press it flat against the wall. I feel paralyzed with fear. I can hear him say some departing words and the creak of the bed as he gets up.

I force myself to react and scurry down the hall, slipping into the adjacent free room. It must have just freed up because minutes ago I know it was occupied. I wait until I hear movement before trying to catch another glimpse of the mysterious man. Maybe he lives here and that's his bedroom. Or maybe he is an outsider visiting. With a costume that covers his body from head to toe, he can be anyone. When I hear the sound of the door opening, I wait long enough to ensure I'm not being discovered and then peek my head out. I scan both directions in the hallway but do not see Skeleton. I just see the shadowed back of another guest who is dressed in jeans and a black long-sleeved shirt.

I pull out my phone and engage in a fake text message chain with myself just to look like I am not paying attention. I snap a picture—even though it is mainly of his back, ass, and legs. When I focus my attention back to see if Skeleton Man appears again, I see that the guest who I thought came out of the adjacent room has the same pair of Converse on. Black and white. With little scuff marks around the top toe area. When I look at his height and frame, they are the same too. I snap one more picture just to make sure the first one is not blurry.

When he turns his head, I see clearly that it is the smoothie cafe worker, Paul. The same Paul who has a connection with Mark Tanner. The same Paul who found Monica at the last frat party and "rescued" her.

Or was he the one drugging her—along with two other agency girls? Maybe his goodwilled gesture was actually a way of following through on his task, or maybe it was his way of taking the suspicion off himself.

"Angie?"

I look up from my phone and see him staring back at me with a broad smile.

"Hey?" I ask, trying my best to act unsure. "Wait, we met before, right?"

He gives me a slow nod.

"Yes, yes," I say, "you introduced me to my now favorite smoothie. Is it Paul?"

His smile lights up at my realization. "It is." His eyes scan over my body. "Nice costume."

I stare down at my hideously sexualized flight attendant attire and mutter a simple thanks. "Why are you not dressed up more?" I ask, knowing full well that minutes ago he was. Why did he change?

He shrugs. "I'm not much for costumes. Want to go grab something to eat or drink?"

"Yeah." I make an attempt at a flirty smile, not really knowing if it is working or not. The closer I can get to him, the better my chances at figuring out why my number one suspect is being so secretive.

"Here, follow me." He takes my left hand into his.

I allow Paul to lead me into the basement where a whole bar is set up with liquor bottles and mixers. In the huge open space rests two pool tables, a ping pong table, and a big-screen TV with several rows of couches. While the upstairs seems to have undergone some cosmetic renovations, down here is very much the stereotypical outdated bachelor pad.

"You seem to know your way around here. Is this your fraternity house?"

"Yeah. I transferred here at the start of the school year and was able to pledge in easily."

"Pretty cool." This would explain why not too many people seem to know him. He is new to the group. "What's your major?"

"Communications," he says, going behind the bar to mix up some drinks for us.

I make a mental note that either he is lying or the alias Skeleton Man—who said he was in grad school—is lying. Communications or business. Maybe both are just bogus majors. This is messing with my mind. He obviously has something to hide. I am almost certain there is a connection between him and all the crazy things that are happening to female agency workers.

Only a dozen or so people are down here and most are watching some fight on the big-screen. Beer cans and bottles litter every end table and coffee table. If I lived here, I would make everyone pay a cover charge just to use the money to hire a cleaning service after every large party. This is disgusting.

I watch carefully as Paul only pours liquor and mixers from their original containers into a shaker. Should be safe for me to consume then. He retrieves two glasses from the cabinet and fills both to the brim.

"What is it?" I ask, taking the first sip.

"A cross between a cosmopolitan and a Moscow mule."

"Moscopolitan."

Paul chuckles. "Sure."

"It is really good." It is true too. This guy knows how to make drinks—with the female palate and alcohol tolerance in mind.

He takes a sip of his and agrees. Then he pulls down a huge snack bin from the top of the fridge and allows me to pick something to munch on. I choose the trail mix. When I struggle to open the package, he takes it from me and rips it with ease.

He points to my bandage. "I bet you had to relearn how to do a lot of things with your hand."

"Yeah and it sucks majorly too. Especially brushing my teeth."

His smile is warm and for a second, I almost want to believe he is trustworthy. "Want to play some pool?" he asks.

"I haven't played in years."

"I don't mind winning." He flashes a sultry smile.

"What are we betting?"

"Any ideas?"

"Let's just turn it into a drinking game. Make it easy," I suggest.

"Okay…so whoever loses does a shot."

"So you want me to die?" I joke.

He chuckles over my exaggerated question. I have him exactly where I want him. Overconfident and soon to be drunk.

Paul racks the balls, and I send Claire a quick text saying I am safe. She texts back a selfie of her and Ethan with the caption—*Apparently my butterfly costume was a mistake or one of my more genius moves*. Ethan looks happy to be with Claire, despite not having any costume on except a shirt that says, "Here For the Boos."

"Ladies first," he says, handing me my stick. "You sure you can play with your hand like that?"

"Yeah, I'll be fine."

I chalk up the tip and then lean over the table to line up the cue ball. I pull back on my stick and gently rock it. Back and forth. Back and forth. Then, back one more time and forward hard. The pressure hurts like a bitch but it's worth it. The sound of the balls cracking together fills the room over the sound of people beating the crap out of each other on the TV screen. Three stripes go into three different pockets, and I jump up and down wildly—like I just won the lottery.

"Stripes," I call out.

Paul groans as he watches me sink two more balls before I miss and it's his turn. Paul gets one of his solids in and then misses. I clean up the table and then land the black into the end right pocket, securing my win.

"I thought you said you hadn't played in years."

"I haven't. But I never said I sucked when I did play." I laugh the entire way over to the bar. I grab a shot glass and fill it with some 160 proof vodka that I see skirting the back rail. The rim is nearly overflowing when Paul tips it into his mouth and down his throat.

He shakes his head as if that is going to make it magically taste better. Yuck. I need to keep winning if I want my plan to work and to avoid that nasty crap. I was never big on shots.

We go another two rounds, and while some matches are close, I end up pulling in the victories. Two more shots go down Paul's throat, and I forgo my mixed drink just to keep a clear head for my next goal.

Between the three vodka shots and whatever else he had been drinking prior, Paul is definitely feeling the effects and convinces me to rest on a free sofa with him and watch the next fight.

I wait until his snores are steady and then dart back upstairs. I find the room where I first located him on the phone, but it is locked. I carefully remove the bobby pin from my hair, bend it, and jam it into the lock. I bite my bottom lip as I move it around. When I hear the click, I sigh with relief.

I sneak inside and lock it behind me. I look in drawers first, not seeing anything worth noting or photographing. Next, I check under the bed and find the skeleton costume rolled up and thrown into a mesh laundry bag. I take a picture of the size label and designer. I never know what details are necessary or not. But being thorough during data collection is way better than having regrets later on.

In Paul's closet, I find a bin that has Rosetta Stone foreign language books and translation guides. One for Spanish and one for Russian. These are the two languages I heard Mark and his business associates speaking in. I snap a few pictures and then organize everything back into the order in which I found it.

In the very back on the floor, I find a lock box that requires a key. I kick myself for not bringing my pick kit. This lock is way more sophisticated than what my bobby pin and my skill set can tackle. Beside the box, there is a paper bag, and inside I find five nameless prescription bottles. The only identifying descriptors are little numbers written with black marker onto the sides. One through five. Five bottles, all containing some type of pill. I reach into my luggage and pull out some collection zippered baggies. I take two pills from each bottle and place them into their own separate bags. Each set of pills look similar to each other—only with very minor differences. One set is more oval than round. Another is a fraction less white. Some have slightly different print style lettering—despite all being pressed with a P23. I take more pictures and then am jolted from my snooping by a loud scream from what seems like a few doors down, followed by the sound of more commotion.

I jump to my feet and gather my accessory luggage. I make my way to the hall and see a group of people surrounding a pale female who appears to be having a seizure. Holy crap.

I stare at her powerless body as it convulses and thrashes on the floor. "Someone call 9-1-1?" I ask suddenly. My voice is shaky, and I feel my own blood rushing from my face. I feel sick. I burst into the neighboring bathroom and get to the toilet just in time to expel all of the snacks and drinks I just ingested. I lean over the bowl while I finish with my dry heaving spell that usually follows the first wave.

I rinse my mouth to remove the bitter aftertaste. I undo the scarf around my neck and remove my recording device, shoving both into my luggage bag. I make it back to the girl who I now recognize as Tracy. From the agency. Gossip Girl Tracy.

Why is this happening? Was she drugged? Is she hurt? How did this happen? What is wrong with her?

I hear the sound of the sirens outside the house, and I know the paramedics are here. My shoulders slump with relief. Help is on the way.

Arms hug around my back, and I turn to see Claire behind me. She looks like she has been crying. Her nose is red and she keeps sniffling.

"Why is this happening?" I whisper to her.

"I have no freaking clue. But whoever is doing it has some balls."

We both stare in shock. This could be either one of us. We could be next. Seeing it all play out in front of us has us both shaken to the core.

Ethan pulls Claire back into his body and cradles her head to his chest to keep her from watching the scene. She is always so strong that it destroys me to see her this visibly upset.

My phone buzzes in my bag, and I see that it is Graham. I am glad I changed the ringtone back to normal, because the last thing I need right now is to take attention from Tracy who is trembling on the floor. Some guests have her turn to her side and are keeping a safe distance from her so as to not get hurt or hurt her.

Tracy is dressed like a daisy flower and looks so pitiful lying helpless. First responders and paramedics infiltrate the small narrow space, pushing us back toward the great room. I stay close to Claire and just cannot stop staring back at the scene unfolding in front of me.

The ringing stops for a few seconds and then picks back up again. I decide to answer it.

"Angie?"

"Yeah, hey, umm," I stutter.

"What's wrong? Why do I hear sirens in the background? Are you hurt? Where are you? I can come get you."

"I'm fine."

"You are not fucking fine. What is going on?"

I start to cry. I cannot keep holding it in. My mouth is dry and I feel faint.

"Angela! What is going on?" His voice is panicked and he sounds out of breath.

"I'm at," I say absently, looking back to the scene. I watch the paramedics turn Tracy on her side. "Halloween party and—"

"And what, dammit? Are you hurt?"

I pull myself together. I take a deep breath and close my eyes to block out what is happening around me. "I think a girl got drugged and is now having a seizure."

"Fuck. I'm coming to get you."

"I don't even know what the address is here. I have Claire and Ethan with me. I'll be fine."

"Sweetheart, give the phone to Ethan, please."

I do as I am told and offer my phone to Ethan. I'm not even sure how well they know each other, but knowing that Graham has access to all of the clients in the Entice database, I assume he has done his research—even if it is from the sidelines.

I stand in silence as the men exchange some messages back and forth with minimal clues from the lack of words Ethan speaks. When he hands the phone back to me, I am shocked when Graham sounds like he is already in his car.

"Stay with Claire until I can be there. Do not leave her side. I mean it. It should only take about ten minutes," he directs. "Just wait for me, baby."

"Okay, I will wait."

6

Ethan guides me and Claire out onto the front porch, and we watch as the ambulance drives away with Tracy. I keep alert for anyone who is on their phone or looking guilty. I want to force myself back into the house to look for Paul. I want to keep snooping in his room. I want to find out who Tracy was seen with prior to the episode.

Claire links arms with me. "You are getting too close to all of this."

I give her a weak nod. She is right. But I cannot stop seeing Tracy's convulsing body in my mind. I am way too involved to back down now. For the sake of protecting us girls, I need to find out the answers.

"I mean it, Angie."

I look up into her bloodshot eyes and give her a sympathetic look. "I know," I mouth. What else can I say? When I have my mind set on something, I cannot just give up easily. Maybe it's a character flaw, or maybe it's some quality inside me that I should embrace rather than try to keep contained.

I watch the curb as Graham pulls up and exits the driver's side in a hurry. He trots up the steps, pushes past a cluster of people loitering at the top, and finds me instantly over in the corner. It's as if his whole body knew where I was located like a magnetic force.

He pulls me into his arms, and I melt into him. He smells like expensive soap and a rainforest. It is my new favorite scent on him. His five o'clock shadow makes him look edgier, and I revel in the feel of his body pressed up to mine. Strong fingers rub into my hair, and I moan at the tingles running up my spine. He kisses the top of my head with lips so gentle and reverent.

I want to stay like this. Just like this.

"Let's go," he says gruffly.

I pull away a few inches just to look up into his eyes. "Where?"

"Anywhere but here."

I nod. I am one hundred percent okay with that.

"Thanks for looking out for her, man," he says with a nod directed at Ethan. He ignores Claire entirely—probably blames her for bringing me here in the first place.

I can only wish that he stops using her as a scapegoat for everything bad that ever happens to me. She isn't going anywhere in my life, even if she decides to move out of state for her dream internship. She is my family. Distance will never change that fact.

Graham grabs my hurt hand and kisses the bandage. For a second I forget that I don't belong to him anymore. But the way he charges in and commands the space makes me feel that in his head, nothing has changed. He has not changed. He is still the same controlling Graham. He is just reining in his obsessive tendencies and wrapping them with a shiny layer of charm.

I follow Graham quietly to his car. He opens the passenger side and helps me in. His touch is so feathery and gentle that I almost don't even feel him snap the belt around my waist. He shuts my door and types something into his phone before finding his place behind the wheel.

The purr of the engine comes to life, and he zooms away from the frat house.

I lean my head against the cool window and try to keep myself from freaking out. I want to ask Graham questions. I want to weasel more information out of him that I know he is keeping from me.

He clears his throat, but his eyes stay straight ahead on the road. "I don't want what happened to Penny to happen to you."

I sit in silence and wait for him to continue.

"You and she are a lot alike. Determined, stubborn as hell, and smart. But in the end, she got caught up in something that was much bigger than she was. She paid the price for her naivete. Angela, I need you to stay out of this mess. I need you to trust me to handle it. I am handling it."

"I can't," I whisper.

He slams his hand down on the steering wheel, making me jump upright over the sound.

"And why the hell not?" he asks angrily.

"It's complicated."

"Not to me it isn't."

"Well, you don't know everything."

"Enlighten me."

I turn back to my side window and watch as the trees and houses blur by. I have so much I want to tell him but can't. I cannot have him sabotage my efforts for my last chance to let the past four years have some sort of worth.

At least I have a chance. Sometimes life doesn't give you a dress rehearsal. Sometimes there are no do-overs. If I have any hope of achieving the goals I made for myself, then I cannot let the fear of failing keep me from taking the risk. I have not gotten this far to back down now. It's like I am on the cusp of figuring it all out, and if I can report on it first, then I will lock in my future.

"Just trust me," I say softly.

"Trust you?" He looks over at me as if I just said the most asinine thing. "*Trust* you?"

"That's what I said."

"Trust you how?"

"Trust that I can stand on my own. That I am strong enough to make my own decisions."

"If something…" His words trail off, as he takes a deep breath. "If something happens to you, I will never forgive myself."

"Forgive yourself for what, Graham?"

"For not putting a stop to you joining my agency in the first place. For allowing you to gallivant around town putting your nose where it doesn't belong."

I shake my head at his words. "Allowing me? I am not a toddler!"

"But most importantly, for not forcing you to accept that you are mine and to know without an ounce of doubt that I protect and cherish what is mine. When you finally come to realize that truth, you will let me do things my way."

I look over at his stern face. Is he for real? What decade is he living in that he thinks he can do this caveman talk and women actually obey? "Graham, I'm not some shiny object. You cannot put me on a shelf and take me down when it suits you. You cannot use the situation with Penny to draw a correlation to what could happen to me. We may be similar, but I am my own person. I make my own decisions. You are not responsible for my safety."

"You are everything to me, Angie. Everything. It took losing you to really understand how much my life needed you in it."

"Graham…"

"I'm tired of this dance we keep doing back and forth. It is fucking with my mind."

"Where are we going?" I ask, changing the subject back to something else that will most likely cause a conflict. Seems to be the common theme these days.

"My place."

I know not to argue. There's really no point to it. I am just glad to get away from the party. There are so many thoughts running through my head, and I lack the energy to fight about anything more.

"For the entire night?"

"Yes, Angela. Any other questions you need to get out of the way?"

I swallow hard. I rest my hands in my lap and fiddle with the curling end of my bandage. The wound site hurts a bit more tonight from all of the games I played. I hope I didn't pop a stitch.

"Are you in a lot of pain?" His rough voice cuts through the silence.

I give him a shrug and respond, "I think playing three rounds of pool wasn't the best decision."

He opens his mouth to talk but then closes it. I can tell he is mulling a response around in his head but resists saying anything out loud. Instead he just nods and pulls into the parking garage at his building.

Graham parks, gets out, and opens my door. Once my belt is undone, I am pulled from my seat and tucked close to his side.

"You look enchanting in this costume, Angie," he says softly while calling for the elevator. "Wish there was more of it, though. And only for me to see."

I roll my eyes at his overly conservative—only in public —nature.

"Lucky for you, you are not in control of what I choose to wear or not wear. So don't worry your pretty little head about it."

He narrows his eyes down at me. He is going to bite his tongue completely off if I keep goading him like this.

I look up at him with innocent eyes and bat my eyelashes. I feel this unexplainable need to tease him. Tempt him. To make him fall over the edge and snap. I'm smart enough to know the game is dangerous. I just lack the willpower to keep myself from playing.

"I know what you're doing," he says calmly.

"Is it working?"

The metal doors pop open, and he pushes me inside the elevator against the rear wall. I let out a high-pitched yelp. His body molds against mine, and my luggage purse slips to the floor. He lifts my skimpy dress over my head as the doors shut, tossing it behind him. I am shielded with his body, completely consumed by everything that is Graham Hoffman.

His mouth suctions to the side of my neck, and he bites down. It's like he is branding me. My good hand grips his hair and tugs with unbridled need.

I moan and hoist my leg around his thigh.

Hands grip my ass cheeks, and he lifts me high up in the air, kissing my bare stomach. One arm holds my weight, while the other shoves his keycard into the slot that allows access to his penthouse floor. As we ascend, I grind my crotch against his growing erection.

"This changes nothing, Graham," I remind. My voice is airy.

"Whatever you want to think, Angie." He pulls back on his hips just to thrust them forward.

I jolt backward with each round. My left hand tugs at his shirt, making him growl from his diaphragm. It sounds animalistic.

"I'm still pissed at you for lying to me."

"Be pissed."

"This is just sex."

He snarls and ravishes my mouth to shut me up. My bottom lip gets bitten, and I instantly feel my gray cotton boy shorts dampen. His facial hair scrapes against my skin, and I love the rough friction it provides. My breasts mash against his chest, and I feel my nipples harden underneath my mismatched blue bra.

His mouth pulls away reluctantly, and he holds my back against the cold paneled wall. One hand is under my ass, while the other grips my jaw so I am forced to look at him.

His eyes darken. "Pretend whatever you want, my sweet and salty Angie." His mouth closes in on the exposed skin of my shoulder, and he nibbles at it before coming up for air. "But it has never been *just* sex."

I swallow my pooling saliva and moan as his cock twitches beneath me. I want him.

"I feel as if you are overdressed."

He chuckles and smacks a hand against my ass cheek, making me cry out. It feels that good.

The bell rings and the doors slide open. Graham kicks my discarded dress and bag into the foyer and carries me right into his home. I kick my shoes off and they fall to the floor somewhere between the kitchen and living room. Up the stairs we go to the king-sized bed where I lost my virginity to him a few weeks ago. He tosses me gently onto the center. I try to conceal my body by bending my knees and holding them to my chest. It is like he is seeing me for the first time.

"If I was smart, I would tie you to this bed and keep you hostage. Never let you leave," he says smoothly, removing his shoes, shirt, and jeans in one continuous string of motions.

I swallow at his words. In this moment of need, I would not resist. Adrenaline is running through my veins, and Graham brings out a side of me that I never knew existed. He makes me want things I shouldn't want. He makes me crazy.

Once naked, he crawls to me on the bed and tugs my

legs apart. He buries his nose into my clothed pussy and breathes. It's like he is inhaling a drug.

"Fucking ripe and ready for me," he exhales. His warm breath makes my skin prickle with goosebumps.

He turns his head and kisses each of my inner thighs as he yanks my wet boy shorts down my legs. My bra is discarded next. Before I realize what is happening, I am flipped over in one fluid movement, lying flat on my belly. Graham's hands grip my ass cheeks and pull them apart, enabling him to see every vulnerable inch of me. I tense under his gaze, nervous that he is going to take me *that* way.

"Relax," he says calmly. "You are nowhere near ready for me to take you there."

I gulp. I am not sure I will ever be ready. Especially with how big he is. And how *inexperienced* I am.

"Yet."

"Fuck," I gasp. I try to look over my shoulder to see what he is doing.

His chuckles don't help my apprehension. "On your elbows and knees," he orders. "Do not put pressure on your hands."

I hesitate for a moment to mull it over in my head. I press my forehead into the comforter, groaning at how I managed to get myself back in Graham's bed. Do I really want to put myself in such a vulnerable position? Do I really want to continue on with this "enemies with benefits" program I somehow enrolled myself in full time?

He bites my shoulder, making me jerk my head back to catch his sexy toothy grin.

"Be my good girl."

My eyes glass over at his words. He makes me so hot

for him with just a few simple words.

"I thought you liked me bad?" I purr.

"I love you any way I can have you. But my preference will always be with you writhing with ecstasy underneath me while I pump into you."

Well, okay then.

I put my weight on my elbows and pull my knees up. I keep my ass high up in the air.

Graham gently pulls my knees apart so that the air hits my pussy, making me want to scratch at the itch.

"You are glowing," he says softly—almost reverently. "So beautiful."

I feel the bed dip behind me as he settles himself between my legs.

"I'm not going to be gentle, Angie."

I nod at the warning.

"I'm going to be rough," he continues. "So you fucking remember this moment for days. I want you sore this time. I want you aching for me. Yearning for me to sneak into your room and rub you raw over and over again. But for this to continue, I need your verbal consent. I want your words that this is what you want."

"Yes, dammit." I push my ass back and feel the hardness of his cock at my swollen lips.

"Oh no, sweetheart, you are not the one in control. We are doing this my way."

I whimper when he pulls himself away from my entrance and grips my hips so tight I know I will be bruised in the morning. But I don't care. I want his mark on me. I want the physical reminder that everything we are doing is real and not some figment of my imagination.

I feel the velvety head of his cock again, and I resist the urge to push backward in fear that he will stop. I rest my head on the soft comforter and allow my pelvis to relax and open up. I close my eyes tight in anticipation. I haven't had sex in a while and miss the feeling of being full.

Graham leans over me and wraps his arm around my body. He tweaks each nipple and kisses the sides of my neck. I groan into the mattress at the sensations he is eliciting from me. When he straightens back up, he rubs down my belly with his palm, until his fingers stop on my clit. He presses the bundle of nerves hard, making me jerk up from the mattress.

"Easy," he soothes. "I got you, baby."

He continues to push hard and then softens his touch. Over and over. I can feel my moisture drip out and onto my thighs.

"Hmm, more..." I moan.

"I will give you everything you have ever wanted, if you let me."

His words rattle my soul, because I know he is referring to more than just sex. But right in this very moment, I need this to just be about sex. Nothing more.

When I am so on edge and primed, with my juices flowing out of me, he resumes his position with his cock between my folds—hovering right at my entrance. I lift my head up in anticipation and brace myself for what is inevitably going to come next. Graham rocks his hips, and then slams forward so hard that I slide forward on the bed.

I scream out from the mere force.

My own chant is reciprocated as he gets used to being inside me again.

"You are squeezing me like a vise. So tight." He pulls back, just to plunge forward again.

My head falls back to the mattress, and my thighs quiver to stay strong enough to withstand his thrusting. At this angle, I am able to feel him to the root—his balls smacking against me. He repeats this hard pattern until he finds a pace he enjoys and can maintain.

"How does it feel, sweetheart? You okay?"

I can barely form a word so I just nod.

He gives my ass a slap, and I yelp at the surprise.

He thrusts into me. "Fuck, you are such a bad little girl." He pulls almost completely out. "Getting extra wet when I treat you like my wench." Thrust. "You are only lying to yourself if you claim you don't enjoy everything I do to you." Pull back.

I yell out his name as he drives back into me again. I feel my walls clench and relax as he shifts his hips down so he can get a different angle inside of me.

"Ahhhh," I belt out. Every time he pushes back in and hits my spot, I yell his name.

"Yes, take me. All of me."

My breathing increases, and I start to get lightheaded from the pleasure he draws out of me. I am so close. I squeeze my walls and my vision blurs as the orgasm overcomes me.

"Yes, baby, oh fuck, you are so tight."

His moans mirror mine—our two voices merging into one.

Graham pushes one last time into me and unloads as I pulse around him with my own release. I collapse my hips forward onto the bed and he follows me on top—still buried inside me. I pant from the sheer force of my orgasm. It is like I am high up on a cloud, never wanting to come back down to earth to face the consequences of giving in to him.

Graham wraps his arms around my stomach and rolls us to the side so we are spooning. His cock slips out, and I instantly miss the warmth. A comforter gets wrapped and tucked underneath me. I drift off to sleep in the safety of his arms.

I wake up in the night with the only light being from the moon filtering through the open blinds. I need to use the bathroom. I slip out of Graham's hold and sit along the edge of the bed just staring. His breathing is steady, and he looks like he is dreaming peacefully.

I meander into the bathroom. When finished, I make my way to the bed with an itch growing between my legs that needs attention. I am a good kind of sore, and the more we have sex, the more I want it. The clock on the end table reads 4:17 a.m., and I am surprised I am not more tired.

I pull back the comforter from Graham and lie upside down next to him on my side. My mouth waters, and I lick the tip of his cock with one long stroke. I use my left hand to hold him at the base and then cover my entire mouth over the first inch of his length. I suck on him like a lollipop before he jerks in my mouth, and I hear him stir above me.

"Angie…"

His voice cracks with sleep.

"Mm hmm," I hum, making him grow between my lips. He tastes good, and I can't help but get wet over the thought of sucking him after he has been in me.

Hands grip my waist, and I am elevated so that I am on top of hard muscle. My legs spread to maintain my balance, resting my knees on each side of his torso. His fingers part my folds, and his mouth locks onto my pussy lips with hunger. I moan deeply over his cock.

"Watch your teeth, woman."

"Mumph swowry," I mumble.

He continues to lick me and tongue my hole, as I slurp and suck and slide him farther into my throat.

"Fuck," he growls, ripping his mouth off of me. "You trying to end this before we even get started?"

"Hmm hmm," I hum. I love when he loses his control and unwinds. It gives me the illusion that I hold some of the power.

My weight is mainly on my elbow, as I experiment with my breathing and how much I can take at once. I suck him in, and my cheeks hollow with the suction. I slide him out and then slide down even more with my lips. I take a deep breath and breathe through my nose each time I pull up and then push down. I keep my lips tight around his girth and when I think I can't take anymore, I go just a bit farther.

I hear Graham's guttural groan and know that I am doing it right. He is enjoying this. His mouth is lazy along my pussy, and I am relieved that he is not putting forth the normal level of effort—otherwise I may lose my own focus. I hop off his upper body and turn so I can get the best angle without getting lockjaw.

I lick up from root to tip and feel his hands grip palmfuls of hair. My scalp tingles as he pulls and tugs and encourages me to keep going. I lick up again and then completely slide him into my mouth until my nose is pressed against his belly. He screams my name in the darkness, and saliva leaks out all over his groin from my mouth.

I pull back so that only his tip is inside and do the same thing again. I keep my gag reflex in check and do it one more time. I feel the first pulse and taste the salty pre-cum that serves as a warning that there is more to come.

"If you don't want to swallow," he starts, his voice airy and out of breath, "I suggest you get up here. Now."

I smile and ignore him. I know what I am doing. He just doesn't know it yet. I use my good hand to reach under and grip his balls gently. I give him a squeeze at the same time I push forward all the way and hold my breath. I fear I may pass out but I stay still and hear my name echoing in the room.

Graham jerks in my mouth and warm liquid splashes against the back of my throat and down into my esophagus. I pull back and push forward again as the next wave erupts from Graham's cock. I slurp and suck and inhale through my nose just to do the whole routine again. His hands massage and squeeze and pet my upper body—anything he can reach from his position. When I know he is spent, I allow him to fall lazily from my mouth.

Graham pulls me gently up and cradles me to his body. He turns so he is facing me, grips my chin in one hand, and makes sure I am staring right into his eyes.

"You are such a surprise to me. You are everything I didn't think I needed in my life, Angie. And everything I am trying desperately to hold on to."

"I don't want to talk," I whisper. "I just want to be here with you and not think about the hundred reasons I should leave right now."

I can tell he wants to talk. To say something. But he chooses not to ruin the moment. Instead, he pushes me to my back, mounts me missionary style, and makes slow love to me until the sun rises with the first sign of morning.

We both drift back off to sleep, and I dream about the man I thought I knew. But in reality, everything I do know is what he has fed me.

I wake up alone. At a glance at the clock, I find it is almost ten in the morning. I notice the first aid kit is on the nightstand, and my bandage on my right hand got changed. I must have been really tired to not even feel it being done.

I glance around the room and don't see Graham in the bathroom or closet. I search the floor for a shirt or something to wear but come up empty. I roll out of bed and pad across the room. I slide open the door for the walk-in closet and am overcome with surprise. The last time I was here, Graham's clothing took up the entire space. Now, over half the racks and shelves contain female clothing. I run my hands over the elegant fabrics and leaf through the hung-up shirts to see that everything is in my size. The folded pairs of jeans have my length and waist measurements correct. Skirts and dresses are all tailored with me in mind. At the end, I find a variety of shoes that are meant for my feet. I am overcome with—

I don't even know. Gratitude? Shock? Confusion.

I don't want to have a beautiful wardrobe here. I don't want to let my heart open just to have it stomped on again.

I hear Graham's voice downstairs and assume he is on some business call. I really want to find my own phone. Thus, I pull a pair of gray leggings and a long-sleeved cranberry Henley down from a shelf to wear. In the dresser, I open several drawers until I find the sets of bras and panties. I knew if Graham spent this much time and effort on clothes that he would not skimp on the undergarments. He is an attention-to-detail kind of man. I select a black ensemble that feels like they were handmade using the softest silk and lace trim. Next, I pull open the bottom drawer to see his secretive items are still in the same location. I will need to find a good opportunity to pick the lock on the boxes. He mustn't be too concerned over me snooping if he left everything right where I found it last.

I carry my items back to the bed and get dressed. I wash my face and brush my hair before making my way downstairs in search of my fake luggage bag. I vaguely remember Graham kicking it into the foyer after our heavy elevator petting session.

When I get to the main floor and round the bend into the kitchen area, I find Graham and another man talking in low voices. The man has sandy-brown hair that is cut military style. He is Graham's height but has a bit more muscle on his bones. He looks to be about thirty and has chiseled jaw bones that make it hard for him to show much expression other than indifference.

The talking stops and both men turn to where I am standing—just staring. "Oh, hi," I say in a breath. I rock on my feet, not sure what else to say.

Graham's eyes focus on me, and I can tell he is on edge. Something has changed in his mood. He is no longer laid-back. Just by the way his back is so rigid and his face is stern, I can guarantee that Sex Crazed Graham has retired. Replacing him is now Calculated Graham. The steel look in his eyes makes me think I did something wrong. He saunters over to me, and I gulp at his no-nonsense attitude. Shit. What did I do?

"I, ah, I'm just going to go find my phone," I say, pushing past him only to be halted by his arms that dart out to wrap around my waist. "What the—"

"It's on the table," Graham says, pointing to its location.

I pull out of his arms and glare at him. Why is he doing this in front of his guest? And why is no one introducing me? Awkward. I make my way over to the dining room, a room I have never actually spent time in, and feel both men shadowing me. My hair stands on end, as I spot my luggage and phone. When I get closer, I see my bags of pills and recording device out in the open. I spin around to find Graham just inches from colliding into me. I yelp at his angry expression.

"You went…" I stop my sentence and turn back around to make sure what I am seeing is actually true. Yup. This most definitely looks like he is violating—once again—my personal boundaries. Now some mysterious person on the sideline is witnessing his levels of overstepping. Lovely. Just lovely. "You went through my belongings?" I ask, venom dripping from my mouth. I'm not sure why I phrased it as a question, when the answer is so obviously a *yes*.

"Yeah, and you have basically made it impossible for me to trust you." His voice is devoid of humor. "Yet again."

This entire situation seems so hilarious to me. As if, how can this be real life? I let out an exaggerated laugh.

"Are you serious?" I ask. "Do you even hear yourself? Trust me? What the hell, Graham! You are the one snooping through my stuff."

"You have overstepped," he says. "You keep interfering. Putting yourself in danger. You are going to get yourself kidnapped or worse."

"What? How?"

"This isn't a movie, Angie. You are not messing with amateurs. You are putting yourself at risk and actively looking for trouble. Collecting pills? Really?" He closes the distance between us, forcing me to back up to get some space. He shakes a bag into the air, causing the pills to settle into the corner. "What if the person knew you took them? What if they had a count on them?"

I frown over his words and back up a few steps. I could be in danger. But right now, I am so invested and so determined to find out what is happening to the agency girls that I cannot back down now. Their lives, as well as mine, are affected.

"I'm sorry that you think it's necessary to boss me around, but I have just as much riding on this as you do with your need to find justice for your sister. I have friends in the agency and am also affected by this craziness. This isn't—"

He stalks toward me and slams his hand on the surface of the table. "Stop!" he bellows, seething with anger. "This stops. Today. Right now. Give this up."

"No! You don't own me or control me." I am pissed. Who does he think he is?

"I will do *anything* to protect you."

My eyes shoot daggers at him. "What does that mean, Graham?"

He looks between me and his guest. "Well, I guess now is a great time to get acquainted with the new bodyguard."

7

I shake my head frantically back and forth.

No.

Nooo.

I stomp my feet over his overbearing caveman tendencies. There is no way I am going to go about my normal life with a freaking bodyguard attached to my hip. Graham is nuts. He has lost it. Gone clinically insane.

I watch in silence as the man steps out from his stance in the corner and walks hesitantly over to us. He has been watching this tirade the entire time.

"Who's he a bodyguard for? Me or you? Because if you keep this up, Graham fucking Hoffman"—I wave my finger angrily in his face—"I'll make you wish you had protection from *me*."

A sexy smirk slips from his stern expression, and I want to smack it right off his face.

"Are you really stomping your feet?"

I stare down at my angry foot. I guess I am. I look back

up to his eyes and narrow mine. "Do not turn your actions into humor! There's nothing funny about this!"

Graham turns his attention to his hired man. "Angela, this is Trevor. Trevor, this is my feisty and sassy woman."

Trevor tips his head in a single nod. "Nice to meet you, ma'am."

I give him a weak smile and focus back on Graham. "No."

"You didn't even hear what I have to say."

"No."

He sighs. "Angie, be reasonable."

"No!"

He shoves hair off his forehead, grasping the back of his neck with the palm of his hand. "You are the most exasperating and frustrating woman I've ever come across on this entire planet."

"Good. But the answer is still no."

"Listen to—"

"I'm not doing this, Graham. There is no us. It was just sex."

He flinches at my words.

"It was good sex too," I admit. "But I cannot do what you are trying to do here. Nope. No. No!"

"Angie…"

"Stop. Just stop. In the next three minutes, I am going to pack my bag up and gather my belongings. Then I am going to walk out your door. Alone. And if you are lucky, I may consider associating with you in the future." He can be a booty call, if he's lucky.

I do everything I claim to do, except for putting the pills back in my bag. Because I am pretty sure Graham will pounce on me if I try. I slip my phone, recording device, and wire back into the luggage. Then I walk out into the foyer where I find my shoes and dress on the chair. I slide my heels on and hit the call button for the elevator. Graham and Trevor watch my every movement from the sidelines.

When the elevator arrives and the doors open, I step inside. Before I can hit the button for them to shut faster, Trevor is at my side.

I look up at him and groan. Then I snarl at Graham as the doors shut.

"First day on the job and probably have a migraine already, eh?" I ask trying to break the ice—before I completely ditch him once the doors open. When he doesn't engage, I continue. "Listen, you look like a nice guy. I'm sure you are highly qualified and really good at taking orders from Big Boss Man, but he has pretty much gone off the deep end and is breaking all kinds of stalking laws and well, I don't need that type of negativity in my life right now. So, when these doors open, I'm going to go about my life as if Graham Hoffman never invaded it. To me, he doesn't exist anymore. He crossed a line, and I am tired of letting him get his way like a tyrant toddler."

I think it's the calm silence that pisses me off the most. Or the fact that when the doors do open, he hovers from a safe distance while I text Zander to come and get me. If Trevor is going to follow my tail, he might as well follow it to some other man's house—and then report back to his boss.

Prior to snooping through my belongings, Graham had to know I was serious about staying away from him. I am still very much pissed at him. This bodyguard stunt only adds more fuel to the fire. He's not an only child, yet acts like one. This type of behavior can only be explained by being spoiled during those fundamental years of life. What else would justify why he thinks this is his world, and we all just live in it? With his permission, of course.

I walk outside to wait the rest of the time for Zander and already sense Trevor's presence. I spin around and put my hands on my hips. "Any chance you can be paid off?"

I see the barest movement of his lips. If I wasn't looking specifically for a reaction, I may have missed it.

"No, ma'am."

"How about a quarter million?" It would be the best way I could spend the money Graham tried to bribe me with.

"No, ma'am."

My mouth gapes. "Not enough? You want more?"

It's the last question I ask because Trevor has now put himself into super silent mode and refuses to talk to me—even if just to tell me no.

Well, if I am forced to endure this crap, I might as well make the best of it. I pull open my camera app and select some animal filters. I switch it into selfie mode and wait for the app to add cat ears and whiskers to me. Trevor behind me is adorned with some dog ears and a puppy dog nose.

"Selfie time," I announce and snap a few pictures of us. He looks as thrilled as I would expect of someone who takes his job seriously and has a brat who keeps annoying him. Maybe if I keep this up, he will just quit. There has to be easier jobs than following me around while I harass the shit out of him.

I send the picture to Graham first. And then to Claire. I

get Grumpy Man to bite first, which I can't say is surprising.

Graham: For the love of God, Angie! Please do not distract your bodyguard!

Angie: I am trying to get him to quit. This shall be fun.

Graham: Don't think I won't come down there right now and carry you back to my cave.

Angie: Whatevs

Graham: Tying you to my bed is not off the table.

Angie: Kicking you in the balls isn't either.

Graham: Such a filthy mouth.

I am about to text him back a snappy response when Zander pulls up to the curb and winds down his window.

"Ready to go?" He flashes me a genuine smile.

"More than you know," I grunt, sliding into the passenger side.

I watch from the window as Trevor pulls out his cell and speaks into the device. I wave at him and mouth, "buh-bye." I feel immature but hopeful that I can escape his shadow for a few hours.

"Who's that?" Zander asks.

"Oh, no one important." I turn my attention back to him. "Where we going?"

"Where do you want to go?"

"Any place but here, please."

He glances over to me. "Want to go to Paint Night at Bliss? The guys are going too, but I need to swing by and get them so they can drink away their sorrows. Apparently they had dates who backed out last minute and now have two unclaimed tickets."

Bliss is a trendy stand-alone restaurant and bar in the Pearl District that caters to hipsters and the younger crowd.

"Um, yeah, sure. Am I dressed okay?" I look down at my leggings and long-sleeved shirt. I'm sure they cost way more than I ever would have paid, but I also don't want to stand out in a social setting.

"Of course. You always look amazing, Angie. It's just a casual thing."

I relax into my seat, ready for something fun and carefree. "I don't need to actually have skill, right?"

He gives me a lopsided smile. "Have you seen my stick figures?"

His lightheartedness makes me smile. I have missed this. Zander and I have spent many afternoons over the past few years playing video games, watching TV, and chatting about life. He has always been a rock for me—even though I am positive I do not deserve him. He is always the better friend.

When he pulls into his parking spot at his townhouse, he turns in his seat and studies my face. "Everything okay with you, right? I heard there was some drama at the Halloween party last night, but I am getting my information from those two jackasses." He points up to his place. "And we both know how their stories get embellished."

"Yeah, I'm fine. But there have been some girls getting caught up in some campus drugging cases. I'm not sure if the girl there last night was drugged, but she was having a seizure. Super scary to witness." I cross my arms over my chest as a shiver runs through me. "It all just freaks me out."

"Never expected you to go to a party. If I knew that, I would have told my dad no to dinner."

I frown over his words. "Your dad probably misses you, Z. I would—" I stop. The words get caught in my throat, and I just shrug to avoid talking anymore about it.

He takes my hand in his and squeezes. "I'm sorry, Angie. It was an insensitive thing to say. I'm glad I had dinner with him, of course. I just wish you would stop putting yourself in potentially dangerous situations."

Join the club, buddy.

"Well, I'm fine. Everything is fine. I just want to put last night behind me and move forward."

"The paint event doesn't start for another hour. So do you want to come in and hang out before we all have to leave?"

"Sounds good." I exit the car and step up on the sidewalk.

"Go on up. I am going to clean out my backseat so we all have enough room to ride together."

When I get home from the night out, Zander and I loiter outside my door.

"Thanks for a wonderful afternoon and evening," I say and give him a hug. I genuinely had a great time laughing with him and his obnoxious roommates. It was exactly what I needed in this moment of struggle.

His arms wrap around me and squeeze me tight. "I enjoyed it as well. More than I was expecting to, to tell you the truth." He pulls back to look at me. "Sometimes hanging out with the roommates can get crazy. I'm glad you can handle my friends."

I can see what he is saying. They are definitely over-the-top. But they are harmless. "They aren't so bad."

Zander rocks on his heels and shoves his hands into his pockets. "So, when my dad left, he asked if I could come home for a weekend and see my sister."

"Something wrong?"

"Miss McFee?"

My name being said makes me jump a few inches into the air. "What the hell?" I spin around to see Trevor standing on the sidewalk. "Do not do that to me again!"

"Who is he, Angie?" Zander asks.

I frown. "Graham's newly appointed henchman." I turn back to Trevor and wave him off. "Please just leave me alone. I'm fine. Everything is fine." I look up at Zander. "Let's go inside."

I unlock the door and guide him inside so we can finish this conversation without listening ears. Ugh. How did my life get this messed up? Again. Everything always ends up being complicated.

Zander relaxes into a chair, and I kick my feet up on the sofa adjacent to him.

"Sorry about that," I say, pointing to the outside. "I

don't even know where to start with that whole situation. So, let's just forget it. Please tell me, is something wrong with your sister?"

"Nah. I mean, maybe." He gives a shrug. "I plan to take a long weekend and go see her. Maybe she'll open up to me, since my parents seem at a loss at what to do."

I reach back behind me and grab an elastic band from the end table. It is resting beside Claire's favorite cupcake-flavored lip gloss. I swear that girl has twenty of them scattered about this place. "When do you plan to go?" I pull my hair away from my face and wrap the tie around it, securing it into place.

"Well, that depends."

I straighten my posture. "Okay…"

"I'm a little flexible over the next two weeks. But I was hoping to make a road trip out of it. I have a friend in San Fran who I can stay with for the night or just use as a rest stop."

"Oh cool."

Zander clears his throat. "But I was wondering if you wanted to come with me."

I swallow hard at his offer. Wow. I have always wanted to go to California and see some sights. I love to travel and see places, but over the course of the past decade, I haven't been able to see much of anything—other than missed opportunities. Family vacations stopped immediately with momma's first diagnosis of ovarian cancer. It pretty much sealed us off from the world of germs. And when she died, going anywhere seemed like a waste of time and a nagging reminder that she was gone. Then after James passed, I moved across the state and haven't really left since. Claire and I would work during the summers and maybe drive to an Oregon beach for a day.

"I, ah," I say with hesitation.

"Don't answer now. Just think about it."

Zander's eyes turn hopeful, and it pulls at my heart. We say goodnight to each other and I see him out. I lock my door and set the alarm system that I never asked for but that I suddenly feel compelled to use anyway. I guess being a little extra safe is not a bad thing.

Picking up my phone, I dial Resa's number. When her recorded voice message plays in my ear, I take a deep breath. "Hey, Resa, it's um, Angie. Just calling to see how you are. Things have gotten really rough here. Girls are getting drugged. I hope you are doing well."

Once I end the call, I feel the familiar vibration alerting me of a text.

Resa: I'm sorry I've been MIA. I found a therapist in my hometown and talking to someone about the whole thing has helped. Just a lot going on inside my head. I heard of the Halloween party incident. Please don't get involved, Angie.

Angie: I'll be safe.

Resa may not have been drugged, but she was at the Campus Smoothie Cafe when other girls were drugged. Paul is in the middle of this mystery and whatever he is hiding, I will find out.

I see my painting near the shoe rack and carry it into the living room. My interpretation of the cherry blossoms never took on the full appeal of the instructor's version; however, the memories made tonight will always make me smile. Especially the one where Zander drank from the red Solo cup of dirty paint water and spit it all over his canvas. I laughed so hard, amaretto sour came out of my nose, burning the inner lining. His face was priceless.

A few hours of fun snapped me out of my funk. It was exactly what I needed. In those little moments, I forget about the dark cloud hovering over my head, as I try to unlock the mystery happening around campus.

Graham may want to protect me, but I have an obligation to protect these innocent girls who are falling victim to some madman.

8

I wake to the smell of food that is not bacon and groan to myself in sadness. Oh no. I knew this winning streak would eventually come to an end. Something is wrong with the dynamic duo. Even my nose senses it.

I throw on some clothes and quickly get myself ready for class. A glance at my clock tells me I have plenty of time. However, I need to address the situation downstairs, and that may require a lot of tiptoeing around some conversational landmines.

When I make it into the kitchen, Claire is in the dining area with a bag of carrots, and I instantly feel faint. *Please, God, no.* Please no. I cannot revisit the shredded carrot diet again. I just can't. As her roomie and bestie, I always feel compelled to go along with her initiatives. Oh, and because I'm scared of her.

Claire gets up from her seat, spots me, and gives me a half smile. I smile back and watch, paralyzed by fear of the future, as she goes over to the skillet and stirs what I know without a doubt is fake animal meat. The smell indicates it is plant-based and void of an appetizing flavor. Any sane person knows there is nothing organic or natural about trying to force the earth to be a mammal.

I lean my back against the island and watch her flitter robotically about the kitchen. Her silence is unnerving, and I am not used to it at all.

I look back at the table and see the start of a dream board that is situated beside the pile of freshly cleaned carrots. She has cut out her favorite flower—the sunflower—and glued it on the middle of the tripod board. Around the vibrant yellow centerpiece, she wrote the words *empower*, *cleanse*, *detox*, *independence*, and *reflection*.

Claire moves to the sink area and starts peeling overripe spotted bananas. Then one by one, she grinds them down the garbage disposal. Eek. Ethan better watch out or his manhood is next.

"Claire?"

"Hmm?"

"Hi."

"You're just in time for breakfast."

Lucky me.

I am going to vomit on sight. I watch with disgust as Claire plates up the "meat" and carries it over to the table, pushing her dream board to the side to give us more room. The fact she is here for breakfast and not at the gym tells me this is something major. I would even go as far as saying *monumental*. Shit!

"Thank you," I mumble and walk over to where she is setting down my plate. I stare at the nasty inedible strips of fake-bacon. They are not even the correct color, which is just disturbing. Ew. "I'm surprised to see you this morning."

"Why? I live here."

I swallow and try to keep my tone lighthearted. "I know, but you are usually off saving the world."

"Sometimes I just want to have a low-key day and not have anyone expect anything from me."

I sigh and relax my shoulders. "I hear you, sister."

I sit back and watch as she eats her food. When her fakin' bacon is done, she shreds off the outer layer of carrot using the peeler and chomps at the freshly cleaned skinny end—like you would expect a cartoon bunny to do. It is so hideous and bizarre to watch. Almost painful.

"Want one?"

"No, thanks. When are you going to be ready to talk about it?"

"Never."

"Claire? C'mon, let's just get it over with. Then we don't have to talk about it anymore."

She shakes her head adamantly.

"Can you at least tell me if I am going to have to eat carrots for most of my meals that I enjoy at home?" I soften my tone. "So I can mentally prepare myself."

She breaks off another piece with her molars, looks down at her teeth marks, and then bursts into tears.

I scoot my chair over and embrace her in a hug.

Her sobs shake through her body, and she can barely get the words out. "He…is…an ass."

I rub her back and fix her hair to stop sticking to her face. "I know." Whatever she shares, I know it is his fault. I will forever be on Team Claire. "Tell me what happened."

"Things might not be over with him and his ex-wife, Deena. I should've seen this coming. For starters, he has baggage. What would I expect from a guy who pays for dates? I think he used me to make her jealous."

"You don't know that, Claire."

"Deena wants to go on a family weekend trip with him and their son. She says that it is for Finn's sake, but I don't know. I just have a bad feeling."

"Have you tried talking with him?"

"No. What's the point? I don't want to just delay the inevitable."

"So, what do you plan to do?" I ask cautiously.

This is the point in the conversation that may involve something on my part. Are we eating just carrots? Are we limiting how much trash we put into landfills? Perhaps we are going to consume all meals through straws. Or are we just going vegan? I can pretty much fake any of those options—except the carrot one. That one by far is the worst. I am pretty sure my hands still have the calluses to prove that I peeled way too many carrots in this lifetime.

"I just need to clear my head," she says sadly. "Think about my own goals and execute a plan for my vision board."

I nod my head over her suggestion.

The doorbell rings. I'm glad to excuse myself and not be pressured to eat whatever it is that Claire cooked up. I check the peep hole and see Dr. Saber standing on the step. He is dressed in jeans and a button-down.

I open the door and welcome him inside.

"I wasn't expecting you, Dr. Saber."

"Mitch," he says with a smile. "Graham wanted to make

sure you are fully healed and that your stitches could be removed promptly."

"In other words, he wanted to control the situation," I mumble, regretting my words as soon as they escape my mouth. My brain-to-mouth filter seems to be broken. "Sorry."

Dr. Saber throws back his head and laughs. "Wow, Graham has finally met his match in you. Never thought I'd see the day."

I give a shrug. I am just calling it as I see it.

I show Dr. Saber to the main floor bathroom so he can wash up. Claire introduces herself and then goes upstairs to get ready for the day. It takes about three minutes for my stitches to be out and for a smaller bandage to cover the area while I continue to heal.

"How does it feel?"

"I have been having some pain."

Dr. Saber takes my hand in his gloved one and examines my range of motion as I bend my fingers. "Hmm…you definitely do not have nerve damage. You healed up beautifully."

"Is there any way I can just get a few pain pills to help me cope with the recovery of using my dominant hand again? To get by as I adjust?"

His brows furrow, and I take a deep breath. I hope he doesn't tell Graham my request and make it into something that it's not. Then I'll have him breaking down my door to try to rescue me.

"I don't typically prescribe medication for situations like this due to the addictive nature that those drugs can bring to innocent lives. Give it a few weeks. Things should improve naturally. But if they don't, I can recommend an occupational therapist and they can probably come to your house if that is convenient for you."

"I doubt my insurance will allow that," I mumble. I have the cheapest package specifically designed for poor college students like me. After being blacklisted from Entice by the cranky boss-in-disguise, I refuse to use their healthcare services either. "Speaking of which, how much is all of this going to cost?"

"Angie, don't you realize that Graham will cover everything? I have known him for years. I guess the benefit of being someone he cares about is that you will always be taken care of."

Yeah, against my will.

I walk Dr. Saber out and enter my car. I have just enough time to get to the coffee shop and to class before Bryce will start blowing up my phone. He just does not handle change very well. I can relate.

After class, I go back home and find Claire watching recorded infomercials while wearing a shirt that is four sizes too big. Wow. This is getting worse and worse.

I look at her sad face. "How much did you buy?"

"It was a good deal."

I groan. "Like the vegetable spiral thingy?"

"Better. This will actually work."

I look at the screen and see the miraculous demonstration of the foolproof hair-cutting gadget set for women. No way in hell is she using my head as a test dummy. I draw the line there.

"I need your help," I say with hesitation.

Claire looks up at me skeptically. As she should, because this was a very last-minute plan I constructed in my head during my morning class. But I figure, if she doesn't have a daily goal, she is going to just mope around and be sad for herself. She and Ethan could have just had a misunderstanding. Regardless, I need to get Claire out of this slump she seems to be content living in and change the course of her day so she can figure out what to do next.

"Go on."

"I think I'm ready to try out that dancing class at your gym but am afraid that I won't be good at it."

"That's nonsense," she scoffs, "everyone is good at it, as long as they move."

"I dunno…"

"You will love it. You loved the other ones I have taken you to, so why would this one be any different? There is actually a class this afternoon."

I bite my bottom lip and pray that she takes the lead.

"Let's just go together," she suggests. "You'll see how much fun it is."

Yes! "If you insist."

"I insist. And let's go now so we can day drink and still be sober enough to dance."

"Umm, do you think that's a good idea?"

"Best one I've had all day. Nothing puts a better sway in my hips than a delicious margie."

"Let me go change."

I run upstairs and dig out something suitable for the bar and pack a bag for the gym. From a selfish standpoint, I'm glad we can spend this time together. I miss it just being the two of us.

Once I get downstairs, I slip on my sneakers and double check my gym bag. I reach into the bottom, making my way out the door with Claire, trying to verify that I did bring my cell phone. A message from Graham appears on the screen, making me blush and laugh at the same time.

Graham: I miss you like your tongue misses my lollipop.

Even though we aren't together, his words still affect me. He is the first man who has ever made me feel alive. Even when I'm mad at him, he still has the power to connect with my emotions—even if just via text. But his disregard for my own wishes makes it easier to walk away from him. To take a step back and figure out what I really want. And what I can't live without.

As Claire locks the door, I make my way down the steps. In my peripheral vision, I catch a dark figure in the afternoon light, making me jump and squeal. My bag falls to the sidewalk, and I hold my hand up to my heart. The suited man stares back at me, groaning at my reaction.

"Sorry, ma'am," he responds apologetically.

Claire turns on the doorstep and sees what the commotion is about and narrows her eyes at the polished man.

"Who are you?" she asks blankly.

"I'm Parker, ma'am. Mr. Hoffman instructed me to drive you ladies wherever you may need to go while he is across the country for business."

"Oh, please," she huffs. "We have cars, you know. Oh, and we're not twelve. We also do not answer to that man's orders. 'Kay, buh-bye." She flutters her fingers at him, as if he is a petulant child.

"This has to do with the Halloween party incident," I whisper, trying to tamp down my own anger. Of course one guard would not appease Graham; he would need to hire a whole security team to deal with me. Ugh. The man is lacking boundaries. It's as if he has never been told *no* in his life.

Despite the shock, I grab my bag off the ground and make my way toward Parker, who is taller than Collins but thinner. He eyes me carefully, ready to pounce if any bad guys jump out of the shrubs. I contemplate tripping on purpose just to test his reaction time. Instead, I sashay to Claire's car and slip inside the passenger side when she unlocks it from the key fob. I slam the door shut and reach over to adjust my belongings and strap in. Her amused expression lets me know that she is on board with my spike of independence. I slide down my window with Parker's persistent tapping.

I muster up my sweetest voice. "How can I help you?" I undo my ponytail only to twist the band around my gathered hair again.

"Mr. Hoffman gave me strict orders to drive you personally. And to not let Miss Nettles do it."

"He did *not* just say that," Claire says, staring straight ahead. "But he did, didn't he?" She stews from the driver's seat and then turns suddenly toward Parker. Her eyes narrow into slivers, making her look mean and angry. Parker looks like he is going to piss his pants. "Listen here, dude, you better not insult my driving skills. And right now, I hate men, buddy. All. Men. So scurry off and go tell your Mr. Hoffman to leave us the hell alone. Buh-byes."

I stifle a giggle at Claire's usage of *dude*. Classic. "Where is Trevor?" I'm not sure it matters; both he and Parker are equally annoying. But I can't help but wonder if he is lurking around somewhere.

"He was reassigned."

I nod. "Oh, so that's code for fired?"

I watch as Parker shifts his weight from foot to foot. Part of me wants to ruffle his perfectly ironed clothes or spill something on the pure white dress shirt that he wears underneath the suit. He's too put together for Claire's and my mood today. He definitely does not blend in with the students who live in our row of townhouses.

"We'll be safe," Claire promises, not easing the tension tic of Parker's jaw. "So Mr. Hoffman doesn't fire or demote you to cleaning his toilets, how about you follow behind us with your ride? And if you want, you can even come inside the gym we are headed to and break a sweat. After, of course, we get drunk."

Claire is having way too much fun with this whole thing. I think she actually wants him to join us on our mission. She hits the button for my window and flutters her fingers to wave goodbye again. She starts the engine and backs up—almost over Parker's foot. He jumps back just in time.

"That felt good," I admit, watching her pull out of the parking spot.

In my rearview mirror, I see Parker's black car, most likely loaded with every safety feature on the market. For a few-mile trip, who needs an entourage? Apparently Graham thinks I'm incapable of handling myself. I swallow hard at this realization. Is it going to get better as we progress with this non-relationship?

I hear the buzzing of my phone, and I dig it out of my bag. I look at the caller ID, not recognizing the number. I slide the bar to accept the call, and the disapproving sigh alerts me to who is on the other end.

"I hope that you realize that you are getting me out of a very important meeting right now. Midflight, mind you."

"I—"

"No, do not interrupt me." My shoulders slouch. He is pissed. Well, I am too. "When my security guy is in charge of your well-being, I do not take that lightly. Why do you have to defy me?"

Oh, come on. My anger boils as I try to keep my temper in check. I feel like hanging up on him, but I know that will just lead him to more panicked thoughts about my welfare.

"Parker is tailing us. I told you at your place I don't want a bodyguard when you tried to stick Trevor on me. I hardly think that anything bad can happen to me when I'm with Claire."

"Your car is decrepit," he states matter-of-factly. "And she drives hers like she has a death wish."

"Your security guy scared the shit out of me by lurking outside my door this morning. You're making it easy for me to want to run away."

"Pull over the damn car, Angie, and ride with Parker. Claire's driving isn't safe."

A growl releases low in Claire's throat. "I heard that, Teddy Graham!"

He does have a point. I can't tell if her speed is to try to throw Parker off, or if this is just her normal amount of recklessness. It is usually the parked cars I worry about; now it's the moving ones as well. "We're fine."

"I'm so tempted to turn this plane around right now and fly back to the states just to lock you away in my tower."

"Graham…"

"I protect what is mine," he snarls.

Oh the nerve of him. We are doing this dance again? Same story, different day. "Get over it." I push back. "I don't plan on having you dictate my life. You already single-handedly laid me off work. You are by far the worst boss I have ever had," I yell into the speaker in true dramatic teenage fashion.

I can hear him laughing at me on the other end. How we can be in a serious argument and him end up laughing about it is so mind-boggling to me.

"Just stay out of trouble so I don't have to fly home early, please."

"When are you set to come back?"

He lets out a breath. "Saturday or Sunday. It all depends on how the negotiations go."

Wow, basically the entire week. I can tell from his apprehensive tone that he doesn't want to be gone.

"I'm not yours to worry about, Graham."

"You became mine the moment we met. You have a propensity for getting yourself involved in bad situations. And as soon as you accepted the position at Entice, you became more than just a personal responsibility, you became a moral one."

I try my best not to let his words affect me. But they do.

I have never had someone care so much about me outside of my immediate family. I mean, Claire and Zander care. But this is next level. "I'm going to go now, Graham. Enjoy your trip. I will try not to get murdered."

He growls. "Stay safe."

I giggle. "Just going to day drink with my bestie at a shady bar. What could go wrong?"

"You drive me mad, woman."

"I know."

"Be good," he urges.

I blush and lean back against the headrest, praying that Graham's voice doesn't extend to Claire's hearing range. "I'm always good." I hum sultrily and end the call.

Claire glances over at me with wide eyes. "Wow, he seems like he crossed into another level of overprotectiveness."

I shake my head back and forth. "You have no idea. It is getting worse with time too."

9

Claire and I arrive at The Shack around three o'clock, and by four o'clock we are completely intoxicated and loving life. We are sitting at the bar, ordering sex on the beach and blow job shots—just for the increased eye rolls from Parker. He really is a funny man. I thought he would have waited for us in his car, but with Graham being in uber paranoia mode, he was probably given the directive to be up our asses like a thong. He blends in as much as a clown would blend in at a country club.

"D'ya think I'm prettttty?" Claire slurs, leaning against the wooden rail of the bar, clutching her chin in her hand as if her head will fall off if she lets go. The question is directed at Parker, who keeps ordering water and chugging it down. I giggle at the fact that it is most likely from the disgusting county reservoir supply—the kind with all the nasty additive chemicals.

Parker swallows hard and nods his head twice. I want to ask the same question, but for the past hour, I've been met with narrowing eyes and looks of utter disapproval. If he could kill any more of my joys, I might slip into a depression.

"Quit being so damn uptight," I urge, waving the shot glass into the air toward him. "Have a blow job!"

Claire and I laugh so hard that we snort. When I try to drink my concoction, I dribble some of the whipped cream topper down my lips, making Claire about lose it. We are definitely a sight. Too bad that our quest for men at three in the afternoon came up short-handed. There's only, like, eight patrons in the entire place. Some are missing teeth. Our posse takes up three in total. Because poor Parker needed to call for backup. Lame-o.

"I hate fractions."

"Well, no shit," Claire agrees. "But why must you express this random info now?" She is acting completely sober—which, by the way, is my undoing. She sucks at acting.

I laugh to the point of pain, slipping from my stool and thumping to the ground. Claire squeals at Parker. "Dude! Your reflexes suck ass! You are totally not a ninja warrior."

The three men surround me but none want to physically help me up. Probably because I look like a disabled jellyfish. My arms are pulled nearly from their sockets—courtesy of a drunken Claire—but I manage to find my feet.

"Ouch, that hurt," I moan, rubbing my hand against my sore hip. That'll definitely bruise.

"We are leaving," Parker snaps.

"Yes, Ninja Warrior," we both chant in unison, slurping down our last concoction before we get escorted out military style.

We settle into the backseat of what I assume to be Graham's car. Everything about it is luxurious and safe. Parker hands us each a bottle of water and makes us drink it. Then he passes us two more each and holds us hostage until we have consumed it all before he pulls out of the parking lot. I feel like a little kid getting scolded and can only imagine what Graham has in mind when he gets his daily progress report on my activity.

"'cuse me? Mista Killjoy?" I call up into the front seat. I laugh with Claire as she spits a little water on her shirt.

"Yes, ma'am?"

Ugh, I hate the formalities. Loosen up a little, bubs. "Can you not share all of da deets with Boss Man?"

Parker doesn't entertain my question with an answer. Instead he just concentrates on driving.

"Hey, where we going?" I ask, as he pulls into the Tasty Tots Burger Palace's drive-thru.

He ignores me, focusing on the person talking through the speaker. "Yes, I will have numbers one through six. Yes, the meals. Surprise me on the drinks."

"Holy hungry?" Claire announces. "I hope you ordered something vegan."

When the food arrives, Parker passes it back to us, and we dive into the greasy grub. He pulls out of the parking lot and merges back onto the main street.

The car doesn't have a privacy screen, so Claire uses this opportunity to talk loud enough to try to get a reaction from Parker. Good luck; he ignored me.

"So, my rag is coming soon," she yells, her mouth full of the burger toppings but no actual meat. That last shot of tequila did her in. "Might need the Parker to stop at the drugstore for some Midol and tampons."

"Mine too. But I'm sure the Parker already knows that information from the extensive file Grumpy Graham probably has been developing on me. Right, Parker?" I ask, attempting to appear innocent.

"Ah, ma'am"—he pauses and looks down at his cell—"excuse me, I have to accept this call." He puts his Bluetooth into his ear for privacy and says a simple, "It's Parker."

He is such a law-abiding citizen. I try my best to listen intently, despite how distracting Claire is beside me trying to sing the alphabet song backward.

"Yes, sir. I have them, yes. I understand, sir."

"Big Boss Man going all kamikaze on your ass over us?" I pry. Claire stifles a giggle and tries her best to keep it together. It feels really good to be able to joke around with my bestie. She needs this just as much as I do.

Parker meets our eyes in the rearview mirror, and the sight of his terse look makes us just burst into fits of laughter, spitting out little pieces of burger bun. Poor guy is going to have an aneurism over us.

We spot a Smart Drug and point frantically out the window, tapping on the glass for added emphasis.

"I de-Claire you stop!" Claire, through her tipsiness, discovered how cool it is to incorporate her name into phrases. Yes, it is as obnoxious as imagined. I must admit that it is working for her, because we get our way.

When the car is safely parked, our gatekeeper keeps us locked in the back until we have proven that we consumed some food.

"I think the six drinks was overkill, but who am I to judge?" I say, sucking three straws to sample them all at once. I make a face. "Ew, that's gross. Not doing that again."

When we meet Parker's expectations, we get out and all walk up to the entrance. It's just the three of us, but I assume the other two add-on men are not far behind.

"Do you think we should be taking one of these wheel-y things inside?" I ask.

Claire scratches her head as if what I am saying is the most intriguing thing she has ever heard. "Uh yeah, they are cold out here."

I burst into fits of laughter over her concern over their temperature. "But…but what if I hit something? Can we get arrested?"

Claire's eyes squint together, and she cups her hand near her mouth, leaning into me. "We make him drive it," she whisper-yells, pointing with her other hand in the direction of Parker. I completely forgot he was still with us.

"Good idea." I smirk. "Oh, Parker, honey, will you, fine gentleman, help us poor defenseless ladies with our shopping?"

Shopping is pretty awesome when you are too out of it to look—or see—the price tags. Because it's fun, we make Parker go up and down every aisle. When we hit the junk food section, Claire goes a little crazy and fills up half the cart with snacks for tonight's reality TV show viewing party. It's at our place again.

It isn't, however, until we get to the pharmacy section that we get a little cruel. As Parker pushes the basket through the cosmetics, shampoo, and medicine sections,

Claire and I throw in box after box of tampons and pads. She even tosses in several packages of condoms—the mega size ones.

"Don't let the mags fool you. Size most definitely does matter," she announces.

Like perfect angels, we make Parker unload all of the items. He allows Claire to swipe her credit card but only because she throws a minor temper tantrum.

"You are not my sugar daddy," she reminds him.

"Or mine," I echo. I twiddle my fingers in the air, marveling at how the tingly feeling is starting to disappear. The alcohol is wearing off. But I miss the feeling of having zero fucks to give.

We load up the trunk and fall into the backseat ungracefully.

"Take us to the gym, Captain!" Claire yells, way louder than necessary for only being a yard away from Parker, who appears to be having some anxiety in the driver's seat.

My phone buzzes with a text, and I open the app to read it.

Graham: Behaving yourself?

Angie: Nevvvvva!

Graham: Can you at least try to be a good girl?

Angie: Tried it. Failed. Being bad is more fun.

I toss my phone into my bag and lean my head against the window. I groan at the dull throbbing ache starting to form. There is no amount of alcohol that will help me forget Graham Hoffman. I don't even know why I tried.

Blake goes shirtless for Zumba and all the girls go wild. He shows off with his bright yellow cargo pants that are made from the easy-dry material and with a lot of snaps. Despite sweating like a dog, his spiky black hair stays intact. He looks very urban chic with his elegant script tattoo curving over the top of his chest, in some language that I cannot identify due to the high speed of his movements. It looks rather fresh from the red outlining. Even Claire is surprised that he actually went through with it.

"This is exactly what we need!" I yell over the Zumba-specific music. It is like an island-rap version of techno beats. I am glad I sobered up relatively quickly. Otherwise, I would never be able to keep up with all the moves. I'm in a neon green tank and bright blue capri pants; Claire has the same type of outfit but in orange and pink.

When the music changes to "Boom Boom Pow" by the Black Eyed Peas, Blake leads the group into a cool suggestive dance with a lot of hip thrusting and shimmying. Everyone laughs at his endless energy. At the end of the mix, he lets us go freestyle for fifteen seconds, and I simply try to mimic whatever shake-shift-swivel thing that Claire does—feeling completely out of my exercising element. At least in the twerk class, the room was dimly lit. Zumba is like a neon light block party. I can't even fake it when there's a spotlight permanently on me.

Upon Blake's request, he switches places with Claire

and gives her the stage for an LMFAO number, which she rocks and releases a layer of stress that she still carries from the weekend.

"No more Ethan," I inform Blake, as he eyes me questioningly about Claire's attempt to mask her emotions. "It was a bad night. I'm trying my best today to keep her together."

He gives me a lopsided frown and a nod. "He's not good enough for her."

"I know."

I have to agree, but I am biased when it comes to her. For her sake, I hope she is able to move on, but not rebound. However, I am not entirely convinced it is over. Claire has a history of overreacting to situations like this. And she is an expert at self-sabotage.

"Please tell me she's not going to do the twenty-day vegan thing again," he says with a groan, knowing that her food choices sometimes carry over into our entertainment parties. We all suffer as one.

"I'll do my best to defer her from that line of thinking. But we both know how she gets when she's upset. And needs to gain control."

"At our expense."

"Yuppers."

"We should all go out guy hunting. It'll be fun."

My change of facial expressions must give everything away, because Blake eyes me knowingly and nods his head slowly. "Teddy Graham got to you, didn't he?"

I giggle at Graham's new nickname that Claire must be using often enough that Blake is adopting it. "We aren't really together."

"Perfect, so you're game for the man hunt."

The two of us groove and move to the beat and try our best to follow Claire's high energy moves. She's in her element, and I know that with time, she will be back to herself. Although, angry and single Claire is pretty fun—from the entertainment aspect only.

"See you tonight? We are hosting again."

"Hell to the yes!"

After sweating my face off, I use the gym's shower and get dressed into a fresh set of clothes that Claire had stored in her locker. Despite it now being dark out, I feel rested and rejuvenated. Maybe doing this more often is the way to go.

Straight from the Graham Hoffman Security 101 Protocol textbook, Parker is waiting in the lobby of the gym and greets Claire and me with a professional nod. He looks the polar opposite of rested and rejuvenated. Something tells me that he would rather do anything right now than tote our butts around Portland.

We arrive in front of our townhouse, and I notice that Claire's car is already parked safely in her numbered spot. We slide out of the backseat, and Parker unloads all of the snacks and feminine hygiene products out of the trunk. He carries them into our entranceway and exits quietly. We wave goodbye—well, Claire blows kisses—and shut the door.

"So," she says, "you want to try the Werewolf Diet with me?"

"Come again?" I ask, flopping down onto the couch.

"It is an amazing cleansing and fasting diet that goes in accordance with the lunar phases of the moon."

I just stare at her, trying to read her body language to see if this is a serious topic or a bullshit topic. I silently pray for the latter.

She plops down on the couch opposite me. "Only the cool celebrities do it."

"Obviously."

The sound of the doorbell makes me jump. I glance at the clock on the TV and see it's time for the show to start. Wow, time really flew today. Claire skips to the kitchen to set up the food, and I open the door to find Zander arriving first.

"Hey, Angie."

I give him a hug. "Hey you."

"Everything okay?"

I'm sure he can tell I'm not myself. That's what happens when I'm away from Graham for this long. I miss him. And I know deep down in the pit of my stomach that it wouldn't be fair to go on a road trip with another man when my heart hasn't fully healed from the breakup.

"Can you all look up the moon phases for the next two weeks?" Claire calls out from the kitchen, completely changing my mind's focus.

"She wants us all to implement the Werewolf Diet," I whisper, to answer Zander's questioning eyes.

"What the fuck is the Werewolf Diet? Do we have to eat humans? Because I draw the line at cannibalism."

"I'm not quite sure yet. Maybe we'll have to make moon water and drink it."

"She broke up with Ethan, didn't she?"

"The actual verdict is not out yet on that. But to her, they are over."

"I had a feeling they wouldn't last."

My eyes dart up to his. "Really? Why do you say that?"

Zander shrugs. "It just seems like when couples start out really strong or heavy in the physical department, things fizzle out fast. I mean, I could be wrong, and this is all just my opinion."

I think about Z's words and wonder if that is what happened between me and Graham. Maybe this whole time I put on blinders and allowed him to infiltrate my heart without really knowing who he truly is.

It's as if we were destined to fall, but also destined to fail.

"Have you thought anymore about coming on the road trip with me?"

I suck my bottom lip into my mouth. I would love to get away. But this doesn't seem right. "I can't." I don't know what else to say. "I'm sorry."

The doorbell rings, and I hop up to let Blake in, desperate to escape Zander's sad eyes. I know I disappointed him.

I know I would have had a lot of fun on the trip, but leaving Portland right now—despite desperately needing a change of scenery—doesn't feel right. Maybe it's because I know Graham would go ballistic. Maybe it's because I don't want to add any darkness into the pureness of Zander's and my friendship. I'm not my best self mentally right now, and there's no need to drag anyone else down with me.

I give Blake a weak smile. "Hey again."

"Hi," he greets me with a hug. "I stopped over at Resa's, and her roommate said she was still visiting home. She also said that Resa may drop out entirely."

I frown. "I called her and left a voice message. She actually texted back. Never mentioned officially dropping out. This all just sucks."

Resa has pretty much been isolating herself from the group, despite us all trying to be supportive and keep in contact with her. I guess some people handle trauma differently, and the night that she was chased may have been too much for her to endure—while still being a college student. I, of anyone, should understand that the human brain copes however it can to survive.

Claire brings in the snack tray and a pitcher of spiked punch. We all take our seats, make a toast, and start the munching. However, in the back of my head, I think about all of the girls who have already been victimized by what is happening on campus. Am I next? What about Claire?

"Ready for the drama?" Blake asks, making us all laugh and snapping me from my depressing thoughts.

I cannot allow fear to paralyze me. I cannot let these bastards win.

Claire sighs heavily. "I'm ready for any drama that is not my own."

I grasp my drink in my hand. "Same."

"To drama that is not our own!" Blake chants.

We clink glasses. "Cheers!"

10

I can blame it on PMS or the cold temperatures of early November or the contagious bad mood of Claire. But in the end, I know that the source of my grumpiness is centered around Graham.

I miss him.

It has been twenty-four hours since I last talked to him on the phone—albeit it was a one-sided conversation with him yelling at me to follow the orders of his security detail. I know that he is across the country—who knows where—and I do have several contact numbers to reach him. However, loneliness does not constitute an emergency by any stretch of the imagination for me to reach out *just because*.

I do not want to be like one of those girls. The type of girl who waits by the phone, going through life as if having a man is the only way to feel free and alive and loved. I want my independence. I want my own desires to dictate the type of things I do each day. But something deep within me

—under all of the layers of pain and disappointment from the past—yearns for the release and comfort of having someone make decisions for me. For someone to come along and care for me so deeply that my happiness is their ultimate mission.

But does that even exist?

In Disney movies it does. In fairytales, yes. Seriously, the romantic novel genre is the number one selling genre for…decades? Yet, why is divorce so prevalent in society? It's because women are led to believe that fiction equals reality. That if we just wait long enough, our prince will come. That we just have to be patient and say "no" to all of the anti-princes. Then, when we least expect it—when we aren't even looking—bam! Love.

Blah.

No. Love like that does not exist.

Nothing lasts forever. The more I keep telling myself that, the better it will be whenever Graham finally leaves me alone for good. And he will. Everyone, with the exception of Claire, who I ever cared about left. Why will he be anyone different?

There's a pattern in regard to falling in love. Almost like stages, rather than pathways. First, there's attraction—also known as lust. Second, the romance stage. Then, the power-struggle. Followed by the trust. And hopefully that leads to commitment bliss.

Graham and I have no problems in the attraction stage. He has made it clear to me—on more than one occasion—that he wants me, and his body language supports his verbal language. The feeling is mutual. As much of a hard-ass as he claims to be, he is definitely romantic. It is just not textbook romance. No, it is a security system and random erotic gifts and a safety entourage. It is unconventional, at best. But it is still a way of showing he cares about me.

Now, the power-struggle stage is something that I constantly feel that we are in. As if the broken record keeps playing over and over and over. I never met someone like Graham before—ever. He wants everything his way. He thinks his opinions are the best. And he rarely compromises. It irks me. It thrills me. It overwhelms me. I love it and I hate it. I can't figure him out. We are playing a game of tug-of-war—where there is never a winner. No one wants to bend or give in. We are always at a stalemate.

As much as he wants to delve into my life, discover all of the mysteries and get to know me more, he very much wants to keep things hidden and buried in his own closet. Which makes me wonder if we are even compatible or if we will forever bump heads. Even when I try to stay away from him, he is there.

I don't trust easily. I blame that on many years of trusting freely and having it shatter my life. I trusted that my mom would be around to help me pick out a prom dress. I trusted that my dad would step up to the plate whenever she couldn't. I trusted that James would be around to celebrate all of our birthdays together. I trusted myself to not let anyone else get close to me. Because everyone either dies or walks away from me.

Now I am conditioned to do the complete opposite. I constantly look for hidden messages and ulterior motives. It's not a great way to go through life, but protecting my heart from being broken outweighs my need for a deeper level of relationship. People can only hurt me if I let them.

If Graham and I can just skim the surface, I will be just fine. I tried to stay away from him and it didn't work. I can't stop thinking about him—especially after spending the night together.

He comforted me while I got stitches…

He took care of me after the Halloween party…

There is a comfort knowing that he is around. And as selfish as I am, I want him to be available.

I slip out of bed and go downstairs to evaluate the damage. The Monday night ritual was intense—both on the TV and in the living room. I spent half the night sleeping at the foot of Claire's bed to make sure she was alright, finally returning to my room after three in the morning. I almost stayed with her longer to clean up the clutter in her room while she slept, but I couldn't turn on the lights without waking her.

After receiving a call from Ethan asking her if she could hang a scarf he left over here on the doorknob outside, she had an emotional break. Quite frankly, it was scary. Not even Blake and his ability to make the guards at Buckingham Palace smirk worked on Claire's mood. In the end, I sent everyone out the door after the show ended and helped her get settled in upstairs.

Once I saw Ethan trot up the steps to our place, I swung open the door and gave him a piece of my mind. One of the new security men who Graham hired got out of a discreet-looking car in the lot and instructed me to go inside as he escorted Ethan from the property. It took everything in me not to jump on his back and beat him from behind. I have no shame in playing unfairly. You piss with Claire, you piss with me.

As expected, wrappers and chip crumbs are all over the coffee table and hardwood floors. Partially filled glasses of some alcoholic concoction are left on coasters around the room on every available flat surface. It's a mess.

A carton of ice cream and the plastic container of chocolate-covered strawberries were victims of last night's episode. Both disappeared without a trace, but Claire cannot be completely responsible for the binge. She had a partner in crime.

Knowing that thirty minutes is not enough time to clean up the disaster, I go back upstairs and prepare for a trip to see Dr. Williams. This can all wait until I'm back.

"What did I tell you about tampering with a police investigation, Miss McFee?"

I frown over Dr. Williams's tone. He has gone from encouraging me at the start of the semester to trying to persuade me to find another topic entirely. I don't have time to find another topic. It's already November and the semester ends right before Christmas.

"I, um, am not interfering."

"You are essentially acting like an undercover police officer. Without a degree, without a badge, and without the skill set."

Sadness rushes through me. He is wrong. I am not doing anything differently than I would as a typical college student. The only difference is that I am privy to a pattern that may have otherwise been overlooked. Only agency girls are becoming victims to a string of druggings happening on campus. I have connections and am able to do more than a police officer would ever be able to do, because I am smack-dab in the middle of the chaos. I am in college. I am a girl. And I am—*was*—a part of the agency. While I don't have the skill set to protect myself like a police officer would, I do have the skill set to see connections that may not be otherwise revealed.

"What would happen if I continue this topic of research for the class anyway?"

Dr. Williams narrows his eyes at me. "You are willing to jeopardize everything you have worked toward to follow a path that might lead you to a dead end?"

"I think it might be worth the risk."

"I see."

"What are my consequences?"

He pulls back from his desk, straightens his glasses, and turns to look out the stained-glass window. "I like you, Miss McFee, I do. I think you are smart and determined and passionate. However, I am not comfortable letting you be disillusioned to the fact that these events you are investigating may not end up anywhere. It may take years to uncover the truth. And we do not have years, Miss McFee. We are down to less than two months' time for you to complete the class and earn my recommendation for an internship. Without my recommendation, you might as well kiss your dream goodbye, because all the internships will be filled by the end of January. And you will have what to show for it? A partial story? A story lacking real evidence? Or the stigma of interrupting an ongoing investigation? Are you willing to risk everything?"

I hear what he is saying. But I disagree. Sure, I may fail

his class—again. But this situation is bigger than the grade. This is something bigger than me. If I can show the world that I have what it takes to rise above the challenge, maybe I can get an internship without Dr. Williams's approval.

It is risky, but it's a chance I may have to take. Right now, I have nothing else. The campus drugging story is all I have. I am all in on this.

"The first draft of your article is due in a few weeks. There will be a signup outside my office for you to select a time slot. A large portion of your grade will be from this draft. Please spend some time in discernment to think about what you really want to achieve. Right now and in your future."

"Thank you," I mutter and scurry out of his office as fast as I can.

I walk at a brisk pace to my car and rest my head on the steering wheel. It wasn't like Dr. Williams didn't warn me. I just thought if he heard the added information I collected, he would be more on board. I was foolish to think that my passion and determination would be commended, instead of snuffed out like a flame in a jar.

My phone rings and I see that it is Graham. I slide the answer bar without really thinking it through.

"Angie? Everything okay?"

I forget that he has been having me followed and look around at the parked cars near me in the lot.

"Holy shit, are your men giving you minute to minute updates on me?"

"Updates, yes. That frequently? I wish."

"You are crazy," I huff. "None of this is normal, Graham. Make it stop. Make it stop now."

"Why are you loitering in a parking lot, sweetheart? What's wrong?"

I open and close my mouth. He is too much. It is all too much. My life was so boring and inconsequential before he crashed into it. Now I don't even know which way to turn or hide. It's like he has eyes on me from across the country and it is treading on my free will. I just cannot do this. Not right now. And maybe not ever.

"Please call off your guards. I beg you."

"How am I supposed to function on a workday when you are day drinking and frequenting the exact place where you got slipped a drug? Tell me how I—"

"I was with Claire. We were both safe."

"Yeah, right, safe," he grunts. "You basically do the opposite of everything I ask. So, think of the security as being something for me—rather than for you. It is my way of being able to conduct business from a distance and not have to get distracted by all the shit you get yourself into."

"This is all unnecessary, and it is just drawing more attention to me. If some enemy of yours pays even half attention to where you are putting your efforts, then I am an even bigger target if retaliation is in the plan."

He remains silent for several seconds. I can tell that my words have affected him. We hang up and find ourselves at an impasse again.

I drive home and channel my inner frustrations over my fizzling dreams and my complicated relationship into how I'm going to help Claire snap back from the breakup with Ethan.

Once inside, I run up into my bedroom, put on some

Red Hot Chili Peppers music, and lose myself in the mindless chore of folding laundry.

There is a soft knock at my door. "Angie? You in there?"

"Come on in, Claire."

She walks in, and I can tell that she is in desperate need of a friend. She sits on the bed and helps me fold the clothes I have left in the basket.

I look at her somber face. "What's up?"

"Nothing. I've been canceling Ethan's requests for dates for next week and allowing other men to fill up the time slots."

"Why are you avoiding him? Seems like he is back to trying. Maybe the whole scarf thing was a way to try to interact with you." And maybe I yelled at him prematurely. I clearly have an incomplete picture of what is happening in their relationship, because Claire is so tight-lipped.

"He just doesn't want me with anyone else—even if it's platonic. Like I could fall for someone as fast as I fell for him. Pretty sure I'm going to swear off men entirely for a while. What were we thinking getting involved with agency men?"

"We weren't thinking," I answer. Both of us got wrapped up in lightning-fast relationships with men who have their own issues and baggage. And once the storm is over, the wreckage could take a long time to clean up.

Once she is done folding the last item, she falls back onto my bed and stares up at the ceiling. "I'm so looking forward to doing nothing this weekend. I just want to veg out and go into coma mode."

"I feel the same way. My body craves to relax and detox from Graham."

"Has he been showing his face?"

"Apparently he's on a business trip. Won't be back in the area until Saturday or Sunday, depending on how the meetings go. But I'm focusing on me this weekend. If the man needs me, he can wait like any other normal human being. And he can shove his dictator ways up his ass."

Claire pumps her fist toward me. "Yeah, I love that my Feminist As Fuck girl is back!"

I smile down at her and nod my head. "Me too."

Wednesday rolls around, and it's another wash and repeat day. My mood is just as drab, and I chalk it up to hormones. With the start of my period, I know that for the next three days, I will be fighting the pain with the non-recommended dosage of ibuprofen and Midol. The mixing of meds is the only thing that can get me to survive the monthly torment. If it wasn't for the freaking pill that was prescribed to me several years ago, I think I would be hospitalized during this time. Luckily, most of the pain will be over in twenty-four hours. I reach into my purse and grab the Altoids container that I used to save my last special pills. I pop one into my mouth and chew. This should fix my PMS even faster than the OTC stuff.

The line at the coffee shop irks me. Parker's scowl doesn't lighten my mood either. He has taken it upon himself to follow me on foot—rather than just safely wait in his parked vehicle outside. I wish I could say I was growing desensitized to him, but it is the opposite. He doesn't get that it is my turn to buy. By the time I make it through with two pumpkin spiced chai teas—a seasonal limited-edition flavor—I am already two minutes late to class. It's the stinking rain. You would think that living in the Pacific Northwest, people would be born with these prerequisite driving skills. Nope. It's like the rain makes everyone's headlights and windshield wipers stop working at once.

The sudden stop-and-go flow nearly makes me want to hurl, despite being behind the wheel.

The smell of the teas and pastries tickles my nose and reminds my stomach that food is good once again. The cinnamon flakey-thing is a worthwhile splurge especially during a class that seems to drag on and on.

I sneak in from the back—exactly seven minutes tardy—and find my awaiting empty seat next to Bryce who is sporting a shit-eating grin. The professor is already in full swing with her lesson on the human behavior behind addiction up on the projector screen.

"Shut your face or no pastry for you," I warn, dangling the soggy takeout bag at eye level.

"Aw, Teach. You are sweet." He is wearing his fraternity hoodie and baseball cap, managing somehow not to look like a drenched rat.

"Ya, thanks. This rain sucks." You know what else sucks? Feeling like a finely sharpened ice pick is being rammed up into your lady parts, poking holes into your uterine walls and continuing to twist and tug until you bleed out and die. Yeah, that fucking sucks. Oh, and having the guy who I can't-bring-myself-to-refer-to-as-boyfriend out of the state and not here so I can use him as a punching bag. It would feel so good to take out my aggression on why I was born with a homogametic double X chromosome—resulting in the production of a vagina—and have to endure this nastier-than-nasty pain. Transferring that aggression onto said guy would cause temporary relief I so desperately need.

The entire back of my coat drips with the saturation I endured from refusing the huge umbrella that Parker wanted me to use. The thing was big enough for avoiding the sun at the beach. My hair feels like a mop of sodden spaghetti. My hood did nothing to help it stay dry. At least my feet aren't wet. That is a relief.

"What did I miss?"

"Well, there was a great moment when Pencil Skirt glanced at me. I just know it meant something."

"Oh, yes. The infamous random glance. She *totally* digs you."

"Not everyone can have people falling at their feet, Teach. Let me live vicariously through you."

I grimace at the comment. Is that what is really happening?

I spend the rest of the class taking notes, self-reflecting, and trying not to let Bryce make me laugh.

The rain picks up—*of course*—when it is time to go back to the car. I run and make it inside in less than two minutes. It's the back pain that really kills me though—the dull nagging ache that debilitates me and makes me act irrational.

When I get home, I strip my clothes off and lay my naked back onto an electric heating pad on my bed. I pop some more meds—fantasizing about having a morphine drip—and fall asleep for an hour.

When I wake, I pad downstairs. I open a can of sodium-infused soup from my hidden stash in the back of the pantry and watch trash TV—the kind with the only plot point being to hook up or get off the show.

I check my phone for messages, seeing a bunch fill up the notification screen.

Zander: I'm leaving early morning for Cali. It's not too late to join me.

Claire: Going to work an extra shift at the gym. Catch you later.

Zander: Would love for you to come with me…

Zander: If the answer is still no, then I'll probably leave today instead and drive through the night.

Zander: You would love San Clemente.

With the last text, he includes a stock image of the nearby beach, making me feel a mix of emotions—the main one being guilt. Sure, I would love to take a spontaneous vacation, but the timing is all wrong.

Maybe the elusive concept of the perfect timing just doesn't exist.

11

"Rise and shine."

"What? What's going on?" I gasp, trying to sit up. I am so disoriented that it takes me a minute to even realize where I am. Glancing around the living room, my brain defogs and I slowly remember falling asleep and dreaming about Graham. The man is infiltrating every area of my life, and I no longer feel empowered enough to stop him.

Claire stares at me. "You fell asleep." She speaks to me like I'm a five-year-old.

Pulling my leg up on the sofa, I readjust. The sun is rising and casting a warm glow through the spread curtains at the window. "I must have been tired." Glancing at the clock, I see that I slept for over twelve hours. I never do that. "What's on the agenda for today?" I try to sound chipper, but I think it just comes out as fake. I am feeling sluggish and emotionally drained.

"Nothing."

I rub my eyes. "Then why did you wake me up, Claire?"

"I was bored."

"You were bored?"

She shrugs.

I'm three seconds away from tossing my hands up in the air. This whole Ethan madness needs to hit a boiling point so she can stop living her life in limbo. I hate seeing my friend so mopey. She's my bestie and we are in this boat together. That's how it has been from the start. I very much sink with her, when she's going through a low. And when she's on a high? Look out.

"Let's throw a party."

Has she lost her mind? There's really no other explanation to justify her mood swings. "A party?" I feel like we are on completely separate wave lengths right now. Gah, this woman is confusing. "Who's invited?" I'm not sure why I'm even starting to entertain this idea.

"Just us."

"Okay… Then what will the theme be?"

"Single AF," she answers with confidence.

"Ha," I laugh. "Seems fitting."

She doesn't even need to think about it, which tells me that she probably spent the better half of yesterday brainstorming. That's the thing with Claire… When she has time on her hands, she lets her crazy ideas come out to play.

"So, let's go to the liquor store and pick up champagne for a mimosa brunch."

"Claire, it's seven in the morning."

"So?"

"There's no liquor store open right now."

Her bottom lip pouts out. "Then let's go get dressed

fancy so when they do open, we are ready. Actually, do you think alcohol can be delivered?"

I don't even answer. I simply just brace myself for all that I'm about to endure.

"I know it's hard to narrow down my great ideas because I have so many of them, but I feel like this party for two tops the list."

POP.

I jump back on Claire's bed as the cork flies up to the ceiling, coming down to land somewhere near a pile of unused clothes from her closet that were pulled out during our earlier fashion show. At least I convinced her to wait until noon to open up a bottle. And alcohol can be delivered if you have friends like Blake in your life.

I smooth out the layers on my fluffy pink chiffon dress. Claire insisted we look *freaking fabulous*. "What are we celebrating again?" I genuinely can't remember.

She fake scoffs. "Us. We are celebrating us."

"I can cheers to that. Except, where are the glasses?"

Claire sets the bottle down on the nightstand and slips out of the room yelling, "Be right back," as she darts down the hallway.

Grabbing my phone, I check my messages for the first time since I fell asleep yesterday. Damn. I guess I shouldn't be surprised.

Graham: Where the fuck are you?

Graham: Answer your damn phone.

Graham: Are you trying to make me go ballistic?

Graham: Are you okay?

Graham: I am worried...please call or text me.

Graham: ANGELA!

Graham: You best be glad I'm away from Portland right now.

Graham: Woman, you are driving me insane...

The first message is timestamped yesterday at nine at night. I was asleep. Each message thereafter is minutes to an hour apart. Closing the app, I look at my missed calls and all nineteen of them are from Graham.

Oops.

Well, good thing we aren't together. Otherwise, he'd be calling in the special forces. Heck, nothing is really stopping him from doing it now.

I hear talking in the hallway. Sitting up on my bed, I listen as Claire yells at whom I can only assume is Ethan calling. She ends the call as she enters her room, carrying two flutes.

"Everything okay?"

She looks at me as if I didn't just witness her tone and partial conversation on the phone.

"Yes. Of course."

I give her a nod. I could write a book on how to avoid situations, so I get it. But I could also write a sequel on how avoiding problems can prolong pain.

"You know how you always tell me I'm a horrible liar?"

She hands me a flute. "You are."

"So are you."

Ignoring me, she pours us both champagne until it's bubbling over the rims of the glasses.

"Don't drink any until I make a toast," she scolds, stifling a laugh as my hand gets covered in fizz. "Cheers to being dickless. Um"—she shakes her head—"no, that came out wrong. Free-balling. Er, no." She stares up at the ceiling, and then as if the idea falls from the sky, raises up her glass. "Cheers to being dick-free!"

I can't help but laugh. "How about a simple cheers to our singleness?" I counter.

"Sweet and simple. I like it." Claire clinks glasses with me. "Cheers."

My phone buzzes on the bed, drawing attention to it. He is relentless.

"Let me just text Graham and then forget about him." I write out a simple message, mainly because I want to detox from him and enjoy my girl time while he's away. I will stay connected just enough for him not to go crazy. However, I really want this time to detox me and restore my mind.

Graham: Baby, I know you're mad at me still. But I need to know you are okay.

Angie: I am fine. Please do not worry about me.

My phone vibrates immediately with an incoming call from Graham, but I decline it. I then see the dots on our text chain indicating he is in the process of typing out another message. It takes seconds for my phone to ping with his reply.

Graham: Stop avoiding me.

Angie: I need space.

Graham: I need YOU.

Angie: Respect my wishes. Shutting off my phone for a bit.

I turn it to "do not disturb," ignoring whatever it is that Graham wants to bark about. How am I supposed to get over him if he is constantly inserting himself into all of my waking thoughts?

"Well, you handled that better than I thought," Claire says, taking a sip from her glass, reminding me that I haven't tried it yet.

"Hmm, that's good," I say, shifting my weight onto a pillow. "What did you expect me to do?"

She shrugs. "Give in."

"We aren't together anymore. I mean, we aren't exactly apart either. It's just"—I struggle for the right word—"complicated."

"Always is."

"I had a chance to go on a road trip with Zander to see his sister. But I declined."

"Oh yeah?"

"It didn't seem right to go. Not now."

Claire nods but doesn't say anything more. I'm still not quite sure why I didn't go on the trip. Even though Graham is across the country, he is very much still present in my life. I just need more time to cleanse him from my world.

Another day finishes.

And another one passes.

Claire cleared her weekend work schedule to have this time for just us, and it is basically the best thing we could have done for ourselves. We've been dressing up in her fancy designer clothes to go absolutely nowhere on a Saturday. Each night so far has consisted of exfoliating our skin and applying a facial mask, while chilling in bed together and chatting about anything and everything.

It feels a bit nostalgic to have these uninterrupted moments together—just like when we first met and didn't have the male population dragging us down. We bonded instantly then, and the ties between us have only gotten stronger throughout the years.

In these moments of bonding, I am simply reminded that my life needs Claire in it. That the thought of her going to California to pursue a passion causes my chest to tighten. It's not because I don't want her to be happy but rather because I will miss her.

Even if ninety percent of her ideas are crazy.

Like the game we are playing now, which requires us to take a sip of our drink every time Ethan tries to call or text her. But gone is the fancy champagne. No, tonight we are going back to the basics with tequila and whiskey. Luckily Claire agreed to allow me to bring in some mixers for the alcohol. Otherwise, we would be a lot tipsier than we are currently.

"Has Teddy Graham contacted you again? And more importantly, have you responded?"

"Yes and no. Graham has been unusually quiet over the past day. He's only texted a dozen times. Maybe this is him trying to give me space."

Claire throws her head back so fast in laughter that she falls off the bed. "Shit."

"What is wrong with you?"

"Everything," she says with a giggle, climbing back up onto the bed. She looks so beautifully disheveled. "But that man isn't giving up. He's probably just waiting for the perfect opportunity to pounce."

"Hard to pounce when he's away on business."

"Surprised he didn't kidnap you and take you with him."

"I am too."

I look at my phone and see the messages highlighting my opening screen. For the past couple of mornings, Graham has been greeting me with a sweet message, followed by a series of frustrated messages, and then ends the day with a simple, "Dream easy, sweetheart." He is being tame, despite being ignored by me. Maybe he's learning that pushing me only causes me to push back.

We are more alike than we are different when it comes to wanting control, being stubborn, and—dare I say it—battling jealousy. Even I know myself well enough to understand that if Graham were to move on without me right now that I would want to claw the bitch apart. Yet, until I am privy to just how interconnected Sophia is with his life, it's hard to jump in heart first.

Oh, and the fact that he's a liar.

Claire's phone rings, causing me to take a sip of my drink. Ethan probably didn't realize how amazing he had it until—

"She's having a threesome." My eyes dart to Claire's as she waves me off with her hand. "She's enjoying it—even though you didn't ask. Figure you should know." She bites her bottom lip and spins out of reach as I lunge for her phone. "The men are smooth, wickedly dangerous in large quantities, and easy to swallow."

Oh shit, oh shit, oh shit. I can hear Graham's boisterous voice boom from the other end of the phone. He called Claire? Was harassing me via texting not enough? The man seriously has boundary issues.

"With guys named Jose and Jack," she says proudly, giving me a smirk.

Please, Claire, don't poke the bear.

"Oh, who cares about last names. The three of them are just on a first-name basis right now. Which is weird that they can even talk with their mouths so full. But since you will just look them up anyway, Cuervo and Daniels. Buh-byes now."

"I can't believe you did that. What did he want?"

She sighs and shakes her head as if I'm a child. "You, Angie. The man only wants you."

I toss my head back onto the pillow that rests against the headboard. "I want him too."

"Oh no." She waves her finger at me. "No you don't."

I feel the sting on my thigh. "Ouch, you hit me."

"Needed to snap some sense into you. The only guys we need right now are the ones who never disappoint and are consistent." Tipping up her glass, she downs the amber liquid, completely bypassing our drinking game.

"I'm going to make dinner before things turn south fast."

Getting up from the mattress, I make my way down the stairs. And—

"Ahhh!" My throat is raw from yelling, as our eyes connect.

"Angie," Claire says in a rush, as she races down the stairs. "What's wrong?"

Taking the next step, my foot slips, causing me to fall to my ass onto the floor. Fear paralyzes me as I stare up into the eyes of Parker.

"Miss McFee, are you alright?"

"You broke into my house," I bellow, trying to stand up as Claire helps but doesn't really help—her drunkenness now showing.

"Dude, you took that one step too far," she says, giving Parker a tsk-tsk.

His strong hands help me stand. "Mr. Hoffman is worried about you."

Rubbing my ass, I stumble into the kitchen to get an ice pack out of the freezer. Parker follows, causing my blood to reach boiling point. "Tell your Mr. Hoffman that he over-stepped. Big time."

"I just—"

"This is his fault, not yours. But please go."

Parker slips back out the front door, setting my security

system. I could have had a heart attack. I plop down onto the sofa, watching Claire join me—almost missing the cushion entirely.

"Wow," Claire mutters. "Well, that was fun."

"Fun? You provoked him."

"Me?" She has the nerve to look innocent. "I simply helped him realize what he's missing."

"He's missing a piece of my mind."

I get up and stomp out of the room, with one hand holding the ice pack to my ass and the other propelling me up the stairs. I retrieve my phone from Claire's bed and then make my way into my room for privacy.

Without thinking, I dial Graham's cell.

"Finally."

"You fucking had your minion break into my home? Have you lost your mind? You know how messed up that is? Surely, you do. How do you get to this stage of your life and miss these types of things?"

"It's not breaking if he enters without damage."

"Yup. You have most certainly lost your mind. Listen here, Mr. Hoffman. Back the fuck off. And never do that again." My tone is stern, and if Graham knew what was good for him he would heed my warning.

"How badly did you fall, sweetheart?"

I shift on the bed and remove the ice back from my tailbone region, placing it on my nightstand. "Enough to probably be sore tomorrow. But I'll be fine."

Graham sighs, letting out a whoosh of air. "I'd massage you if I was there."

"Stop."

"You better the hell not be having guys over."

"Oh yeah, give it to me, Jose and Jack." I try to perfect my best fake slutty voice.

"I mean it, Angela."

"Right there. That's the spot. Ohhh…"

I giggle over Graham's growl. He can't possibly think I'm being serious.

"So help me, Angie."

"They are some mighty fine twins, mind you. I always had a thing for twins."

"You are going to force me to make rash decisions…"

"Tequila and whiskey, you nutball." I laugh over his sigh of relief. He is so irrational sometimes. "Claire and I have been playing a drinking game with some liquors that happen to have some masculine sounding names."

"Sounds highly irresponsible."

"It's our girl time," I defend, pouting out my bottom lip despite him not being able to see. "We haven't left our townhouse since Wednesday."

"What are you wearing?"

"A scowl on my face," I deadpan.

"Sexy."

I burst out laughing. "Only you would find a sour face hot."

"You're my sweet and sour girl."

"I'm not your anything, Graham."

"You're mine in every sense of the word. You just need to accept the fact."

"I have to go."

"I want you to stay."

"Bye, Graham." We stay on the line a few more

seconds, listening to each other breathe, and then I finally hit the end button.

I need to maintain an emotional distance from him to determine what I can't live with and what I can't live without. The problem is, when he's around, my heart chooses what my brain is too afraid to accept.

For years, I told myself lies. I convinced myself that I didn't need anyone. People let me down. I forced myself to believe that happiness was an illusion—some made-up feeling to survive. Then, from the first time I met Graham, he lit a fire inside of me from a candle that I thought melted long before he ever entered the scene. He made me believe in the impossible and gave me a reason to hope.

Of course, everything that Graham represented was also a lie. He runs by a different set of rules, where he is the author. He is unapologetically controlling and yet compelling, in equal parts.

He is dangerous and lethal to my already broken heart.

12

I wake the next morning to a series of texts from Graham. One is a picture of him with a sad face and the caption—*My entire body misses you...especially my lips.* He even has the nerve to accuse me of giving him the early signs of carpal tunnel. I laugh over his playfulness. The next message is an excerpt from *A Midsummer Night's Dream* about the path to true love never being easy. I let those words marinate in my head. It has been years since I have read anything from Shakespeare. But that quote is powerful and holds meaning to my own life.

Do I love Graham? I have never experienced romantic love with anyone else. So, I have nothing to compare. I have never allowed anyone to get that close to my heart. And yet, here I am, with a man who has forced himself into my mind, and even though we are hundreds of miles apart, it is like our hearts still beat as one. The separation has only made it clear to me that I am not over him. Even though I am furious with how he continuously affects my life, there is an undeniable connection between us.

After breakfast, I dedicate my Sunday morning to looking for a part-time job. I load the River Valley Connection page and click on the job postings specifically geared toward college-aged students. The tab opens to a virtual bulletin board with openings for positions on and around campus. I scan through the listing and my eyes narrow in on the one for the Campus Smoothie Cafe. Ever since Resa was chased the night she left the cafe, I've been trying to get more insight on what is happening there.

And I know Paul is involved. I click on the link and read through the job qualifications and description. This would be a great way to get to know the mysterious man on a different level. I fill out the online application and cross my fingers that I get a call back for the opening.

I close down the search engine and move over to my text messages. I don't respond to the two messages that my dad sent, mainly because they are asking me to wire him money. Money that I do not have—at least not any I actually earned. And for the first time in what feels like weeks, Mark messaged me.

Mark: Hey Angie. My newspaper recruiter friend wants to have dinner with us over the weekend. Are you still game? This could be your big break.

My heart leaps from my chest. I forgot that Mark showed him my resume and portfolio to gauge his interest in meeting with me. I don't have very many standout accomplishments related to the field, however I hope to sell myself in person on my work ethic qualities and my willingness to learn.

Angie: Yeah, I should be free. We meeting at Fortune?

I don't have to wait long for his reply.

Mark: I will send you details this week. I saw you are off the agency's database. Everything okay?

How do I tell him I was laid off by my dictator boss without raising more questions and outing Graham? I settle for being my elusive self and type out my vague response.

Angie: Everything's fine. Just needed to take a short hiatus to focus on school.

Mark: We'll catch up soon. Looking forward.

Angie: Same

An energy zings through me, making me feel hopeful that I'm on the right track with my career goals. Maybe—just maybe—I have what it takes to pursue my dreams.

Hopping out of bed, I go in search of Claire, finding her sitting in her closet looking lost.

"Hey you. Everything okay?"

"We need to go face the world, Angie. The time is now."

"Okay…"

She rolls onto her side and grabs ahold of my knees to try to get up, avoiding my offering of my hands. Stumbling forward, she climbs my thighs, nearly knocking me down. Finally getting upright, she looks at me with purpose and says, "Go get dressed into something worthy of pancakes."

"Alrighty."

"I'm so full," I moan.

Claire licks syrup off her fingers, making a popping sound as she ends with her thumb. "This place has the best pancakes on this side of the river."

"True story." It also helps that there really isn't much competition.

I excuse myself to use the bathroom, feeling my phone vibrate inside my handbag with a notification. I don't even need to look to know who is texting me. The man is relentless in his pursuits. I wonder when he'll be back in town from his business trip. Taking out my phone, I open his message.

Graham: The next time you get the urge to dress in a hot little minidress to go get pancakes, you do it with me.

I roll my eyes and glance around the space, half expecting him to pop out of the woodwork. I guess I should be alarmed that he figured out the exact location of where I am, but that man has no boundaries when it comes to acquiring information. He is some information ninja or a secret agent man.

Or he has Parker following me. At least it's better than

him breaking into my house again. I'm not going to respond as tamely as I did if it happens a second time.

Feeling bold, I type out a message.

Angie: Do you have a tracking device on me?

Angie: Maybe you injected one into my neck while I was asleep.

I see the dots that indicate he is typing.

Graham: I wouldn't do that to you. You hate needles.

Angie: Like that would stop you.

Graham: I'm a less invasive type of stalker.

Angie: But a stalker nonetheless.

Graham: Most women like that level of attentiveness.

Angie: Pretty sure we already established that I am not like most women.

Graham: You definitely break the mold.

As I start to write out another text, I see that Zander is trying to call, which I accept. "Hey Z, how is the trip going?"

"I'm actually just a couple of hours away from Portland."

"San Clemente fun?"

"We actually never left San Francisco. My sister wanted to get away. It worked out."

"Oh cool."

"I was actually hoping I could see you later so I can give you a little gift I got you."

"Oh, that is so nice of you. Yeah, um"—I mentally run through my plans for the day—"I should be free."

"Great. I'll pick you up around six and maybe we can go for a walk at your favorite park across the bridge."

"Sure. Sounds good. But can you pick me up on the street behind the townhouse? I'll go through the back gate."

"Uh, yeah, sure."

Luckily, Zander doesn't ask me a thousand questions about my reasons. It's just easier doing it this way so I don't get followed like what is apparently happening while I'm here eating pancakes.

Claire might like agitating Graham for fun while he isn't in town to retaliate, but I know better than to pull it off successfully. Throwing Zander in his face won't have a good outcome—regardless of where he is currently located. Thus, it's best he doesn't know that I'm going to be hanging out with a friend.

A male friend.

It is rare for me to see Zander so dressed up, so I allow myself a few seconds to take him all in. His tailored gray dress pants and light-gray button-down shirt look good on him. The blond locks that typically flow freely around his face are tamed and styled off his forehead. He looks different. Sophisticated.

He clears his throat and his eyes bore into mine, as I settle in the passenger seat and click my belt into place. "Ready to go?"

I look down at my black leggings and ankle boots. "I, um, feel a bit underdressed."

Zander's eyes come to life. "You always look amazing. I went shopping while in San Fran and picked up a few items. Just trying them out."

"Your sister okay?"

"Yeah. Her boyfriend actually drove up during our stay at my friend's and he proposed to her. Apparently she was terrified he would leave her if he found out…"

"Found what out?"

Zander pulls onto the street and drives between the rows of townhouses to get onto the main road. "She is pregnant."

I turn in my seat to get a better look at his facial expressions. "You're going to be an uncle."

He nods. "I am." His face beams with pride. "And I'm so excited."

It's good to see Zander so happy. Genuinely elated. That's all I ever want for my friends, so to be a witness to their joy helps me to find my own—as small as it may be.

When we get to the park near the river, Zander cuts the engine and grabs his coat from the backseat. We exit and walk along the pathway that leads to the riverfront. The sun is setting and the view is breathtaking.

"So, I bought you a little gift." His voice is a bit unsteady, making my stomach twist with nerves.

"You didn't have to do that, Z." I hope it isn't too expensive. Pricey gifts make me feel…inadequate?

"I wanted to."

I watch with bated breath as he reaches into his coat pocket, pulls out a little box, and hands it to me. With shaky hands, I pull the ribbon from the top and lift the lid. "Oh, Zander. It's beautiful." My fingers touch the silver heart that hangs from a linked chain. Turning the pendant over, the shape of the state of California is engraved on the back. "I love it."

"Yeah?"

I nod eagerly, giving him a hug. "Thank you." I undo the clasp and turn around, pulling my hair out of the inside of my coat. "Here, put it on, please." When Zander has it secured, I turn back and touch the heart with my fingers, feeling the smoothness of the metal. "I really love it."

"I'm so glad."

I tuck the box into my coat pocket and we walk along the pathway, enjoying the view of the setting sun. "I'm glad your sister is okay."

Once we are at the park's end, Z turns to me and smiles. "Me too. Seeing her happy and overcoming some of her fears with her boyfriend helped me in a way."

"Yeah?"

He nods. Then he leans his elbows on the wooden rail, looking out at the river. "Have you ever thought about what we could be?"

I almost don't hear his question from the whistling sound of the wind and the splashing water. I tug at the locks of my hair, as it whips and swirls around my face. Taking a band off my wrist, I twist it and secure it into place.

Zander turns his attention back to me and fixes a piece of loose hair behind my ears.

His touch feels different.

Everything feels different.

I'm not unacquainted with loss and yet I know. I just know. That nothing—*nothing*—is going to be the same again. And the grief that fills up my entire body pushes me down and down and down…

"Have you ever thought about me"—he glances down at my lips—"as more than a friend?"

I grow lightheaded at the implication. I look up into his eyes and see them droop from the weight of his words and probably from my confused silence. I look out at the water and try to ignore his question. I try to focus my brain on anything other than how this moment in time is going to be a turning point—one I don't want to endure. But I can't. Because Zander says my name with so much reverence that I think I may be sick.

Gone is the boy who would sneak me candy when Claire wasn't looking. Gone is the man who would help me in the computer lab when I was on the verge of tears. Gone is my friend who I could lean on for emotional support as I stumble through life with half a heart.

Gone.

"What are you talking about, Z?" I whisper. I feel out of breath. Like his physical proximity is sucking all of the oxygen out of the air and carrying it away with each breeze that blows past. That with each inch closer he becomes, the harder it is to go back in time and undo everything that is about to happen.

I fear that if Zander continues with this conversation,

there will be no going back. That nothing will ever be the same. And I want to resist that change. I want to stay the way we are…as friends. Amazing friends. So I want him to stop talking. I want him to forget what he just asked me—twice. I want the now darkness of the night to swallow me up and transport me away, so I don't have to remember this moment as the time in my life that my best guy friend stopped being just…

A friend.

If I knew that accepting his invite here tonight would end like this, I would have said *no.* I would have delayed it—even if it was inevitable—just to preserve us. To have a little more time of things fitting perfectly into place, just as it has always been. I would have kept our friendship whole—without cracks and uncomfortable silence.

I would have avoided this very moment with every ounce of my being.

Zander takes a step toward me, and I am frozen stiff—unable to move or breathe or think. His hands move to the back of my head and pull me toward him as he meets me halfway. His lips press against mine. I just stand there. Paralyzed with uncertainty. He stays there a moment, and I push my hands gently on his chest to stop. *Please, make this stop happening.*

He fixes my hair and kisses my forehead. These are the exact same acts that Graham has done to me. And yet they are giving me night and day reactions.

"Somewhere between freshman year and now, I have fallen for you. I love you, Angela McFee. I've loved you for a long time. I was just too afraid to act on it."

"I…" I pause. My voice catches in my throat, and it is

like I am trying to talk after swallowing a strong shot. "I don't even know what to say. I love you too. But I don't think it is the same type of love you have for me."

"Maybe with time? Now that I have finally admitted my feelings for you, maybe you can take a leap of faith and a chance on us?"

His hopefulness stabs at my heart. Deep down I feared this exact moment. Having a guy friend who is an amazing listener, catches me when I fall, and cheers me on in my endeavors is a rarity. And now, it is like an unspoken understanding, that if I don't continue on with Zander as more than friends, I will no longer have those supports. That he will somehow cut the strings and this into an all or nothing type of friendship. The crushing feeling on my heart carries the weight of my decision.

"Zander, I just," I say slowly, "am caught off guard." I look out at the moonlight dancing on the water.

"Does no part of you wonder what we could be? You don't think about it at all? I have been deluding myself for years thinking that maybe, just maybe, you would stop and say 'let's try.' But no, Angie…you always saw me as just a friend. Please don't give up on a seed of hope before it ever gets the chance to be watered."

I listen to his plea. His voice is shaky, and I can tell he is stressed about my answer.

"I just don't know." But I do know. I don't need time. I know that I cannot consider Zander as a love interest because I am still attached to Graham. My heart knows. And it has always known. "I'm wrapped up in a bizarre on-again, mostly off-again, relationship and—"

"He is a horrible partner for you. You put blinders on to his abusive tendencies, and it makes me want to snap."

I flinch at the harsh words. Graham is definitely not perfect. But my heart is drawn to him. He is inimitable. I never had that pull with anyone else. It is undeniable.

"Can you just drop me back off at my place? I need time to think. I just don't know what to say."

I want to ask him if he thought this out. If he knows how much work being with me really is. I want to ask him if he can forget about everything and have it all go back to the way it was before he shook up my life.

He gives me a nod and puts his hand on the small of my back, as we walk back to his car. It is a simple touch that now feels different despite it being done numerous times in the past four years. Now I know his intentions. Now I know where his heart is. He opens the passenger side door and lets me in. Everything feels different. His demeanor. His actions. His glances. And I mourn the loss of the past—when things were still uncomplicated.

The drive to the townhouse is painfully quiet, and every side glance that Zander gives me, I try to ignore. I am sick to my stomach over which path to take at this crossroad. It seems like no matter which way I go, someone gets hurt. And I cannot figure out which will give me the least amount of collateral damage.

When we are just a mile from being back, Zander turns to me at a stop light. "So, this is how it's going to be? You are just giving up on us and not even thinking about how this will impact our friendship?"

My fingers twist in my lap, as I let my lungs deflate. "Trust me, Z, I'm thinking about it." *Just not in the way you think.* "How can I not think about it? It has consumed the free space in my brain right now. And I am freaking out in my head."

"Over what? This shouldn't be that hard to decide."

I look at him bluntly. "It is not that easy." I go back to looking at the road, hoping that my mind is even capable of staying in the present—all while my heart feels twisted in a million different ways—and looking for an escape route.

"It can be."

"No, it can't." My words come out as a bark, making Z flinch. "You basically flipped my life upside down with your declaration."

"You only see it that way because you are trying to find an excuse as to why this can't work out. But it can. We can date. Do the things we always have done before"—his voice catches—"but now with the knowledge that we are moving past just friendship. I can help you get to that place. We can get there together."

Tears fill my eyes. I wipe at them frantically with the back of my hand. "I'm still working through my feelings for Graham, Z. It's not fair to either of you to get strung along for a ride that may end up just crashing."

I straighten out my legs and reach for a tissue from the center console. I wipe my eyes and blow my nose. I just want to curl up in a ball and forget about all of this.

Zander pulls into the parking spot beside Claire's car and offers me his hand when he makes it to my side. I take it out of reflex, something I've done many times over the past four years. However, this time is different from all the rest. My heart craves for things to go back to being easy between us. Yet my mind knows that the turmoil is only really beginning.

I shut the car door, and before I realize what is happening, Zander cups my cheek and turns me to look at him.

"I wish I could say sorry for making things weird between us." He glances away and then refocuses back on me, with eyes so determined that it stops my breath. "But I'm not. I would have regretted letting another day go by without you knowing how I feel."

"Z, please," I whimper. I don't want to do this right now. I just want to go inside and lock myself away.

He walks me back against the door, and I struggle to keep my balance. His arms drape around my back, and he dips his head to capture my mouth. I push at his chest. I do not want to muddy the waters any more. *Stop!*

I see a shadow, and suddenly Zander is pulled back and his mouth releases from mine. I wipe at my lips with my arm, as tears blind me. I try to remove the image of my best friend stealing yet another kiss from me that I didn't want to give. I close my eyes for a second and wait for my quivering legs to stop shaking.

When I open my eyes, I am staring straight into the blue abyss.

Graham.

But not just any Graham.

No. This is Livid Graham. Feral Graham. Doesn't-Give-A-Damn Graham. And…

He is about to go ballistic.

His piercing look roots me to the ground, immobilizing me with the fear of the unknown. Except I do know. He's going to lose it.

Fuck! Where did he come from?

"Go inside, Angie," he barks.

I try to look around his towering body to find Zander. Graham glares at me and tries to nudge me toward the steps.

"Go, Angie," he snarls.

I stand my ground. "No."

"No? You fucking think it is wise for you to say 'no' to me right now as you make out on the street with someone I always saw as a real threat but tried to ignore it?"

"Threat? Really, Graham?"

"Anyone who comes between me and you is a threat, Angela."

I swallow and prop my hands on my hips. On the other side of the wall of muscle, I see Z running his hands through his wayward hair. He looks more stressed now than he did at the river when he first shared his true feelings for me.

I clear my throat. "You need to calm down." And then I see Graham's focus shift from my face. Down my throat. Settling on the base of my neck.

Shit.

His finger hooks the chain—the one I completely forgot I was wearing—pulling it free from the shield of my coat. I can feel the tension build from the stiffness of his back as he examines each side of the heart. Protectively, my hands move up to cover his, worrying that he is going to yank it and break the one reminder I have left of Zander before everything changed.

"Please…" My eyes beg for him not to do anything rash.

"I never want to see you wear another man's jewelry," he snarls. "Ever again."

My hands fall to my side, and Graham releases his hold

of my silver heart. He looks disgusted, and I feel the pang of remorse for putting both these men in this position. I never wanted this to ever happen.

"Let's just all go home, and we can work this out tomorrow," I suggest softly. I need to de-escalate this fast or there is going to be a brawl on the sidewalk.

"Work what out, Angie? What is there to work out? Huh? Did you run off with him the second he got back into town?" Of course he was keeping tabs on Zander. The man has a shattered moral compass. "Are you two *together*?"

I flinch over his words. I know he is referring to sex. He thinks so low of me. That is always his go-to reaction.

I hold my hands up. "Just stop. I am in no mood."

"And you think I am in an amicable mood? You disappear for a couple of hours, then come back swapping spit with some boy and wearing his heart around your neck." He tosses his hands up. "How the hell do you expect me to react?"

I see Zander approaching from my periphery, moving around Graham. "Listen, this is on me. I initiated. I have zero regrets. But this was not her doing."

Graham narrows his eyes and looks from me to Zander and then back again. I can tell he is trying to work out the timeline in his head. Trying to figure out why he didn't see this coming. Good luck. I am as clueless as he seems to be.

"I'm going to go in my house and go to bed. Good night, you two." I stomp up to the door and then turn to look down at the two men who each want something I can't give them. "But for the love of everyone who lives on this block, please don't make me call the cops."

I open my door and lock up for the night. I don't have

time for the testosterone comparison showdown happening on the sidewalk. They can size each other up until their dicks freeze and fall off. I am in no mood for this pissing contest.

When I am about to climb the stairs up to my room, Claire catches up with me. "Angie? What's wrong? What happened?"

"Zander told me he loved me." I choke on the words.

"Oh shit. Wow. I knew he had a thing for you—all of us could tell. But I never thought he would act on it. I mean, he took long enough to act on it. I thought he had given up," she rambles.

I start climbing the stairs. "I feel like I could throw up. I just want things to go back to the way they were. I would rather live life without knowing this added information."

She gives me a hug outside my bedroom and rubs my back soothingly with her hands.

"Well, this sure complicates things," she mutters.

I relax into her arms and cry.

When I get myself together, I go into my room, take off my new necklace, and do a watered-down version of my nighttime routine. I toss on sweats and crawl into the comfort of my familiar bed.

I close my eyes, but every time I relax my mind, thoughts of Zander's disappointed face creep in, haunting me with the memory that my friend is gone.

I broke his heart. But my heart is broken too. Because hurting him, hurts me. Right now, I cannot see a future with Zander. I doubt I ever could.

Needing a distraction, I grab my laptop from my night-stand and open up my blog specific email. I sift through the dozens of questions until I find one that I could have written myself.

Dear Bad Advice,

My best guy friend has just admitted that he loves me and wants me to take a chance on "us." I have never seen him other than as a friend. I doubt I can get to the place his feelings are at. Advice?

-Friends First

I read and reread the entry. I don't have any advice. Not even bad advice. I close that message and try to find an entry that I can advise on—even if it is just satire. Although, in my current state of mind, it may be best that I keep all of my thoughts to myself.

Feeling frustrated, I roll to my side and try to fall asleep—hours before my normal bedtime.

I just want this day to end.

13

I wake up the next day to the smell of bacon and fresh coffee—two of my favorite things. I roll to my back and smile up to the ceiling. *Thank you.* Maybe Claire and Ethan can make it work after all. Perhaps this time apart was exactly what their relationship needed to move to the next level. My stomach growls with the thought of being able to eat greasy breakfast meat at home again. The ban has been lifted. Today is going to be a good day. I can already feel it.

I get dressed in a long black maxi dress and pair it with a lightweight white denim jacket. I take my long wavy hair and work it into a loose chunk braid to the side, so it drapes over my right shoulder.

I stomp down the stairs to alert Claire of my arrival, just in case Ethan is here too. He is ninety-nine percent the reason why she makes bacon, so it is a safe assumption. While the verdict isn't out yet on my approval of Ethan, I will forever be in favor of anyone who makes Claire happy. I round the corner into the kitchen and see the muscular bare back of a man wearing just low ride jeans. As soon as my eyes graze down and make contact with the shape of that behind, I am rendered breathless.

Hot damn. One could fry an egg on that ass.

I clear my throat, causing him to turn around with a spatula in his hand, coming face-to-face with a pair of sapphire blues.

"I shouldn't be surprised and yet—"

"Good morning, sweetheart."

"Good morning, Graham," I mutter, narrowing my eyes at him. I look around for Claire.

"Just you and me," he chirps, obviously proud of himself.

I can't take my eyes off his abs. I bite my lower lip and try to stay focused. "Claire let you in?"

"Sure."

"What does *sure* mean?" I snarl. "Did you break into our place again?"

He turns back to the stove and hums. "It is not breaking in if I know the code."

"You are insane. You know that?" I snatch the spatula out of his hand from behind and turn off the bacon before it burns. He might be pissing me off with his overbearingness, but burning the food will take it up a level for my bad mood.

"I missed you and your sassiness," he says, giving me a smile. "You seem passionate this morning."

"It's called angry."

"So, some extra bacon it is." He throws another two pieces on my plate. Then winks.

I can't help but shake my head at him. He makes me go completely crazy.

Graham steps closer to me, and I back up until I am pressed against the island. His thumb comes up and rests on my bottom lip. "Why did you let him touch you?"

"Everything happened so fast," I whisper, looking down at his hand.

He wipes at my bottom lip, then moves up to the top and does the same swiping motion. It's as if he is trying to remove the memory of Zander's lips from my brain. Wiping me clean.

"When are you going to realize that you are mine?"

I close my eyes and feel the weight of his lips on mine. Yours.

"Yes, mine."

I don't even realize I am talking. He has me in a trance—some vortex that I get sucked into every time his fingers graze me with his worshipping touch.

"He has some fucking nerve to buy you jewelry." His words are harsh. They vibrate against the softness of my lips.

My mouth opens at the sheer force of his, and I breathe into the kiss. I accept him and let him in, leaning into his embrace. His arm bands around my ass, and I get lifted up onto the island. He rips his mouth from mine and lifts my dress only to insert his head underneath—parting my thighs to accommodate him. I lean my hands back on the surface of the counter to brace myself for what will be a wild ride.

Graham pulls my red satin panties to the side and shoves his tongue hard into my crevice, probing and searching for refuge. He is hungry—starving—and for nothing that resembles actual food. I grab his dress-covered head for support and scream out his name. His thumbs pull my folds open to give him better access, and it only takes him a few strokes of his tongue to have me trembling with the force of an unexpected orgasm. Hot damn, he is efficient when he wants to be. He laps up my juices and crawls out of my fabric.

He fixes my outfit, smoothing down the fabric over my bent knees. It's like he can be chivalrous and deranged at the flip of a switch. One second he is calling me sweetheart and the next he is giving me a mind-blowing orgasm with just his mouth.

"I—" My mouth opens and shuts, while my thoughts try to form. "I—"

"I can think of better uses for your mouth," he grinds out, capturing my lips again with his. His mouth covers mine in a sloppy kiss and brands me with a bite. He pulls away reluctantly, and my hand moves up to rub at the wound he just inflicted on me.

"You are going to leave a mark," I say in shock.

"Good."

I am dumbfounded. "Good?"

"I want every fucking man who sees you to know that you are taken. That you are claimed. There is no part of you that I do not want."

"We are not together!" I yell, sliding off the island. The audacity of this man to just storm into my home and make me breakfast and then give me a toe-curling orgasm—all without permission. "And where is your freaking shirt? And your socks? You look homeless."

He stifles a laugh, knowing that his body is having a

positive effect on my libido. "On the couch with my other belongings," he says nonchalantly.

I walk into the living room and see his suitcase. His shirt is draped over the chair, and his wallet and keys are resting on the coffee table. I sense Graham at my back, so I ask without even bothering to look. "You spent the night?"

"I wanted to wake up to you," he says softly.

"I'm impressed that you were able to stay out of my room." My words come out as sarcastic as I intend.

"Oh, I visited there. You always say the cutest things when you are drowsy with sleep."

My mouth gapes open like a fish. "You got issues, dude."

"I get what I want, Angie. Always."

I let out an uncomfortable giggle. "You sound like a petulant child that needs some sort of grounding."

"I mean it. You are mine."

I let out a sigh. "I'm asking you nicely to respect me enough to give me some time to figure things out. I'm on the verge of losing it from stress. And I just need to be by myself without you or Zander clouding up my vision."

His eyes twitch at the mention of another man. "How long?"

My mouth dries over him actually considering this. "One week. No contact, no calls, no texts. Call off your guards too."

"Hell no to the guards demand. How am I supposed to know you are safe?"

"Trust."

"I don't trust you. Not after you let a guy, who has been pining for you probably since the beginning, touch you."

"Quit changing the subject."

"It is a valid fact."

I raise my brow. "It is blatantly an opinion."

"Fine."

"Fine."

"Guards stay."

"That is not how negotiating works, Graham."

"What are your terms?"

"No guards. And I mean it. None. And if I see one or suspect one is following me or tampering with my life in any way, I will do two things. First, I will call the cops and file a restraining order. Second, I will cut you out of my life completely. Think of this as a test."

He walks over to the chair and pulls his T-shirt over his head. He runs a hand through his hair, and I can tell that he got a haircut recently.

"I don't like this, Angie. I just do not like it."

"You don't have to like it, Graham. This is not about you liking or not liking something. This is about me. And my requirement to have breathing room. If you want any chance to get me to stop being mad at you and to stop wanting to kick you in the balls on a regular basis, I need you to do this."

He nods his head. "When does this dry period start of keeping my distance?"

"After bacon," I say with a smirk.

"You sure love your meat," he chuckles softly.

I click my tongue. "And you sure love to feed it to me."

"So, let me get this straight," Claire says as she throws back a shot, "we are doing this bar crawl simply to see if Graham has stayed true to his word and is backing off."

"Yup. Because if he is having me followed during this break that I instituted, then my reckless behavior should overpower his need to stick to the deal."

"Genius."

"I know, right?"

"Does that mean you are staying away from Zander as well?"

"Yeah. I need to stay away from all men before I get any more wrapped up in the cluster fuck that is my life. I don't even trust *myself* to make good decisions right now. But enough about me. What's going on with you and Ethan?"

"Next."

"Oh, come on," I whine.

"*That* is something I do not want to talk about. I want to have fun." She holds up her glass of melted ice and diluted margarita. "Cheers to screwing a bunch of men!"

I look at her with confusion. "Not exactly the vision I was going for, but sure, cheers!" I say, smacking my diminishing drink glass against hers. "Pretty sure we are bringing some bad luck to ourselves with these pathetic looking beverages."

"Fill us up, bartender-oney!" Claire announces to the bartender, who just shakes his head at her. I do the same. "It sounded better in my head," she grumbles.

"What do you ladies want to drink now?"

"Something that makes our lips turn numb but our nipples stand up," Claire answers.

He chuckles. "Coming right up."

We hit up another three bars in the Pearl District—getting an appetizer and beverage at each. As we walk to the last stop, Claire grabs my arm and points. "Look."

I follow her finger to a little French bistro. I stand paralyzed watching Graham and Sophia share a bottle of wine and what looks to be comfort food.

"At least he makes it easy for me to want to stay away from him," I whisper—as if my words will somehow make it to his ears. "I hate how he affects me."

"Guys are such asses. But maybe this is just business."

"Even so, they are so embedded in each other's lives that one of us will always play the *other woman* role. And I have too much self-worth to constantly compete with her."

"Let's go home. I am one drink away from busting in there and throwing up on his shoes."

I fall into a rhythm over the next few days and channel my energy to creating a dress for the meeting on Saturday. Mark told me to dress as if I am going on an interview for a swanky job that I am desperate to get. After perusing my wardrobe—as well as Claire's—I realize that I have nothing that would say "hire me," and that is very sobering. If I want to get headhunters to notice me, I need to stand out in the crowd. The best way to do that is to perfect my outfit to help give the illusion that I have my life together.

I hit up the *Thread Count* store and spend hours looking through modern dress catalogs that are scattered across a cutting table until I find the best pattern for my body shape. I settle on an A-line ruffle skirt dress that is sleeveless and fitted on top. The style is a conservative knee-length. I choose a deep red fabric that will be bold—but still be in the fall family of acceptable colors. I purchase black lace to use as an overlay for the top half, just to add a bit of flare.

With time factored in to learn the new pattern, I set myself up to work at the sewing machine on my desk in my bedroom. I carefully lay out the pattern and fabric on the floor to pin, chalk, and cut. I jam out to some U2 music from their earlier albums and spend the next five hours completing a beautifully sophisticated dress. I try it on and look in my floor-length mirror at my image, adjusting pins as I go. I do a slow spin and see if any other parts need altered. I complete the finishing touches and then retry it on.

While my creation is very pretty, I feel like something is missing. Digging through my random part box, I find some sparkly embellishments that would look amazing along the waistline. So, I strip down and get back to work.

Once I am satisfied, I place the dress on a hanger over my closet door and steam out any wrinkles. I pad down the hallway to find Claire who will be able to handle the shoe dilemma.

I give a knock at her door and hear her yell to come on in. I push open her door and meet some resistance. I manage to sneak my head in and notice that there are clothes on every surface of the floor, dresser, and bed. It is the biggest mess I have seen from her and definitely worse than the last encounter I had here. It's as if she just gave up trying. If it wasn't overstepping, I would come in here and straighten up when she was at the gym or in class. It surely could use an intervention.

Claire gives me a sad frown. "Sorry about the mess."

I shrug it off. “It’s okay. Really. Your turf, your rules."

“I just lost my OCD mojo.”

I give a weak smile. “Well, I hope you get it back soon.”

“What brings you to my abode?”

“I have a sort of interview tomorrow, and I just finished sewing my dress. I just need to figure out shoes.”

“Oh, let me see,” she says, pushing off the bed.

She follows me back down the hall, and when she sees the first glimpse of my dress, she gasps.

“Too much?” I ask, suddenly self-conscious.

“Hell no!” she exclaims, touching the ruffle skirt. “It is stunning, Angie. I cannot believe you are choosing journalism over fashion design.”

“Humph, not much designing when I just follow a pattern.”

“But you made it your own. It is one of a kind. I love it.”

I give her a hug. “Thanks for always cheering me on. I know I don’t say it enough, but I am so glad you are in my life.”

She squeezes me harder and pulls back to give me a sad smile. “So, we will be graduating soon, and I’ll eventually need a real job. I am considering going to Los Angeles for that internship in January. This opportunity could lead to more doors being opened for me.”

“I know.”

“You know?”

“Yeah. I accidentally saw the letter that said you applied,” I whisper, ashamed that I have not admitted the truth until now.

“I just don’t know what I want to do. And this whole thing with Ethan is causing me a lot of grief.”

"I know these are not my typical words of encouragement, but I really do believe that things have a way of working themselves out. Sometimes all it takes is time."

"Yeah." She gives me a nod. "So, you aren't mad?"

"I'm selfish to expect you to always be in the same city I'm in. And caring for someone means letting them fly. If you decide to go to Los Angeles, then I will be cheering you on."

"You're such a good friend, Angie. I really do appreciate you." She claps her hands together and bursts with the biggest smile. "But enough of this sappy talk. Let's get back to the shoes. I think I have the perfect pair. Let's go find them back in my room."

I follow her down the hall and wait until she clears a path to her bed for me to walk without tripping on stuff. She pulls a long plastic bin out from under her bed that is labeled with big Sharpie letters across the top that say "DOOMSDAY SURVIVAL BIN." I stare at the words and try to stifle my laughter.

"Why would there be—"

Before I can finish my question, she whips off the top, and lo and behold there are a beautiful pair of strappy black stilettos. New ones. Perfectly polished ones. My mouth gapes at them. There they are, lying right beside a wad of cash, a few canned goods, four flashlights, Tylenol, an inflatable raft, bug spray, and one of those emergency blankets made of reflective plastic.

"Claire, why are there stilettos in your Doomsday bin?"

"Because you always have to be prepared for whatever life throws at you," she says matter-of-factly.

"This is so true."

14

It's crazy how fast a person's life can drastically change in just a matter of moments. I go from failing my last semester, to repeating it, to being told my research topic is unsuitable, to waiting to be picked up to meet with a recruiter from *Pacific Press*. Just when I think all is lost, I get a glimmer of hope—something to hold on to and work toward.

It takes me an hour to get ready for the meeting with Mark and his friend. I agonize over my dress and whether or not it exemplifies professionalism, without having the look of trying too hard. I was confident I nailed the look a day ago when I sewed it, but when I am smack-dab in the middle of the preparations, I let doubt creep in. Hopefully my work ethic will be my selling point and not my attire.

Claire is holed up in her room. Hopefully she's not stalking Ethan's social media page and making comments on his posts that she will later regret. She has not been herself since she decided to avoid him. Graham has followed through with my demands. It has been almost a week since we have seen each other, conversed, or fought a winner-less battle. Five days of silence. It is a record.

I wait downstairs in the entryway until Mark's car pulls up. Then I grab my handbag and portfolio, give my dress one last smoothing, and exit through the front door. I lock up the house and set the security system that I am finally getting accustomed to using. Mark slips out of the driver's side and watches me make my way down to him.

"Angie McFee." His eyes coast down my body, lingering on my curves. "You look radiant."

"Thank you."

If one positive thing has come from my work at Entice, it is finally learning to just accept a compliment when one is thrown my way. The opportunity to meet a variety of men and their eclectic personalities has helped me to learn how to adapt to the situation I am thrown into. No longer do I feel like the timid girl who is afraid of her own shadow.

"Do a turn."

My mouth gapes. So much for feeling confident. "Right here? On the sidewalk?"

"Yeah, why be shy? You have to know how sexy you look."

I reluctantly spin around, trying not to stumble in my sky-high heels.

"Hmm, ready to go?" he asks me, his voice gruff.

I nod my head and make my way over to the passenger side. He doesn't have a driver this time, and I am glad we are not forced to stare at each other in the backseat.

"Don't be nervous," Mark soothes, rubbing his hand

along the ruffle of my skirt. He plays with my hem before smoothing it down and giving my leg a light squeeze. "You really know how to make a man want for more. Just be yourself and things will go smoothly."

I get goose bumps, but they are not the "feel good" kind. "I'll try."

I stare out the window as Mark maneuvers his car on the busy streets. For a Saturday evening, there are a lot of people out and about. We cross the bridge and enter the downtown area. He pulls up to the valet booth, signs a form in a lazy scrawl, and hands over his keys. I slide out of the car and shut the door. Mark joins me and places his hand on the small of my back.

We enter Parkhouse Plaza—where I went on my very first date with Graham. It is hard to be here and not think about him. The selfie we took on our way to El Pastel, the decadent chocolate desserts, and the bantering that began that night and that we still can't stop ourselves from doing when we are in each other's presence. All of the memories saturate my mind, warming me from the inside out.

I hate that I miss him.

I hate that we see the world so differently.

I hate that our common ground is often used as a battle ground.

I follow Mark to the elevators, and we take the car up to the fourteenth floor and get escorted to our table at Fortune without any fuss. We are the first to arrive, and I look over the menu. Since my stomach is tied up in knots, I settle for a seltzer and a small plate appetizer. Mark orders wine and a lamb entree.

"Should we have waited to order until Steve arrives?"

"He is notoriously late for most things, so it's best to just go ahead like we did."

I nod and then take a sip of my water.

Mark's phone buzzes, and he picks it up to look at the screen.

I watch as his face changes to a frown. "Something wrong?"

"Steve has another meeting running over next door at the Maylord Hotel. He says to meet him in his suite for drinks and to look at your portfolio. That work for you?"

I swallow hard over this change in our original plan. Prolonging my energy for making a good first impression is wearing on my nerves as is. I just want to get it over with and have him decide if I have enough potential or not.

"Okay," I answer hesitantly. Surely going to someone's hotel room isn't the most professional, but I would regret backing out now and not seeing this opportunity through until the end. Plus, I would rather hear from Steve's own mouth if I am not cut out for this line of work. It is one thing to have my professor hint at it. However, to have someone in the actual field express it would carry more weight.

I excuse myself to the restroom and freshen up my hair, which I straightened to lay long down my back. I reapply some lipstick and make sure it is not on my teeth. I check my cell for texts, even though there haven't been many this week. It's like I fell off a lot of people's radars. Or I just forced them to stay away this time and they listened.

When I make it back to our now table-for-two, my

seltzer and appetizer have arrived. I squeeze the lime into my drink and take a sip. My food looks amazing, so I dig in.

"How's the pharmaceutical business going?" I ask, to break the silence. I try to feign being casual, even though I am always trying to gather data and information.

Mark gives me a warm smile. "Better than expected, actually. Thanks for asking."

"Can you tell me anything about it?"

"Most is highly confidential, but I can tell you that we are making breakthroughs on some testing."

"Oh yeah? That is great. Do you test on animals?" I have read a few articles about how vaccines were made, so I feel like I have a tiny amount of knowledge on how trials work.

"We are actually doing trials on humans—using the actual test drug and a placebo."

"Wow. That is fascinating."

He winks. "And super lucrative."

"I bet."

"If this all works out for me, I may retire early and just live off my dividends."

"Now that sounds like something worth striving for."

"Do you miss the agency line of work?"

I think about the question for a few seconds and then nod. "I miss having something to do." Which reminds me, I better continue looking for a part-time job—even if just a few hours a week. I like to stay busy, and waiting around for opportunities to land in my lap is never the best strategy.

Mark smiles, pays the bill, and then helps me from my seat. We get back on the same elevator and walk through the same lobby that we did just an hour before.

"Here, hold my arm so you don't fall. The hotel is just across the street."

I link Mark's arm and try my best not to break my ankle. These doomsday shoes may be the death of me. When we enter the Maylord Hotel, we walk straight to the elevators. It's as if Mark has done this dozens of times before. He knows where everything is, selects the correct button on the elevator, and knows the direction we should walk to get to Steve's room without even a glance at the arrowed sign that directs which way to go based on the room number ranges.

"Steve is finishing up a meeting at the lobby bar, but he texted me while you were in the bathroom to let ourselves in."

My heart rate increases, and I clutch my portfolio to my chest. The pressure does not slow it down and only makes it accelerate faster. What am I doing? Something seems off. It's like every warning bell in my head blares its siren at once.

Danger!

Leave!

I watch as Mark pulls a keycard out of his back pocket and inserts it into the slot on the door. He mumbles something about doing a lot of business in this room so the hotel reserves it for those purposes.

Nothing makes sense.

My head fogs and I lean sideways, catching myself on the door frame. I drop my handbag and stumble to the floor to retrieve it. I push items that have escaped out of the side flap back inside, struggling to keep them there. I look up and see Mark eyeing me with a smirk. It is the opposite of comforting. I hoist myself back up, as ungracefully as one could while wearing five-inch stick heels. I lean against the frame and hunch my shoulders forward. I am so tired. It's like my neck is in charge of holding up my head and is failing miserably. It slumps forward, hitting against the wooden plank.

"Come on, Angie," Mark coaxes.

His words echo in my ears, as if the phrase is set to loop. My vision blurs and I blink hard to refocus. I glance around the space from my stance, reluctant to cross the line between the hallway and the actual room. Nothing seems unusual just from a visual perspective. There is a table set up with some file folders. I can almost see the newspaper's logo across the top one, but my vision keeps fading in and out. I am too far away to see the details. There is a bed along the right side of the room. A stocked minibar, as well as an ice bucket with what looks to be champagne resting in it, is set up along the back wall.

"He should be here soon," Mark comforts.

His words sound distant in my ears. Like he is in some tunnel and the echo is what you would hear if you were trapped in a seashell. He saunters over to me and squeezes my elbow gently. He guides me inside, despite my feet feeling like they are encased in cement.

"Let's have a drink," he says calmly. "It will help you relax."

I try to shake my head no, but I can't tell if I actually do it or not. It is like I am able to see my surroundings but not have much control over my own body. I hear a thump and look down to see the portfolio I thought I was clutching scattered on the floor. Heaps of papers just lay at my feet. I stare at my work…at my articles and my writing papers and my graded documents over the course of four years. All of my hard work just littered all over the carpet of a luxury hotel room, like trash.

I disentangle my perceived expectations from reality. What I thought was going to happen and what is actually happening are two vastly different things. I look around at my surroundings as if I am seeing them for the first time, trying to figure out how I managed to get myself here.

"Sta-sta…" I stutter. "Eve is is…" My mouth feels like it is stuffed with marshmallows. "Isn't co-co-coming is he?" My words are sad even to my echoing ears. Mark guides me over to rest on the king-size bed. The room is exactly what it should be—warm, open, comforting. For about four hundred dollars a night, this hotel room should be worth every penny. I might appreciate the beauty if I wasn't chin deep in dilemma after dilemma.

He shakes his head. "Had to cancel last minute."

So here I am. In a position I thought I would never find myself in again, at least not with a man I barely know. A man I have been warned against. When in reality, I am nothing more than a naive girl who fell for a trick.

I didn't fall asleep and wake up in this nightmare. No. I got here by my own two feet. And that's the worst part of this all.

I did this to myself.

This is all my fault.

I feel nauseous and stupid. Like I just made a colossal mistake by even stepping foot in the lobby of this hotel.

Now I am stuck without a clear path to escape and no one to come to my rescue.

Mark presses against my shoulders gently and massages the tension that seems to be building with every passing minute. My temples throb from the loud voices inside my head screaming to get out. Get out now! But I cannot make my legs and arms work. I cannot get them to do the things I need them to do. So I lie here and stare up at the ceiling. It is high and has a scalloped pattern.

Mark nudges my bent knees, causing my legs to spread about two feet apart, trembling and weak. I'm repulsed. At the man, as this level of degradation is unforgivable, but even more, I am disgusted with myself. Despite now knowing that the whole thing was most likely a ruse to get me here right now, he doesn't know the other side of the coin.

Nope. Not a clue.

The other side is that deep down I know that this is the only way of using his sexual predator-ness to get what I want in return. I find thankfulness in knowing that when I used the restroom at Fortune, I was smart enough to start the recording device that is secured in my handbag. I may have entered this room on false pretenses, but I am at least going to bring hell upon his life once I exit it.

According to key physics principles, every action has a reaction. But according to life, not every action has a justifiable consequence. And rarely are those consequences equal in dynamic.

No one deserves this.

No one.

Sure, I chose to meet with Mark. I chose to believe him.

I chose to see hope in something that otherwise was hopeless. My consequence tonight might be that I can no longer live with myself; it might be more than I can bear. Or maybe the consequence will be that this is all for nothing. That I am going to be brutally violated and be left with broken dreams, as well as a broken body.

"Wha-a do?" I ask, amazed that my mouth can even express itself. My words sound incoherent, but the understanding in Mark's eyes lets me know that he heard them for the intended purpose.

"Just relax. I need to check your reflexes. See what I can do and not do."

Huh?

"Yoo draa me?"

"Perhaps not enough. It's not personal, Angie," he says, moving over to the minibar to fix some drinks. "You've just been hand selected for the trials. And we are still trying to figure out your tolerance levels. You are definitely a special case."

I try to roll and am unable to feel my limbs. It's as if I am paralyzed. My mind races at what to do. How to get out of here. How to alert anyone in the hall that I need help. Whatever he has slipped into me may wear off if I can keep him busy long enough to regain my wits.

The pressure on the bed alerts me to Mark being back again. He sits me up against a mound of pillows and grips my chin in his palm. He squeezes it to hold it in place. A pen light shines into my eyes, and I blink over the brightness.

"Fascinating," he mutters. He pulls out a folded piece of

paper from his pants pocket and jots something onto it with a pen.

"Oww?" I manage to squeak out. My head still has some range of motion, so at least I can turn my neck.

"Shhhh…"

He grabs a hammer tool, and I watch stupidly as he hits my knee with it. He then puts it back into his briefcase and rubs at my feet.

"Let's have a drink," he suggests, walking over to the ice bucket to retrieve the bottle of bubbly. The popping sound echoes in my ears. He pours two flutes and fiddles with his briefcase, pulling out a vial. He adds it to one flute, emptying it entirely into the bubbling liquid. He moves over to the bed and presses that glass to my lips. "To help you be more"—his brows rise—"amicable."

He tips back the champagne glass into my mouth, since I cannot use my floppy hands. No! I slam my head forward in a rush. The glass knocks out of his hand and onto the floor.

"Bitch!" he snaps. "That was my only expendable dose!"

He just confirmed my fears. He drugged me tonight. And planned to do it again. Maybe I still have a chance to get away. Maybe the first dose, which he must have slipped into my seltzer when I was in the restroom at Fortune, did not take as much effect as he wanted. Maybe I can get this nightmare to have an ending that is less tragic than he planned.

And then it hits me. A series of events merged into a video montage starts to play in my head. Graham has been warning me from the start not to drink anything from Mark. At El Pastel, Mark sent over a drink to our table which was returned. On the night I met with Mark's business associates, Graham warned me not to drink anything. The handoff with Paul at River Valley U was probably drugs. Graham knew all along that Mark was drugging the women he employed. He probably just didn't have enough evidence to prove it. But he knew. That is why he has been trying so hard to get me to stay away from Tanner.

And then there is his sister, Penny, who probably got caught up in the crossfire. She is the reason why Graham has been on this manhunt from the beginning. He has a personal investment to prove who drugged her.

"Howww?" I exhale, watching Mark's eyes grow dark. He is frazzled, and his demeanor is scary. "Waa eee?"

"I'll tell you, my sweet and naive Angie. But only because you won't remember a thing in an hour or two."

I swallow hard as he continues to speak.

"After a few failing businesses, I discovered that the easiest money to be made was to manufacture some newer age drugs. Test them and then distribute them using my pushers. Narcotics for pain. Drugs that can cause temporary paralysis…you know, for men who want some easy fun with the ladies. Sleeping pills that actually work. But the FDA is a nasty organization that is controlled by politics and deep pockets. So I am just bypassing all the red tape bull-shit. Selling my product locally—but with hope to expand internationally. Mexico, Russia, China, and the Middle East surprisingly have a high demand for easy-to-access pills. It is the new culture."

"Sick."

"It is basically like self-help in a pill form. There's something for everybody."

I sit in silence as he talks. I try to lock on to certain keywords—despite him warning me that my memory will be gone. He is crazy. He is a criminal. His business associates Benjamin, Samson, and Edward probably are too. And Paul.

"So here we are, my helpless Angie. And while this trial of the testing did not work out one hundred percent as planned, I think we can still have a little fun, right? Why waste a perfectly good supplemental dose I snuck into your drink back during dinner?" He leans in closer to my ear and hovers at the shell. "We better hurry since you will probably metabolize the strains faster since you ate food." He glances at his watch. "And since it has already been an hour, let's see how immobile you can be. Don't worry, though; you don't have to perform. This is more for me than it is for you. So just lie back and enjoy the ride."

Mark pushes me into the pillows and forces my mouth to his. I'm going to be sick. I squeeze my eyes shut as he pulls at my dress and curses over how to get it off me. There is a hidden zipper in back, but I cannot even focus on how to make my mouth talk, and I definitely do not want to help him out. I scream. But the only one who hears is me. I no longer have a voice. It is like someone suctioned it out of my throat, leaving me verbally impaired.

I hear a ripping sound. My eyes fly open. Panic wants to rise, but I shove it into another section of my brain, compartmentalizing my protest.

Tears fall down my cheeks as my lungs seek air. The throbbing of my head escalates, making my eyes want to shut. *Don't close them.* Look for a way out. I need to be coherent and not get inside my headspace and zone out, even though every preprogrammed self-preservation mechanism in my brain is telling me to go there. To hide. To curl up and wait out this hellish nightmare. I swallow hard and urge my mind to stay still and wait for the effects of the drug to work its way through my bloodstream and then dissipate. I just need time.

Panicked thoughts lead to physical trauma.

Stay calm, Angie.

I want to escape the present and travel to another time. A time when decisions didn't seem so tough. I can't go there, though. I need to stay alert to try to protect myself.

Fabric slides down to my curvy hips, and the carnal groan vibrates in my ears, furthering the disgust of what I am physically unable to stop. My knees are forced apart, and the animalistic stare of Mark makes me want to die. He wants me. As clueless as I am at times, this I know with certainty.

Mark Tanner is going to rape me.

And I very well might not remember a thing.

His shadow lassos me back to the present and keeps me there. When he leans his head down to capture my lips again, I throw mine forward and smack my forehead against his teeth. Blood splatters onto my naked stomach. I stare at it and let out a wail. One that is heard. It startles Mark so much, he whips his hand back and smacks it so hard against the side of my cheek that I see spots.

I float to a time when things were simple. Like James and me deciding between vanilla and chocolate pudding. Momma would make the best homemade pudding out of heavy cream. It was thick and creamy—not like the kind you get in the little cups in a pack of four. This was decadent. But both flavors were so delicious. It was hard to tell which one was better. It all depended on our moods.

She would let us lick the beaters. It became our ritual. If we were really good, she would swipe them into the batter to give us extra. That is love. Momma would go through her day doing these little gestures to show us how much we meant to her. We were her world.

I miss her.

My eyes flutter open and the light burns like acid.

"Oh good, you are awake again. Just in time for the main event. You won't tell, will you?" He bends to kiss my nose that appears to already be swelling. "This can be our little secret?"

He is standing above me along the side of the bed. My face throbs with the pain from him hitting me. I can bet I am bruised with shades of blue and purple. I watch through my hooded eyes as he pulls his black trousers down, throwing a few wrapped condoms on the nightstand in presumptuous glory. I stare at the yellow foil-wrapped coins and think back to all of the moments leading up until now. This is it. This is the exact day that I get…I can't even think the word again. Saying it in my head will make this real. My head flops side to side.

He saunters over to the other side of the bed, silver silk boxers highlighting his erection, begging to escape. The mattress dips with his weight. His strong hands grasp my naked ankles, pulling them down to the foot of the bed. The weight of his body crushes me. He readjusts his forearm at the side of my neck, his free hand roaming up underneath my bra. His blood has now dried on my stomach and part of me wishes it was mine. And that I was dead.

Lips press to the curve of my neck. Acid and bile burn my throat as the nausea persists. How the hell am I going to stop him?

Mark's fingers pull at my bra, tugging gently to undo the snaps. His eyes marvel at my rising breasts.

"I usually don't play with my test subjects. But you are so fuckable that I can't resist. Plus, taking something from your fucker of a boyfriend will bring me great pleasure, knowing that every time he looks at you, he will see the possession of another man written all over your body."

A wicked grin plays on his lips as he bends down to suck at one of my breasts. They are heaving, not because of pleasure but because of panic. He moans at the heaviness of the globes, weighing them in the balance of his hands like ripe fruit. I whimper from the injustice of my situation. It is entirely my fault for thinking that his friend was waiting here for me. A series of horrible choices and bad cards to play. I am doomed either way I move.

My hands regain some feeling. Just my hands. I ball them into tight fists of sheets, in an effort to distract myself. Illusions of doing this with a man I love drift away like lighted lanterns in the night.

Suddenly, something hits my head, and the sound ricochets off the walls as more beads fly and skitter across the floor like scurrying insects.

My dress. It is completely ruined. All of my hard work—the embellishments and details—destroyed.

"Yum." He grins, his eyes sparkling with pent-up desire.

I am naked except for my panties. The last piece of self-respect I have left.

The once tender Mark is now the I-need-to-get-my-money's-worth Mark. And that idea alone makes my stomach sour with the realization.

I don't even have time to process what is happening as his hands roam over my body. I can feel the pressure. I just cannot get my body to turn away from the unwanted prying and squeezing and pulling and smoothing. Only one last lacy strip of sheer black panties stands in the way of my fleeting modesty. I am nearly naked. The panties are see-through in all the right places, except at the crotch. That is my only saving grace. Ironically they are a gift from Graham.

Graham.

And out of all times to force him to stay away from me. To call off all of the guards and security team…I do it when I need them most. He has never listened to my wishes any other time I have asked him to—except this week. He has been completely silent. He has not texted or called or stopped over unexpectedly. No one has followed me or trailed my movements around Portland.

So here I lie, helpless. On my back, dressed only in a pair of lace panties, as Mark rubs at his cock and preys on me like the devil in flesh form.

The light from the room seems to get brighter. More painful. It blinds my vision, and I blink hard to try to keep the queasy-floating feeling from consuming me. Everything blurs and refocuses in time with my beating heart. Damn light. Things would be so much easier if my vision was shielded. Maybe make it less real.

Images of my mom taping up the time capsule box and making me and James swear that we will not peek until we are past the start of freshman year in college flash over my vision. "*Angie, maybe you will meet a nice boy by then and you will need this box more than you know. But you must wait until you find the right one. And you definitely must not spend too much time crying over me whenever I go. Promise, baby? Promise me you'll wait. Promise me you will fight for what you deserve in this life and not settle for mediocre.*"

Her sweet voice penetrates my senses and alerts me to what I need to do.

Promise me you will fight.

I can't get the words out of my head as they play on loop over and over again—driving the little ounce of sanity that I have left over, over, over…the edge.

Stop! Stop! Please stop!

The voice in my head screams and panics. STOP! Please! I can't do—

Before Mark has a chance to tear at my virtuous shield, I rationalize a plan of action out of this predicament I voluntarily put myself in.

I must make noise, because he goes into soothing mode.

"Shhh, darling," he cuts in breathily. "Give me a chance to make you feel good. You may even have some fun too."

His finger draws a line from my chin all the way down my shoulders, over my arm, across my belly, around my hip, and then takes a plunge. In between my clenched thighs. The intrusion causes a jolt of pain as I desperately try to keep them tightly together—having no such luck. Or strength. Even though I cannot get my brain to make my body move, I can still register the intrusion—the violation.

He is not listening to me. He is going to rape me. And I may or may not remember what happens. I cannot figure out which is the lesser of evils. Always wondering? Or remembering every violating detail?

I panic and thrash out of his hold, convulsing on the bed like a child in need of a priest from a horror movie. I am amazed that I have regained some mobility.

"I see you feel a little alive again," he snickers. "Fun. Well, I like my whores to have a *little* life in them when I fuck them, so this will still work out in my favor. Feel free to fight me, so I can show you who's in control. I get off on the struggle."

He slams me back onto the bed and pulls my panties to the side. He mutters something disgusting and is about to finish stripping me when a loud deafening crash resonates through the room. I can hear a high-pitched squeal, similar to how a frightened girl would sound. It takes several seconds to realize that the girl is me. And I can't seem to stop the screaming.

It is like I finally have my voice back. Like I can finally make my mouth function. And now I can't shut it up. I wail. I whimper. I cry out.

My heart stops for half a beat as I roll my head into a pillow in a frantic move to hide from the impending danger. My body attempts to curl up in the fetal position, naturally trying to protect myself. I tremble in fear. My heart launches blood throughout my limbs, but they are still heavy and stationary. I am stuck. And in this moment, I cannot tell if it is voluntary or involuntary anymore.

My breathing staggers as I gulp for fresh air, unable to fill my lungs to capacity. Fuck. I am going to have a panic attack. The all too familiar feeling of the past pushes my senses to the limit. Everything is in slow motion. My eyes flicker open to see three suited men surround the bedroom in the invasion. Is this a robbery? A shoot-out? Maybe Mark's business associates came to subdue me and offer him backup. I squeak as I see hands moving closer to hurt me. But I feel nothing except the bed bouncing. Am I hallucinating?

One man snarls out obscenities, his back to me, arms gesturing in thin air at the animated showdown. I never get a look at his face. I shiver over his anger.

My mind is in chaos. Every noise sounds like it is being passed through an underwater cave. Images and flashes flying like blips on the radar of my conscious thoughts. Mark is facing the livid man, wide-eyed.

The man lifts his fist and wields it forward with Olympic speed, connecting with Mark's chiseled masculine jaw. His head flies sideways as if on a spring. Blood spews out of his mouth—reopening the wound I already caused—squirting on the clean linen sheets of the bed. I quiver in repulsiveness at the crimson splash, rolling farther away from it into the corner of the mattress. My throat feels raw, and I can no longer produce the words that scream from within.

"You want me to fight, right? Isn't this what it's all about!" he screams at Mark's limp form. "Get up and be a man!"

This cannot possibly be just a robbery. I know I should escape, but my fear and lack of adequate oxygen keep me in place. My head feels light and heavy all at once, vertigo hitting in waves. My blurry eyes give me the impression that I am moments from passing out. Black spots fill my vision of the suited man nailing punches to Mark's midsection. A knee jerks up, throwing him back even farther. Spit and blood and sweat speckle the surrounding designer ivory furniture.

Vomit rises in my throat and catches in my passageway, making me choke for air. It's the sight of blood that sends me over the edge. The crimson stain of red. The smell of rust. As if my head is submerged under water, I hear a string of muffled orders snapped out of the violent one's mouth. One of the two non-fighting men nods and they move in my direction, faces emotionless. Not even a slight twitch of their brows or lips. They are like soldier robots moving in synchronized steps toward me.

A noise escapes deep from within my belly that is unrecognizable to me. Acid tasting air fills my lungs in a rush of pure fear. The sounds I'm making startle me back to the present situation, making the men stiffen their shoulder muscles. It is my turn. I scream and kick at the hands trying to get ahold of me. I can finally move. The drug has worn off. The taste of freedom makes me thrash and punch. My lungs inflate and my fighter side unleashes. I will not go down like this. "HELP! HE—"

A hand covers my mouth in a mere second, and my eyes dry and water simultaneously from their wide exposure to the stale air. Another hand reaches around my naked torso and pulls me up against a strong chest of muscles. I search the room for an exit, and I use my unrestrained arms and legs to fight. I pinch and kick and pull and flail and yank and claw. I wiggle and shift in the arms holding me prisoner. *Let me go!*

Fuck.

The main man in my field of spotted vision turns and growls angrily in my direction. The piercing blue eyes electrify my insides, sending charges throughout my limbs.

Graham Hoffman.

Angry, fierce, virile, and sexy.

Shit.

Damn.

Fuck.

15

"Enough!" Graham bellows, flashing a look to the man holding me captive. "Restrain her before she hurts herself! Dammit! NOW! And get ahold of Nic!" His snarl is laced with a deadly warning that sends the feeling of liquid nitrogen down my spine. My tongue catches in a cage of teeth. I am chilled by the freezing numbness and then left scorched from the afterburn effect.

As Graham's concentration leaves him, Mark strikes out, connecting with his left cheekbone. The sound of tenderizing meat with a mallet penetrates through the tense air. Graham's head slings to the right to absorb the blow. His hair sways in the swiftness of the fluid motion. I gasp over the pain he must be feeling.

"Ah, fuck!"

It is then that I feel the other hands on my bare skin, attempting to immobilize me on their boss's orders. I squeeze my eyes shut to hide from the embarrassment. I do a blind inventory—six total. One pair on my naked arms, holding me firmly as I continue to squirm. One pair on my calves, circling me into a steel, deadlock vise. The newly introduced third pair wraps my exposed torso in a blanket. Shivers run havoc down my spine, circulating the coldness all over. I go limp—all fight extinguished—as I try to process what is happening.

Five men have witnessed my state of undress. And each one has had the opportunity to touch my body in some capacity. Mortification strikes down on me like an anvil. How can this be happening? Why is it happening? My heart beats loudly with the beat of every punch Graham throws at Mark's grounded form. It is a rhythmic song of sorts. Shit. Why aren't any of the men trying to stop him from killing him?

Maybe Mark should be dead for molesting me and nearly raping me. Maybe I should wish it. But I don't. If Graham does end his life, then where will that send him? To prison?

I get passed to a different man. His fingers are rough with calluses. As I flicker open my eyes, I see short lighter brown hair.

Collins?

He helps me hold the blanket around my fragile body.

"I'm so cold," I mutter. I look down at the fabric and discover that it is actually a charcoal suit coat.

Collins carries me to the opposite side of the suite, in a cheap attempt to keep my eyes off the violent display of bloodshed. I feel safe in his arms but fidget to get free. The other two men leave the room hastily.

"Ma'am. Keep still." His voice is soothing in my state

of shock. He doesn't seem stressed at all. His impeccable manners are even intact.

"He…he…he's going to kill him!" I shriek, tears flying violently down my cheeks. Each tear stings my raw, chafed skin. Feels like dumping hydrochloric acid in a wound and then rubbing it with sandpaper. I relish the pain, but fear the aftereffects of processing the damage.

"He knows when to stop." It is short and to the point. Not a question, just a matter-of-fact statement.

How does he know that? Has this scene played out before?

"Can…get down…dressed? Please?" I sniffle and choke out the words. My homemade dress is destroyed, but I can still wear the scraps. Perhaps it is on the bed? Under the bed? I crane my neck to look for my outfit. It is then that I remember the splattering of blood from Mark's open wounds and shudder.

I have no place to hide my shame; not even my logical side wants the soiled garment as a protective shield. It becomes yet another sacrifice from tonight, and a waste of an entire day I spent making it.

"No time. We'll be leaving any minute. I'll get you more clothes, Miss McFee. And a first aid kit for your lip and nose." Collins examines my face briefly, his eyes darkening with an emotion I cannot quite distinguish. "Nothing appears to be broken, so that's good. Just try to calm down. Everything will be fine."

Fine? Fine means that everything is excellent, first-rate, splendid, exquisite. How can he think that? Everything is *not* fine.

Collins's dark eyes stare into mine, and I glance away

out of reflex. I catch my reflection in a wall mirror, and I can see that my mascara has streaked down my cheeks. I look like a clown.

Collins's jaw twitches, as he adjusts me in his arms. "Delay them," he barks an order obviously not to me. The gruffness of his voice makes me think that he must have some sort of undetected communication device. Perhaps an earpiece? "It's nonnegotiable."

I am carried toward the fight scene. I jerk with each echoed smack, unbelieving that Graham could be so unyielding when delivering his wrath. I whimper and shift, trying to divert my eyes away from the scene.

"Boss? It is time." Four words. That's all it takes to pull Graham from the fight ring. He mutters what I assume are profanities at Mark's limp form. Graham reaches into his tailored pants and glances at the screen of his phone. He then spits at Mark's crumpled body beneath him—disgust radiating from his pores.

Moving over to the minibar, he dampens a napkin and wipes the blood stains from his knuckles, bending his fingers to check for damage.

"Parker cleaning up?"

Collins shifts me in his arms as he looks at his Rolex. "Done, sir. We have approximately three minutes."

They speak in code that I do not understand. Graham blatantly disregards me. Not a glance, not a touch, and definitely not a word. It's as if I am an appendage of Collins.

"Get her out of here and get me backup."

Her. It hurts to be referred to as just a pronoun. I feel small and insignificant. A nobody. He is furious and hateful, a combination that I hope to never see again. Especially directed at me. I feel the scold take effect on my insides. I want to get swallowed up in the suit coat and suffocate inside the designer wool fabric. I cling to Collins like a lifeline, using his body to hold me together before I completely have a meltdown.

"Get Parker's ass up here now. I want it spotless! And Nic better sure as hell have the footage destroyed so our hands are clean," he snarls. "Handle any witnesses. We cannot afford to take a wrong step right now."

"Yes, sir."

In a blur of movements, I am transferred from the room, down a hallway, and then into a service stairwell. It is there that I break down from the force of the events finally being processed in my fragile head. The image of Graham's disgust toward me shifts to the primary focus of my mental assault on my own shameful regard of myself. Who could blame him? If just a man grabbing me at a bar could cause him to react violently, what did I expect him to do with a man lying beside me naked and about to rape me? A man I barely know. A man I have no intention of having a relationship with, but yet followed him willingly to a hotel room.

How stupid can I be?

Lock me up and throw away the key. I am certifiable.

While I have made many bad choices in the past, it is this incident that tops the list of being the most horrifyingly traumatic.

I could have been raped.

I could have been killed.

My body heats and thaws rapidly as I am bounced down each step leading to the exit.

Her.

That's all I am right now to Graham. Just a *her.* And for the first time since meeting him, he has managed to knock down my wall to my heart and decimate it. All with just one flipping three-letter word.

"I can't"—gasp—"brea..." My eyes widen with panic as Collins shifts me in his arms, his biceps flexing as he darts down a series of stairs, often taking two steps at a time. I count them as we descend—looking for even a minor distraction. My lungs wheeze for air as Collins transports me even faster through the winding maze of steps.

"Through your nose. Small and shallow, Miss McFee," he instructs, authority present in his tone. I sense his tension through his grip on my body. Despite his pace, I know that he will not drop me. Especially with a boss prone to starting wars. *Where is he?*

"Grah...Graha—"

"No talking. Just focus on breathing." He bursts through the steel exit door and into his invisible device says, "We are out."

The night air hits my exposed legs, traveling up to my waist. I don't even know what happened to my shoes. I scrunch my face into the white starch dress shirt of the man holding me, trying to avoid any observer's gaze. I am sure I look as hideous as I feel.

Fuck. What the hell was I thinking? I continue to go back to that line of questioning. My throat clenches like a valve on the water faucet. Open-close-open-close.

Silence. Black spots fill my vision, changing to red and green in color. I squeeze my eyes shut. Make it stop! *Open.* I gasp and then continue the assault on my lungs again in perfect OCD form. Close-open-close-open-close.

"Not good, sir. Yes," Collins answers, actually frazzled. "The shock is wearing off. I'm on it."

The light airy feeling of floating comforts my fraying resolve. Noise of a car door stimulates my awakening senses. Collins sits on the backseat bench and pivots, swiveling in with me still in his arms. I rest on his lap in his coat. How humiliating. My eyes flutter open as my lungs beg for air. I give in. *Open.* Then I quickly make the valve of my air passage *close.*

"Breathe, dammit!" He jostles me like a sack of potatoes. "You are going to pass out!"

I whimper and tremble at the sudden jolt to my body. *Don't hurt me! Leave me alone!* He sets me down, and I feel the cool seat beneath my thighs. Hands rub my arms. Shakes. My mind wants to retreat, but my body keeps getting jostled. *Stop, please! Leave me alone!*

My vision blurs, and my head slumps to the side as my mind starts to—

Smack!

Son of a—

SMACK!

"Stop it!" I scream, my hand instantly going to my bare leg. Ouch! The rush of heat radiates underneath the palm of my tingling hand.

He hit me.

Right on the thigh. Hard.

Tears bubble as I stare blankly at Collins's determined eyes. He hit me.

"Good. Now fucking breathe!" His snarl is on par with Graham's. And it is equally annoying.

"You hit me?"

Everyone is pissed at me.

Plastic pushes against my lips, wetting them. Coolness pours into my dry mouth, filling the reservoir. It is juice. Orange. I swallow before the next flood comes—one after another. I am barely given a chance to pull away as I empty the contents of the bottle in one sitting. Some dribbles out of my parted lips, streaming down my chin. My mind returns to earth.

Don't think about it, Angie. Forget about tonight. Focus.

"Graham." The word is more movement of my lips than actual sound.

Collins reads my concern. "He's fine and on his way."

He removes something from his ear, slipping it into his pants pocket, and drapes a fleece throw over my shoulders as a double layer. I clutch the material tightly around me, making my knuckles almost crack open from the strain.

"Drink more," he demands, twisting the protective seal, handing me a fresh chilled bottle. This time it is water. "How do your mouth and nose feel?" He studies what I assume is a cut at the corner of my lip, and then turns my face with the gentle touch of his hand to look at the bridge of my nose.

I glance away, trying to force myself not to relive the moments in the hotel room with Mark. "I'm fine."

Collins exits the car and rummages around in the front seat. He returns with a first aid kit. Opening it, he removes a pair of latex gloves, some antiseptic wipes, and a one-time-use ice pack. He slides on the gloves and opens up several individual wipes.

"This may burn," he warns, pressing the dampened cloth to my split lip.

I close my eyes as he cleans my face and disinfects my wounds. Every time I open my mouth to talk, I feel the pulling of my cut and the faint taste of blood. "Thank you," I mouth.

Collins snaps the cooling pouch in half, moving the inside particles around to activate it. "Put this on your nose and cheek to help with the swelling."

I just nod and keep my eyes cast downward to avoid feeling any more vulnerable. The ice helps to numb the pain radiating from my swollen flesh.

He removes his gloves and gathers the wrappers for the trash bag. "Are you hurt anywhere else besides your face?"

I think about the question. "No. But I was drugged."

Collins nods and growls, "We are aware."

Damn.

His eyes darken. He looks murderous but not shocked. I can tell he wants to say something but resists, keeping his impeccable manners in check. All along, Graham and Collins must have suspected Mark; however, maybe they weren't quite sure to what extent.

Did the same thing happen to Penny? Did Mark try to do to me what he may have done to her?

Eight couples pass by in the parking lot before Graham shows up—dressed in a pair of easy wash jeans, a gray hoodie, and a black ball cap—with his union of guards in tow. Collins exits the backseat and shuts the car door quietly behind him, joining the men.

I watch the animated debriefing unfold. Graham's twitching jaw, his ready-to-pounce stance, and his sapphire blue eyes all show evidence of his unrelenting rage. Apparently beating a man to a bloody pulp did not help alleviate some of his anger issues. It probably only helped fuel his hunger for revenge.

I watch in quivering fear as his hands make punctuating gestures in the night's air to what I assume is about me. He rips off his hat, runs his fingers through his hair, and tips his head back to look up at the night sky. He whips his cell phone out of his back pocket and rapidly talks. The car is soundproof, so I can only read lips.

One of the guards opens my door from the other side of the car—away from the conversation—and hands me a duffle bag. "Put these on, ma'am."

"Here?" I choke out.

"The windows are tinted. You have privacy."

I scoff to myself as he closes the door. *As if privacy matters after tonight.* Everyone has seen everything. Being modest now is almost a joke.

I grab hold of the bag and pull out similar attire to Graham's—all in my size. I flinch when I search the bag in the dark confines of the town car, finding the soft lacy cups of a replacement bra. My other one most likely got tainted with the sins of the night. Please tell me a girl was in charge of picking these items out. Yeah, right. This shopping excursion, most likely in one of the ground level stores of the hotel, was done by one of the men on Graham's payroll.

At the bottom of the bag is a small pack of wet wipes. I pull out several and wipe at the dry blood that is crusted on my stomach. It is revolting to look at, so I just rub vigorously all over and toss the trash into the empty bag.

I slip out of the charcoal suit coat and quickly hook the pink lace demi bra in back. I discard my current panties because they feel tainted with Mark's touch and pull on my new pink pair. I slip into the softest denim jeans, buttoning the entire fly. The wash looks trendy in the dark, yet completely meant for comfort. I could sleep in these—they are that luxurious. The solid black hoodie serves its purpose by providing warmth; the silver thread at the seams and pocket provide just enough edge to make it a bit more than just casual attire. Burgundy sequined ballet flats complete the look. The fit of everything impresses me. Someone has done their homework. The thought alone unsettles my stomach.

The men finish up and diverge into two separate vehicles. I watch as Collins disappears into the driver's seat—the privacy screen blocking my vision.

I stare out the window as Graham paces a trench beside the car. His hands clench and relax like he is squeezing an imaginary stress-relief sponge ball. His knuckles are stained with round bloody sores—a reminder of tonight's event. The clotting agent starts the process of his scabbing. I want to kiss each knuckle, one by one, and express how sorry I am that I was stupid enough to fall for Mark's ruse.

But true to form, he has rescued me from a horrible situation. The thought of what would have happened to me if he did not show up makes me want to shrivel up into a ball.

Confusion washes over me as I try to speculate how Graham knew I was at the Maylord Hotel. Did he know Mark and I were having a meeting? How was he able to locate the exact room we were in? Has he been keeping tabs on me, all while giving me the illusion he was ignoring me? I doubt it. If he was, then Mark would not have gotten as far as he did.

Beneath the ball cap, a purplish shadow darkens under

his left eye; he needs ice. I want to go to him, to comfort him. I try to open the door. It is locked.

I am a captive. To my own mistakes.

I slink back into the leather, pulling my legs up to my chest after kicking off the flats to gather on the floor. I curl my toes, and my body leans against the coolness of the window. I press my face against the glass. I don't even realize the tears are flowing until my face slides from the slickness of the stream of moisture. My eyes shut and become prisoners to the deafening silence.

Like a lamb to the slaughter, I await my fate.

The jerk of the door sends me barreling sideways in free fall.

"Geez, Angie," Graham admonishes, scooping my limp form up before I hit the pavement.

The crisp air awakens my senses. He situates me back into the car with trembling hands, careful not to graze me with his wounds. He then slides in beside me. His shakiness rattles my insides, but hearing my name off of his lips sends a thrill through me.

His hand grazes along my cheek at the place where Mark hit me. Even the slightest touch is making me flinch—maybe from the memory or maybe because it is still so sore. His thumb gently glides over the corner of my lip and up to the bridge of my nose. His eyes turn dark and murderous. What is he going to do with me? I am frozen in fear of what will happen next.

"Did he—" Graham's words catch in his throat as he scans down my body.

"No. You got there just in time."

Without another word, Graham buckles my belt and

places the throw blanket on me. I grip the fabric, tugging it tightly against my body. I feel so cold.

Once I am settled, he scoots out of the car and shuts the door, leaving me wondering the extent to which he hates me that he can't even be in the same section of the car with me.

I sniffle quietly in the silence of the backseat as the car starts to move. I assume Graham is in the passenger seat, but the screen keeps me completely isolated from those in the front. We weave throughout the heavy weekend city traffic, heading north. Collins takes a hard turn and follows the road to a parking garage. I am limited to only see out my window. I watch as he drives up the ramp to the second level and parks near a silver sedan. Dr. Saber gets out upon recognition of our vehicle. The sound of the back door unlocking makes me jump.

"Hi, Angie," Mitch says softly, getting into the backseat.

I must look confused because Mitch gives me a small smile.

"Graham wants me to run your blood in my private lab to see what you were slipped."

"Okay," I whisper, moving the blanket off of me.

"Did you leave your drink unattended tonight?"

I nod my head shamefully. "I know better too. But between using the restroom and the waiter delivering my seltzer, I bet Mark drugged me."

His warm fatherly smile makes me not freak out over my confession.

I cough into the sleeve of my hoodie. "He told me that I would not remember anything. But I do. I remember everything." Every detail. A small part of me wishes that my memory was wiped clean.

"That's good."

"Is it?"

He frowns at my words, knowing without saying that I am referring to more than just the trauma from being drugged. I can tell he wants to give me a hug but doesn't want to overstep a boundary. He is nurturing and patient, warm and inviting. A natural helper.

And then it dawns on me. "You helped Penny after she was drugged, too, huh?"

Dr. Saber doesn't verbally confirm, but the hard press of his lips tells me that I am correct in my assumption. No wonder Graham and he mutually respect each other so much.

"How long have you known the Hoffmans?" I continue, trying to distract myself from the situation. I close my eyes at the sight of the latex gloves and rubber band tie that get removed from his briefcase. The pain from Mark smacking me hurts way worse than a silly needle. I have been through worse, I remind myself.

Like with the stitches, Dr. Saber does his job of rolling up my sleeve and tying the rubber band around my arm without any commentary. I close my eyes, stay still, and just focus on breathing. Just breathe.

"I got to know Graham when he was in high school. I was a new physician and was working at his school in their sports program. After Graham graduated from college, our paths crossed again. He offered to hire me to be on retainer as his primary doctor, and I accepted."

When I hear the snap of the briefcase, I know that he is done with the blood draw, and it's safe to open my eyes again. I look at the Band-Aid and press my fingers against it, before pulling down the sleeve of my hoodie.

"Thank you," I whisper softly. "For always helping me when I need it most."

Out of his shirt pocket, he removes a light and shines it into my eyes and does so a couple of times until he is satisfied. "I'm sorry this happened to you. I really am. No woman deserves this."

Tears pour out of my eyes. I close them tightly, trying to keep from breaking down.

"Angela?"

"Hmm?"

Dr. Saber's eyes soften, as he gathers his belongings. I know he wants to say more, but he refrains. "You're going to need to drink lots of fluids to wash out the drug from your system. You appear to have little residual side effects, and that is amazing. The bruises and swelling on your cheek and nose may look worse than they actually are. Your face has a lot of sensitive spots, and once the blood breaks under the skin, it could look pretty gruesome. So I'm going to leave you with several one-time-use packs of ice." He notices the already used one resting near my feet. "These are similar in function. All you need to do is fold them in half, shake for a few seconds, and then take off the plastic protector. Try to do so every few hours for the first twenty-four."

"I have a huge headache. What can I take for it?"

"Nothing right now."

"Nothing? Why?"

"Because the drug that was slipped to you needs to be completely out of your system before you introduce any other blood thinners. This is serious, Angie. You could have been really—"

"I know," I mouth. I know I could have been…

Raped.

I don't want to keep thinking about how fortunate I am and what could have happened. I just want to forget about tonight.

Dr. Saber leaves the ice packs on the seat between us and exits his side. He shuts the door and stands at Graham's window—most likely to give him an update on my condition. For some reason, I feel like HIPAA rules do not apply to Graham Hoffman. I suppose that if he can shell out money for a doctor to be at his beck and call, the doctor would be able to follow a set of pre-decided upon orders.

Once again, I am alone in the backseat. I feel empty. Insignificant. Everything that I am wearing—including my underwear—doesn't even belong to me. I do not have a piece of jewelry on. There's nothing in my hair. Whatever I did own at one point is up in the hotel room or being taken away by Graham's worker bees. I have nothing. I own nothing. Yet, I am responsible for everything.

I slouch in the leather seat, slipping down under the confines of the belt.

I must doze off, because it is the clean, masculine scent of Graham that awakens my senses, followed by the sound of the car door shutting.

The acceleration of the car pulls me back into my seat. I glance in his direction. His bloodshot eyes meet mine for a split second and then go back to facing forward, staring emotionless at the opaque privacy screen.

We sit in silence for at least ten minutes while I become

more coherent and realize that we are still driving, except we are way beyond the outskirts of the city. I stare out the window at the unfamiliar landscape of the interstate. "Take me home," I sniffle and choke out. I want to curl up in my bed and waste away in the privacy of my own room. Claire is probably home, and I can wallow in self-pity with her the rest of the weekend. I need to flush out the craziness from my system.

Perhaps a fasting would be necessary and allow me to meditate and cope with my loss of reason. Shredded carrots and moon water sound good to me right now. At the very least, I will have my bestie's support to surround me while I navigate the ruins that my life continues to find itself in.

Tonight I was introduced to a new version of Angie. She was completely different than the old me and nothing remotely close to the new me. But the one thing I know with certainty is…

I don't like her.

Tonight I turned into a desperate version of my old self. I became reckless and stupid the minute I instinctually felt that Mark was dangerous and still chose to follow through with my original plan. I treated tonight like a game of poker where I was anxious to see the last card on the table instead of just folding the horrible hand I was dealt.

I give a side-eye to Graham. "Are you not going to talk to me?" I whisper, trying to keep my gaze on the trees outside. A few still have color to them. Reds and oranges and browns.

Silence.

"Did you kill him?" I don't even recognize my own

voice. It is hoarse from screaming, raw from crying, and weak from breathing.

He grunts, and his nose twitches just enough to tell me that he is pissed at my question. "He's breathing." *Thank heavens*. "Barely."

When Collins got me out of there, I wasn't sure if Graham was just waiting for me to leave to finish the job.

"He needs medical attention," I hedge, knowing that my words could be confused as being genuinely concerned for Mark's welfare. I only care that Graham could be in some type of trouble with the law.

"And he's getting it." His disdain tightens my muscles into a compact ball.

"Take me home, please."

"No." His voice is arctic ice.

Is he mad at me? His anger can't compete with my own self-hatred. I stare at Graham for answers, wordlessly begging for him to speak to me. To him, I am a child. I am something he seems to want to take care of, but doesn't really want to engage in an equal relationship. We have been on uneven playing fields since we met, and I am tired of losing. Panic rises at his eerie calm. It feels like my heart is going to break through my rib cage.

My fists ball, and I slip my feet back into the shoes. I start to feel along the door handle for a button to open the privacy screen. I need to tell Collins to stop the car. Surely there has to be some way to open the screen. I swipe my hand over the walls and panel of the door, trying to hit any button that I can get my fingers on—willing to beg, plead, bargain. Maybe if Collins is alerted that my door is open, he will slow the car down enough for me to jump out.

And then I see it—a button on Graham's side. I quickly undo my belt and move my body toward it, elongating my arm to reach. I stretch my fingers and—

"Let go!" I yell, twisting to get out of his grasp.

Graham's eyes tell me to *stop,* but I am too stubborn to listen. I flail my arms out and push at his chest.

Graham and I struggle, but I manage to kick a row of buttons in the darkness, hearing the sound of victory as the privacy screen rolls down.

"Everything alright back there?" Collins's voice sounds out over my pants for air, as he looks at us cautiously in his mirror.

"Can you please take me home?" My words come out staccato as I try to keep the quivering from my voice.

Graham clears his throat, moving me back to my side. "We are fine."

I glare at him as I watch dumbfounded as the screen slides up again. I feel a wildfire break out through my body, and the heat of my temper explodes in another rage.

"Do something!" I scream. "Make Collins turn around!" I lunge toward him again, but he instantly has me pinned beneath the weight of his leg, turning just at the last moment to capture his victim.

"Settle the fuck down"—he looks into my soul—"before you hurt yourself more tonight."

"Let me up."

With one hand, he tosses his cap to the floor. "Not until you calm down. Have you lost your mind? Do you really think you can out muscle me?"

My vision fogs and I see beady eyes. I hear the low-pitched snicker of a demon, waiting to consume me. Take me.

Mark.

His smirk invades my thoughts, and he hovers over me, ripping at my dress. His touch repulses me. My hands tremble as I pull at the fabric. Stop! Don't hurt me! His fingers snake down my stomach, coating me with a vileness fit for the devil. Stop!

And then I fight. With everything I have in me. I fight.

I smack.

I punch.

I hit and kick and thrash.

Every cell in my body comes together in a force that I have reserved to fend off the evil that radiates from him.

"I hate you!" I scream, my mouth raw.

My body lashes about.

"Angie!"

My hands fly around me, swinging at anything they can to connect with. To feel. To defend. To finally fight back.

"Let me go!"

He turns my hips so that I am straddling him, pinning my wrists to the leather seat beneath me. His gaze penetrates through me, as if he isn't even seeing me. Like I am a ghost, haunting him.

"I'm not Tanner, dammit!" he snaps. He shakes me. Jolts me.

A scream bubbles from deep within the pit of my stomach, unleashing into a fiery blast out of my mouth. The sound scares me so much that it feels like my body detaches from its soul.

I blink, and there, sitting underneath me, is the man that saved me. The man who prevented me from getting—

My body goes limp as the flood of anger rushes through me, causing me to deflate into a shriveled up ball of emotion. Quivering, my voice trembles out the words, "I… hurt you."

It is like the life is sucked out of me, and the only thing left is a shell of the person I used to be. How will I ever be the same again when I can't even stand to be with the person I have become?

"Oh, baby, please don't cry."

But I can't stop it. I wail and quake with every fear that I experienced in the hotel room at the forefront of my brain.

Helplessness.

Immobility.

Violation.

Every time my mind is idle, it seems to drift to Mark. His nasty hands on me. The way he found pleasure in my pain.

"He…" My lips shake. "He…"

Graham's arms hug me to him, embracing me in a cocoon of warmth. "You are safe. I will always keep you safe."

Tears continue to fall, soaking into his hoodie. I clear my throat of the sobs racking through my insides, wave after wave. I can't seem to make them stop. His hands rub at my back, one under my shirt and the other over it, drawing circles. When I stop shaking, I lift my head to look at him. Under his left eye, his skin appears to swell. Mark got a good hit on him when he was distracted with me.

With one hand, Graham traces over my wound on my

cheek and my lip, trailing his fingers gently over the tenderness. We don't talk. Instead, we just melt into each other. It's as if the weight of the entire evening has finally taken its toll on our shoulders, and we are unable to bear any more without leaning on each other.

We stay interlaced for some undeterminable amount of time. Once I have fully calmed—and am too exhausted to move—Graham puts me back on my side and snaps my belt into place. His ability to hand select which rules to follow and which ones to break is confusing. He acts like he doesn't just own the law, he creates it for his liking.

We ignore each other for some amount of time. I count the mile markers on the highway that we merge onto. Graham goes back to stewing on his side of the backseat. I focus on my breathing and another plan out of this mess. Graham taps his fingers against his knees. Neither of us are at peace. No. We are highly strung and ready to bite.

"Claire is going to wonder where I am."

"I notified her."

My eyes snap to his. "Notified her of what exactly, Graham? And when are you going to allow me to be privy to all of this information?"

His teeth make a grinding sound, he is pushing them so tightly together. I imagine the bones turning into powder at the fierceness of his rubbing. "You need to trust me that I know what's best for you right now." He removes his ball cap—I didn't even realize he'd put it back on—and runs his hands through his hair. "I could have been too late tonight. And the image I've created in my mind of what could've happened will haunt me for the rest of my life."

We are both traumatized by what happened in that hotel

room for different reasons. But I just want to go home. I want to shower. And cleanse the repulsive feel of hands from my body. I still feel grossly naked despite being clothed from head to toe. I want to be alone. Breaking down and reevaluating my priorities does not require an audience.

My eyes well with tears, and I look pleadingly at Graham for any indication that he will fulfill my wishes. But I am met with indifference.

His hand reaches for me, and my vision fogs. As if stuck in a horrible nightmare, his face morphs into Mark's, and I scream out in fear. "Get away from me! Don't hurt me!"

"Fuck!" he bellows, grabbing my wrists between his strong hands, immobilizing my upper body.

I twist and turn and knee him with any force I can muster up from my lower half. A hand gripping my wrist loosens just enough for me to wrestle it out of his hold, throwing myself full force into my attack—while still confined by my seatbelt.

"Dammit, Angie!"

The fog lifts, and I see him.

Devastated.

Hurt.

Graham.

I must have been hallucinating. I can't tell if it is from the drugs in my system or from the trauma I endured at the Maylord. I whimper and lean into Graham, as he undoes my belt—yet again—and envelops me in his arms.

"What is wrong with me? I'm going crazy. I'm"—I shake my head as a shudder runs through me—"sorry." My nose runs with my eyes, and my lower lip quivers. I can feel my teeth click against each other with a chatter.

"Shh…"

Graham hugs me so tightly to him that I fear I may break into pieces. I *am* breaking into pieces.

"I am broken," I whisper-choke.

He places gentle kisses on my forehead. His hands gently weave into my hair, while his thumbs rub against my cheek bones. "You are strong, sweetheart. But you have been through a lot tonight. I'm going to do my best to help you get through this, but you have to be honest with me and yourself, and give yourself a chance to feel all of the emotions."

After a long pause, I finally conclude what I really need from him. "I need you to talk to me." I rotate in his arms and slide on the seat so I can look at him better. "I won't be able to move forward if I don't deal with these uncertainties. The unknowns are festering inside my head and eating at me from the inside out. Tell me what's going on. Please. I know you are holding back."

"This was targeted, Angie."

My eyes twitch. "What do you mean?"

"Tanner had to know I didn't have my eyes on you, at least not to the normal standard. He waited for the perfect chance to try to hurt you. And he basically succeeded."

"But we had this meeting set up to meet his friend Steve from a newspaper for weeks. How would he have known I wouldn't have you following my trail?"

"Maybe he didn't know it would work out that way. Maybe he had a backup plan in case my men would have kept him from getting to you easily."

"He told me I would have no knowledge of the evening. But I remember. And it is unfortunate that I remember how scary it was being helpless to whatever drug he slipped…" I choke. I turn my head to stare out the window. I try to forget how his hands felt on my skin. How he destroyed my dress. How he smacked my face.

The growl coming from Graham's diaphragm snaps my attention back to him. He grips his hair in angry fistfuls, and for a second I think he is going to yank all of it out.

"Did things go further than you are letting on? How far did he force you?"

"Far enough to make me hate myself," I admit meekly.

He takes my bruised cheek in his hands, and his thumb caresses my swollen skin. Keeping one hand on my face, he reaches down and retrieves an ice pack. I hear the popping sound and then feel the coldness as he presses the pad to my abused face. He holds it in place for me and stares into my eyes.

He opens his mouth to speak but stops before any sound is made. After several long minutes, he finally breaks the silence. "I'm pissed at you for not listening to my warnings about Tanner. I'm pissed at you for falling for his trap. But him ripping your clothes off. Him drugging you. Him touching you. That was never—and I repeat never!—your fault. Do you understand me? Abuse, of any kind, is never okay."

My eyes water in a distorted blur, as I try to regain focus. "I was stupid."

"Nothing justifies abuse. Ever."

I swallow a sob as it shudders through me.

"He'll pay for the rest of his life for what he did to you. Don't you know by now that I protect what is mine? And you are mine. Whether you like it or not. If I have to dismantle his entire organization and blacklist him from the entire United States, I will. And I'll have zero regrets about it."

My shoulders hunch forward. "I can't believe how stupid I was. He kept telling me his friend was finishing up a meeting at the Maylord. I went this long waiting to meet him, so I figured why would I back out now? I fell for the sunk cost fallacy."

Graham's eyes soften, and he reaches for my hand to gently massage, encouraging me to keep talking.

"Mark told me during our first agency date about Steve. Mark had me polish up my resume and get excited for this potential internship possibility. So, we get to the Maylord, and then he tells me his friend is at the lobby bar finishing up a prior commitment. But by that point, I was already drugged. I was getting a headache after I came out of the restroom at Fortune and sipped my seltzer. Sometimes nerves make me feel that way, so I thought nothing of it. I was feeling fuzzy. By the time he got me to the hotel room and then to the bed, I was paralyzed from the neck down. I knew something was wrong with me before I entered the room, but he kept pulling me and pushing me forward with his ultimate plan."

"I'll make him pay, Angie. I swear it."

I have no doubt. "Despite losing the ability to move my limbs, I could still feel everything. I just could not get my brain to signal to my body to move." I choke out a sob over the memory. How horrible and helpless I felt. "I just think Mark messed up on the dosing. Because even he was shocked I was still able to move my head and form some words. He just thought I would not be able to remember anything. He was counting on it. But I do remember. And I tried to record what I could."

He studies my face, my reactions. I try to shield him from discovering the truth about my research project for my degree being wrapped up in all the Mark drama. I pray that my emotions do not give any more away. Because even though I plan to stay away from Mark, that doesn't mean I'm giving up on this story. Now, this is *my* story. One I need to tell. I have a voice, and my voice needs to be heard.

"You need to stop this nonsense." His words are final. Not up for negotiation. "The recording and the interfering. You are going around Portland acting like you are some undercover cop. It has to stop. You're going to get yourself killed. You have no idea how far he could have taken things tonight."

"Then why is he even part of the agency if he is so bad? Why risk all the other girls, me included?"

"It is not that easy. I have to choose my next steps carefully. Things are not always black and white. You just don't get it."

"Apparently not," I snarl, removing the ice pack from my skin and placing it on the floor.

"I want to be honest, I do. But there are things that I cannot share. Yet. Just trust me that I have your best interests at heart. That I would do anything to protect you."

"But what about the other girls?" I press.

Graham sighs. "I'm taking precautions. As much as I can without setting off warning bells. But remember, Tanner doesn't know I own Entice. I need to keep that fact a secret so I can maintain a certain amount of anonymity."

I take a minute to cool down before I ask what has been

nagging me all night. "How did you know I was at the Maylord?"

"I know a lot of people, Angie. I maintain a lot of connections—both in the business world and in my personal life. Someone saw you with Tanner leaving the Parkhouse Plaza and decided to pay me a favor. Thankfully I got to you in time. I had my men check with the front desk to get the room number."

I look to him for clarification.

"Anyone can be bought off when the price is right."

I nod. "Thank you for coming to get me."

"I'll always come for you, baby." His voice is gruff with angry need.

Tears stream down my cheeks at how mad I am at myself. Nothing about tonight happened the way I expected. Despite logically knowing I am a victim, I can't help but think how badly I messed everything up.

"Tanner is using you as a way of getting to me, Angie. Can't you see that? He knows that I'll react in regard to you. You're my kryptonite. My biggest weakness. You seem to always find some way to put yourself in danger, with dangerous people, and in dangerous situations. Hell, if danger didn't exist, you would fucking dangle yourself in front of moving traffic or volunteer your body to science just to get what"—he makes a face—"a thrill? Is that what you are living for right now? A fucking thrill?"

Oh for the love of— "Fuck you!" My hands get tossed up into the air. What is with him? Dangling myself in front of traffic? What an imagination.

He laughs. Hard. He's fucking laughing. I think he might cry. Bipolar bastard.

"Let me out of this damn car!" I demand, this time trying to open the actual door with sheer force, until my wrists are pinned tightly to the seat for the umpteenth time tonight.

"You are mine for the rest of the weekend," he growls, pressing down on my skin, making my flesh turn white. It doesn't hurt, but it definitely doesn't feel good.

"What do you mean the *rest* of the weekend?" So, we aren't just driving around aimlessly, like we did after open mic night at The Shack? He's taking me someplace? As in overnight?

"I need time to clean up this mess before we can return to Portland. Get all my ducks in a row and figure out my bearings."

"Where are we going?"

"Does it matter?" He releases my hands, crossing his arms over his chest.

"Are you always an asshat bastard? Or just when you are around me?"

"You drive me mad, woman!"

"I can't stand you!" I lie.

His grin is boyish. "Love and hate are very strong emotions."

I glare daggers at him.

"And they can be flipped very easily," he explains. "I'll take whatever I can get, even if it is hate, Miss McFee. But at least you are safe."

"Am I?" I ask, more out of trying to piss him off. "From you?"

"Yes, dammit. I would never hurt you! And that is why we are not hanging around Portland for the weekend. While my men clean up the shit that you put into motion, I am guaranteeing your safety. If only for a day or so. And you being safe is something I do not fuck around with. Not anymore. I am done following the rules. I am tired of making concessions where you are concerned. It ends tonight."

I mull Graham's words in my head, trying to decipher their meaning. Based on his body language alone, I know he is being serious—in the literal sense. "I'm sorry you had to rescue me tonight. But I'm not your responsibility."

His eyes flash with an emotion I cannot distinguish. He almost looks angry. "You became my responsibility the moment you crashed into my life. You knocked me off balance. I have never felt this way about another female in my entire life, Angie. You consume me. Beguile me. I'm done letting you top from the fucking bottom though. I let you have your taste of freedom this week, and we know how badly that went. I'm back in control now."

Oh.

His honest stare bores into me. "And I'm still not done being fucking pissed at you for your stunt back there with Tanner. His actions are not your fault, but going to him in the first place—well, you should have known better."

"I just need space to think," I plea quietly.

"You are mine."

His words penetrate me, but I need time to myself. Time to think and lick my battle wounds. "Please just take me back to Portland or at least tell me where we are going."

"No."

I pound on the privacy screen, yelling Collins's name.

"He answers to me," Graham responds, in the most

annoyingly nonchalant tone. He loosens the strings that hang around his neck from his hood. "I know you think this is a punishment, Angie. But it's not. I'm so spitting mad at you right now, but I would never hurt you or not put your best interests first."

I watch as his fingers curl into fists, as if the air is his stress ball. Being taken away from the very city that keeps causing me harm might be karma's intervention. Perhaps the time away will be good for me.

I curl my legs up into the seat, stretching the seatbelt to accommodate my change in position. I lean my head against the cold door and stare out into the emptiness. It is just trees for miles and miles. From the signs, we are still heading north. The Washington border is just a few miles away. I go back to counting mile markers and feel the hypnotizing effect of keeping my gaze peeled on the endless supply of guard rails. As my eyes droop with the weight of the day, I hinge them open and continue to force myself to count to stay awake.

16

It is the odd feeling of free falling that pulls me from my sleep. I blink a few times in the shadowy darkness as my eyes try to adjust to my whereabouts. A pillow of ultra-soft denim presses against my cheek, and it is then that I realize the dampness.

Ugh. I am drooling.

I hoist myself up from Graham's lap, biting my bottom lip as I analyze the wet spot on his pants leg courtesy of me.

"Where are we?" I mumble, moving over to my side of the backseat. My eyes cast downward in a wave of embarrassment. "Sorry about"—I point to the darkened patch of denim that is saturated with my spit—"that."

"Lake Chelan. And I don't mind."

"Really?" I look through the tinted glass window, squinting to focus my vision. I remember crossing into Washington state, but I was not following the routes closely enough to see any clues as to where we were heading.

"Yes, Angela, you can sleep on me anytime."

"No." I shake my head. "I mean, that's not what I meant. I'm just shocked you are taking me to a lake. That's pretty far away, right?" The moon shines brightly in the clear sky. I wipe the sleep from my eyes and rub at my neck, which twinges with a dull ache from the sleeping position I was in on Graham's thigh pillow. I don't even remember laying my head on him. Everything is just a blur. I stare in awe at the glimpses of beautiful landscape. Despite the darkness, I can see the different shades of orange, red, and yellow on the changing leaves. It is like driving through a postcard—spatial, quiet, and picturesque.

"We are five hours from the city," Graham comments, leaning in closer to me to see what has me so entranced.

"Oh." I soak it in. The scenery. The excitement. It is my first time in this part of the state. I have only seen pictures.

His warm breath tickles my ear as he fixes a piece of hair to be secured behind it. "I'm glad you calmed down."

I pivot in my seat to glare at him, knowing that his words are serious despite his relaxed tone.

"Well, I do not take kindly to being kidnapped."

"And I do not take kindly to being called an asshat." The corner of his lip lifts slightly, baring a few of his pearly whites. He looks sexy—and a tad bit cocky—in his half-grin and ball cap.

"Pretty sure I said asshat bastard."

"That you did," he says with a chuckle. "And I'll accept my title with pride."

I look out the window of the country road that barely has visibly painted lines. "Why here of all places?"

"I have a house on the lake. We need to be free of distractions and hammer out this…*thing* between us." As he says *thing* his hand moves emphatically through the electrified air between us.

"Interesting choice of words."

His eyes smolder and take on the look of the hottest level of fire. "I really want us to relax and talk openly. I don't want any reservation that sometimes can be there when we are in Portland—surrounded by the chaos of the city."

I stare out into the water as we move around the lake. It is calming. Serene.

I watch in awe as a burst of wind rakes through the water's surface in the moonlight, causing ripples of waves, similar to the swirl of emotions floating through my nervous system. One second I think I have everything together. The next, I am trembling with fear.

"Sweetheart, don't cry." His hands rub my cheeks, spreading the moisture from the tears into my flesh, hydrating my pores.

I am not even aware of my own emotions. They keep coming to the forefront in flashes.

"I…I…"

"Shhh," he soothes, rubbing my back and hair. His touch travels from my arms to my neck. He lifts me and embraces me in a tingling warmth to the point where goose bumps sprout and multiply into colonies all over my sensitive and charged flesh. It's as if his touch is the plug and my body is the outlet. "Right now, I just want to get you inside and lay you down to finish off your sleep. Tomorrow is a new day. A fresh start."

The thought of talking overwhelms me, so I try to ignore it and hope that he forgets. *Yeah, right.*

"Are we here?" I wordlessly ask, using just my eyes, as Collins comes to a stop in front of a house that appears to be built on the bank of the lake.

Graham kisses my forehead. "We are here," he whispers.

I sniffle during the entire walk from the car to the front porch. The lake house is lit up with many outdoor lights. It is a beautiful mix of equal parts modern and rustic. The exterior is mostly stone and brown wooden siding. Huge windows of all different sizes and shapes allow light in, making it easy to be one with nature instead of being encumbered by it.

"I'll give you the grand tour tomorrow. Let's get to bed."

I give him a nod and try to dry my eyes to keep my nose from being a leaky faucet.

He guides me through the foyer and living room until we encounter the main floor master bedroom.

"Do you come here often?"

"Not often enough. But this time of the year is the best with the leaves changing. And I think we are in the middle of peak bloom."

I follow Graham inside the room, which consists of nearly all oak and iron furniture. Exposed wooden ceiling beams give the room a rustic feel, while still keeping with the natural theme. Potted plants fill every corner of the room, and I can't help but wonder who waters them when he isn't here. There is a beige and red plush area rug over the hardwood floors, adding to the coziness. Two chairs and ottomans face the large fireplace, as well as a sofa along the posterior wall near the dresser. The room is spacious and beautiful. Inviting.

"This is absolutely exquisite. I love it here."

Graham wraps his arms around my front as he stands behind me. He kisses my shoulder. "I'm glad you like it."

He guides me into the attached bathroom, which has a similar style with dark beige colored tiles that surface both the floor and the walls. There is a large basin bathtub that looks like it could fit four people. It is halfway above and below the floor level—accessed by climbing tiled steps and descending inside the tub. It is huge. Unlit candles surround the exterior. The shower is also equally impressive by sheer size alone.

"I'm going to make a phone call and check on a few things. How about you freshen up and get ready for bed. I'll join you soon—if that's okay with you." It is phrased as a question—but with only one answer.

I smile and nod. No matter how frustrated we get with each other, the bedroom seems to be the one place where we do get along.

I see a medium sized travel bag on the long vanity, beside a very modern bowl sink and faucet. I dig through and find my favorite hygiene products. This man, or his overpaid henchman, has thought of everything. I can't figure out whether or not I should be relieved or disturbed. I brush my teeth and wash my face. My makeup was on thicker tonight so it takes me a few rinses to get it all off. When I do, my cheek bone looks to be a nasty shade of purple, much darker than it originally appeared.

I reach my hand up to touch my swollen skin. Mark hurt me. Flashes of memories snap one by one in front of my vision. His satisfied eyes. His mouth on my skin. His hands ripping apart my dress. His fingers touching my…

A solo tear slides down my cheek. I angrily wipe it away but then whimper at the pain shooting through my upper jaw. Damn him.

I lift up my hoodie in the mirror and examine my bare stomach underneath. I see the droplet of dried blood that I missed with the wipes. I lean over at my waist, my stomach churning wildly. Vomit explodes from my mouth into the empty porcelain sink. I grab my stomach to stop the cramping, as wave after wave of liquid acid expels from my body. I huddle over on my elbows, as sweat beads on my forehead.

I run the water and then stumble into the shower to wash down my pain. I turn the faucet on hot and allow the water to heat as it sprays me—fully clothed. The steam rises as my skin burns underneath the fabric from the temperature. I scratch at my arms and stomach, probably leaving angry red streaks. My vision clouds, causing me to lose my balance, falling back against the wall and sliding down to the floor. I bend my knees and curl my body into them, shielding my face from the force of the spray.

And I cry.

An ugly cry.

I weep for what could have been.

"Oh, sweetheart…"

Graham. He showed up. He always shows up. Even when I push him away, he knows exactly what I need, and that is to not be alone right now.

My eyes blur with my tears and the water pelting down on me. He is at eye level, kneeling at my crumpled up body, ready to be of service to me—just like he was when I was mad at him for his betrayal. He is with me. He is always with me. Even when we are separated by distance, my heart still carries the memory of him.

His gentle hands tug me closer, placing me on his lap.

"I just…" I don't even know. I feel so broken inside that I doubt I can ever be pieced back together again.

"Let me take care of you," he says simply.

I nod. I can't get my mouth to form a word, my throat is quivering too much. We stay like this, glued to one another on the tiled shower floor, while the water pelts against us. He kisses my neck and wraps his hands into my hair, cradling me to him like a fragile child.

I feel small in his arms. Like if I move too much or breathe too deep that I will shatter.

After my fingers have already pruned, Graham helps me stand and then as if asking for permission, starts to slide up my soaked shirt. I lift my arms, granting him access. One by one, I am shed of each article. I do the same with Graham's clothes.

He hands me the soap. I take the white bar into my hands, starting at my stomach. Graham's hand covers mine, and together we run the soap over every inch of my body, cleansing me of Mark's sinful touch. The water tinges brown as it washes off of me, mixing with the tainting of blood from the incident. I can only pray that the memories branded into my brain from tonight don't haunt me forever.

Like they are haunting Penny.

So many girls could have been hurt worse.

Resa.

And Monica. Tracy.

At least I am aware of what I went through tonight and hopefully can continue processing it. Penny is still dealing with the unknown. And at this point in time, I'm struggling to determine which is worse.

"I am sorry about Penny," I whisper.

"I know, baby. And I'm going to do everything in my power to make sure you both aren't victims again."

As Graham washes my hair, I release all of the tears that I have accumulated inside. The only sounds I hear are my own sniffles, the beating spray of the water, my staggered breathing, and Graham's soft words of comfort.

I turn toward him so we are face-to-face, mouthing the words, "I'm sorry," so softly that the only sound that exits is that of labored breathing.

His hands rest at the small of my back, so feathery light that I may just be imagining them there. "We are going to get through this together." He places a kiss to my forehead, and I take a step closer to hug myself around him.

"I sure hope so," I choke out.

Graham turns off the shower and exits first to retrieve some towels. I have completely lost track of time. I walk into the plush cloth he opens for me, allowing him to wrap me in its warmth. His care for me makes me feel even more vulnerable and exposed. He dries my hair, while I brush my teeth. Just my reflection in the mirror causes me to wince. Purpling skin. Swollen eyes. And an expression of defeat.

I walk beside Graham into the bedroom to find a long-sleeved set of pajamas laid across the bed. "You always think of everything."

"I'll always take care of you, sweetheart. Every want.

Every need. Every desire. Let me be the man to give them all to you."

My eyes fill with tears over his tenderness. He can be such a rugged and demanding man, yet be so soft and accommodating. I stretch up to kiss his lips, feeling the pain bite at my lip from where I was slapped.

Sensing my discomfort, Graham pulls away. His thumb gently grazes over my bruised skin, as if he is trying to erase my pain—and the memory of it—from my body. He slips into a pair of black pajama bottoms and then helps me into the softest cotton pair of pants and shirt. I rub the fabric up on my cheek and revel in the feel of a luxury thread count. Graham has a way of spoiling me and making me appreciate designer clothes. As much as I have resisted before, I know deep down that I could get used to this level of pampering.

"I'll be right back," he says, helping me get settled under the fresh linen-smelling covers.

I lay under the weight of the blankets, staring up at the ceiling. It is in the quiet that I can decompress and think about what happened tonight.

I must have dozed off when Graham enters the room, because it is the flames coming from the stone fireplace that cause me to stir. His muscular body looks even more appetizing in the flickering light. He is only wearing pants, and if I wasn't so emotionally and physically exhausted, I would want to be intimate with him, to erase all memories of—

"If the light from the fire bothers you while we sleep, I can try to put it out or find a scarf to put over your eyes."

I nod and whisper *thanks*. I pull back the comforter to welcome Graham and roll farther to my side—my back to him. The bed dips as he gets in. I feel his arms circle me and rest against my midsection. I thought it would bother me more, with Graham taking initiative to touch me, but it is exactly what I need. My body craves his possession. He is my safe haven.

His body is warm and molds easily to mine. My eyes grow heavy. I listen to the crackle of the wood, and it lulls me into a much-needed slumber. It is in the half-awake and half-asleep phase that I pray my own lingering pain doesn't become a fuel source for my nightmares.

I fall asleep and wake up without the hovering backup of an alarm clock. Usually on weekends, I program my phone with a later wake-up time. Except today. Today I allowed my internal clock to decide for itself when it was time for it to get up.

Foggy memories from last night sift through my head with only a few details recalled. There was lots of cuddling and the disentangling of limbs. I remember at one point my arm falling asleep because it was tucked so deeply under Graham's weight. The heat that radiated off of his body was more powerful than any fireplace could have offered. At one point, I was ripping blankets off of me from being so hot.

It could have just been my hormones. Perhaps it was the way he whispered my name in his sleep-drunk state.

My eyes flutter open, but I don't need to look over to know that Graham isn't here. The bed is back to being cold. The only sound I hear is my own steady breathing. The room is so dark with thermal curtains pulled across the windows that it is difficult to even tell what time of the day it is. Based on how rested I feel, I imagine the sun has been up for a while now.

I stretch and grimace over my growling stomach. How can I possibly want to eat when there is so much still on my mind? I roll out of bed and move into the bathroom. I slide on a bra that is part of a new stack of clothing, folded perfectly on the edge of the vanity, but keep my original pajamas on. They are so comfy.

I dig through the hygiene bag, pulling out all the items I need to appear human.

Sunlight beams down through the skylight, casting a warm glow throughout the room. If Graham is anything, he is thorough and accommodating; the man thinks of everything. Everything that I could possibly want or need is at my disposal, even though we are tucked away at a secluded lake house—sequestered from the rest of the world.

At the sight of my blotchy face, I quickly dig out the regimen of cleanser, scrub, toner, and moisturizer and go to town repairing the damage. I dust on makeup to cover my bruising as best as I can. The reddish-orange hued rays warm the air in the chilly room. I sit down on the edge of the huge bathtub and give a quick brush to my teeth and hair. After I feel human again, I make my way to the bedroom door. The quiet of the house does not give away the time. Not knowing frustrates me. I need to find my phone.

I open the door leading out to the huge two-story living room and hear the muffled low toned voices coming from a hallway. I quietly tiptoe across the large area rug and through another corridor until I find a more formal living space. And it is there that I find him.

Dressed in a pair of black low-rise drawstring pants and a royal blue fitted crew neck T-shirt, it is obvious even clothed that Graham's body is that of an athlete. I allow my eyes to coast lazily down his body, enjoying my view with the freedom to linger longer on my favorite zones. His back muscles, the strength of his torso, and the pull of the fabric over the front of his crotch.

I rarely see Graham this dressed down, so it is a welcomed treat for my senses. His feet are bare and his hair looks sexily tousled—most likely washed and left to dry as is.

Damn, this man is hot. Ten out of ten, I recommend.

Graham is more captivating than any man I've ever met. But he also exceeds every book boyfriend I ever fantasized about. Hundreds have made naughty appearances in my dreams, so I have a lot of comparison data.

If it wasn't for the periodic tic of his jaw, I would actually think he was relaxing. However, I know better. He doesn't relax. Even in his sleep, he seems tightly wound.

Graham and Collins sit adjacent to one another with all of their electronics on display. Laptops are open on the coffee table, iPads are in hand, Bluetooths are in ears, and phones are plugged into chargers.

At the sight of my phone, I open my mouth and then quickly shut it, not wanting to be caught. I am not shocked it is being babysat, but that doesn't remove my desire for wanting it back.

"Figure it out. Now. I hired you for such matters. Do not disappoint."

I cringe and shimmy back a few steps as if the venomous tone that Graham gives to the poor person on the other line catapults me away from the scene. After last night, I know his capabilities when it comes to a physical fight. His heavy sighs cause me to stay rooted in my spot, if just to gain information so I am less in the dark.

"I damn well know you provided me the information on her. I need more. Dig. Give me a fucking address, bank statements, some sort of timetable."

Her. As in, me? Or another *her*?

"Yes, I know I have it! Well, you aren't in any position to be making the demands. Pretty sure the day I step away will be the day I also get my life back."

What does he mean? Who is Graham talking to on the phone?

"Fine, I'll look at it and consider my options when I please. You aren't me! Remember that."

I watch behind a huge decorative column in awe as Graham turns to the side, snatches a folder off of the coffee table, and shuffles through a series of papers.

"Get me everything you have. Summon the workers, witnesses…I don't give a fuck how you do it. Get me the damn information!"

He must hang up because the earpiece is ripped out and tossed onto the seat cushion beside him. Collins has enough sense not to react. I imagine he has seen a variety of moods from his boss.

Graham grabs his phone from the table and appears to make another call. "You have a watch on him? Yeah, I want it around the clock. I know!" he snarls. "Don't you think I know what he is trying to do? I let him walk so you could track. Remember that. I get this is not the original endgame plan. But we need to adapt or be discovered. There is too much at stake now."

I shift my weight and watch as Graham takes a sip of his coffee, looking thoughtfully at the artwork hung on the wall. He is edgy and bothered.

"I give the asshole credit for choosing the Maylord. But if he really thought I wouldn't have friends who would have seen the two of them eating at *Fortune*, then he really is a freaking idiot. Unless..." Realization crosses Graham's features, as he turns to Collins.

I swallow hard as Collins receives whatever silent message Graham passed on to him. He jumps from his seat, grabs his phone, and steps into the other room to make a phone call.

Graham grips the back of his neck, while still holding the phone to his ear. "He wanted me to find out. Son of a bitch," he snaps. "I thought not having eyes on Angie was the setup to leave her vulnerable. But now I think he actually wanted me to find out and make a move. That was all part of the plan. Dammit!"

I watch in silence as he grimaces and paces several yards in front of me.

"It was a setup," he echoes slowly into the phone. "Inform the team of my theory. See if they can dig and find out anything with the underground. See if there is talk going down." He sits back on the couch, strumming a few fast fingers on his laptop before resting into the cushions. "No, no one has contacted me with a proposal. It's been quiet for a while." He places the cover back on his iPad, groaning into the phone. "Yeah, I want it to stay that way. I'm not going back. I refuse."

What does he mean by the *underground*? Is he involved in illegal business? This would explain his secretive behavior. I wish I had my phone so I could text myself notes so I don't forget anything.

Graham ends the call, and Collins enters the room again.

"Since that first night, Tanner has been planning this whole time? Dammit," Graham hisses. "And I could have stopped the whole thing from the start if I wasn't so—" He slams his hand on the coffee table. "Fuck!"

"Sir, we will shut down the operation. You have my full support on this. Trust me in that I can handle whatever task you throw my way."

"I do trust you, Collins. But I don't see a way out right now. I feel suffocated." He tosses the file beside him and leans back, stretching his torso. "I want Angela protected. I mean it. At all costs. No matter what. Something happens, I will never forgive myself. I'll plant additional devices, do whatever it takes. I want arrangements made in case something happens to me. I need to know she'll be taken care of."

If something happens to him? I rock on my heels as I listen to their exchange, feeling lightheaded.

"Of course, sir. I'll notify the staff and do any briefings that need to be done. Now that we know his angle, we can be more efficient."

A phone rings and Graham moves to answer it. "Hoffman," he greets with one word. He wipes his hands down his face, as if trying to wash off the tension he has in his brows. Something big is going down. And I feel like I—unknowingly—started it. Maybe joining the agency was the spark that started the wildfire. Maybe this whole time, I have been playing with the enemy. Mark Tanner might be the one person capable of destroying Graham, and I could be the weapon to deliver the final blow.

I brace myself for a new reality. Even after I get back home to Portland, I will most definitely have watchdogs. Graham is in full protective mode, and after last night, I may finally be on board. Only problem is, I will have a harder time getting my field research done while I am being followed. I still have a paper to write. I still have an internship to strive for. I still have justice to deliver, to give all these victims a voice.

My movement hits Collins's attentive hair-trigger senses. His eagle eyes catch mine, and I can no longer pretend that I am not eavesdropping. He rises instantly and greets me. "Good morning, Miss McFee." He bows his head slightly, gathering up files and closing lids on laptops.

I know that his words serve a double purpose—respect to me and a warning to Graham to filter his phone conversation. Collins does not look at me, and I can't help but feel weird. I round my shoulders and stare at my feet. My hands pull at the hem of my shirt, stretching it further over my butt. He saw me with just my panties on. He also was probably instructed to take pictures of me while Graham and I fooled around at the dance hall. How will I ever feel the same way around him again?

It is silly; I know this. At no time has this man been disrespectful or off base. But, I can't shake the nausea of the realization that more men saw me next to naked last night than the entire sum of men who have seen me naked prior. I keep my eyes to the floor as I continue to stretch my clothes, embarrassment plastered all over my stance, my expressions, and my gestures. Collins must have sensed my unease because his body retreats instantly, leaving me alone with the boss.

Graham acknowledges me with a sweet smile, completely contradictory to his continuing verbal tirade. "I said handle it! We are done for now." He tosses his phone onto a stack of files on the table.

"Hey sweetheart." His change in voice shocks my insides, rattling my bones.

"Um, hi," I answer sheepishly, rocking back and forth on my heels.

"Hungry?"

I glance around the room, as if noticing it for the first time. Last night I was too tired to care or even take notice of much as I was escorted to bed. The blinds are open to the view of the lake. It is small enough to see the steep bank on the other side of the water. Small ripples form on the surface from the wind. It is calming. I turn back to Graham as he prompts me with another question.

"Hmm?" I ask. I must still be groggy with sleep. Yet, I feel rested.

"I have waffles and all the toppings ready to go." His eagerness is similar to that of a little boy ready to show off his model airplane. It scares me that he has the ability to flip a switch on his moods. One minute he is yelling at some person on the phone and the next he is talking sweetly to me.

My stomach growls at just the thought of food, but I can't bear to eat with my rampant thoughts. My physical reaction is hunger. My emotional reaction is to suffer through the pangs. "I'm not hungry."

"You lie worth shit. I can hear your stomach." He gestures toward my belly with his hand, his tone edging with anger. "Come," he coaxes, strolling toward me and taking me by my elbow to guide me through the house.

I follow him into the kitchen.

Graham turns to Collins, who is hovering in another room, and shoots him a knowing look. "Field my calls."

"Yes, sir," Collins responds on cue, catching Graham's phone that flies through the air with ease.

The kitchen is open and inviting. Floor-to-ceiling windows surround the huge rectangular table, allowing in light and the connection with nature. The entire layout looks magazine-worthy with quartz countertops, stainless steel appliances, and a custom backsplash.

"Sit."

"You change your mood so often, you know? I swear you are bipolar or something," I mutter at the overbearingness of his single-word demands. I park my butt onto a stool that I pull out from the island. "I mean, if you are, then that is"—I try to think of the right words as I fumble this ball majorly—"fine. It is just that if you are, then you probably should—"

"I'm not bipolar, Angela."

His words aren't angry. If anything, he is resisting laughing.

My eyes narrow. "Glad I am entertaining."

I watch him move around the kitchen with ease, dumping batter into the waffle maker and pulling out several prep bowls from the fridge. Blueberries, strawberries, chocolate chips, whipped cream, and raspberry syrup are the toppings. He arranges all of the fixings on a large flat wooden plate. It is basically a waffle charcuterie board and it looks spectacular.

There's something very sexy about watching a man move around a kitchen. Chore porn. I admire this new version of him with a smirk. It is much different from the authoritative version of him I got just a moment prior while he was on the phone.

After several long minutes of silence, Graham arranges my plate with two cheesecake flavored waffles and gestures for me to add whatever toppings I like. I choose a little of everything and salivate at the sight and smell of the comforting scent of a country kitchen. Besides having bacon on some mornings when Claire is with Ethan, it has been awhile since I actually ate a hearty breakfast.

"Did you sleep well?" he asks, passing me a mug of freshly brewed Colombian coffee, fixed with cream and a sprinkle of sugar.

"I think so." I breathe in the scent before taking my first sip. I could get high off the smell of a delicious cup of coffee. "How about you?"

"I would have slept better if you weren't propositioning me for sex every couple of hours."

I choke on my coffee, sputtering some onto the surface of the island. "I did not."

"You most certainly did. Multiple times." He forks a piece of waffle and blueberry into his mouth and chews, while meandering about the kitchen. "If I wasn't trying to respect the side-of-the-bed boundary that you implemented as a rule, then I may have taken you up on your frequent offers."

My mouth drops open. "No way."

"No way?"

"You were the one who started snuggling up against me before I even fell asleep. And there's no way I would be so brazen to beg for sex in my sleep."

"I just want you to respect my whole self and not just worship my body."

"Oh my goodness!" I belt out.

A huge smile bursts over Graham's face, and I realize now that he is just teasing me. He's just trying to get a reaction and it worked. I throw a chocolate chip at him, and he opens his mouth just in time to catch it on his tongue. That man never ceases to amaze me with what he can do with his mouth.

"Eat."

His smirk brings a boyish sexiness to his features. His playfulness with me is only making him more attractive. I like this fun side to Graham. It balances out all the other times when he is an asshat bastard.

For once, I do as I am told without giving lip, rolling my eyes, or resisting. I cut off a piece of waffle with my fork, containing a little bit of each topping. I shovel it into my mouth and struggle to chew it with my mouth closed, but I have to give my compliments to the chef.

"You're pretty"—I pause to chew a bit more—"good at this."

"What can I say? You inspire me."

"Inspire you how?" I ask with a laugh. "To not get takeout?"

He puts on a serious face. "Inspire me to not order my men to get me takeout."

I roll my eyes.

Graham joins me at the island with his half-nibbled plate. We eat in silence, except for my little moans breaking through, all over the deliciousness of the meal.

"These are really good."

"Thanks. It's my mom's recipe." His smile is adorable. Despite the stress, he seems younger. Lighter. I'm amazed at how quickly he can shut off his emotions, like a switch.

"Is your mom a good cook?" I have never really learned much about his family, so I see this as the perfect transition into a discussion—since he was the one who mentioned her first.

"Almost as good as my grandma, who would make everything from scratch, using the freshest ingredients. But my mom has the gift of making everything she touches look pretty. Including her food."

My heart smiles with memories of my own grandparents. While they are no longer living—on both sides—I still have pictures of the time we spent together. To remind me of what I had, and what I want to have for my own life in the future. As soon as the thought crosses my mind, I stop and think—

It is like an epiphany. I never really cared about what my future would look like, beyond having a career, but here I am wanting the same things that I grew up seeing with the generation before me. It's like my entire universe shifted with a new outlook on life.

I went through a long period of time thinking I had nothing to live for, but now I can see that maybe all of the things I once thought were impossible are really just at a fingertips' reach.

I want the connection with someone and a home with a

foundation for making memories and traditions built on love. My heart that I thought was incapable of that level of emotion was just scared of another crack in it.

"I can tell something heavy is on your mind," Graham says, frowning.

I fake a smile. "Are your parents in Portland?"

His eyes twitch but he doesn't apply pressure with another question directed back at me. "They spend most of the year in Hillsboro and the coldest months usually in their Florida home."

Must be nice to have multiple homes. I imagine his entire family comes from wealth. It is easier to make more money when you have a chunk to invest. I know being an investigative journalist will not bring in a hefty paycheck, but at least the work will feel rewarding. It just seems so out of reach right now. Like I am running a race that has no course.

"That sounds nice."

"Although this past year, they haven't been traveling in case Penny needs them in Seattle."

"Makes sense."

I stare at Graham's throat as he swallows a mouthful of waffle and takes a sip of his coffee.

His eyes darken. "It's hard to continue talking about my family when you are looking at me like this."

"Just enjoying my view, Mr. Hoffman," I hum with a smirk. It is refreshing to move away from the serious talk.

He leans across the island, his fingers moving in heated slow motion, gliding through the air toward my parted lips.

The soft touch on my cheek sends electrifying pulses through my entire body. I lean into his palm, my eyes drifting shut at the magnetic pull, the sound of static sizzling and crackling through the air. His touch is like a wildfire, coursing through my body, extending all the way to the tips of my fingers and to even my littlest toes.

I feel his thumb rub the corner of my lip. I open my eyes and am met with a smoldering gaze, locking on mine as he makes a primordial alpha male sound. His thumb leaves my skin wanton and needy, the fleeting heat liquefying my flesh and melting me in a delicious feeling of euphoria. I watch in disbelief as he sucks on it between his dry—yet surprisingly soft—lips. I shift in my seat, rubbing my bottom into the surface—hard.

I need friction, dammit!

He skirts around the island, like an animal anticipating the next move to hunt its prey. My breath catches in my throat. My backed stool turns in his direction—fully at his mercy. If he knew that I would do anything at this point to have more of his touch, he could take advantage of me willingly. I would give him an open-ended invitation. He just needs to ask.

The same hands that caressed my face grip my waist at my hips with a level of urgency. In a fluid motion, I go airborne and am situated on top of the cold surface, my empty plate sliding out of the way in a hasty retreat as my butt settles down in its vacant spot.

"Grah—"

He silences me with a look. His hips zero in on the junction between my thighs, as he uses his weight to part my knees. He slides between with ease, crushing his body into my heat. I feel the humidity of his sweet smelling breath on my face as he nuzzles his nose into my hair, my name falling off of his lips in a chant of seductive whispers.

The back and forth of are-we-together-aren't-we-together is messing with my mind. I need to stop him. I need to tell him we can just be friends, to stop blurring the lines. Ha, like that is even a possibility with us. The rational thinking side of my brain gets overruled by the irrational side that says to take the leap.

I need him.

I want him.

I squeeze my thighs against his waist, bringing him closer. His groan escapes, vibrating my neck into a delirious state—sending pulsing sensations due south.

Message received. Loud and clear.

My nipples poke at the material of my bra—standing proud but begging to be free.

Graham's hands on my hips slide up and down my sides, over my top, pushing it up a few inches in the process. "I want you so badly," he whispers with carnal desire evident in his breathless plea. "Even when I am mad at you for pushing me away and ignoring me… Even when I am pissed as hell at you for kissing Zander."

"He kissed me," I mouth.

"And even when I am furious over you putting yourself in grave danger last night. After all of the things you put me through, I still can't walk away." His gaze levels with me. "You are so freaking beautiful. You know that, right? The prettiest thing I have ever seen." His eyes search mine for a response, but I give none.

I toss my head back and press my chest against his

upper body as his mouth claims the hollow valley at the base of my neck.

When did this spot become an erogenous zone?

Utter pleasure flows through me. I never thought that anything could be more intimate than kissing on the lips. I am most definitely wrong. At no time do his hands turn greedy or does his mouth lose concentration. He calculates every move with certainty, reining in his control. He deliberately is keeping me on the edge. Seducing me. We have kissed before—numerous times. But it is like we are dancing with music from our souls now, without ever touching our lips together.

It is raw.

It is intimate.

I shudder at the mere capability of his hands and sexual expertise. Every time he touches me, it feels like he is relearning my body—memorizing every little detail with just his hands and his mouth.

I wiggle my behind on the counter's edge, my fingers gripping the surface with white knuckles, anchoring my body to keep from melting into a puddle. Every nerve in my body erupts and declares war-like havoc on the reasoning system of my brain. I should stop him before this goes too far. Before Collins walks in. Before I get so involved with Graham that I will never be able to walk away from him without destroying myself.

He is a wrecking ball knocking down every protective wall I have ever built around myself before I can erect another one in its place. I should not allow someone to get emotionally involved when I am incapable of reciprocating at the same magnitude.

What if I am not enough?

His firm lips search along the vein in my neck—kissing and teasing the pulse point—while his fingers caress my clavicle over my shirt, moving my hair back as my spine crumbles into a pile of dust at the slow torture.

"Sit still," he warns me, gripping my hair and tugging to get my attention. "I'm enjoying myself."

I yelp and huff out a laugh at the same time. As if I can control my involuntary movements. *It's not my fault!*

"Just let me taste a little more. Here, mmm," he hums, brushing over my earlobe with his warm haunting breath.

Did he just lick me?

Why does he keep doing that? And why do I freaking like it?

Tingles run through my entire core. I feel lightheaded with need. *Do not pass out, do not pass out, do not pass out.* Why does it feel so damn good? Like I have never been touched before today?

I teeter even further on the proverbial cliff's edge. My hips plant firmly into his, stretching me to accommodate his width. I can feel his cock jump with each little movement I make. I push off from the counter, sliding along his length through the thin fabric of his lounge pants.

"You should wear these pants again," I say casually.

"And why is that, baby?"

I ignore him, shooting him my best attempt at a sexy smirk. I think it works because his fast breathing turns into a groan—a deep, guttural plea.

"Tease," he hisses.

To stop or not to stop?

We have had sex before. But this all feels different. It is

about the slow buildup. The anticipation. It's like he is waiting for me to confirm what he already knows. That I am his.

Our eyes lock. I can see my reflection in the glassy shield of his. He studies my face, and his hands steady me, rubbing soothingly up and down my arms—lifting and squeezing my hair into loose fistfuls. What is it about someone touching my hair? Pure heaven.

"You feel this?"

Umm, your cock? Why, yes sir, I do.

"Angie, this thing," he says, moving his hand through the minimal space between us emphatically. "It's not going away. It's definitely not getting any easier. Nor do I want it to."

"I know," I whisper. My butt bumps against the island's base. "I know."

"You are scared, sweetheart. I'm aware of that. Saving you last night did not help my cause. But when I found out you were with Tanner"—his eyes look away for a second and then return—"I lost it. All I could focus on was getting to you. I knew within my soul that you were in trouble. And I had to keep myself together long enough to teach Tanner a lesson but get you out of there with minimal harm."

I nod, eyes on the floor, ashamed of the position I put myself in. Graham's anger is palpable as he attempts to express his thoughts.

"I wanted to *kill* him for getting as far with you as he did. I should have cut off his hands."

I gulp but do not question the authenticity of his words. If given the chance, I bet Graham would resort to archaic methods to punish his enemies. "I acted impulsively. I never wanted or planned to have any type of physical encounter with him. Looking back, I know I acted stupidly and should have seen the signs that he was full of bullshit. I was terrified and helpless and repulsed. Then when you arrived, I feared you were going to murder him and go to prison for life."

"That's the only reason I left him breathing. Remember that," he growls, anger sparking off of him, making him back away from me. He runs his fingers through his hair, pushing back stray strands. What a sight. Like a model stepping right off the advertisement for—

Toothpaste.

Or fitted shirts.

Or male enhancement pills.

Hell, the man could sell tampons or anti-fungal cream, and I would buy it. I clear my throat at that wayward thought.

"I'm sorry," I mutter absentmindedly, if only to fill the silence and end my blatant eye ogling.

He quirks an eyebrow and crosses his hands at his chest.

"I don't even know exactly what for." I grimace at my pathetic excuse for an apology, but decide to continue. "I guess for getting myself involved in something that only caused me more pain in the end. I feel stupid and compelled to keep saying sorry." I peek up at him through my lashes, catching his eyes softening on me. "I guess if I'm really being honest with myself, then I have to admit that not seeing you or talking to you for a whole week—" I furrow my eyebrow as I gather my thoughts.

"Tell me."

"I missed you." My three words come out in a rush, as if saying them out loud makes me weak.

"I missed you too, baby. I wanted to contact you. I did. I just am trying so hard not to smother you. But like I said last night, I'm done with going against my better judgment and allowing you to put yourself in impossible situations."

His gaze moves away from me and focuses somewhere behind my head, then refocuses back. He looks surprised that I even said as much as I did in one turn; it is not in my character to bare myself this much. Perhaps his lips on me double as a truth serum.

"Let's go relax," he says softly. "I have some place I want to show you." His hand on my elbow guides me out of the kitchen, through the living room, and into a heated sunroom with three walls of glass windows. He moves me to line myself up with a wicker cushioned seat and then presses down on my shoulders to get me to sit—never saying a thing. I shake my head at his still controlling nature, even though he improvised and adapted.

"Give me a minute." He turns and leaves the room in a hustle.

The lake glistens with the sunlight—golden rays peeking out over the hill on the other side. The blinds are pulled up, and the windows are so clean that it feels like we are in the open air. There is a stone patio down below and a private outdoor pool and hot tub. It is like a lakefront spa. Floating out in the water is a small dock with two boats attached to cleats with rope. The boats do not look extravagant and are probably the least expensive of all his possessions.

I still don't know what time it is, and the minor issue is making it easier to give in to living in the moment.

Graham is gone for about five minutes. When he returns, he sets a large bag down on the end table and flops into a chair next to me. "Okay, I have a proposition for you."

Huh? "I think I should refrain from any more propositions. We know how badly those have worked out for me in the past."

Graham breaks out into a laugh. My attempt at a joke works and lightens the mood. "So, how about you hear me out?"

I nod and he continues. "How about we play your favorite strategy game?"

I sit up straighter in my seat and eye the bag with curiosity. I would be lying if I said I wasn't a tad bit intrigued. From the playful gleam in his eye, I know he is up to something. "We are playing Monopoly?"

"Of course," he says proudly, pulling out the game board.

"I can't wait for you to lose."

He makes a face. "Haven't you learned by now that losing isn't what I do?"

I smile with all my teeth. "This shall be fun."

17

It seems like a lifetime ago that we were dancing at the charity gala, and Graham was asking me inappropriate questions about my number of sexual partners. We joked about how Monopoly was not a real game and the alternative way I could pay for landing on his hotels if I ran out of money. I just never thought that our silly bantering would become reality. Today is the day—apparently.

Graham pulls out the brand-new game box from the bag and smiles brightly at me. "Ready to become a slave to capitalism?"

"What's at stake?"

He grins. "I like how you think."

"Well, I know you are all about winning. So it is super fun to get you to lose."

"Touché. Are you up for adapting the rules?"

I think about it for a second. "What do you have in mind?"

"How about whoever lands on the opponent's property will either have to pay rent or answer a question?"

I swallow hard. "Anything?"

"Within reason," he clarifies.

"And the overall prize for the big winner?"

"How about whoever has the most money and property value at the end of an hour gets to decide how we spend the rest of the day?"

I let out the air I am holding, puffing out my cheeks on the exhalation. "Are you sure you want to play this with me? I am reallllly good at it."

He looks at me as if I have ten heads. "So you are saying you are good at luck?"

I make a face. "Skill. I have skill. And sure, winner gets to plan the rest of the day, although that doesn't really seem fair since I don't know the area."

"I doubt you'll have trouble coming up with something."

I rub my hands together, constructing a plan for if I win. "Do you think there are some male strip clubs out here?"

Graham shakes his head at me as if I lost my mind, and it makes me burst out laughing. "Well, that isn't happening."

"Oh?" I put on a straight face. "It will definitely happen if I win."

"You aren't going to win."

"You may be able to control the stock market and all of your employees, but you cannot stockpile luck. Just get your dollar bills ready as backup."

We slide down to the floor to sit on pillows and use the

square coffee table to set up the board. He shuffles the yellow and orange cards, while I dish out the rainbow play money.

"I have your game piece," he says, handing me a shiny trinket.

I look down at the tiny silver candy bar and then back up at him. "Huh? This is not one of the original pieces."

"I had it custom made for you."

I rotate my game piece between my fingers. "When?"

"Back in Portland," he says with a shrug. "I figured we would be playing the game eventually. I just got it delivered."

I smile. "Pretty cool. Thanks. What is your piece?"

Graham holds up a miniature bag with bills coming out.

I shake my head at him. "Suitable."

He chuckles and wiggles his eyebrows. "I cannot wait for you to lose to me."

I shift my legs. "You wish."

"Sir?" Collins clears his throat loud enough to halt our conversation. His unyielding stance is in the doorframe leading to the sunroom. His look is of concern, and maybe fear of getting reamed for interrupting us.

Graham glances his way and a message is exchanged. I almost miss the subtle nod that Graham gives his right-hand man.

"Miss McFee, your father texted you, and Mr. Worthington called you. Would you like to access your phone to respond?"

I slouch my shoulders, and my face turns cold from the blood washing out of me. I feel the double stare bore into me from both men as they wait for my answer.

"Do you need to contact either of them, Angie?" Graham asks. "You can." His voice is velvety smooth. I feel like it is a test though.

I shake my head rapidly. "No, I can handle it later. No biggie. Can I get my phone back, though?" I look toward Collins, who suddenly looks agitated.

"No," Graham answers for him.

"Why not?" I challenge, wrinkling my forehead with my glare.

"Because I need to know if Tanner makes contact with you. And—"

I cross my arms over my chest and sigh. "You don't trust me to tell you."

"I refuse to apologize when your safety is my first priority."

"You refuse to apologize for much of anything," I point out.

"This is not up for negotiation. We are doing this my way from now on so I can guarantee you are safe."

"Fine." There's really no point arguing. What am I going to do, tackle two full-grown men for the usage of my cell phone? I can only pray that Zander doesn't say anything that will push Graham over the edge. I cannot handle that right now. And I already feel guilty for pretty much leaving him in limbo with my emotions. As for my dad, I would bet that he is most likely needing money I do not have. That has been his theme for years, and I can't keep enabling him.

Collins turns to leave, and Graham is eyeing me from his side of the table. "You okay?"

"I'm fine." The words are classically female and classically an avoidance of the real issue. I know that if I look him in his eyes, he will catch my lie on his radar. My eyes shut to hold back the tears that pool. Why do I turn into a pile of emotional girl goo at every turn when it comes to him? If my pain was a knife, I would be shredded right now —bleeding out onto the floor of the flawless tweed carpet.

"Shhh..." He is at my side before the first tear drips from my chin, down on bended knee.

I push away his hands at his comforting touch, not wanting it now. I clear my throat and straighten in the chair. "I'm ready to play."

Graham's confusion is evident in his wide eyes and raised brow. He looks at me incredulously, and I can see the fight he has with himself as to whether or not to keep pressing me for more information. When his eyes soften back to the mystical blue, he rises from the floor and retreats into the main living area of the house. He comes back with two huge mugs of coffee, and I sip on the hot beverage and try to relax.

We each roll one die to see who goes first. Graham gets a four, and I have a two. He then shakes both and rolls a nine. It is no shock to me that he buys Connecticut Avenue. I roll a five and buy Reading Railroad. Graham lands on St. James Place and sweeps that property up. I get Virginia Avenue. We go back and forth buying up properties, picking up cards, and performing the tasks. But when I roll and land on his green Pennsylvania Avenue land, I decide to pay and avoid answering a question.

"You're going to run out of money," he says smoothly.

"Always do," I say. It is true. This is what happens to me in real life. I am accustomed to it.

"Interested in a personal loan?"

I narrow my eyes at him. "No strings attached?"

"Oh no, there will be a lot of stipulations. I wouldn't be a good businessman if I let you have it interest free, now would I?"

I stick out my tongue. "I would rather mortgage my properties to the bank for the cash."

"I would offer you a better deal," he persuades.

I pick at my fingernails. "Doubtful."

His laughter makes me join in. When it's his turn, he rolls doubles which result in him buying the last of the light blue properties to complete his trio and obtaining the Electric Company.

I roll and move my chocolate bar to pass go. I land on Baltic Avenue and buy it up to complete my duo. I have just enough money for a house on each of the two properties, with a little left over in case I land on one of Graham's. They are the cheapest on the board, so I am not expecting to get rich from them.

Graham rolls, lands on free parking to get the jackpot, and uses his money to buy two houses per property on his light blue collection. We just created residential row. That street is going to be dangerous.

When I land on his newly acquired Electric Company, I groan at the implications that I could lose a lot of money. There is a multiplier involved on the amount on the dice.

I take a large sip of my now lukewarm coffee and fix my hair behind my ear. I count and recount the little bit of money I have. I can feel Graham's stare burning into my resolve. He knows he is in a way better position. Even though I own more properties overall, he owns more clusters that he can build on.

"I think I will do the question," I say nervously. He could basically ask me anything, and I would feel obligated to tell the truth. I have not been truthful with him in the past to protect my career prospects. But with a game, I would never cheat. I like to play fair.

Graham rubs his hands together and looks like he just won the entire game already. So smug. "Stop biting your lip before you cause it to bleed, sweetheart. You really that nervous?"

I release my skin and take a deep breath as he thinks about what to ask me.

"Okay," Graham begins, "do you have romantic feelings for Zander?"

I frown at the mention of his name again. It causes me pain that I have not been in contact with Z and that things are now strained between us. "I care about Zander." I ignore Graham's slight flinch and continue. "We met during freshman year and instantly became friends. He has been there for me when I needed him most and always cheers me on. But I do not feel romantic love toward him. I never saw him like that."

Graham gives me a nod and seems to accept my answer as truth. "He is still a threat to us."

I shake my head. "No, no he's not. He will move on and hopefully find someone who is open to having a relationship with him. He's a great catch. I'm sure when the right girl comes along, he'll know."

Graham shrugs. "Or he can pine after you and never commit to anyone else."

"Ugh, please don't say that. I already feel horribly for not seeing the signs and potentially leading him on because I enjoy his company."

"Did things with you two ever go beyond kissing?"

"No." Thankfully. "And it seems like you got your facts wrong, because I never kissed him."

When it is Graham's turn he rolls and lands on the Chance spot, so he takes a card and reads it. Of course, it gets him to move to "Go" to collect two hundred dollars.

"Are these rigged?" I ask, looking at the cubes.

He chuckles. "That would be some pretty high-tech cheating if they were. You give me way too much credit." His eyes lock onto mine. "Maybe you are just unlucky."

"Maybe so," I grumble. I roll and land on Kentucky Avenue—the last red property I need before I can start building houses with the money I do not have. The only way for me to even have a chance at winning is to get some houses. "I'll sell you my panties for two hundred."

His eyes sparkle with mirth. "Done." He reaches into his pocket to pull out his wallet.

"No, not real money," I giggle.

Graham's laughter makes me laugh more.

I smile like the cat who just got the canary, as I snatch the two bills from his hand. He leans back and watches me intently. Waiting. It's almost like he is afraid to blink.

"Expecting a show?"

"For two hundred dollars? Damn straight."

"Too bad I'm not wearing any," I say cheekily. "Sorry." I reach for a little green house to plop onto my property but am thrown backward and pulled on top of a very sexy Graham.

"You tricked me," he growls, making me laugh.

"Not my fault you made a bad business transaction before checking for accuracy." I try to wiggle out of his hold. Collins could walk in on us or boaters could see through the wall of windows. And that little lingering fact that we could get caught makes me hot.

His hands slide from my back to my ass and give it a squeeze through the flimsy cotton fabric of my pajama pants. I grind my hips into his and rub myself onto him.

"What are you doing to me?" His voice is rough with need.

I bite my bottom lip and then release it, while licking the edge. "Whatever it is, I better renegotiate the cost. I don't want to get ripped off."

He tickles my sides, making me bolt upright. My core grinds even farther into his cock. He feels so damn good.

When my breath settles, I rest my head on his chest and tip it back to kiss his neck. He is so warm. Our encounter in the kitchen only made me want him more. He teases me. Seduces me. It has been this way from the very beginning. Until we both can't take it anymore, snap, and give in to our desires.

I continue my grinding—turning both of us on. It's like we have gone back several steps and are now resorting to dry humping, and it feels so damn good that I don't even care.

"I'll pay four hundred for your pants."

I remove my lips from his neck and look down into his almost black eyes. "Make it six hundred and it's a deal."

"Done."

I don't even know if he has six hundred dollars, but the way my body melts when his is around it is making me do irrational things. His fingers play with the elastic waistband and then roll it back to peel the fabric from my bare skin. It is sensual and slow. I lift my weight off of him in sections, until he takes his foot and brings it up to assist with the removal.

He grabs my bare ass and rolls me to my back. His hands slide up my shirt and palm my breasts over my bra. So many contrasting sensations run through my body. He is rough and gentle. But both types of touches have the same effect on my pussy.

Graham's mouth is on my ear. "I can feel your juices leaking all over my pants."

I look up into his eyes and moan. What used to embarrass me is now fuel to get me even more turned on. Our lips lock and his hands go into my hair. The weight of his body feels good on me and has the comforting effect of a security blanket.

"I should charge you for those too," I say with a smile, as I continue to kiss him.

"Would be worth every penny."

We tease each other until the brink of release and then halt at the last second. It surprisingly feels exhilarating to get to the edge and then to stop and wait it out. What used to frustrate me while I would attempt my own release in my bedroom all those years has now become a fun challenge.

Graham reluctantly lets me up, and we situate ourselves back on pillows so we can finish the game. I have a strong competitive side that he seems to bring out in me, so I am eager to see who wins. He hands over the six hundred dollars. I count and recount it. And then do it again.

His laughter booms through the room. “Think I would cheat you on the money?”

“A girl can’t be too sure these days,” I chirp. His eyes burn holes into me as I turn the bills over and over. I hold one up to the light coming through the window. “Are these counterfeit?” I feign shock, until I can’t take it anymore and burst out laughing.

“What am I going to do with you?”

“Hopefully take me to a club to help me stuff bills in other men’s pants.”

His growl is animalistic. “You know that will never happen, right?”

“Whatevs.”

Once I get myself settled, I spend my newly acquired money on some houses for my red trio.

I don’t know how to sit without Graham being able to stare at my naked lower half and get me distracted. His amusement is evident in how he undresses the rest of me with his eyes. Only two more articles of clothing keep me from being completely exposed.

“Can I buy you out of the game?” he asks, his tone serious.

“No.”

“So, you don’t have a price?”

“You make it seem like I am your property—beyond the game.”

“That’s the plan,” he says seriously. “But I need to play my cards right.”

"The game we are playing does not translate to real life, Graham."

"It can."

"But I cannot be bought. Especially now that you basically fired me from my job." I really need to continue looking into another part-time position. Maybe work as holiday-help or something.

"You make it sound so dramatic. Like I won't provide for you and everything you need or want."

"For someone who has a sister and has been exposed to the female gender, you would think you would know that we are capable and that some of us actually enjoy working. This is not the 1950s."

"I have no problem with you working. Hell, I'll even offer you a job in my other companies. But you are not working at Entice. That is a hard no."

"What job would you offer me?"

"Personal assistant," he says with a smile.

I huff. "Are you serious?"

"I haven't given it a ton of complex thought. But, yeah," he says shaking his head, "I would love for you to work for me in a non-dangerous position. I would give you a great salary and a comparable benefits package. Bonuses for being easily available."

"Are you kidding me? Easily available? What does that even mean, Graham? Are you looking for an assistant—which you have currently—or an office fuck doll?"

"Well, when you put it so eloquently…"

My mind runs crazily with images of being in the same building as Graham daily. What would he want me to do?

Prance around in pencil skirts and silk blouses while making him coffee? Bring him his mail?

He just fired Hanna, but seemed to find a replacement efficiently. Pretty sure if I was under his employment again, I would not have many job duties other than to serve him. Or *service* him.

"It would be ideal so I could have access to you all day long. Bend you over my desk, pull up your skirt, and sink into you easily."

The image he creates is so hot that for a moment, I want the exact picture he painted. I close my eyes and try to regain my stance on the topic. Even though I would read these types of boss-employee scenarios in my romance novels—and it was hella sexy—it is not like I would be able to do actual work if Graham was hovering around my same space and soliciting me for office sex.

I shake my head at him. "I already had one taste of what it would be like to have you as my boss. And quite frankly," I say, picking at a piece of fuzz on my shirt, "I wasn't very impressed. Horrible benefits pack—" A flash of a shadow passes and I double over as his fingers wiggle against my skin. "Stop," I gasp and start to giggle. "It tickles!"

Graham relents after tears of laughter fill my eyes. "You drive me mad, woman."

"You drive me mad, caveman."

"Grrr…"

"Did you really just *grrr*?"

He laughs. "Yes. Yes I did."

"Let's get back to the game. I actually see some hope."

Graham analyzes the board and glances over at my dwindling money. "Is that so?"

I play with the hem of my shirt, rolling it up inch by inch to show off the skin of my belly. I have a new spark of confidence, and my alter ego wants to be unleashed from her cage. And she is a sassy thing.

I stretch my arms up over my head, pulling the fabric another few inches upward. "It's so warm in here too."

Graham's eyes darken to cobalt blue. I am playing with fire and tempting the beast within him. I can see his wheels turning as to how he is going to gain control back in this game. He watches as my thighs spread open like a butterfly's wings. He knows what game I am playing and doesn't seem to care that I am taking the lead. Maybe he even likes it?

"How much for your damn shirt and bra?" he growls.

My eyes light up. "How much do you got?"

He counts and recounts his money. "Seven hundred forty-five dollars."

I make an exaggerated pouty frown. "Oh no, that's too bad. They cost seven fifty." I shrug and then click my tongue against the roof of my mouth.

Graham's eyes narrow.

I lick my lips for dramatic effect. "Also too bad, I would have given you a blowjob for a thousand or for the transfer of your houses to my properties. But it looks like you are a poor saver. "

His growl lets me know that I am getting to him. It feels powerful and freeing. Dare I say *fun*?

"Using sexual favors as currency, I see. Smart alternative strategy for a game that only has one," he says shaking his head at me. "I underestimated you once again, Miss McFee."

He rolls for his turn. He lands on one of my railroads and, because I own three of them, owes me one hundred dollars. Or he can opt for the question.

"Question." His voice is hoarse.

I love that we get to each other. We know each other's buttons and know exactly how hard to push them. It is a dangerous game of edge play. The push and pull. Give and take. Rise and fall.

I just never thought Monopoly would be the catalyst that would bring out these sides for us.

"How many sexual partners have you had before me?" I blurt out in a fast string of words.

"Fuck, Angie. Really?"

I move my head up and down. "Yes, really." I have been curious since we started heating things up. Plus, he already knows my sexual history, although it lacks any real experience. Only seems fair I should know his. I watch as he tilts his head back and closes his eyes. Ugh. How many does he have? "Do you need an accountant to help with the addition?"

"Twelve," he spits out.

So I am unlucky—or lucky—number thirteen. I am not exactly sure how many I thought he would say. But I think any number other than *one* would make me have the rush of jealousy that is currently smacking against my heart. I knew he had a past. You don't get as good as he is with his hands and mouth without having some type of practice. Porn can only provide so much education.

I let the number marinate in my head a bit more before I ask a follow-up question. "What do they all have in common?"

"They are all female."

A boisterous laugh bursts out. "Smart-ass." I should have expected it. Neither of us like openly talking about our personal lives. "Can you be more specific?"

"They all had vaginas."

I scoff. "Graham!"

"What do you want to know, Angie? I barely remember most of them. Some were just sex partners and nothing more. It's not like I have had many actual relationships. I fuck and forget. And a few times, I fucked *to* forget."

"Eww." I make a disgusted face. He makes it sound so nasty and clinical when he puts it like that.

"You have been the only person I have ever really wanted *more* with."

"What about Sophia?" There. I said it. The one woman in his past who makes me want to spit nails…into her eyes.

"Right now Sophia and I are strictly just business associates. She is employed under Entice as an escort and under Jealousy as a signature model for the jewelry line. We had an on-again but mostly off-again"—he pauses to search his brain for the right word—"partnership."

"Romance."

"It is not what I would call romantic."

"Would you guys go to restaurants?"

"Yes."

"Over to each other's places?"

"Yes."

"Remember birthdays and holidays?"

"Yes."

"Then it was a fucking romantic relationship, Graham." How can he be that obtuse?

"There was no love, Angie. I care about her welfare. But I do not love her romantically. Never did."

"Does she love you that way?"

"No." He runs his hands through his hair. "Maybe?" A frown forms on his lips. "I don't know. Can we freaking get back to the game?"

I want to close the door to my heart that I was just starting to open. "I feel like I'm competing with her for you in an invisible game of Tug-of-War. I've heard it in her voice and seen it in her eyes. She is not over you, Graham. Are you really that dense to not see the signs?"

He scoots closer to me and holds my cheeks in his palms. His thumb passes over my bruising skin. "I never wanted *more* with her. I never took her to meet my family. I never took her to this lake house. She never tied me up in knots. She never made me see into the future." His eyes soften. "You do. Angie, you make me think about the future. You make me delirious with all of my overprotective tendencies. You bring out the best and the worst in me. You blur the line between right and wrong."

"That last part is not a compliment."

"It isn't meant to be. It is the truth. I should let you live your life freely. But I can't let you walk out of mine without a fight. You are my weakness and my strength all rolled up into one overarching emotion of obsession."

"I'm just scared," I whisper. "Scared to get my heart broken."

"I know, baby." He moves me on top of his lap and kisses my forehead, then my nose, and ends at my lips. He pulls back to study my face. "I am scared too. I don't want to break yours or get my own shattered. I love you so much."

He hasn't tried saying those words in so long that I wondered if he didn't feel them in the first place. My lips press against his as I snuggle in closer to his warmth. "I love you too." I can't keep them contained inside any longer. It is the first time telling him. Maybe all of this time apart and all of the time I had to discern my emotions has brought the realization to the forefront of my mind.

"Say them again," he whispers so breathlessly that I struggle to even hear him.

"I love you."

His mouth swoops in and captures mine. I am held prisoner to his binding arms and melt into his hold. He feels warm and safe. He is my home.

He releases my lips and stands up. Within seconds I am airborne and carried to the row of windows that look out over the lake. He places me gently onto the furry irregular shaped rug and pulls my shirt off over my head and then unsnaps my bra. He strips down to nothing and settles himself between my parting legs. I don't need much buildup because I am already primed and ready for him. Staring into my eyes, he pushes into me and rocks his hips back and forth to stretch me and get me reacquainted with his size. I love the feeling of fullness and how we fit so well together. It is like our bodies were designed with each other in mind.

"You are so freaking tight," he whispers out a moan. "I want to lose myself inside you."

I thrust my own hips upward, trying to get more of him inside me. I wrap one ankle around his ass and grind my hips in a circle.

Graham holds his weight up on his elbow and pushes my hair off my forehead. The sun is coming through the windows and warms my skin. We get lost in each other's eyes as we make love slowly. It is different from the other lustful times when we were intimate. And for some reason, I needed this moment more than I realized. We both have our release and bask in the afterglow as we come back down to earth.

18

"Do you forfeit?"

I lean up on my elbows to look at Graham's hungry eyes. "Never." Plus, I am pretty sure I am close to winning.

"Have it your way."

His tongue trails down my neck, over my breasts, and then down to swirl around my navel. Expert fingers pull my pussy lips apart, and the hypersensitivity of my freshly fucked sex causes me to tremble.

"Graham," I gasp. "What are you doing to me?"

He ignores my question and thumbs my clit, while scooping up the product of our arousal and pushing it back inside. It is such a territorial move and one that makes me melt even more.

"I love seeing you like this." His words come out raspy. "Laid out and open for me. Dripping with my seed. Your whole body is glistening. You are perfection, Angela. Your beauty captivates me."

I try to sit up and feel myself leaking. Graham brings up a finger to my lips in offering.

"Taste us."

I lick along the pad of his finger, savoring the unique taste of our combined releases. I feel my hair matted to my head and my face flushed from sweating so much. There is no way I can be as sexy as Graham just described, yet seeing him with a similar unkempt appearance is ramping up my own desire again for him. So, who am I to argue?

Multiple fingers push into me without warning, and I throw myself backward onto the fur rug, arching my back to accept the pleasure Graham doles out.

"Ahh!"

He pumps them a few times, and as soon as I think I am going to come undone, he rips them out of me.

"Dammit, I was close," I yell.

"Do you forfeit?"

A smirk dances on my lips. "No."

"Have it your way, Miss McFee."

He pushes in his fingers, adding one more, judging from the fullness I feel. I writhe with pleasure, waiting for him to hook his fingers just like—

"Oh hell!" I grunt, thrusting my hips upward to try to get more friction. I am so close. And then I feel it—his mouth. I suck in air through my teeth that can't seem to do more than just grind together. Just when I think he will finish me off, he stops. I deflate like a balloon.

"Do you forfeit?"

"Yes, dammit! I forfeit!"

Graham chuckles and then runs his tongue along my cleft until he suctions his entire mouth onto my clit. I thrash on the floor, as he holds me down from trying to roll. He breaks the seal just to scold me and give me a warning to stay still. Then he shoves his fingers inside me roughly and gets me to orgasm again, as I forfeit more than just the game.

I give my body to Graham.

He crawls up my body, kissing every part as he makes his way up to my face. Pushing back damp hair from my forehead, he gazes into my eyes that no longer have the will to stay open. I feel like I just reached the biggest high of my life.

"I win."

"Pretty sure we both won." I hum, feeling the bones return to my limbs. I am the laziest starfish.

He plants a kiss on my nose. "I think so too."

When my body has feeling again, I try to sit up to see what kind of puddle I am resting in.

"Oh no…" I bite my bottom lip, feeling mortified.

"What's wrong?"

"I think I peed."

Graham stifles his laughter. "Sweetheart, you just squirted. No pee involved."

"Oh. I thought that type of thing was just some urban legend."

He looks at me like I am the most interesting person on the planet. "You sure are one of a kind."

"Thanks?"

He pulls me up by my arms and then carries me into the bedroom to rest on the bed while he pads off into the bathroom. I enjoy the view of his naked ass from my perch. The sound of running water and the sweet smell of toasted coconut and vanilla fill the air as the steam permeates the room.

When he returns, I get scooped back up and then lowered into a sea of bubbles. I moan at the sensory overload. The bordering candles are lit, flickering around the walls of the room.

Graham joins me from behind. His hands wrap around my midsection, and warm lips breeze across my neck, traveling up to nuzzle against my sensitive ear lobe. I melt farther into him as I rest my butt between his legs. *The man is good.*

My lobe feels the prickle of his sharp teeth, and I groan in response to the pulsing sensation that shoots down my torso. I swear I hear him mutter something about me liking it *rough*. I can't argue the truth.

I stare out of the surrounding windows, seeing only the changing leaves and a partial view of the lake. Surely, Graham owns enough land around his lake house to keep this particular room private from any neighbors or curious eyes.

As I adjust to the water, my skin tingles from the heat and Graham's expert hands. He moves me from his lap, and I sit on the adjacent bench. He finds my feet in the abyss of bubbles and massages the soles. I slink into the side of the tub and rest my head and neck against the rim—my body completely hidden under the surface.

He pulls my foot from the water to kiss my big toe and then repeats the same action on the other foot. "Did you mean what you said back there?" he asks, looking at me for a reaction.

I said a lot of things, but I know which specific words he

is referencing, because I was shocked over my declaration as well. “Yes. It felt weird saying it finally after all this time, when deep down I think I knew all along.”

“I’m glad you didn’t wait a second longer.”

I melt farther into the water as his fingers press along my arches. “I love when you rub me like this.”

His smile is genuine. I actually think he likes to perform services like this for me. He never makes it seem like a chore to touch me and almost always initiates. His hands slide up my calves and massage the tension out of my muscles. He hedges his way farther up my legs and I welcome him. I flinch when he makes contact with my pussy, not even aware of how sore I am.

His eyes dart to mine. “I hurt you?”

“Still getting used to your size. It’s a good sore.”

He gives a small nod. “I should have spent more time prepping you.”

“I don’t mind being sore, Graham. I actually kind of like the reminder of where you’ve been.”

His thumb teases my opening but doesn’t enter. I get pulled onto his lap and our bodies slide against each other. We share a kiss and then he turns me to face away. This time he presses his fingers into the tense muscles of my neck. I groan and shift in the water as his hands go to work at the knots and tension being stored in my joints and tissues. He chuckles at my moaning that I cannot hide or mask. The feeling is incredible, and I never want it to stop. His hands move to the front of my neck and dip down to my clavicle bones and then back up over my throat. His minor choke-holds cause pleasure pulses to travel through my nervous system. He is careful not to press too hard and knows exactly where to place each pad of his fingertips to produce the exquisite feeling that keeps me wanton and pliable putty in his hands.

After the massage, Graham uses a cup to wet the top of my hair. Every time I try to resist and do things for myself, he hushes me and coaxes me into submission with his soft lips on my neck and ears.

"I'm enjoying this as much as you are," he whispers, sending tingles up my spine. "Let me take care of you. Just relax."

My face is damp from the thin layer of sweat. Graham squeezes sweet smelling shampoo in his palm and runs his lathered hands into my scalp. I wiggle and twitch at the amazing feeling of having my hair played with and washed. If I thought that nothing could top the neck massage, I stand corrected. The hair therapy session is by far my favorite act. After I am rinsed, Graham reaches behind me to the basket of supplies and takes out a wide-toothed comb. He gently brushes through my long locks, getting out the knots. His attention and gentleness make me smile and close my eyes as he cares for me. When the water starts to cool and my skin reaches full prune-like status, I am lifted and wrapped in a towel the size of a blanket.

Once dried off, I slip into a fluffy white robe and am taken back to the room where I am presented with a beautiful red and black striped skirt and a red silk long-sleeved blouse. It's a bit bolder than what I would typically wear, but the quality of the fabric and seams spell designer. The ensemble includes a silver belt, red-soled high heels, and a black clutch. I resist getting giddy over expensive footwear and frown at the amount of money that the outfit must have cost.

"You are worth it, sweetheart," he intercepts my thoughts, making me shiver at how he knew what I was thinking. "You are going to look amazing in this, I just know it. We will be leaving in forty-five minutes. Is that enough time?"

I nod. "Where are—" I start to ask but stop, knowing that it is pointless. He loves to surprise me. "You've thought of everything, haven't you?"

"This is just a small taste of how I am going to spoil you."

I bite my bottom lip and then release it. "What would you have done if I won the game?"

He shrugs. "I never planned to lose."

I roll my eyes. "Bye, Graham."

"Goodbye, Angie."

I admire his retreating backside as the door is shut, and I am left alone with my thoughts and a whirlwind of emotions. We must be alone if he is walking around without clothes on in this house. Either that or he just doesn't give a damn what anyone else thinks of him.

I dig through my supply bag and find the tools needed to prepare my face, body, and hair for the date. As I finger the clothes set out for me on the bed, I find a thin black box with a white ribbon and bow across the top. My breath catches. I take the box into the bathroom and place it on the vanity. I pull at the bow and lift the lid, pushing back the tissue paper to reveal a beautiful red and black bra and panty set, with black nylons and matching garter belt. Along the side of the lingerie, there is a smaller silver box with

Jealousy's logo embossed along the top. I open it to reveal a necklace. Diamonds make up the length and sparkle in the light from the sky window.

Holy shit.

I finger the stones and marvel at the gesture Graham has done. I fasten the chain around my neck and cannot stop staring at the glistening diamonds in the mirror. I guess the perk of being with the CEO of a jewelry company is that I get to model some of his creations. Or perhaps he's still pissed over Zander's gift to me from California.

Next, I pick up the bra and examine the intersecting strips of velvet and satin that go over the cups. The appearance is that of a cage for the breasts, with sheer fabric in between the horizontal and diagonal stripes. The panties can barely be called such due to the limited coverage. They match the same type of design as the bra. I know that my supple ass cheeks will be peeking out of the bottom lace. The nylons and garter belt have the same type of thread theme and textures—tying the entire ensemble together with grace and elegance, despite the overly sexual nature of the look. Although I never splurge on expensive undergarments, I like to buy things on sale at Victoria's Secret. They make me feel pretty and feminine to wear them under my clothes. A guilty pleasure. These pieces, however, must cost a fortune.

I just hope Graham doesn't like them enough to rip them off of me. He seems to do that with his favorites.

I blow dry my hair, brushing through the wave of curls to tame their springing volume. I dust on a light amount of makeup, but choose a bold shade for my lips. I slip on the lingerie. Looking in the mirror, I can't help but groan at how sexual I look wearing just undergarments and diamonds. I smile wickedly at the thought of walking out to greet Graham in just this. I hope he was the one who actually picked it out. The thought of Collins doing lingerie store shopping—even if just online—freaks me out. He has already seen too much. Graham, being the overprotective man he is, probably has limits as to what his men are in charge of in regard to me and my *needs*.

The skirt and blouse fit like a glove. When I am done with the last-minute touches, I shut off all of the lights and slip out of the room.

"I want an update hourly. Collins will be fielding my calls. I get that she is upset. I'll be back soon." Graham's tone is all business and no nonsense. He paces in the giant living room with his Bluetooth device in his ear. Our eyes lock, and he stares at me shamelessly. "Got to go," he responds hoarsely. He takes his device out while moving his gaze up and down my body painstakingly slow—as if he is trying to commit every part of me to memory. "Stunning. You take my breath away."

"Thank you." My mouth is dry.

He saunters over—meeting me halfway—and leans down to kiss me on each cheek. His thumb grazes along my bruises that I hope are covered up enough with the foundation I used.

"I am one lucky man."

He trails his fingers along my neck, settling them at my shoulders. He plays with the springiness of my soft curls. I can smell his cologne on the collar of his pressed light-gray dress shirt. The darker shaded suit, sans tie, looks to be professionally tailored and originating from

Italy or some other place in Europe. He looks smoking hot.

"Maybe I'm the lucky one."

His hands slide down and play with my belt, using it to tug me closer. "You are a feast for my eyes. I am nearly speechless." He stands for several long seconds and admires me. And I realize how much my happiness is tied to his approval. "How about we take a quick tour of the house before we leave for our date?"

I accept Graham's hand as he walks me through the house and points out the home library, office, gym, and several guest rooms. The house is bigger than I thought. The basement has a walkout and provides access to the pool and hot tub.

"We can get in later," he whispers into my ear.

I look up at his beautiful eyes and smile. "I would like that."

He wiggles his eyebrows and says, "Clothing optional."

I laugh as he tickles my sides. I would love to rest with the jets at my back while looking out at the lake, under the stars. This place is magical and private. It is a safe haven away from the hustle and bustle of the city. We walk out onto the floating dock, and I use Graham's arm for balance. Walking with stilettos on a wood plank surface definitely has its challenges.

He lets go of me at the end and has me turn around to face him. Pulling out his phone, he holds it up.

"I want to try to capture just a frame of your beauty," he says, snapping a few pictures. I don't even think I am looking at him when he takes them. "I love that you are wearing my jewelry. I need to get you more pieces."

My hand moves up to my necklace. I forget I am wearing it because it feels so good against my skin. It fits perfectly. "Thank you for getting it for me." I stretch up to kiss his lips. "You spoil me. I'm not sure I deserve it."

He pulls back from me and cups my cheek. He looks closer at it and confesses, "I love having someone to spend my money on. I want you to want for nothing. And I have the means of giving you whatever your heart can dream up, Angie."

I snuggle in closer to him, as a wind gust across the lake chills my body. "Just know that money is not a quality I look for in a person to be in a relationship with. I need trust and honesty and respect."

"I love that you don't want me for my money. But please just try to accept that I do have a ton of it, and I want to use it on you. You don't have to struggle for anything anymore. Let me have the honor of providing for my woman."

"I can try," I whisper. It is definitely going to take a lot of getting used to.

We snap a few selfies with the trees and the water in the background before walking off the dock and back up through the house to the front entrance.

I am helped into the back of the car and strapped into the seat. He definitely has a liking for doing this task; I'd hate for him to be deprived by doing it myself. I stare out the window as we round Lake Chelan, as it glistens in the afternoon sunlight. I reach for my phone to take a picture and remember that Collins has it. Knowing Graham's over-protectiveness, there is no point asking for it now.

"Such a splendid view," he whispers in my ear.

I turn in my seat to catch him looking at me instead of the picturesque landscape outside. I swallow hard over his inability to keep his thoughts or his intentions to himself. I am not used to a man being blatantly obvious about his feelings. And I am definitely not used to actually enjoying it.

"Where are we going?" I ask softly. "I'm so excited."

He chuckles over my girliness. "To a winery."

"Oh, I love wine!"

"Remember, Miss McFee. You are," he says, pausing to kiss me on my nose, "a lightweight."

I frown. "I am not."

"You very much are. And if you get drunk tonight, I might just have to devour *you* instead of the wine."

I furrow my brow as the car leads us up to a rustic looking building with a huge sign in the shape of a wine bottle stating "Majestic Valley."

He leans over the seat bench and suckles on my exposed skin at the V of my shirt. "Mm hmm." He licks over the sensitive spot, and I fear he has left a territorial mark. Reluctantly, he pulls himself away from me, eyes hooded and soft.

He has a point about my tolerance. My track record in regard to alcohol is nothing to brag about. Pretty sure the last time I really had a drink, I landed flat on my ass.

"We are going to go on a little tour since the lake is known for having a variety of grapes, which make quality wines. There are over thirty wineries here," he elaborates. "We only have time to visit a few."

I smile and scoot out of the car with the help of his hand at this first stop. We follow the path up to the building, and the place looks deserted of all other customers—despite being a perfect weather Sunday afternoon. Our hands remain entwined. There is something extremely innocent about the act, which is odd because nothing about Graham resembles innocence.

"I wanted privacy," he responds boyishly with a shrug, answering my unspoken question about the lack of customers.

"Oh," I mouth silently and continue to follow him through the doors. Excitement bubbles. I have never done a wine tasting before—especially not at an actual vineyard.

"Mr. Hoffman, Miss McFee, I'm so glad you could make it," a black-haired lady greets us, breaking our skin to skin contact by reaching out her hand to be shaken. I smile at her warmth and French accent. Her all-weather jacket sports the embroidered Majestic Valley winery logo. "Shall we explore the property?" She starts walking, never waiting for an answer.

Perhaps she understands Graham's hatred for wasting time.

We follow her out to an awaiting golf cart. Graham's hand that was once enveloping my own now rests at the small of my back—another hot spot. We sit on the back cushion together, as the guide takes the driver's seat. A young man steps out of the shop that we just left and hands us each a glass filled with their award-winning Cabernet Sauvignon named *Purity*; it is a delicious bold tasting wine that takes me a little bit of time to get used to the flavors. The worker also hands us an oversized fleece blanket, big enough for the two of us to bundle underneath to keep warm from the fall air.

The tour guide pulls out into the field with the cart and

explains the process on how the particular vineyard harvests the grapes and how they determine what type of wine will be produced based on the season and type of fruit. She explains how each winery around Chelan Lake is unique in flavor due to the different types of soil surrounding the water and the different harvesting methods and time frames used to collect and utilize the fruit. Graham and I sit and enjoy the warmth from the wine and our own body heat.

Under the blanket, Graham's hand rests on my upper thigh, just a few inches above my knee, and his fingers draw little circles on my nylon-covered leg. The simple motion soothes me, and the working of the wine relaxes my joints to the point that I am leaning up against him and snuggling into his side.

"Are you flirting with me, Miss McFee?"

"Maybe," I whisper softly, savoring his light mood.

He bends down and licks along my earlobe. "Don't worry. I like it."

I shiver.

"Cold?"

My eyes narrow on him. "You know damn well what effect you have on me. Don't start something here that you can't finish," I warn.

Graham's hands find my waist and with little use of his strength, I am tugged from the soft leather seat to the firm cushion of his thighs. Somehow the slack in the blanket allows for me to sit comfortably in his lap, and our rapid heartbeats merge into one big vibration. He turns me so I am straddling him and readjusts the blanket to cover my now exposed behind.

His breath is in my ear. "You think I won't pull your

panties to the side and fuck you right here? Do you honestly think I care if anyone knows? So do not suggest otherwise. I am keeping myself a gentleman in public for your sake." He punctuates his blunt words with a bite to my neck, making me jerk up in surprise.

"Ouch," I hiss, rubbing at the mark I know he left.

His fingers dig into my side, and the pain pulsates through my lower region, sending electric currents to my sex. He knows my limits and rides the fine line between too much and not enough.

"Maybe I don't want you to be a gentleman," I goad, mimicking his tone.

With a motion of his hand, the golf cart comes to a stop. Within seconds, I am lifted into the air. The blanket falls off me onto the dirt path. The sudden burst of cool air awakens my senses. I yelp as my butt gets a hard spank, and I am carried like a sack of potatoes toward a renovated barn building that is covered with caution tape and do not enter signs.

I am too embarrassed to look back at our guide, who I am sure is as confused as I am.

"Put me down!" I beg, anger simmering to a boil. "This is embarrassing!"

Graham pushes open a thick red painted door. He sets me back on my feet, and I fix my skirt into place but keep my eyes locked on his.

"What are you doing?" I snap.

"Being the bad boy you crave."

19

"For fucks' sake, Angie. I am going to teach you a lesson about tempting me in public. For one, I don't give a flying fuck about right and wrong. And second, to prove my point, I am going to take you—hard—in a temperature controlled room with barrels of aging wine. Standing up."

I gulp and look around the room. There are stacks of oak barrels with years stamped on the sides that house the wide range of award-winning wine. The room is dimly lit, and it appears we have total privacy. Several sawhorses are set up with wooden boards resting across the top. Power tools and carpentry supplies are scattered about the perimeter.

Graham stalks me with his eyes, and I inch backward infinitesimally, putting the barest distance between us. I am sexually charged, and I want him. But I want to make sure he follows through, and teasing him seems to get him to loosen the reins on his control.

I bolt away as fast as my shoes will allow, knocking over the wooden plank that is leaning against a pillar. "Have to catch me first," I giggle. I make it a few more feet before I am flipped midair and hauled backward against the smooth wood of a barrel.

"You are such a tease."

Graham bites my neck and then moves to my lips to suck them dry. My legs wrap around his waist, and the skirt accommodates the span of his hips. With one hand on my ass, he uses his other to unbutton and unzip his fly with ease. I pull my lips from his and kiss his neck as I run my nails along his spine. His fingers pull my panties to the side as he lifts my hips higher. He pulls me down onto him and slides right into home base. He doesn't give me time to adjust. Instead, he pushes his weight against me and bends his knees before lifting up—pinning me with his cock against a wine barrel.

It is dirty. Gritty. Every cell in my body is exploding with pleasure and worshipping this man who takes no prisoners and breaks every rule.

"Is this how you want me? Losing control? Fucking you hard against a wooden barrel?"

I try to arch my back to take him deeper. "Hell yes!"

And that is what he does. He continues to thrust upward, each time pushing me farther up the smooth wooden surface.

It is wild. It is raw. It is heaven.

I come screaming his name and him mine. I flop into his arms, completely spent. Sweat beads on my forehead, despite the room feeling chilly.

Graham tries to pull back so he can look into my eyes, but I just clutch on tighter to his upper body. "Are you okay?"

I exhale. "That was amazing."

He kisses me on top of the head, refastens his trousers, and fixes my skirt into place—all while I am still wrapped around him. "Don't wash me away. I want you to ooze out for the rest of the evening while we make friendly conversation with the local folk."

I swallow the spit pooling in my mouth. I am pretty sure I can already feel him seeping out of me. The scrap of panties I am wearing will not be able to withstand the volume.

"Do you want me to carry you like this out or do you want to walk?"

I am not sure I can even move, but I whisper, "walk," anyway.

Graham sets me down gently and we make our way hand in hand toward the door. He comes to a halt, and I look up at him with confusion. A scowl appears on his face, and he reaches into his pants pocket and pulls out his phone, answering it. He then turns all business in his demeanor and tone after a minute of silence.

"I want someone on him twenty-four seven," he demands. "I don't care the cost. Well, then hire another person!"

I watch as Graham struggles to keep control in front of me. His eyes move to mine, and the heat behind his gaze warms my insides.

"And you provide protection round the clock as well until it is determined what his true motive is. I have my theories, yes. Put every available person on it. I trust you to do what is needed. We are leaving tomorrow, yes. We will connect in person then."

He ends the call and runs his fingers through his wayward hair.

"Everything okay?" I ask dumbly after he slips his phone back into his pocket.

"Tell me everything you know about a Paul Sutterland."

It is in this moment that my heart stops. I am sure Graham can be perceptive enough to see the absolute fear in my eyes. I think fast at what would appease him, knowing that coming clean now would only put my entire research article at risk. If Graham knows what my end goal is, he will just try to sabotage me—just like he did with my escort job.

"He's a frat boy who works at the Campus Smoothie Cafe. I didn't even know his last name until now."

"Then how do you even know I am talking about the same Paul?"

"Because when Monica got drugged, I went to see her at the hospital to see how she was doing. She told me Paul was the one who supposedly helped her get medical help. Basically saved her from being assaulted. But you knew all of this already." His eyes look at me with confusion. "Because I saw you enter her room to ask her questions after me."

He opens and then closes his mouth as he puts the pieces together. The genuine shock on his face lets me know that he was clueless that I was there prior to his arrival. Monica must have kept that information to herself.

"My friend Resa was chased one night after leaving the Smoothie Cafe. She may not even return to school."

His eyes narrow. "What aren't you telling me?"

Shit. He knows I'm hiding something. "That's all I know." It is a half-truth. Because what I discovered at the frat Halloween party is all speculation. I don't need any more interference in getting to know how Paul fits into this big drug scheme.

"Quit lying."

"I'm not lying."

Graham's snarl rattles my composure. "You don't get it, Angie. I have Collins monitoring your phone as we speak. I have men back at home working at figuring out the missing puzzle pieces. You have fucking texts coming in from Zander. And from this frat boy Paul. I know what Zander wants. But why is Paul texting you?"

"Probably because I applied for a job at the smoothie shop he works at."

"Why did you apply there of all places?"

"Because you fired me! Remember?" I snap, tossing my hands into the air in frustration. "Because I actually need a job if I want to pay bills. Because I actually like having something to do with myself other than go to classes or be spread eagle in your bed."

He glares at me over the last part. Good. Maybe he will finally get the point that I have a brain, and it is one I plan to keep using.

"Are we together?" he asks boldly.

"Yeah, we are."

"Then no girlfriend of mine will ever work at a cafe making drinks for minimum wage. You are better than that."

"What an elitist thing to say!"

"You have an entire benefits package that you can still utilize through Entice despite being laid off—*not* fired. I did *not* fire you."

"Semantics."

"That's not the point. You don't need to worry over your bills anymore. Whatever debt you are carrying, I'll wipe clean."

"I don't like going through life with IOUs."

His eyes level with mine. "You will never have to pay it back—even if something happens to us—the money is yours to keep."

"Graham, I know you are trying to do something nice. But you really need to understand that you use money to gain control. We keep doing this back and forth dance over my need to hold on to my free will. I will relinquish many things over to you, because you have made it clear your need for that is like air, but I have to make my own money. Thus, I need a job. So either accept it or get ready to go to battle over this one. I am not budging."

He runs his fingers through his hair, and I can tell he is visibly stressed. He is about to argue, but he sighs and looks down at his pocket again. He wrenches out his phone, hitting the answer button and shoving it to his ear.

"Hoffman," he snaps. "Yes, you can. I need you to pull the archived footage from Saturday. I'll be back in town by midday tomorrow. I suggest that the team starts with the first layer of analyzing. Run anything concrete through the software to be thorough. Try to get credit card records. Be prepared for a briefing late afternoon, five sharp. Yes, all hands on deck."

I watch as Graham's posture straightens and his jaw clenches as he listens to the person on the other line. I use this delay to gather enough willpower to stand my ground. I am so deep in thought that I lose focus and realize that my name is being said.

"Angie? I am talking to you."

"Sorry, what?"

"Where did we leave off? Oh yeah, you agreed to let me take care of you. Including debts."

"I never agreed to that. But I do remember you agreeing to tone down your cranky controlling ass long enough so I do not freak my shit and bolt before you even enjoy me being your girlfriend."

His eyes darken to a richer shade of blue. He pulls me closer at the waist. "Girlfriend. It does have a nice ring to it."

I give him a squeeze. "It does, doesn't it?"

He pulls back and grips my face in his hands. His thumbs rub over my skin, and it instantly calms me. "I know your first instinct is to push me away when times get rough. Maybe it stems from some deeply rooted trauma, but I'm holding out for the day that you run to me when things get tough. Just know that I will be here, with arms wide open, waiting to catch you when you take that leap. I won't let you fall, sweetheart. Let my words be a promise to you."

I give him a weak smile. I am afraid to admit to him how much I already lean on him. Building my own strength while using other people as my rocks is dangerous architecturally, because as soon as those essential people disappear, I am left with a crumbling foundation of just ashes.

We table the discussion, knowing that it is far from being over, and walk out into the fresh air. The tour guide makes zero eye contact with us as we get situated in the back of the golf cart once again. She drives us back through the vineyard and points out the different types of vines and which types of grapes would grow from each. November starts the dormant period and signals the end of the harvest, so the only grapes on the vines are dead. I listen as well as I can with Graham's hand running up my thigh and spreading his leaking cum all over my folds from under the confines of the blanket. I shift uncomfortably in my seat as I get hungrier and hungrier for more friction. He is turning me into a crazy person who has one thing on her mind—him.

The tour ends with a drop-off at the store. Graham casually orders a mixed variety case of wine and tells the worker to send it to his Portland residence. We shuffle into the back of the car again, and Collins passes me a coat that he must have had delivered or had waiting for me from the front seat. I am thankful for the added layer, if just to help conceal my nipples from poking through my layer of clothes and cutting someone. Graham helps me into the black leather jacket that has a light fur lining. It pulls the chill out of my body. I sit back into my seat while Collins drives us to our next destination, Paradise Vineyards. Graham and I engage in small talk. We find ourselves laughing and enjoying each other's company.

Every bump we hit causes my thighs to clench. I try my best to keep my resolve as Graham shoots me knowing smirks from his side of the backseat.

He leans over the center and whispers, "Am I dripping out of you, sweetheart? Or are you clenching your inner walls and trying to keep me inside longer?"

I bite my lower lip. It is such an odd feeling to be this sticky and completely okay with it.

"It's turning you on, isn't it?" he asks.

All I can do is silently agree. I can't get enough of his dirty mouth. It's like he lacks a filter.

"Show me."

My eyes dart to his. "What?"

"You heard me."

It's true, I did. I glance to the rearview mirror and can see that Collins is paying absolutely no attention to us. And if he is, he is doing a damn good job acting unaffected. I spread my legs but keep myself covered with the fabric of my skirt. With my right hand, I snake it underneath and pull over my panties, just enough so my index finger gathers up the moisture that is part me and part Graham. I carefully remove my hand and hold up the finger of proof for Graham to witness.

He grabs my wrist and guides my finger up to my cherry-red lips. He then pushes my glistening fingertip inside my mouth. "Suck it," he demands.

A thrill runs up my spine as I do as I am told. It's as if he has me in a sexual trance. I suck on my own finger and taste the combination that is uniquely *us*. I never tire of him making me do these acts.

As soon as my finger gets pulled from my mouth, Graham's lips are on mine. Tasting and licking and seducing. It is the feel of the car stopping that makes us finally cease the foreplay. We detach, straighten our clothes, and smile a knowing smile at each other. He gets out of the car first and moves to the side so I can exit. The feel of his fingers pinching my ass cheek jolts me upward, and I shoo his hand away with my own.

"Stop," I scold.

He wiggles his eyebrows boyishly. "Why?"

"People will know."

He leans down in line with my ear. “Know what, sweetheart?”

“That you are a”—I pause to think of the correct word—“horndog?”

His cheesy, satisfied smile makes me laugh. “Oh, that’s cute.”

Once inside the main building, I enjoy a variety of different wines in the tasting room. Like the other winery, the place is empty and the workers are attentive and amenable to whatever we want. As we sample some of the award winners, plates of cheese, crackers, nuts, and fresh sliced fruit get brought out for our enjoyment. For certain samples, dark chocolate wafers are given to us to enhance the flavors of the wine. There are so many that I like due to the sweeter qualities in the flavors. My favorites are Simply Red, Birth Berry, and Petite Paradise Riesling Ice Wine. Graham takes note of my likings, hands over his card, and instructs a worker to form my wish list into a case and have it delivered to his penthouse.

“You’re going to need a wine cellar to store all of the bottles you are buying,” I joke, making him laugh.

“I got extra to take back so Claire can enjoy some as well,” he states. “Do you think she would like a gift basket of goodies too?”

I smile and nod my gratitude at his generosity. I think about offering to pay a portion, but instantly hold my tongue in fear of unleashing Angry Graham. I much prefer Horndog Graham and do not want to lose sight of him.

Our last stop on the wine tour takes us to Chateau De Vin—a beautiful winery with a wooden banquet room where we are able to have dinner. It is evening and all of the lights are on, casting a beautiful reflection onto the water of the lake. Unlike the other places, this winery is full of customers enjoying the elegance of formal dining, with the rustic, country-like scenery. Graham is greeted at the door with a warm welcome. He seems to be known amongst the workers, and his request for a table is met with efficiency. Soon we are seated, drinking more wine and eating a sesame and feta spinach salad with a champagne vinaigrette dressing. Fresh rolls are brought out, and I savor the aroma of buttery delight.

"Did you have fun today?" The question is meant to be light, a deep contrast to the questions that were asked hours before.

"Of course. I have never been to this lake, and it is so pretty. I really appreciate the effort you made to give me good memories here."

"We can come back anytime you want. I need more excuses to visit. I do love it here."

I smile and nod, knowing that being able to go out on the water in one of his boats would be a lot of fun.

"You are like the king here. Everyone seems to know you and respect you."

He takes a sip of his wine. "I bring them a lot of revenue."

"Based on the exorbitant number of bottles of wine you purchased today, I can believe that."

Our stuffed chicken and grilled asparagus arrive, and I dive into the meal, feeling the alcohol and knowing that eating is the best way not to get sick. When I have had enough, I grab my purse and excuse myself to use the ladies' room on the other side of the dining area. Like the rest of the building, the restroom is just as elegant and decorated with the same country theme. Once I exit, I glance over the items in the attached shop and decide to buy a beautiful picture frame made out of corks and a melted glass wine bottle. It is free to ship to my townhouse via an online order, so I do that to keep it a surprise. I pay and start walking back to the dining area when the air gets stuck in my throat.

My feet halt as soon as I see the brunette woman hugging Graham and pulling out my chair to take a seat in my place. Just like that, my house of cards seems to fall. I dip back behind the joining wall and watch as Graham smiles and gestures toward the direction where I just came from. I am careful not to be seen and continue pretending to look at items off the shelf as I spy and eavesdrop on the scene. I open up a wine and food pairing cookbook and go through the typical motions of someone who is interested.

"You look wonderful," he responds, leaning in to squeeze her hand over the tabletop. "As always."

I can only see the side of the woman's face, but from what I can tell, she is beautiful and model worthy. Her little black dress is classic and refined on her thin frame. Suddenly, I am self-conscious of my outfit, despite it being handpicked by Graham. When her hand reaches out to touch his, I get the urge to take off my heel and stab her flesh with it. While I am at it, I might as well stab out her eyes for eye-fucking my man. I know I am being catty, but what the hell? He isn't even moving his hand away from hers. As much as I have fought myself to admit it prior to this trip, Graham is very much my boyfriend. And all mine. I don't share.

I don't know why it is so hard to say it—even in my

own head—but he is my boyfriend. Today, we finally put a label on it.

I think the sound of their laughter is what sends me over the edge. I pivot and make my way to the back of the store where I am stopped by a worker.

"Miss, is everything okay?" she asks. I figure that she knows Graham—everyone around here seems to—and by association, she is probably scared to death that I am displeased with something.

"Oh, yes, everything is great," I lie. Well, half lie. The food, the service, and the wine are spectacular. The broad bitch sitting in *my* seat and flirting with *my* man…well, she can go jump into the lake for all I care.

"There you are." The timbre of his voice penetrates my ears and makes me slump my shoulders in defeat. His hands are on my waist, turning me to look at him. "Where have you been?"

"Oh, just looking around."

He nods, eyeing me skeptically, and then continues, "I wanted to introduce you to Ria. Ria, this is my Angela."

Behind him, the supermodel appears in all her glory, smiling her bleached teeth and putting her hand out to me in greeting. I shake her limp hand but imagine the stems of my stilettos hanging out from between her eye sockets. She is lucky I am only violent in my head right now.

"How do you know each other?" I ask expectantly, feeling the muscles in Graham's body coil. Are you uncomfortable? Good. Serves you right, bastard. What did you expect me to do? Not ask? I put my best smile on for show.

"Well, we…" His words trail off with a sigh, and I can see him trying to collect his thoughts. No need—him not answering right away is my answer. *You slept with her*. If I am number thirteen, I wonder what number that makes her.

"We went out a few times. Had a hell of a lot of *fun*," Ria answers proudly.

Yuck.

"It just never worked out long term," she interjects. "Maybe if I would have moved to the city…"

Her incomplete answer makes me cringe. She still thinks that she has a chance with him. I swallow down the knot forming in my throat and move my teeth to my inside cheek to gnaw. The tearing skin and the wine residue left over in my mouth mix, causing a burning sensation.

"It was a long time ago," Graham mutters, shifting on his feet and staring down at his hand on my waist. His free hand pushes his hair back from his face—a nervous gesture I have come to know very well. "We should go."

"Nice meeting you, Angela." The fake tone of her voice is obvious to me but not to Graham. Ria's perfect veneer smile is more of a sneer. "I'm glad that the coat I brought over fit you. You definitely fill it out." She looks me up and down before finishing her thought. "We only had a larger size in stock. Looks like it works perfectly for you. Yay."

"We have to go," Graham answers before I can interject my own snippy response.

Damn her. And damn him! I start to take off my coat, but Graham is a step ahead of me and holds it firmly in place. I glare at him in the middle of the wine gift shop as I watch Ria's retreating figure saunter back to her imaginary pedestal she so proudly perches herself on.

"Let it go," I whisper, but it comes out like a strangled yell.

"It's cold out, and I asked her to drop it off with Collins since she lives and works in the area. She has her own clothing shop attached to another winery that her family owns."

"How sweet," I bite back.

"I don't need your smart mouth right now."

"Well, I don't need to wear the garment that your ex-fuck-thing picked out." I make a face. "*You definitely fill it out,*" I mock in a pipsqueak voice. I grind my teeth together to keep from saying exactly where he can put the stupid coat. I know I am being petty, but I can't keep myself from changing course.

"Quit being that way, Angie. And quit fighting me about wearing it. You can take it off in the car if you hate it that badly."

"What number is she?"

"What?"

"I am thirteen. So what does that make her?"

He rubs a hand over his face, looking distraught and stressed. "I have no fucking clue. Why are you doing this?"

"There's a bigger issue than the coat, Graham." Although having an ex-girlfriend pick out clothes for the new…

I stop myself from thinking that I am or can be more to Graham than just a thrill or a challenge. I shove those thoughts back inside the comfort of my head. I thrust open the door and walk out into the chilled air.

He catches up with me and stops me with a jerk of my upper arm. "What? What's the bigger issue?"

"Are you really that clueless?" I ask, turning my whole body on him so that I can stand my ground. "You have absolutely no idea what just happened in there?" I ask, pointing back to the restaurant. When he genuinely looks confused, I continue with my rant. "I think the fact that you're oblivious pisses me off the most. Surely you could see how Ria just talked to me. How can you not understand how weird it is for me to be surrounded by your ex-lovers at every turn?"

Graham's sigh is audible. "You are making a scene, when we can have this conversation in the privacy of my car."

He's the one who asked—*no*, demanded!

My stubbornness wins in regard to not wanting to talk to him anymore. I follow Graham down the sidewalk but forgo the idling car altogether. Instead I keep walking.

"Angie!"

"I just need to take a breather."

"Well, do it in the car!"

I turn and glare at him. "No. I'll suffocate in all of your chauvinistic masculine energy!"

"What the hell!"

"You and your double standards," I rant. "I am so over this. You can stuff all of your ex-girlfriends up your ass one by one, because that's where they've been living since I came into the scene anyway!"

"Angie, get in the car!"

I turn and prop my hands on my hips. "How many more are going to pop out of nowhere, Graham? Huh?" I huff the air out of my lungs. "And they all must love your magical golden cock because they all flock to sing your praises!" I stomp my feet as I make my way farther down the road. "Unfuckingbelievable! That's what it is."

"We can talk about this!"

"Leave…"

"Angie…"

"Me…"

"Angela!"

"Alone!"

20

Graham catches up to me, but I ignore his directives and just keep moving along the path. Collins follows beside us in the vehicle. With the headlights, I can see the main road in sight. I don't know where I am going or what exactly I am trying to prove. However, my ego is hurt, and being locked inside the backseat with Graham sounds stifling right now.

"Get in the damn car."

I remove my coat and throw it at him. "No."

"What did you say?"

"You heard me."

I make it another couple of yards before his hand grips my elbow, spinning me around. I want to hit him. I am that mad. Collins is out of the car and is standing on the sidelines. Graham gives him a look that says so much more than a dissertation ever could. Problem is, I have no idea what information has transferred in the three second "look." And these silent *looks* are driving me up a wall.

Within seconds, I am escorted into the backseat by both men. There's no amount of fighting that will allow me to win this battle, so I just submit and settle into the leather.

"Quit treating me like a toddler!"

"Quit acting like one."

I buckle myself in and insist on shutting my own door, with my own trembling hands. The flash of amusement reflected in Graham's eyes is fleeting, and his always polished appearance shines brightly once again. But I saw it. He is entertained by me.

Damn him.

This isn't some dog and pony show. I stare out of the window at the moon over the lake and close myself off to the possibility of being anything more to Graham than *number thirteen*. I need to protect my heart, and I have not done a very good job of that thus far.

The touch of his cool fingers on my arms makes me jump. "Look at me." His even tone masks his emotion. "Please, sweetheart," he coaxes.

I refuse to meet his gaze and continue my blind staring at the passing foliage in the night. I can feel the snap break in his resolve, frustration reaching a boiling point, long before his words start. *Not so intrigued now, are you*? It's hard not to feel that the two of us keep taking two steps forward and ten steps back on a daily basis.

"Look at me, dammit," he demands with his low baritone—intent on making me succumb to his will. I'm sure in the business world, this strategy would work ninety-nine percent of the time. With me, not so much. Even I can admit that I am too damn stubborn.

"What?" I snarl, giving him the attention he wants, but

not in the form he wants it. From his ticking jaw, I am irritating him with my attitude. "What is it, Graham?"

"You are pissed, I get that."

"Do you?" My eyes study his features. "Because you seem pretty clueless on the art of an apology."

"But I haven't done anything wrong. Perhaps you are a bit envious?"

How dare he! "Screw you and your double standards, you hypocrite." But he is right. Every time I think of Graham with someone other than myself, I feel a rush of jealousy flood my entire body, making me not see reason. I know he has a sexual past. I'm just not sure I want to be reminded about it at every bend in the road.

He sighs, bends his right leg onto the leather seat, and softens his voice. "Explain why you are mad. *Please*."

No. "I shouldn't have to."

He lets out the air from his lungs, pulling at his hair. I go back to looking out the window, just to keep myself from getting angry again.

"Do it anyway. Spell it out for me. I don't want you mad at me, and I need to know so I don't have a repeat experience again. Are you mad because I was talking to another woman? Because we used to go out a few times? She doesn't mean anything to me. Nothing. I already know having her deliver the coat was a bad idea. I see that now. But I needed to make sure you weren't going to get sick because I didn't think ahead at how cold it would be up here in November."

I turn to look at him—so he can see just how truly affected I am. "You let her put in snarky digs about my body. You let her sit in my seat. And you let her touch you.

You didn't even remove her hand. You were laughing and smiling. It made my blood boil. Imagine if the roles were reversed, and I had a guy who I used to fuck—who knew my body intimately—sit down in your place and touch me?"

"I would cause him bodily harm." His answer is clear, concise, and predictable.

From everything I have been learning about him and seeing with my own eyes, I don't doubt a single one of his words. "Don't you think that I would feel the same way?"

"But you are a girl, and things are different for girls. Your gender needs protection from my asshole gender. Guys are perverts. It's a given." He gives a casual shrug that speaks greater volume than his words.

I stifle a laugh at his explanation, but only because it is kind of true. "Well, girls can be vindictive petty hussies."

"What Ria and I were doing was completely innocent."

"Doubtful for her. I saw the way she oohed and ahhed over you."

"Sweetheart. I want *you*. No one else."

"You need to consider my feelings though when you are around your harem of women."

His nose turns up in disgust over my comment, but he doesn't correct me. "I apologize for making you feel like she was replacing you. But that is completely ludicrous. Because baby, no one could ever do that. Ever."

Graham's words ignite the flame within me, and the heat permeates into my deepest insecurities—making the emotions scatter to the forefront. Guilt overwhelms me for making such a simple conversation with someone he used to know turn into such an overexaggeration.

"I wish you could understand how easy you have it,

because I have never had sex with anyone but you, so you don't have that to worry about like I do."

His eyes darken with the realization, and a small part of me finds comfort in knowing I got through to him.

I need to get over the fact that he has a past—a twelve-girl past to be specific. And that's just assuming he added correctly. I have no clue how good his math skills are. Better than mine, no doubt. But coming face-to-face with now two girls who have been a part of his life is a bit much. My insecurities about myself blossom and flourish under the inspecting gaze of his ex-lovers. It is much easier in theory to deal with his past whenever it isn't staring at me straight in the eye.

"I'm sorry for making you feel bad over something so small," I concede, making his demeanor soften.

"I get that you don't comprehend just how much you mean to me, Angie. I know that it is utterly ridiculous to like someone as much as I like you after only a couple of months. But there's no competition where you are concerned. No one else compares to you."

Graham runs his hands through his already rumpled hair, stirring the sexual energy in the back of the car. The man lives and breathes sex appeal. Graham's eyes change to a crystal blue and he turns his body to face mine, leaning his left leg onto the leather seat.

"But know that I will slay your dragons and protect what is mine. You enchant me beyond any logical reason. You have the power to destroy me." His fingers move to my cheek, and the gentle caress causes a shiver down my spine. "Just remember. You are mine. And as for any other man who stumbles into your life, well"—

he raises his eyebrows—"I'll be willing to fight for you."

"That's obvious." I don't mean for my words to sound as snarky as they do. I quickly curl my lips to a small smile to convey my feelings. "I keep telling myself that this is just a challenge for you. That you're going to get bored or move on to the next conquest. I keep denying what I feel for you. But I know that it is fear holding me back."

"What are you afraid of, sweetheart?" His question falls from his lips as eloquently as a pianist producing a chorus melody.

"Of being happy," I blurt out. It's a short answer. But it's the truth. This must be the wine talking, because I'm not a sharer.

Graham furrows an eyebrow. "Most people would think that *never* being happy would be their worst fear. But your fears are different. What else do you fear?"

"Being alone." Fuck. What am I doing? *Shut up*.

Graham leans back in his seat and studies my words. "You do realize that those two fears will inevitably cause conflict?"

I shrug. "Then I guess I will just live in limbo."

"What happened to you, baby? Please share this part of yourself with me. I can try to help you then."

I open my mouth and then quickly close it. I look out the window and lean my head against it. I don't want to talk about it. I want to keep it tucked away, inside for good.

"Please, baby."

We arrive back at the lake house, so I get granted a reprieve on having to finish the conversation. Knowing

Graham, it is just giving him more time to construct a plan to get me to open up.

He helps me out of the car and leads me through the main doors of the house. "Tired?" he asks softly, earning an *umm hmm* from me, even as he is pulling me toward the stairs to the basement. "Or up for a soak in the hot tub?"

I look up into his concerned eyes and instantly feel the pang of sadness that they bring. I care about him. "I would like that." My voice is barely a whisper. It feels like there is cotton in my throat.

I follow Graham down the stairs and into a dressing area. He turns me gently and unzips my skirt and unbuttons my shirt. He pulls it from my body and kneels in front of me as he admires my lingerie.

"You are the most gorgeous woman I have ever seen. You enchant me, Angela. I want to get to know every part of your body and your mind—equally." He kisses my knees, then moves up to my thighs. I spread my legs just enough for him to kiss my pussy and then my stomach. "I want to burn the memory of how you look right now into my mind. You are mine. I am never letting you go."

Graham strips me, starting at my bra, and kisses his way down to peel off my panties and then the belts and thigh-highs. He unfastens the diamond necklace and places it with my discarded clothes. He kisses along where my necklace used to be, and I enjoy the wet trail he leaves behind and the way his hands knead the tension out of my skin. He helps me into the skimpiest white bikini that has more strings than actual fabric. I'm not actually sure what the point of it is, other than to accentuate my curves even more. I watch from the bench while he undresses in front of me, and I sit back and enjoy the show.

"Where's a wad of dollar bills when I need them?" I tease.

He throws back his head and laughs from his diaphragm. "You did say you wanted a strip show for your date preference."

I raise my hands in the air. "I sure did."

"But I'm not worth fives?"

"Hmm, maybe a few of those. But only if you give me a worthwhile lap dance. This girl has a healthy sexual appetite, so I expect some fancy moves. Maybe even a headstand or a cartwheel."

He shakes his head at me, and I join him in laughter. That is how it is with us. One second we are fighting, the next laughing. We can go from serious to fun like the flip of a switch. I fix my hair into a messy bun on top of my head and secure it with a band from inside my purse.

When Graham is in his solid black trunks, he wraps me into a thick blanket and helps me into a pair of slip-on shoes.

"Ready?" he asks softly.

"I think so."

The air outside is very chilly, but the steam rises like fog from the hot tub, giving me comfort in knowing I won't be cold for long. Graham removes the blanket from me and places it on a neighboring chair. I kick off my shoes and step down into the tub. His hand on my upper arm steadies me, and I sink into the water.

"Ow, this is hot," I yelp.

"It does take some getting used to," he confirms with a laugh.

Graham pours us two glasses of wine and places them along the decorative brick edge. I eye my glass and take the first sip.

"Truth serum?" I ask with a smirk.

His smile brightens. "Whatever it takes."

He joins me in the water, and I move over to sit on his lap. Being this close to him is therapy for my soul. He feels so good. I cuddle up with my back to his front and lean my head on his shoulder, feeling the hair at the base of my neck getting saturated.

"Is it safe to say I am missing class tomorrow?" As soon as I ask the question, I realize I have a writing assessment for Human Behavior. Shit.

"I'll get you there on time. We are leaving very early in the morning. I know how dedicated you are to your studies and wouldn't want to cause you added stress."

I turn so he can see my face. "Thank you," I mouth.

"But I cannot keep you unguarded. I am not willing to budge on this topic."

"Can we at least discuss it?"

"It won't change anything."

"Graham…" I move so I can sit beside him and still see his face.

"Angie." His face is stern—unyielding.

We sit like this with the only sound between us coming from the roaring bubbles surrounding us and the rustle of leaves from the swaying trees. I lean my head back and look up at the stars and the moon. It's like we are in another world. We are protected here, from any outside influences.

While I know this feeling is only temporary, I yearn to hold on to it with all my might. To resist change with everything in my soul. Here, we are finally coexisting—trying to figure out how to be together without completely jeopardizing the things we each find nonnegotiable.

"I need you to be upfront with me about your plans in regard to my protection. Do you think it is really necessary?"

"Yes," he answers, his volume raised. "It is one hundred percent necessary." His eyes move out to the water, and I can tell his shoulders tense up. When he looks back at me, he is shielded. My heart skips at how affected he is from all of this chaos. Between the Mark situation and the girls getting drugged…to me getting drugged and his quest to find justice for Penny. It is all taking a toll on him.

"Can you please just try to let me know what you plan to do? I'll do my best to cooperate, unlike I have in the past. Can you please still let me drive my car? If you take away all of my independence, I can't keep myself from lashing out in defiance. I've been doing things on my own since I left home for school, and it's hard relinquishing all of the control over to you. Please understand that."

He takes a sip of his wine and hands me mine. It is a delicious blend, and the smell itself is intoxicating.

He clears his throat and places his glass back down along the side. He scoops me back up and I straddle his legs. He kisses the strap around my neck and runs his hands over my bare ass cheeks. This suit barely covers anything. I suppose to him, that is the point.

"Can I buy you a new car?"

"What? No."

"Why not?"

"Because some things have sentimental value."

"Can I buy you a second car and you can keep your other one in storage?"

"No."

"Angie—"

"Graham."

"I plan to have my security team watching you and Tanner. You do not need to know the details. This is something I cannot bend on, so please don't ask. He is trying to set me up, and you are going to be in the crossfire if we are going to continue this relationship. I already tried to keep you at a distance but am incapable of doing that. You should not even notice that they are around. Just go about living your life. Just for the love of God, Angie, please stop dangling yourself in front of the enemy."

"Is he going to press charges?"

"No."

"Why are you so certain?"

"Because he is trying to avoid being on the police's radar at any cost. He wants a low profile right now."

"Then why not report him? He assaulted me."

"He will continue to pay for that. I kept him alive so I can spend the rest of my life seeing to it that he is punished for his crime. But the police are useless when it comes to these types of things."

Don't I know it. When James and I were struck by a drunk driver, they couldn't even find any suspects. None.

Graham sighs. "Trust me, I'll make Tanner pay more than just some bruises and a few stitches. No one touches what's mine and gets away with it. I just have to play my cards right. It is about the long game—and I need him to think he has won a few of the short ones."

Satisfied with his answer, I drop the subject. As long as I am unaware of his security men, then I can pretend they are not there.

Graham hugs me closer, and the heat from our bodies merges into one ball of energy. I run my hands down his pecs and abs. His muscle definition is impressive.

"Are things over with Zander?" he asks softly.

I pull back to look into his eyes. "I'm going to need to have a difficult conversation with him. I fear our friendship will never be the same again. I'm not sexually attracted to Z. He and Claire are my best friends. I am pretty sure he won't want to be around me if I don't give him and me a chance. It makes me really sad. So, right now, I am avoiding him to delay the inevitable and hope that with time he will see that we are not the best match but can still be friends."

He nods. "Okay…"

"Are things over with Sophia?"

"Of course. Has been for months."

"Does she know and accept that?"

He looks off to the side of my face, and I realize that this is his way of coping with blurring the truth. "I think so."

"Have you made it clear?"

"I have made it clear that I am pursuing you. So, yes."

"And does she accept that?"

His eye twitches. "Not exactly."

"Explain, please."

"She sees you as just a fling. She is hoping that—"

"You will grow bored with me," I finish his statement, "and go right back to her." I think about the situation for a minute before growing even more agitated. "Why the hell is my name even being uttered on her lips when she is just an employee, Graham? It's like you allow her special privileges that you would not allow anyone else, and that for me is the bigger problem."

His sigh is drawn out, but it's his silence that says everything I need to hear. "Let's just forget about everyone else." He runs his hands up and down my body, and I get goose bumps under the heated water.

I grind my center into his erection. He has been sporting one for the past twenty minutes; I can't imagine it feels enjoyable. "Do your flings make you feel like this?" I ask breathlessly, as I rise up a few inches and back down. I am a bit salty over Sophia's title for me. I do not want to be a *fling*, and I definitely do not want to be just someone he fucks. I rub myself all over him.

His fingers dig into the flesh of my ass and move up to the strings of my bottoms to pull them apart. He tosses the garment out of the water onto the stone patio. I guess I won't be wearing them again. He does the same routine with my top.

"Do your flings," I whisper into his ear, "make you come undone at the seams like you do for me?"

He growls and stands up with me wrapped around him, so he can yank down his trunks to free himself. The cold air hits my back, and it feels good against the fire that is building inside me.

"I want you to fuck me so hard that the only person I should be thinking about right now is you—and not all of your previous conquests."

Graham plunges into me with one quick thrust, and I

arch my back at the forcefulness of the pleasure. He sits down with me on his lap and grips my hips. Up and down he lifts and pulls me back to him so that I am impaled. He thrusts his hips up as I am pulled down, and we slam into one another. He is controlling the movements as I am too weak to keep up the pace.

My breasts bob in and out of the water, which is now splashing over the sides.

"Graham!"

A few more rounds and I am screaming out in a rippling orgasm that keeps vibrating through me in wave upon wave.

"Yes, come all over my cock," he encourages. "I am right there with you, baby." He pants, thrusting upward as hard as he can, and then pulses his release inside me.

I flop over in his arms, completely spent. I rest my head on his shoulder and allow myself to drift off for a few minutes as my heart rate recovers back to normal.

Graham kisses my forehead and then nose. He sets me on the seat bench and climbs out of the hot tub to retrieve the blanket that I arrived in. He walks over, shuts off the jets, and then helps me out. The warmth of the blanket envelops me, and I am lifted up into his arms as he carries me back inside.

He makes his way through the house and into the master bedroom. He lays me gently on the plush area rug that is a few feet away from the glowing fireplace. He joins me there and covers my naked body with his.

"I'm going to love you now. Every inch of you. That is what separates you from everyone else. No one else has ever gotten that side to me. No one ever will, except for you, Angie."

He kisses down my body and licks up any remaining droplets of water. He places three soft kisses around my belly button and kisses a path down to my apex. He runs his tongue from my entrance all the way back up to my clit—where he spends extra time teasing me. I am held still with firm hands.

"I could make a feast out of you," he says approvingly. "So delicious. And all mine."

It doesn't take long until I am screaming with an orgasm. He crawls back up my body and pushes himself easily inside—now that I am primed and ready for him. His hands join mine, and he pulls them above my head and pins them to the rug. I am completely at his mercy. It feels wonderful and freeing, despite my being in a submissive position. He takes his time this round, and the slow burn is just as good as the explosive, impulsive burn. We release together and then pass out under the flickering light from the fire.

I startle awake with the sound of a zipper. My eyes take time to adjust to the artificial light from the lamps.

"Hey, sorry to scare you," Graham says softly. He is already dressed in dark gray dress pants and a crisp white shirt. "But we need to leave in the next thirty minutes if you want to get back in time for class."

I am wrapped up in a fleece blanket and surrounded by pillows. I must have fallen asleep, because the last thing I remember is Graham worshipping my body. I pull back the cover and remember why I am naked. The soreness between my legs will be a nice reminder this week of where I was this weekend. And who I was with.

"Okay. Yeah, I can't miss class."

"How about you take a quick shower, and we can eat in the car on the way back."

As I start moving around, my head is throbbing. "Can you turn down some of the lights? I have a splitting headache."

Graham moves toward me from his seat on the bed. "Shit. I should've made you drink some water yesterday before going to sleep. Between all the wine and the sweating from the hot tub, you're probably dehydrated."

"Yeah, that's probably it."

He kisses my forehead. "Go get rinsed off, and I'll have a fresh glass waiting for you on the nightstand."

"Thank you."

I scurry off into the bathroom, use the toilet, and then hop into the shower. It doesn't take me long to wash, rinse, and shave with the disposable razor that is still in its packaging. I dry off, brush my teeth, and blow out my damp locks. I apply the bare minimum makeup to cover up my bruising and swipe on some mascara to help my eyes look a little less tired.

In the bedroom, I slip on a more practical underwear and bra set, a pair of gray leggings, and a pink cashmere sweater. Graham may need to continue picking out my clothing, because the man has style. Cute silver ballet flats complete my look. I down the glass of water and hope that my head feels better soon.

I find Graham in the kitchen preparing to-go cups of coffee and some bags of pastries that must have been delivered here at the house. He hands me a few things to carry and locks up the house, escorting me to the waiting car.

"Good morning, Collins," I say softly.

"Same to you, Miss McFee."

I slide into the backseat and kick off my shoes for the long ride. I snap my belt into place and use the cup holder to rest my coffee after taking the first sip. It is delicious and exactly how I like it.

Graham joins me in the back and places his coffee adjacent to mine. We arrived at this lake house angry with each other and are now leaving mutually in love. What a difference a weekend away can make.

"I'm going to miss it here," I say, watching the house disappear as we move up the path.

"We can come back anytime you want," Graham says softly with a smile. "How's your head? I brought you a bottled water to drink in between your coffee." He hands me the bottle after he opens it and holds onto the lid. "Drink."

I listen and take a few huge gulps before handing it back to him to seal.

"Thank you for a wonderful weekend. I really did enjoy myself."

"I did too."

"When can I get my phone back?"

"When you promise me you'll not try to ditch your guards."

"So you are holding it hostage until I agree?"

"Yes."

I swallow a sip of my coffee. My safety is very important to him. And after Mark tried to rape me, I am actually relieved I will have someone looking out for me—despite it making it difficult to get my research done easily. "I promise."

Graham reaches into the back panel of the seat and pulls out a black cloth bag. He reaches inside and removes my phone. He places it into my hands.

"Thank you," I mutter, turning it on and waiting for my screen to come to life.

"I have some business email to tend to, if you don't mind. Feel free to eat something out of the bag or take a nap."

I nod and then get to work at checking my own email. I delete all of the junk mail, archive what is important, and then download the attachments from the Smoothie Cafe employee handbook that was sent to me. I glance over the recipe guide that I will surely have to memorize if I want to work there. I also read through the health protocol information. When my eyes begin to blur and my mind starts to drift, I move to my text messages and voicemails.

Numerous voice recordings are from Zander asking me to meet him. I can't keep avoiding him. It isn't fair. If I meet him at a public place, then I know Graham will get the line by line script of what was said during our conversation. So, I decide that it is best if I go to his place to talk. At least there, we can have some privacy to deal with this limbo we are both in. I type out a message to him.

Angie: Can I stop by your place tomorrow afternoon?

Zander: Of course :)

I hope he doesn't think this is good news. Why does everything have to be so complicated?

Next, I pull open all of the vague texts from my dad and read through them. I decide to cave and message him back.

Angie: Hey dad, what's up?

He doesn't respond right away, so I drink my coffee and enjoy a cream cheese danish from the bag of goodies. I open up my private *Bad Advice* email and answer a few questions on the blog site. The sun is now fully above the horizon and casting a beautiful orange glow on all of the trees. It is a sad reminder, however, that everything is about to die.

In between giving one-word answers to the recipient on the other end of the call, Graham hands me my water to remind me to sip it. I shake my head at his bossiness and ability to multitask and still give me nonverbal orders.

The buzz of my phone indicates an incoming message, and I open up my app and read what my dad typed out.

Dad: I need to borrow $75,000 to pay for some bills.

I stare at the amount. Surely it is a typo. And for bills? He is lying to me.

Angie: I already gave you my entire inheritance to get you out of trouble before. I can't keep doing this.

Dad: I have no one else to lean on. Just you.

Angie: I don't have that kind of money.

Angie: I can't keep enabling your bad habits.

I am still bitter over him using my money that mom left me in her will. What a waste. This is how our messages over the past three years have gone. He asks for money. I give in. Then, I don't hear from him again until he needs more.

Dad: But I am your father.

But I am your daughter. Someone you should have taken care of. And loved. This is manipulation.

"Everything okay?"

The sound of Graham's voice startles me, and I drop my phone onto the mat on the floor of the car. I reach for it and then place it in the holder on the door.

"Yeah, everything will be fine."

He eyes me suspiciously but doesn't press. Why he cuts me slack now, I have no idea. I am relieved, nonetheless.

"Here, give me your feet, and I'll rub them."

I move the pastry bag and prop my feet up on his lap, leaning against the window. "You know the pathway to my heart."

He smiles as I moan in pleasure while his fingers pull the tension from my body.

"What does your week look like?"

"I have classes and my final paper to work on before I can graduate. Nothing really going on this week other than that." And talking with Zander tomorrow. "Maybe go to a workout class with Claire. She used to peer pressure me to attend with her, but this time I may go willingly because I do have a lot of fun."

He listens intently and shows interest without interrupting me. We sip on our coffees and just enjoy each other's company. It's hard to go back to normal life after coming off of a much-needed weekend with Graham. I will have more down time which means I'll have ample time to think about how bad things could have gotten with Mark and have a chance to fully freak out. Graham might want revenge—but I do too. No woman deserves to be treated the way he treated me.

And I plan to make him pay.

21

"What's your biggest regret?"

We are about an hour from the city, and Graham is taking full advantage of me being confined in the backseat of his car with him. I can't run away or escape his interrogating questions.

I don't need much time to think—these emotions have been weighing on my mind for years. "I have two," I answer hesitantly. My natural instinct is to avoid.

He waits patiently for me to continue. His hands have moved up to my calves and knees. I relax into his comforting touch.

"My first one is not saying goodbye."

His lips straighten into a hard line and his mind seems to deposit the information into its bank. "Please explain."

"I'm sure you did an extensive search on my past. You probably have a lot of the information already."

"Tell me anyway." His hands run up my legs, kneading my flesh.

If we are going to be in an actual relationship with each other, then I have to open up some, even if just the slightest amount.

"My mom died when I was twelve. My twin brother died in a car accident when we were eighteen. I never got to say a proper goodbye to either of them." I am amazed at how I am not crying and that I can even understand my own words. Some part of me decides to continue. "My mom had cancer. Breast," I specify. "She went through all of the surgeries and treatments. Had several months to celebrate being in remission. And then of course it came back with a vengeance. Except this time it was ovarian. They are linked, you know? Some people don't realize it, but they are. And the latter type is vicious and more aggressive. Always a death sentence. Both cancers resulted from the same type of genetic mutation." My hands get squeezed, and I get the will to continue. "As a little girl, all the adults around me would speak as if she would get better. That my mom was strong enough to fight it. That I would not grow up from twelve on without her. Everyone needs a mom. And I lost mine."

"Oh, baby." He doesn't say he's sorry and for that I am thankful. He squeezes me tighter and rubs my limbs in a soothing rhythm. His love allows me to open up even more.

"There's a test to see if I'm a carrier and at high risk. It's a fifty-fifty chance I have it. For years, I just couldn't seem to bring myself to get genetically tested. It's just as easy as drawing blood. Such a simple task to determine my fate. Well, when I met with the doctor at Entice, I had them run the test based on my family history. I was already getting stuck with a needle anyway. So I figured that I would like to know now that I am older and can make proactive decisions about my body if I am a carrier."

Graham straightens his posture but keeps his hands on my legs. "And?"

"I have the results in an envelope in my nightstand. Just couldn't bring myself to open them."

"We can open them together," he says softly. "If you would like."

"See, that brings me back to my second regret… Being the girl who always needs rescuing."

He watches me intently. "I don't mind rescuing you."

"But sometimes being rescued has a steep price."

"Go on."

"My twin brother was that guy…the one who would help anyone out. He was always trying to be the father figure to me that my dad couldn't be after mom died. We were all a mess. But James somehow was able to pull his life together the best—even at the age of twelve. Well, no one thought he would ever die so soon. I never got a chance to say goodbye or thank him for getting me through the years of my life that I needed a mom for. He was the strongest one in our family. I was—and in a lot of ways still am—the weak one."

Graham takes my hands in his and massages the flesh, encouraging me to continue.

"My dad sent James and me away when my mom got sick the second time. Gave us to his brother—my uncle. And my aunt. Although she had weird work shifts and wasn't around all the time. I don't remember much from that time." That fact alone eats at me. How can someone completely lose track of a big section of their life? It's as if I didn't even exist during that time. "I was a shell of a person. But really, James and I were obligations that no one really wanted." I take a cleansing breath and continue before I lose the courage. "I just know that James and I harbored a lot of bad feelings toward our dad. It wasn't until my mom grew severely depressed that we were able to come back home. She missed us too much. I would dedicate my time after school to helping her live out her life, knowing that every minute that she was alive was a gift. I would wash her hair and help her dress and spoon feed her whenever she was too weak to pick up the utensil. She lost her sparkle and it broke my heart. Part of me wanted to be valued so I wouldn't get sent away again. But the other part wanted my mom's love…even though she would keep telling me that I never had to work for it. Love just is. Those were her words."

"Oh baby. I wish you never had to deal with any of that. Is that why you don't want to talk to your dad now?"

I am saying too much. And I am jumbling everything together and partially out of order—but talking about it feels better. It is oddly therapeutic. "Well. After James died, I quit my semester in college and tried to keep my two-member family together. I had a few injuries to tend to and it was easier to just take some time off. My dad needed me. But I couldn't keep him away from the bottle. Or the casinos." I stop and try to catch my breath. "And I—"

"Shhh…let it out, sweetheart. It guts me to see you sob like this, but it will make you feel better."

No. Not even a little white pill can do that. I have spent years trying to feel numb. "I had no will to live. I just existed. Nothing could fix what was broken. And I felt just that. I started to gain control of my life by cutting."

"You cut yourself?"

"Not for long. But I would slice at my scars left over from the car accident. That's why some are crooked and some are straight on my thighs."

He has me pulled into his body tightly. I am on his lap weeping and sniffling and purging the memories.

"My dad sold our house in Baker City. That was the last straw for me. I went to surprise him one weekend with Claire when we didn't have too much studying. And we saw a whole new family sitting on the porch and playing in the backyard. He never even told me he was considering selling it. Claimed it wasn't my house and it wasn't my choice. So, Claire drove us back to our dorm that we shared and insisted on me being part of her family, since all of mine were gone." I whisper the last words, as my emotions get caught in my throat. "Granted, Claire's family is not the best at showing love either. She rarely talks about them, but I can read between the lines. So that incident bonded the two of us together more than we could have imagined. We became sisters in that moment." I am rambling, but Graham seems to appreciate me talking, so I continue. "I think my dad sold the house to pay one of his bookies. The house was already paid off. It wasn't like it needed to be sold. He already blew through my inheritance that I was able to start withdrawing from when I turned eighteen. But he convinced me to give it to him. Guilted me over it. So the money I was going to use for college tuition no longer exists. And while I don't know exactly, James's portion is probably gone too."

"Fucking hell, baby. You've been through so much."

"Moving to Portland and making the friends I have now has been life changing. My friends are my family." The fact that I may lose Zander is eating me alive. And another regret will probably result out of that no-win situation.

I let the remaining tears slide down my cheeks and use the sleeves of my shirt to soak up the moisture. As much as it hurts to share my life with Graham, I feel like a weight has been lifted off my shoulders. A burden gone from trying to hide that part of me for so long.

He never takes his hands from my body, always rubbing circles on my back or massaging my palms. For the first time in many years, I feel cherished. And I like it. We just sit. And find understanding with each other.

Graham hands me my water to remind me to keep drinking it, and I realize that I no longer have a headache. He rubs my ankle with one hand and snacks on a muffin with the other.

"But how does this all circle back to you regretting being the girl who needs rescuing?" he asks softly.

"My memory is hazy the night of the car accident. But I am almost positive James was coming to my rescue late that night. He always would be the one I would call if I needed anything. It was rainy and foggy and someone hit us and fled."

"Is this why you have a hard time letting me support you and try to make your life easier?"

His question sets off a lightbulb in my head. I am very stubborn over those who want to help me, and it might all stem from my regrets with James and how he died and I lived. I shake my head. "Yeah, probably. It makes sense when I think back to my fears and regrets."

"And here I am, always swooping in. Trying to fix everything. Because I have this compulsive need for control. I have this drive to make sure those I love are safe and taken care of. When the one woman who needs it the most, resists it the most."

"We are like oil and vinegar," I say with a bitter laugh.

"But together, we make a delicious salad dressing."

I throw back my head and laugh through the tears. Leave it to him to wring out every emotion from me with one conversation. His fingers catch a few tears and wipe them away.

"Will you spend Thanksgiving with me at my family's house in Hillsboro?"

I think about when the holiday actually is. Claire and I usually do a Friendsgiving event prior to the actual date. But with Ethan being annoying and Zander most likely not wanting to show after we have our discussion, I doubt there will be enough people to make it worth all the cooking that would have to occur.

"Is Claire going to be celebrating the holiday with her Virginia family?"

"Doubt it. They will probably be busy with their restaurant biz."

"If she has no one to be with, feel free to invite her as well."

"Thank you," I say softly, "for including her." I can tell he is trying. Graham and Claire's friendship status would be classified as *complicated*—at best. But that is only because "hostile" is not an option on social media.

"So will you come?"

"Don't you think it's too soon to meet the family?"

"Why does there need to be some arbitrary timetable?"

"I guess that's true." But I don't want to fall in love with his family and then something happens to us, and I lose more people. My heart cannot handle another loss right now.

"So you'll say yes?"

"Hmm," I say sweetly, "I'll let you know. Got to check my calendar and see if I can pencil you in."

His growl startles me but I am bound by his arms. He wiggles his fingers along my sides, and I burst into a fit of giggles. I love this playful side to him—almost as much as I love his take-no-prisoners side. But I can't tell him that little secret. Because that is information only my pussy and I need to care about.

"Just say yes. It is faster than saying a thousand nos." His fingers tickle my inner thighs, and I jolt upward to move away from him. He holds me in place. "Say yes and I'll stop."

I squirm and pant for air as he manipulates me into submission. My core rubs along his groin, and I am starting to turn myself on.

"Okay, Okay!"

He pauses his attack. "Okay, what? I need to hear the words."

I compose myself and catch my breath. "Okay, I'll go with you to your parents' house for Thanksgiving."

"See, that wasn't so hard."

I grind my butt down on his thighs and give him a smirk. "Except now we are both turned on and only have ten minutes until we are at my place."

"Then let's use our time wisely," he suggests.

I slip off the seat bench and get on my knees. I start unzipping Graham's pants and start pulling—

His hands move to my hair. "Not what I had in mind."

"Oh well," I say with a shrug. "Some things are just out of your hands."

I finish releasing him before he can stop me and swallow him whole. I hear a string of curse words followed by my name. I go to work getting him to come undone in under ten minutes.

I lick and suck and tease him until I am swallowing every drop he has to give me.

"Holy hell, Angie, where do you even learn these moves from?" he asks, out of breath.

I smile wickedly. "Porn."

"My naughty girl." He zips himself back up and plops me back onto his lap. "I don't even have time to return the favor."

"This time was about you for once. And I am perfectly okay with that."

He kisses me hard on the lips. Collins pulls into the parking spot near my car.

"Sure I can't buy you a car?"

"Yup, I'm positive," I say with a scowl.

"How about I lend you one?"

"Nope." I exit the backseat and Graham follows. "What are you doing?"

"Escorting you inside."

"Why?"

"Because that is what good boyfriends do."

I look at him and give him a slow once-over. "What do bad boyfriends do?"

He pulls me closer and bends down so he can whisper in my ear. "Fuck you until you forget your name."

I swallow hard and try to keep my composure. "Lucky you, I crave all things bad."

He bites my lobe and laughs at my sudden jerk. I pivot and climb the steps leading up to the door. I feel him right on my heel. I am nervous to let him inside. There is no time for a quick romp, and the last ten minutes of the car ride have left me wanting *more*.

"I just need to grab my book and school bag," I say, unlocking the door.

"Sure, no problem. You still have fifteen minutes before we have to leave."

I turn the doorknob and let us inside. I barely make it two feet before we are blinded by a buck-naked Ethan and Claire having sex on our couch.

"Fuck!" they say in unison.

"I wasn't expecting you home today," Claire screeches, trying to cover her boobs with her hands.

I put my hand up over my eyes. "Ugh, Claire! Those cushions cannot be sanitized."

"I have a condom on," Ethan says frantically. "Don't worry."

Graham turns me away from the scene and pushes me up the stairs as I continue to yell back, "I thought you guys were over with! Next time warn me. I can never erase that image, thanks a lot."

"It was makeup sex," Claire bellows so I can hear a floor away, making Graham chuckle beside me.

"That couch is going to need to be burned now," I groan, entering my room and digging through my belongings to make sure I have everything.

Graham clears his throat. "Well, at least they are back together."

"At least I'll be eating bacon every time he visits. Silver lining."

When I have everything I need, we head back to the waiting car, and Collins drives us toward the campus. Within minutes we arrive, and he pulls up as close as he can to the building where I have Human Behavior.

"When can I see you again?" Graham asks, giving me a light kiss on the lips.

"I'm free on Wednesday after class."

"Perfect, I'll make sure I am free as well. I have some business to tend to now, but Collins will bring you back to your place after your class ends. Or wherever else you want to go. I'm trying my best not to keep you in my pocket."

"Okay, sounds good. Thank you."

"Please be good."

I make a face. "I'm always good."

"Right," he says in a disbelieving tone.

We kiss goodbye, and I walk briskly to class. I skip down the steps of the auditorium and look to see if Bryce is here first. I spot the back of his head and the crutches leaning against the seat beside him. Oh no.

"Hey, what happened to you?" I ask, pointing to his gear.

"I wish I had a hero story to share. But I slipped on an empty beer bottle on the stairs and fell. It's as lame as it sounds."

I take a sip of the iced espresso drink that he picked up for me and wonder how he even managed to do so with crutches. "Well, that just sucks. Is it broken?"

"Just a sprain to the ankle," he explains, lifting his pant leg to show me the wrapping. "And luckily, not too painful. Definitely manageable with the help of some good meds."

"Well, that is good."

The professor walks into class and stands at her podium. Today is a writing assessment. I did not prepare much for it —but then again, writing comes easily to me. She sets a timer and has her TA pass out writing booklets. Everyone is asked to sit with a desk between them and the next person to avoid the temptation to cheat. I write my name on the front cover of my booklet and then fold it back to read the first social story about addiction. Several questions follow that require a paragraph each.

The assessment is supposed to last about two hours, and I take every bit of it to complete mine. Bryce reaches for his crutches to turn in his booklet, while I reread my answers to check for any flaws. His fall must have just happened because his coordination is not mastered at all. He clumsily bumps into his bag and knocks a few things out.

"I'll get them," I whisper and bend down to put the items inside.

My eyes connect with a small orange bottle of pain pills. I look at the label and see that he was given thirty pills to last him over a week's time. I glance ahead and see that Bryce is still trying to get down the stairs. I pop open the bottle and take out a small handful—just to get me by when my shoulder pain is excruciating or if I need to take the edge off my stress level. I slip the white discs into my Altoids container and see that they are the same size as the ones I have already and have the same engraved markings. He already said his pain is manageable, so these will probably expire before he ever uses them all. I finish tossing items into his bag and then get up to turn in my own test.

"Do you need help getting to your car?" I ask, handing Bryce his bag.

"Nah, I need to practice on my own, before I am stupid enough to hurt the other ankle."

When I make it out to the parking lot, Collins is waiting for me, right where he dropped me off just hours ago.

The privacy screen is down so I greet him with a wave.

"Where to, ma'am?"

"Back to my place, please."

"Certainly."

"So how was your fuckation?" Claire asks, while shoving a Slim Jim into her mouth.

I laugh at her terminology and choice of highly processed snack meat. "Probably tied with yours." As much sex as Graham and I had, "fuckation" seems like an accurate name for our getaway.

She laughs and breaks off a piece of the encased meat with her front teeth—like a beaver would. "So, tell me how you ended up on a weekend romp fest with Graham."

"It was unexpected really." I turn in my seat to face her while she rests on the contaminated couch. Condom or no condom, there is definitely some DNA evidence on those cushions. Yuck.

"How so?"

Even though our conversation is lighthearted and fun,

my eyes start to tear up when I start to dissect what actually led to Graham and I going to Lake Chelan.

Claire moves from the couch and kneels at my side. "What happened, Angie?"

"Mark Tanner tricked me into believing he had a recruiter friend visiting from *Pacific Press*. He lured me up into a hotel room and tried to—" Tears roll down my cheeks and a knot forms in my throat.

She shakes her head back and forth. "No."

I nod my head as a sob breaks free, and I stutter out the words. "He tried…to rape…me."

"That fucker!"

"He drugged me. Told me I would forget everything. But the dosage wasn't working because I remember everything. I could feel his touch, but couldn't move my body. He hit me on the face before Graham and his men busted through the door and Graham beat the shit out of him. It was a bloodbath. So we fled and went to his place on Lake Chelan."

"Fuck." She wraps her arms around my waist and rests her head against my thighs. "I'm so sorry you had to endure that. I just…I just can't believe he did that. Did he think he wasn't going to get caught?"

"I'm not sure. Graham thinks Mark was setting him up. But I have no idea what to believe. It seems like Mark and his pharmaceutical company are using their platform to make illegal drugs and conduct human test trials on agency girls to check their efficacy."

"He has to have other help."

"Yeah, I agree. I have a few suspects I am checking out."

She lifts her head up from my lap. "No. No, Angie. You need to stay out of this."

"This is my chance to prove to Dr. Williams and any local news stations that I can uncover, research, and write a worthwhile story. And what better way than to use being a victim to illustrate exactly what it feels like to be helpless? Stories like these can spread like wildfire. Soon, other cities will have whistleblowers speaking out. I need to do this for me to heal. However, I also need to give the victims a voice. I want to be the start of the trend—not the dying tail end of another. Change is made by being brave enough to speak out about topics that make people uncomfortable."

"Does Graham know you are still going to pursue this?"

"Of course not. I haven't even told him my career goals or my real major. I'll probably have to wait until I have my article go to print first. He has been literally trying to shut down any attempt I make at figuring this all out."

"Good."

"Good? Really Claire? Whose side are you on? I am less than two months away from learning my fate when it comes to graduation and a possible internship. And you are rooting for me to fail again?"

"No, not at all. Can't you write about something less dangerous? Like puppy mills or how food labels are a lie? Sexual harassment on the job or the hidden costs of MLM businesses?"

"Those are not things I am passionate about. I need that spark of inspiration if I am going to make it in this type of business."

"Zander has texted me a few times asking about you. Are things going to be as weird as I think they'll be?"

I frown. "Yeah, I doubt anything will ever be the same again. I'm going to his place tomorrow to chat and clear the air."

"Good luck."

"Thanks. So, how are things with Ethan? What changed?"

"His ex-wife, Deena, is crazy. Like I have no idea what he ever saw in her. Ethan did a ton of groveling and then he lavished me with some pretty nice…" She pauses as if she lost her train of thought. She sits back and crisscrosses her legs.

"Gifts?"

"Sure." She nods. "We'll go with that."

I shake my head at her.

"So, semi-off topic, but asking for a friend…"

"A.k.a., asking for yourself."

She doesn't deny it. "How often do you clean out the kitty?"

"What?"

"Like do you use a douche?" she asks seriously.

"Aren't those things outlawed by every single gynecologist for causing UTIs? Along with colored toilet paper from the eighties?"

"Well then, why do they still freaking sell them?"

"I have no idea. But why are we talking about this?"

"I used one. Not because he was complaining about my fine china. But because I didn't want him eating from a dirty plate."

I make a face. "Ugh Claire, you and your visuals."

"Well, I didn't want to have any clitty litter."

I burst out laughing over her terminology. "You are too much."

"If you're going to visit my snack shack, then it better not be expired. If you know what I mean."

"I never know what you mean, Claire."

One second we can be crying our eyes out in sadness and the next we can be crying in silliness.

"Not like he ever complained before," she continues, "but now that I know what it feels like to lose him, I am trying my best to impress him."

"So you sprayed some fragrant liquid stuff up inside, and now you think you have an infection?"

"Yeah, pretty much."

"Well, that sucks."

"I keep itching down there."

"Oh no."

"Oh no is right. And it burns a little when I pee."

We both laugh over her mishaps from the weekend. It is always easy with Claire, and if she leaves for Los Angeles after this semester ends, I will miss her beyond words.

22

I wake to the sound of a truck idling outside. I roll out of bed and make my way over to the window. I kneel on the seat bench and pull back the drapes. Four men all wearing navy polos and dark wash jeans lower the back ramp. Stamped along the side of the truck are the words Horton's Movers.

I grab my phone from my nightstand and dial Graham's number. It's nine in the morning, and I am already feeling like my blood is going to boil. If this is what I think it is, then this is not him giving me the freedom I need.

"Good morning, sweetheart."

"Maybe."

I hear the squeak of his chair and the sound of his mug hitting a coaster. "What's wrong?"

"Please tell me this is a mistake."

"You are going to need to elaborate more."

"Please tell me that the four men who appear to be

walking up my townhouse steps wearing Horton's Movers logo polos are not here to move any of my shit."

"We are together, Angela."

"So."

"So, naturally I would want you under my roof so we can spend more time together and get to know one another. This is a normal progression in relationships, sweetheart."

I count to ten. And again. "We have been in a relationship no longer than forty-eight hours. Can you at least exercise some self-control?"

"I did. Hence, why I let you sleep at your place last night."

"Oh, then I should thank you for being so reasonable!"

"Yes, yes you should."

The sound of the doorbell makes me jump and nearly knock the phone out of my hand. I ignore it.

"Graham, this is not how you show me that you can be civilized. You never even asked me!"

"Well, then bring nothing here. I'll provide whatever you need or we can go shopping together. I just figured you would want something from your place that will make you feel like home."

"Being here in my home makes me feel like home."

"I plan to see a lot of you, and I don't feel comfortable with you being there with Ethan walking about naked whenever he feels the need to strip down and wave his dick around."

I giggle at his words. Claire and Ethan definitely like utilizing every surface of this townhouse for some kinky reason. "I don't know…"

"Keep your bed there, visit it whenever you want. You

can have girls' days or nights or whatever, but at least have the understanding that you will mostly be here. If you don't want to bring anything, send away the movers. If you want to bring some of your items, then have them pack them up. Just direct them to do what you want done, and it'll be done."

"Fine," I grumble.

"I'm glad *you* can be reasonable."

I huff at his patronizing tone, tossing my hands up into the air. "Bye, Graham."

I throw on a hoodie and jog down the stairs to let the men inside. I give them directives to pack up all my sewing materials, a few drawers of clothes, my collection of romance novels, and my electronics. Sadly, the job could have been handled by half a man and a pickup truck. I don't have very many personal belongings—and definitely not many sentimental things that are must-haves.

I meander into the kitchen to grab a drink from the fridge and text Zander.

Angie: What time are you free today for me to stop over?

Zander: How about 1? The roommates will be gone.

I check my voice messages and see that I got a recording from the manager at the Campus Smoothie Cafe. My finger hovers over the call-back button, and I decide to just take the leap. No better way to get closer to Paul without blowing my cover than working where he works.

"Hi, this is Angela McFee. I am returning your phone call about coming in for an interview this morning."

"Yes, of course, how about stopping in around eleven? Were you able to study the recipe booklet in case we are interested in moving forward with the practicum part of the interview process?"

"Yeah, I think I have all the recipes memorized, and I read through all of the health protocols."

"Great. I'll see you shortly."

I end the call and jog back upstairs to get ready for the day. I work around the movers and am thankful they are done by the time I need to leave. I grab my bag, slip on my new favorite silver ballet flats that Graham got me, and head out to my car.

I arrive at the cafe with fifteen minutes to spare, so I use the time to review the recipe booklet on my phone. There are twenty different smoothies that have base ingredients. Add-ons cost extra and can easily adapt any drink to meet health, fitness, or dietary needs. Even though there are cheat-sheet cards posted around the prep station, it is best to have everything memorized to speed up the process of getting customers served the drinks fast.

I pull my hair back into a bun and secure it on the top of my head with several bands. I take a deep breath, exit the car, and walk up the sidewalk to the cafe. I see Paul behind the counter and give him a wave and a smile. I haven't seen him in person since the Halloween party—when he got drunk and I snooped through his room. That was a strange night with so many missing pieces to the puzzle. Maybe I can get closer to him and learn more.

"I see you are serious about the job," Paul says smoothly from behind the counter.

I shrug. "Yeah, I need to pay the bills."

"Well, it's all about the tips," he says, pointing to the jar resting beside the register.

I nod my head and then make my way over to the "Employees Only" door that appears to be an office area. I knock and wait.

The door opens.

"You must be Angela," the man answers. He has a name tag on that says "Manager Lawrence Woods" and appears to be my age. "It is nice to meet you. I'm Larry."

"Thank you."

He moves back to his desk and pulls out a file with my name on it. "You have years of experience in customer service, I see. The bakery owners gave you a glowing recommendation. So, really all that's left is the practicum portion. If you get hired, you will probably be shadowing Paul for the first week, since he has a similar schedule to what you are looking for."

I inwardly sigh in relief. I was hoping our schedules would overlap and specifically tried my best to learn Paul's before I put down my own availability. "That sounds great."

"So, here is a new work shirt you can slip on over what you are wearing. We'll head out and have you start making some drinks. Just be sure to wash your hands and not touch your face or hair in any way. If you do, wash up again. All of our ingredients are scooped or poured, so no need for gloves—unless you have a current hand injury. I will sit off to the side and just observe. Try to relax. You have obviously served people before in your previous bakery job. So just treat it as such."

I smile and relax my shoulders. I slip the T-shirt that says "Got Smoothies?" over my head and follow Larry out of the office. I put my belongings in a cubby below the bar and wash my hands. Paul is making drinks for a few people in line. He winks at me as he turns on the blender.

"You know how to work a register, so how about you take the next person in line," Larry says softly, sitting up on one of the bar stools at the far end of the counter.

I make my way over to the register and look up at the next customer. I about choke when I see my asshole ex, Russell, standing there with his tanned face and stupid shades on top of his head. He is wearing khaki shorts and probably still pretending he is on an island somewhere—despite it being a chilly fifty degrees in Portland.

"How can I help you?" I ask professionally. I try to smile, and I'm sure it is more like a grimace. His eyes rake over me, and I feel like I need to shower.

I can feel Paul's eyes on me as well, and I instantly get nervous that I am going to mess this whole job interview up just because my ex has thrown me off my game. I pull my shoulders back and take a deep breath. I can do this.

"Keto Chocolate with an extra scoop of protein powder. Small."

I punch in his order and calculate the total with the add-on. I then move over to the workstation and scoop up the powders, ice, heavy cream, and almond milk. I put the lid on the blender and turn it on. I grab a small cup, write the name of the smoothie along the side with a Sharpie, and then fill it with the blended concoction. It smells better than I think it probably tastes. But I was never one for skipping the sugar. I snap the flat lid on and grab a straw.

"Here you go, that will be four dollars and ninety-six cents." I take the crisp five-dollar bill from Russell's hand. Preppy Boy probably starches and irons his money after he takes it out of his trust fund.

"I want the change," he says aggressively, as if I would have shorted him.

I nod, place the money into the register, and pull out four pennies. He takes a sip of his beverage and his face is expressionless. He then takes the pennies and drops them dramatically into the tip jar—one by one. What did I ever see in him? He is such an asshole.

He moves over to the bar and sits by himself and just follows my moves with his eyes as I wait on the next customer. I sanitize my hands and fall into a rhythm working beside Paul. We don't communicate with words, and I'm careful not to lose my focus.

Larry gets into line, and I make him a medium Peaches N' Cream smoothie—which ends my practicum.

"This is really good, Angie. I think I have enough information to officially congratulate you on being hired. You can start next Monday. I'll email you the schedule and you can confirm it this week."

"Thank you so much."

I reach into the cubby behind the bar and grab my bag. I notice that Paul has his book bag in a separate section and marvel at how easily I would be able to snoop through it if he was taking a break. I say my goodbyes and exit the shop.

It only takes me a few minutes to get to Zander's townhouse. The place is quiet, for once, with the roommates gone. I ring the doorbell, and Zander lets me inside.

"Hey, Angie," he says softly. He looks down at my shirt, and I realize I forgot to take off the added layer.

"I just got hired at the smoothie shop today. I start next week."

He gives me a nod. "Seems like we're both working entry level jobs."

For some reason, his comment stings. Maybe because I have been working relentlessly to follow my dream at being an investigative journalist, and within the next two months, I will either succeed or fail. "It's just temporary."

He gives me a lopsided smile. "Hope so…only speaking for me."

The once carefree Zander who always saw the bright side to life is now just a deflated version of himself. I would only be lying to myself if I didn't take some responsibility for his outlook change. It stabs at my heart.

He points to the couch, and I sit on one end while he takes up the other. The kitten climbs onto my lap, and I rub at its fur.

"Does she have a name yet?"

"Chewie."

"Aww, that's cute."

"Except when she gnaws on all of your shoes like a puppy would."

I laugh at his facial expression. Maybe we *can* still be friends. Maybe this is all just a misunderstanding. Maybe we can go back to how things used to be.

I clear my throat. "I miss hanging out. I hate how we left things, Z."

He studies my face. "Are you willing to give us a chance?"

I swallow and furrow my brow. I can't meet his eyes. "What does that mean? We have hung out for years. Celebrated accomplishments together. It's not that we don't know each other."

"But those things were done under the friends category. I want *more*. I want a relationship. Something beyond platonic hugs and gestures. Can you give me a chance to date you and see if it leads to anything more? I am only asking for a real chance, Angie. This doesn't have to start out as a big commitment. Let's just see where life takes us. But I want to do it with you by my side."

"My heart is elsewhere." I annunciate each syllable carefully, and each word seems to cut Zander like a knife as his once hopeful expression turns to anger.

"You are going to throw away four years of memories to fall at the altar of a guy you just met and barely know?" He gets up off the couch to pace. "He won't care for you and honor you like I will."

"If this was a different place in time…"

"No," he says, shaking his head adamantly. He stops just a foot away from me and glares with fire in his eyes. "Please don't fucking say shit like that to me. Acting like I even had a chance. Don't you dare give me the 'if this was a different time and different place' trash. I deserve better than that."

His frustration guts me. I don't know how to fix this. I am about to lose someone else who I love, and he is slipping through the cracks without a rescue strategy. Chewie scurries off my lap, disappearing into the other room, and I wish that she would return so I had something to do with my trembling hands.

"Please, Zander," I beg. "Can we just keep being friends?" Even though that is what I want, I know there is no way to undo what's been done. I already know his intentions. And he already knows mine. It would be super awkward at best. And just sitting here now on the sofa, where I've spent a lot of time the past four years, suddenly feels weird.

For the first time in all these years, I feel like I don't belong. That I am unwelcome here.

"I hate that you are so perfect for me. And I hate that you are going to hate yourself for breaking my heart. Because Angie, that is what you are doing to me."

"I'm sorry," I mouth. I can't be here anymore. I can't sit here and listen to his heart breaking without mine crumbling apart too. I lift myself up off the couch and head for the front door.

His body fills the door frame as I stand on the top step and look up into his devastated eyes. "When he shatters your heart again—and you know he will—I might be around to lean on. Or just maybe, it will be too late."

I give him a nod and then walk down the steps as tears drip from my eyes onto the concrete. I sit in my parked car and watch as he slams the door shut to his townhouse. I wait until I have some of my eyesight back and then pull out of the parking spot and head back home.

Claire is resting on the couch when I let myself inside.

"Wow, you look like shit."

"Thanks," I mutter, "that is a great way to build up my self-esteem again."

She frowns. "What happened?"

"I told Zander that my heart was elsewhere. And he—"

"Didn't take it well?"

"Understatement."

"Want a distraction?" she proposes.

"The last distraction you gave me had me on a blind date that I never even wanted."

"And we know how that turned out," she says cheerfully.

I scrunch up my face over her prideful joy. "Yeah, it turned out horribly."

"No. No, it did not. We managed to make Teddy Graham jealous, which in turn made him extra obsessive," she says, waving her hands wildly through the air to emphasize each point. "Which in turn helped you achieve the most mind-blowing orgasms of your life."

I look at her as she rattles off all of her event dominoes as if she were the mastermind behind all of Graham's actions. Leave it to Claire to take credit for a bunch of coincidences.

She shrugs. "See? You owe me actually."

"Owe you?"

"Yuppers. You owe me big."

"And how am I going to repay you?"

She rubs her hands together. "Come exercise with me."

I look at her suspiciously. This doesn't seem like a great way to pay her back, which makes me speculate that this is not just a normal treadmill or stairclimber workout. "What is the title of this class?"

"It's a pool class."

"So I need a swimsuit?"

"Sure. But let me pick it out."

"Fine. I'll do it."

"Obviously. You owe me," she says cockily. "Oh, and because I am the generator of the best ideas."

"I'll be the judge of that."

23

"Why are we not going to the indoor pool area?" I ask stupidly. This is happening again. She tricked me. I can feel it in my bones.

"Just chill and follow me. You'll love this."

I grind my teeth together. "Love what? You haven't been very clear."

"Life is all about surprises and taking chances. It's good for the soul."

"So is honesty," I point out, making her sigh.

I follow Claire into another studio room that is dimly lit and has black sheer curtains pooled on the floor below the windows. This is an all-female class and relatively small compared to the Zumba class we attended together. Large metal poles are sporadically placed, spanning from the floor to the ceiling. I stare at them. And then it hits me…

"Claire!"

"What's up, buttercup?"

"Oh no. No. No. No. You said pool."

"Spelled P-O-L-E."

"You cannot be serious. We are pole dancing?"

"It's a surprisingly great workout."

"I'm wearing a two-piece!" My coverup is partially see-through. Underneath I have a solid black, conservative two-piece suit. It looks more like a dance outfit with the boy shorts and tank bustier. But still.

"We can hit the swimming pool up afterwards. But look around," she says, sweeping her hand out in a fanning motion. "You will see other girls wearing much less. So chill your butt cheeks."

She is right. I definitely don't stand out. I set my gym bag next to Claire's on a bench that is along the back wall. I take a gulp of my water and put my phone on silent. I can see that Graham has sent a few text messages, but I don't have time to check them.

The instructor introduces herself, starts the music, and adjusts her microphone headset.

"We are going to start the class by first going over the six basic movements. I will show you what it should look like. Then we will practice together. And then afterwards, we will perform everything to a song and really get into it. Remember that if anything seems too challenging or if you feel like any of your muscles are pulling too hard, either stop or modify your movements. This is a confidence building class. This is not meant to show off or be a class on comparing to each other. We as women are often our own critics—our worst enemies. So as I do these movements, I want you to find your inner strength and focus on that. There is beauty even in the struggle. Embrace it."

I watch in awe as the instructor does each skill and gives

us a fun name to remember it by. She is extremely flexible and agile.

I practice each move as best I can but really just have fun and laugh with Claire—who, despite being extremely athletic, is struggling as well. We won't be joining Cirque du Soleil anytime soon and that's okay. By the time the real workout begins on tempo with the music, I am so worn out and sweaty that hitting up the pool is actually sounding really good.

After I shower and put on my lounge clothes, Claire and I head out to her car.

"What's on the agenda for tonight?" I ask her, looking at the clock and seeing it is only five o'clock.

"Ethan wants my Hershey hole."

"Uh, what?"

She sighs. "He's pestering me to try anal."

My mouthful of water explodes onto the sidewalk. "Can you at least warn me before you blurt things out like that? In public, mind you!"

"What? It's just sex," she says flatly. "Completely natural. No reason to be ashamed. I thought as a feminist, you would be pioneering ways to break the stigma, ya? It isn't just about a man's pleasure anymore. Women have feelings too."

"Some of us have a bit more reservation about talking about it on the street," I whisper-shout. "And who just tries anal as if it's a spur-of-the-moment thing? Aren't you supposed to work up to that?"

"The girls in the porn videos I watched—solely for educational purposes—seemed to be into it."

"Oh yeah, that sounds like really sound research there."

"I just think that giving it over is equivalent to an engagement. So, basically it's a type of commitment."

I don't exactly see her reasoning but don't want to continue any more discussion over her asshole, so I don't ask any follow-up questions. I am sure she will over-share after the act is over with at a later date.

Claire unlocks the doors, and I slide into the passenger side. I check my messages while she tries not to hit a row of parked cars. I really want to know how much her car insurance premiums are. Graham's texts are just checking in with me to see how I am doing. They are sweet, and I can already tell he is trying not to smother me like he has in the past. I dial his number instead of texting him back.

"Hello," the female voice greets, catching me off guard.

"Oh, um, sorry. I think I have the wrong number." I stumble over the words, and I pull my phone back to look at the screen just to double check.

"Hello? Miss McFee?"

I shake my head at the unexpectedness of hearing a voice other than Graham's. "Excuse me?"

"Miss McFee, it's Kylie. From Hoffman Headquarters. I am Mr. Hoffman's new assistant. We met a couple of weeks ago." She rushes to get everything out, probably in fear that I will hang up and get the wrong impression—which is pretty accurate to how I was feeling about thirty seconds ago.

"Oh, Kylie. Hi." Why is she answering Graham's personal cell phone?

"Mr. Hoffman is in a meeting. Sometimes I take his phone to field his messages," she explains politely, answering my unspoken question. "Hold on and I'll get him for you."

"No, no, please don't," I insist, not wanting to inconvenience him. I also need to be extra careful when sending him flirty pics or messages now that I know she can be reading them. Ugh, embarrassing.

"Miss McFee, I have strict orders to retrieve him if you call. Please hold on."

Of course Graham would put the fear of losing employment into the minds of all of his workers. Pretty sure Hanna was the case in point for his threats.

I wait approximately thirty seconds before I hear the sexy breath of Graham vibrate through the phone. "Sweetheart. This is a nice surprise."

"Hey."

"Hi."

"I wasn't trying to interrupt your meeting, but Kylie didn't give me much of a choice."

"Are you in the car? I can hear road noise. You shouldn't be talking and driving."

"Claire is driving."

"That isn't any safer."

"Hey! I heard that, Teddy Graham!" Claire yells over the center console.

"What could I do to get you to agree to having a driver?"

"Hmm…nothing." Well, maybe that thing he does with his tongue…

"Can I pick you up for dinner, and we can go back to our place?"

Just hearing him refer to the penthouse as being *ours* sounds weird. I don't think of it as being a joint property. I surely didn't put a dime into it. Considering Ethan and Claire's plans tonight, I would rather not be home to accidentally witness or hear any of their shenanigans.

"Can we just do simple takeout and chill on the couch?"

"Sure, that sounds perfect. I can be there in forty-five minutes. Just finishing up a few last-minute things here and can drive over."

"I can just meet you at your place—"

"Our place."

"Our place," I correct. "Since it is out of the way to come get me."

"I don't mind the drive."

"Okay."

Claire parks the car. I hop out and make my way up the steps. I open the door and toss my belongings into a pile on the chair.

"We going to do Girls' Night at The Shack on Friday?" she asks from behind me. "Half-priced drinks for anyone with a vagina. No need to flash it for proof."

With my new pattern starting tonight of staying at the penthouse, I will need to schedule time to hang out with Claire more. "Yeah, that sounds good. I'll need something fun this week after all the craziness. Did I tell you I got the Campus Smoothie Cafe job?"

"Seems like such a downgrade from Entice," she mutters, kicking off her shoes and placing her gym bag on a hook near the door.

"Well, now that Graham and I are officially dating, I doubt I will ever be able to reclaim that old job. He would have a complete fit if I bypassed any of the protocols too. Plus, I may murder Mark if I ever see him again."

"I would like to help. Evil bastard."

I slump into the chair in the living room. "Sometimes when I'm bored, I sit still and wonder how my life got so fucked up."

"Danger just follows some people. Like a plague."

"Is Ethan coming over?"

"Yeah." She throws herself onto the couch and covers her hands over her face. "And I am so nervous."

"You know you don't have to do anything you don't want to do. Your body, your rules. Is he still reserving you for dates via the website?"

"Yeah, only because every argument ends up with me threatening to go on a date with someone else—but it's just shits and giggles. I enjoy forcing him to pursue me even harder. It's all about the manipulation."

"Lovely," I deadpan.

"It's a weird game we play. Gets him to really ravish me though. So, I keep upping my game and hoping for the best."

"Sounds like you are throwing mud at the wall and seeing what sticks," I comment absently.

"Yup. Pretty much."

I wish I could say I didn't play a similar game with Graham. But I would be lying. I love it when I get him to lose control. It is one of my top three favorite hobbies.

I glance at the clock and realize I am running out of time. I run back upstairs to pack my bag and throw on a fresh set of clothes. I braid my hair down the side. I dust on a little blush, add some mascara, and apply peach-flavored lip gloss. I throw my schoolbooks and laptop into my tote bag and toss my Altoids container of pills inside the secret zipper compartment—just in case.

I can hear the arrival of Ethan down below and decide that I need to get out of here fast. I jog down the steps, slip on shoes, and decide to wait outside in the fresh air for Graham to arrive. I park my butt on the top step and rest my elbows on my knees.

In a little over a week, it will be Thanksgiving, and I will meet his family for the first time. I am not sure if I am more excited or more nervous about this milestone.

Thoughts of Zander infiltrate my mind, and I cannot shake how his words affected me. Maybe I am making a mistake by dating Graham. Maybe my heart will be broken in the end. And maybe Zander won't be around to catch me when I fall. The more I think about him holding out on pursuing any real relationships with other women, because he was waiting for me, the guiltier I feel. It is like being friends with him has blocked him from possibly finding happiness with someone else. And even though it was not my intention, I still feel responsible.

I love being friends with Zander. He is so easygoing, and I can chat about almost anything with him without judgment. Maybe I used him? Maybe the selfish side of my subconscious wanted to keep him all to myself and not share him with others. Because if there was a girlfriend involved, then I would slide into the "other woman" category. No woman really wants to be labeled as the "other" anything.

I am so deep in thought sitting on the top step that I don't even notice Graham taking the flight up to me.

"Why are you waiting outside in the cold?" he asks, pulling me up and wrapping his arms around me.

He is dressed in full business attire—suit and all—and smells sexy.

"I'm pretty sure Claire and Ethan have big plans tonight. I don't need any more images for my database. Some things cannot be erased. My poor, innocent eyes."

He laughs and guides me to his car. "Pretty sure you only play the innocent act. We both know the truth when you get into bed." He leans down and licks my ear. "You know what they say about a lady in the street…"

I fake scoff as he helps me into the passenger seat. "Only because you've corrupted me with your prowess."

He jogs to his side, settles into his seat, and pulls out of the parking spot. "Hey, a man can't help himself when a beautiful woman dangles her virtue in front of him for the taking."

I turn in my seat and glare at him. "Oh really, Graham? Is that how it happened? You're blaming me for tempting you?"

"Yes."

I smack his arm, and he bursts out laughing. "You are such a troll!"

"There you go with the name calling," he says with a playful smirk. "What do you want for dinner? Any requests?"

"Frozen pizza."

He turns to look at me, and I can tell he doesn't know if I am serious or not. "Like the kind from the grocery store?"

"Yeah. Have you ever been?"

He shakes his head at me and chuckles. "What am I going to do with you?"

I smile sweetly. "Hopefully take me to the nearest grocery store for some pizza."

"But there are four amazing Italian restaurants within a three-mile radius of our place."

"That is wonderful information. But I want something less, umm—" I snap my fingers, trying to think.

"Delicious?" he says with a look of disgust.

"Handsy."

"Handsy?"

"Yeah. I want less people touching my pizza. And you know in those pizza places, they basically molest the dough," I explain. "I'm just not in the mood for that type of hand job tonight."

Graham's eyes focus on me while stopped at a red light. I can tell he is trying his damnedest to figure me out. During our staring contest, I spontaneously come up with a fun game. I reach into my bag and find the lollipop I placed in there when I was rummaging through my nightstand. I pull off the wrapper and pop it into my mouth and suck hard. He is back to watching me out of his peripheral vision, and he mutters something under his breath.

I look up at him innocently as I pull out my strawberry-flavored candy. "What was that, Graham?"

"I called you a little fucking tease, that's what," he snaps.

"Is that so?" I lick all around the sphere shape and make sucking noises as I place it into my mouth. I poke the side of my cheeks, making them puff out. This is so much fun, and I inwardly kick myself for not doing this sooner.

He narrows his eyes at me. "I'm not walking into the grocery store with a hard-on."

"Then ya better start thinking of some nonflattering images so you can take care of your"—I point to his tent in his pants with my lollipop—"situation."

"There's going to be a situation," he grinds out. "When I forgo this entire detour."

My bottom lip sticks out in a pout. "But I'm so craving the three for ten dollar pizzas."

"I'm craving the taste of your pussy."

I smile with the lollipop stick poking out of my mouth and stifle a giggle. A flash of his hand comes toward my face, and before I can move in time, the lollipop is pulled from my mouth and tossed out his rolled down window.

"Hey! That is littering!"

"It will biodegrade," he says casually.

"Why did you do that?"

"I was doing as you suggested and *handling* the situation."

I look down at his crotch and lick my lips seductively. "How's that working out for you, big boy?"

He shakes his head at me, and I can tell he is amused despite his stern demeanor. He pulls into Hank's Market and helps me out of the car. My ass gets pinched hard and his hand lingers there. I yelp as he squeezes the other side.

"Let's go get your damn cheap pizza, woman."

He follows me inside, and I grab a small cart to push. I have never been here before but follow the clearly labeled aisle signs until I discover the candy aisle. Score. I push the cart to the pick-your-own display cases and rip off a plastic bag from the roll. Graham eyes me carefully but resists from commenting. By now he should understand my need for sugar. And my need for him to sometimes go with the flow.

Graham helps me hold the bag as I scoop in an obscene amount of gummies, caramel chews, nonpareils, and taffy. He watches me with amusement as I move about—doing my thang.

"Want anything for you?"

He points over to the display of huge rainbow lollipops. "Just one."

I break out into a giant smile and pull a huge, coiled unicorn-like lollipop from the cardboard holder. I didn't even notice them there.

I cock my hip. "This one better not go out the window."

"How I choose to enjoy my candy is my business," he responds passive-aggressively. But his grin tells me he is just trying to get a rise out of me. "Besides, I may even explore where this could"—his eyes settle in on my groin—"also fit."

My eyes must bulge, because Graham's satisfied expression says more than words ever could. Oh, he thinks he is so cute.

We move on to the freezer section, and I throw some of the lean meals that just take a few minutes to microwave into the cart.

"You don't need to eat that type of low-quality food, Angela. You can order whatever you want and have it delivered to our place. Organic, vegan, farm-raised, whatever your heart desires. Whether I'm there or not."

"But I like these quick meals that don't take any

thought. I don't expect you to understand my peasant ways."

"I just want you to have finer things than five for ten dollar boxed meals."

I shrug and continue searching for what we came here for in the first place. Yes, there it is—frozen pizza. Yum.

"Do you have a preference on toppings?" I ask, scoping out the section.

"Get whatever makes you happy."

"Extra pepperoni it is. Ohhh, they have the cute, cubed pepperonis!"

Graham smiles at my excitement and helps me load up the cart. We move to the self-checkout lane, pay, and are settled back into the car with ease.

When we get to the penthouse, I dig in the bags for my candy and can't find it anywhere.

"Did we forget—" I stop when I see Graham pull the variety bag out from behind his back.

"Hey, candy thief! That's mine!"

"You have to earn it," he says smugly.

"You're holding my candy for ransom?"

"I'm keeping it safe."

I eye him suspiciously. "Until when?"

"Until you tell me about your day. Leave out no details."

"I, um…" Why is this so hard for me to do? It is just my day.

He tilts my chin up and leans me back against the island. "This is what people do in relationships, sweetheart." He kisses me on the forehead. "We talk about our day and spend time together."

I nod my head. It is still so foreign to me to even

consider Graham as my boyfriend. But that is what he is. My boyfriend.

"Can you start first?"

"Nope. You need to get used to sharing your life with me, baby."

"Okay, fine. I woke up to the sound of your moving company truck opening its doors, I went on a job interview, I chatted with Zander, and then Claire tricked me into trying a pole dancing class at the gym."

"Wow. So many things to unpack and ask follow-up questions on," he says, preheating the oven, pulling out a cooking stone, and unboxing the pizza.

"Can we not?" I groan. "I just want to move on to the part where you tell me about your day."

"Why is this so hard for you to do?"

I shrug my shoulders. "I honestly don't know. But it's all still new to me. Me being here. You caring enough to ask me about my day. Us sharing space together, doing mundane things."

"We share and will be sharing a lot more than space."

I laugh over his playful eyes. "True. So, what else do you want to know?"

"How did your interview go?" he asks, putting the pizza into the oven.

"I had to make a bunch of drinks for customers—including the manager. It worked out well, despite my nerves over messing up. But in the end, I got the job."

He nods his head. I can tell he is not thrilled by my choice in work, but he is refraining from expressing his dislike verbally. "What will your schedule look like?"

"I think I will just be working Mondays and Tuesdays. Few hours after class each day."

"And your conversation with Zander?"

I look down at my hands resting on the island. I am perched on a stool. "It was rough," I whisper. Tears fill my eyes as I remember Zander's words and his disappointed face. "Harder than I was expecting to break my best friend's heart."

Graham moves over to me and wraps his arms around my upper body. "I'm sorry you are sad over this. I wish I could take away your pain. However, Angie"—his eyes level with mine—"you are not responsible for making those around you happy."

"I wish it wasn't all or nothing with him. We have been friends for years. Good friends. But I never saw him the way he sees me." I wipe the tear rolling down my cheek with the sleeve of my shirt. "I just never saw this coming. I either am that dense or I didn't want to even consider it as an option. Regardless, it sucks."

Graham's hug is warm and genuine. He helps me off my stool and guides me into the living room where we flop down on the couch. He drapes a soft blanket over my shoulders and we cuddle. Cardboard boxes and my sewing desk are piled in the corner with professional labels on the outside describing the contents.

Graham brushes hair from my forehead and kisses my lips. "I'm glad you are here," he whispers. "I want you to feel comfortable here. This is your home too. Girly the shit out of this place—I don't care."

I laugh through the tears. "You may regret that."

"Doubtful."

"We'll see."

He smiles and bends forward to grab a stack of magazines. "I got a bunch of home store catalogs for you to look through. Order whatever you want."

I eye the dozen or so magazines. They range from super fancy to farmhouse casual. "Where are the tacky ones? With the roosters and birdhouse decor?"

He laughs and gets up from the sofa. He takes two books from the entertainment center and walks them back over to me. "Here."

I look at the cover and see "Country Cottage and Style" on the one, featuring plaid and apple prints. I flip through and see the roosters and birdhouse artwork and kitchen supplies. "This is perfect!" I say, pointing to the floral wallpaper section. "We can wallpaper one of the walls as an accent wall."

Graham shakes his head at my enthusiasm and leans over to see what has me so excited. "How about that one?" He points to the mini sunflower print. "I'm pretty sure you weren't even born when this trend was at its peak in popularity," he laughs.

"Like clothing, everything comes back in style eventually."

We laugh over the other hideous pages of decor items. The oven timer goes off, and Graham excuses himself to dish us up some highly processed cheese goodness.

I place the home magazines back on the coffee table. Graham returns with two glasses of wine from our lake trip and two plates of pizza.

"Cheers to our first night together in our place," he says, holding up his glass.

"Cheers," I say and clink mine with his, "thank you for having me. But you know I still plan to go to my townhouse some nights, right?"

"I don't see the point. But we can negotiate terms later."

"Graham, our relationship is not a negotiation. This isn't a business transaction."

He shrugs and takes a bite of his pizza. Strings of cheese stretch from his mouth, as he tries to make a clean break.

"Good, huh?" I ask, taking a huge bite of mine.

"It is not Giovanni's. But it is pretty decent, if you like unmolested pizza," he admits.

I laugh. "I do."

"The wine definitely makes it taste better."

I sniff my glass and enjoy the aroma. It brings back all the memories of our wine tour, and how he had his way with me against a wooden barrel. "Truth. How was your day?"

He finishes chewing and then clears his throat. "It was a decent day. Nothing crazy happened. Just managing the supply chain for our new line of watches and answering to the marketing team on how to push out our release."

I lean back into a pile of pillows and listen to him talk about his jewelry line. It is sexy listening to him go over some of the process details and how he wears a lot of different hats in his company. I can tell he really likes being involved and not just the one signing papers. It all boils down to being in control. And his need for it.

After dinner is over, we take a shower together, and I put on a set of pajamas from the closet that Graham has supplied for me. He must have known that I would end up here when he decided to proactively buy me a whole wardrobe. I would like to think it was just wishful thinking and not part of some bigger plan.

I climb into bed and see my romance novel that I am currently reading resting on the nightstand. Graham must have unpacked it already for me. I smirk at the cover models. The male character is shirtless, and the female character is basically just wearing lace panties. I blush at how having someone know what I am reading makes me feel very vulnerable. This is why I don't even have an online book profile; I don't want anyone to accidentally see the fantasies that I read about.

Graham shifts on the bed behind me and leans his mouth into my ear. "I have one more question about your day." His voice is airy and breathless.

"And what is that?" I ask, moving my head to look at him.

"Can you show me some of your pole dance moves?"

I wiggle my eyebrows. "Oh, you are in for a treat."

24

I am awakened by Graham fingering me gently. I actually feel rested, despite all the sex we had the previous night. I guess having multiple orgasms is a great way to sleep better.

"You're awake," he whispers, kissing me on my lips. "I have exactly seven minutes before I have to get up and get dressed for work."

I can feel his erection pushing against my thighs. "Then you better hurry."

He pulls out his fingers and slides himself in with ease. He presses me against the mattress as he rolls on top. I thrust my hips upward and enjoy the friction against my inner soreness. Graham sets the pace and angles himself to hit my g-spot with the right amount of pressure.

"You are so beautiful."

We stare into each other's eyes, and I moan out his name with a quick release. Graham follows and pumps himself inside of me.

"You make me feel beautiful," I whisper as he reluctantly pulls out of me.

"I wish I could stay buried in you the entire day."

I pout at his words. I wish that too.

"Oh no, you don't."

"What did I do?"

"Don't look at me like that. Because I would love nothing more than to tie you to this bed and keep you as my little sex prisoner. And I know you like some kink—based on the book you are reading."

"Hey, that's a violation of my privacy," I whine.

"Call it on-the-job training and field research."

"How do you figure that?"

"As your boyfriend, I need to know what turns you on so I can make sure you are fully and utterly satisfied."

"You turn me on."

"Good." He captures my lips with his mouth and kisses me hard. When he pulls away, I can feel how swollen he made them. "You make me crazy with desire."

I smile and roll onto my back. I don't need to get up quite yet, so I watch my man as he gets ready for the day.

"Bend down one more time," I request, licking my lips as he puts on another dress sock.

"I feel like a piece of meat."

"A juicy caboosey one. And I love me some meat," I say with a giggle.

He crawls back into bed like an animal luring its prey. "You're going to make me miss my nine o'clock." He pulls my ankles, dragging me down the bed toward him. "Lucky for me, I don't give a fuck."

"Psst, what did you score?" Bryce asks, sipping his pumpkin spiced latte, with all his weird adaptations, that I got him from the coffee shop. The professor just passed back the writing assessment, and I am flipping through my booklet reading her notes and critiques.

"I got an A, how about you?"

"I got a B and am loving it, considering I never even studied."

"Nice."

I am thrilled over my score and can confidently say that the remaining credits for my minor should now be secured —unless I completely jack up what is left of the semester. Human Behavior is just an elective class. However, without these credits, I wouldn't be able to complete the requirements. Just like if I don't pass Dr. Williams's research journalism assignment, I will not be able to graduate with a degree in journalism—since it requires this final key component. Instead, I will only have enough credits to have an English degree—which is a slap in the face after all of the work I have put forth, including repeating my last semester.

But grades are subjective. And Dr. Williams does not seem to be a fan of mine anymore, especially after I refused to give up on my quest to find out who is drugging college-aged girls around campus. I honestly don't think I am interfering with any police investigations, because I have yet to see any police activity around campus, unless they are patrolling the area in unmarked cars. Notoriously, university presidents and board members often try to hide any negative publicity involving their campus in fear that it will affect admission rates—a.k.a. the influx of money funneling in. It is disgusting how much money affects so many aspects of the world.

"I can pretty much jack off the rest of the semester and still pull a C," Bryce brags, knocking his crutches down on accident. The sound ricochets against the walls of the auditorium. "Shit."

I laugh at his wide-eyed expression and help him put his crutches back in place where he had them.

"You okay?" I ask.

"Yeah, but I have to go pee. I think falling down the stairs has shrunk my bladder."

"Hopefully, not anything else."

He looks down at his crotch and frowns. "Ugh, I better measure later just to be sure. Way to make a man paranoid, Teach."

I stifle my laugh and watch as he gets up on his crutches to excuse himself. On the floor next to his open book bag, I see the orange bottle of pills that must have rolled out with the falling of the crutches. I pop open the lid and take out a small handful. It doesn't even look like he used any from the last time I snuck a few. I have such pain in my shoulder and can't even get any medicine for it other than OTC Tylenol. I place the pills in my tin container and seal his back up. At this point, if he is not using them, then they will just go to waste.

Class ends with a presentation on the different types of human personalities and behavior characteristics. I stop taking notes halfway through because my hand is cramping from where my stitches used to be.

After class, I walk out to my parked car and drive into the city to relax at the penthouse. This morning, Graham left a key and my new credit card linked to his bank account on the island for me to use. He also left me a little Post-it note to tell me to order food from the takeout menus that he has collected in a drawer in the kitchen. It's weird walking into the foyer and being here without him. It is equally weird thinking of this place as anything other than just being his.

I put some upbeat music onto the sound system and move into the living room to start unpacking some of the boxes that were delivered. I carry my book collection upstairs and fill the bottom drawer of my nightstand with them, since I usually read in bed when I have some spare time. I add some of my favorite clothes items to the ones already hung up in the shared closet and dig a little through Graham's side to see if he still has the two lock boxes I was never able to open. I find them in the bottom drawer—exactly where I saw them weeks ago. I grab a couple of bobby pins and paperclips out of my bag and pull open a YouTube video to use as a refresher. I then go to work at picking the first lock.

It takes about thirty minutes to release both locks and open the boxes. It helps that they were made by the same manufacturer and used the same skill to release the pins.

I am careful to keep everything inside in its original place. The first box has several identity bracelets in different types of metals that appear to be the same ones that agency girls wear. In addition, there are several cufflink sets. It is weird that these are valuable enough to lock up—especially when none contain diamonds or gemstones. I rush downstairs and look in one of the packing boxes for my own identity bracelet and bring it up to compare with the ones in the lockbox. Everything appears to be the same—except for the small, engraved numbers on the inside that I never noticed until now. They are so tiny, I barely can make out the digits 09-01 on the one I own. The ones from the lock box are labeled 09-02, 09-03, 09-04, and 09-05. The cuff-links have 03-01, 03-02, and 03-03 as markings. I email myself pictures and delete the ones I have stored in the Camera App album.

I close that lockbox and set the lock again. Then I pull up the lid on the second one to reveal a tiny pistol. I hate guns. They freak me out. I close the lid and set the lock. It is not unusual for people to have guns in Oregon—which is a "stand your ground" state. While the city of Portland restricts owners from walking around with loaded guns on their bodies or in vehicles, the overarching rule for the state still allows residents to protect themselves in self-defense and to protect their personal property.

The sound of the door opening downstairs and footsteps on the tile floor alert me that someone is inside. I quickly close the bottom drawer. The building is a fortress so I know whoever it is has to have access. It is way too soon for Graham to be done with his work shift, so I assume it's either the house cleaner, Collins, or Sophia—who seems to love to help herself inside. I push my shoulders back in confidence and make my way downstairs, prepared to fight with her if it is in fact Sophia.

I round the corner and see the back of a man, sitting at the island eating an apple.

"Excuse me?" I say. My voice is shaky.

He turns around and his eyes grow big as he recognizes me and I him.

"Dominic?" I ask, not sure why I formed his name as a question when I can obviously tell it is him.

"Hey, Angie." He gets up from the stool and makes his way over to me. He gives me a hug, and it seems like it has been forever since our paths have crossed. So much has happened since I last saw him. It's like he fell off the face of the planet.

"Hi." I hug him back. "I, uh, what are you doing here?"

"I was actually just dropping off some paperwork for Graham to sign and was going to leave it on his desk. But—"

"Wanted a snack?"

Dominic looks down at his teeth marks in the apple, and he gives me a big grin. "Sorry. I didn't know you and Graham worked things out to the point where you are cohabitating. I would have rung the doorbell and not just let myself inside."

"I was unaware you had a key." Seems like there is a growing list of people who have keys.

The main door opens again, and I hear Graham's voice. "Angie?"

"In here," I call out. "Dominic is here dropping off papers. And stealing fruit."

Dominic smiles. "I can replace it."

Graham moves to my side and eyes Dominic suspiciously. Something transpires between the two men, and I wonder if Graham has some secret nonverbal code that he trains his associates in. It is so annoying.

He takes the papers from Dominic and moves them to his office down the hall.

"I hope you at least knocked," he scolds. "Angie is living here now, and I need my friends and business associates to respect that."

Dominic nods slowly and glances between us. "You look happy, Angie, and for that I am really glad."

"Thank you." My voice is barely a whisper.

"Graham, will you walk me out?"

"Yeah." He smiles at me. "Be right back."

I watch as both men exit the room and enter the elevator together. Something seems off. I can't tell if it's just that Dominic may not realize that I know he isn't the CEO for Entice Escort Agency. That it is all a charade. He probably doesn't realize that I know about Graham's obsession with finding out who drugged Penny—and in turn, find out who is continuing to do the drugging. Mark is obviously involved, but he has to have minions working for him. The only way to successfully bring down the whole entire organization is to punish every key player.

Graham returns and saunters over to me. I place my arms on his shoulders and mold my body to his. "You're back early."

"It's hard to get work done when I know you are here by yourself thinking of me."

"Man, you are extra presumptuous today, aren't you?"

"But you were thinking of me, weren't you?"

"Maybe."

"Good. Because I have been thinking of you all day. Are you sure you don't want to work at HH? I would be way more efficient at my job if I had midafternoon sex regularly."

I shake my head at him. "I'm not cut out to be your secretary or personal assistant. You know that I don't have it in me to follow most of your orders. You are way too bossy. Plus, with your track record, I would barely make it an hour before you would be searching for a replacement."

He laughs. "True. Except for the last part."

"How many other visitors should I expect this week to just barge in here? You better be glad I don't just randomly walk around naked."

"I'm in the process of getting the locks rekeyed."

"Good."

"So feel comfortable walking around naked."

"Maybe."

"I have a few work related things I need to finish up in my office here. But did you want to use the spare room on this floor to set up your sewing area? We can move your desk together."

"Yeah, sure," I say with an eager nod, "that sounds good." I have never had a whole room dedicated to my hobby. It has always been a small corner of a room or a few bins stuffed under my bed that could be pulled out when I felt inspired.

Graham kisses me on the lips and lingers there for a few seconds before pulling away. "I love having you here with me."

"There's no place I'd rather be right now than with you."

Even though I haven't spent much time in the penthouse cumulatively, I am starting to relax and picture living here as more of a normal thing—and less of it just being an extended sleepover. Graham is busy working in his office, and I'm setting up my sewing room. It's a lot of fun being able to decide where I want the desk situated and where I want all of my supplies to go.

I walk out into the living room and scan through some of the decor magazines that Graham collected for me to use to help make this living space more my own. I find the storage sections in a few of the more modern catalogs and start dog-earing pages and circling my favorite organizers that would be great in my sewing room. I need places to put fabric, buttons, thread, and patterns.

Everything is so expensive but definitely looks to be high-quality. I grab a sour peach ring from the plastic bag of candy and pop it into my mouth. I am chewing the last bite when I feel Graham's lips at the back of my neck.

"Hey you," I say, turning around on the sofa to see him.

He points to some of my circled items. "Find anything good?"

"Too many things. That's the problem. I can't narrow down what I want."

"Just pick the most expensive item. Then you'll know it's the best."

I scoff at him. Is he for real? There is no way that is any indication of something being better than other items—especially when the retailers are completely different.

He shrugs and smiles. "Just order a couple of things and if you don't like them, we can schedule a return pickup. No big deal."

This is something I am not going to get used to no matter how hard I try. The ability to snap fingers and have people come running to make everything better is so foreign. It is like he has the world at his fingertips with people just waiting to help make his life easier.

"Want to go out for dinner?" he asks, sitting beside me and grabbing my legs for his lap.

"Not when you are rubbing my feet like that," I say with a laugh. "Feels so freaking good."

"I can continue after dinner. But we need to eat."

I nod my head. "We can go out. But you pick the place. I don't have a preference."

"I have the perfect idea."

I freshen up my face and hair, as well as change into a more suitable outfit of tights and a sweater dress. I slip on a pair of knee-high boots and follow Graham out the door into the elevator.

I look up at him. "Where are we going?"

He smiles. "It's a surprise."

It takes us ten minutes to arrive at a little tavern in the heart of downtown Portland called Olive Oil. The corner restaurant has tinted windows, and the lighting inside is dim and intimate. We seat ourselves and look at worn cardboard menus that are propped up on the table between the salt-shaker and the metal cup that holds rolled up napkins with eating utensils inside.

I scan over the listed items and am surprised at how small the menu actually is. It makes me think that all the food here is extra good since the venue has had a chance to master the favorites.

"The olive oil bread here is so delicious. We have to get

some."

"Sure," I agree. "I think I want soup too."

He nods his head and looks down at his menu. "We can get one of the market salads with shrimp and share if you want. And a small meat and cheese plate."

I excitedly agree. My stomach is hungrier than I thought. Skipping lunch probably was not the best idea, because now I am starving.

Graham pushes back his metal chair and goes up to the register to place the order. Several men in business suits line the bar with a smattering of a couple of females sitting in groups in the table area. The layout is small but cozy.

An iced drink is put down in front of me, and I smile at the little rubber ducky bath toy floating on top. "It's their signature drink," he responds with a chuckle. "Figured you would find it cute."

I laugh. "Oh, I do. What's in it?"

"A lot of different flavored vodkas and some sweet mix-ins."

I take a sip and my nose bumps against the rubber ducky, making me laugh some more. The drink is delicious.

"How was your day?" I ask. "Living your best life while conquering the world?"

He leans back in his chair and takes a swig of his beer. "It was a little on the stressful side. Not every day can be a win."

"Oh no, does it have anything to do with the stock market?" I don't know much about the market, but figure most businesspeople do, and a lot of their daily moods coincide with the day's stock exchange.

"I lost a million today, but that is just what happens when you gamble with a few side projects."

"A million?" I ask, coughing from my drink going down the wrong pipe.

Graham sits up in his seat. "Are you okay?"

I nod and wave him on to continue.

"Not much to say, really. I'll move some things around with my investments and probably gain back the money in a day or so. It's just a risk you take when you dabble in the European and Chinese markets as well."

Our food arrives and takes up nearly the entire table. Everything looks fresh. Graham hands me a plate, and I fill mine up with items from each serving tray. He ordered two different types of soup, and I start by eating half of the asparagus bisque. Graham digs in on the beef barley.

"How did your day go?" he asks, taking a bite of olive oil bread while handing me a piece.

It is divine, and I can tell the oil is not the cheap kind I buy at the grocery store. "I got my assessment back from Monday."

"And?"

"I got an A."

"Awesome, baby. That is great."

I have never really shared my grades with anyone while attending River Valley—unless someone was sitting beside me and was being nosy. I never wanted to seem like I was bragging or comparing, so I usually just kept things to myself. But Graham isn't comparing himself to me. We are not in competition with each other. So, I find it oddly refreshing to have someone to share these small accomplishments with.

We eat and drink and laugh over stupid things we have done in the past. Tears fill my eyes as I can't keep my emotions in check to get my words out. "I can't believe you dressed up in drag for a dare to get free drinks in college. I guess it's true that women rule the world of getting things for free."

"I can't believe you lost your suit during the polar bear plunge. What is this event anyway? Never heard of it."

"It's where you jump into the river in the winter at Poet's Beach near the bridge and raise money for a charity. They have the event all over the nation—anywhere there is a decent amount of water."

"And this can't be done in the summer?"

I shake my head and laugh. "No, then you would never find sponsors to donate money for the cause."

"Seems unnecessarily horrible."

"I must have shivered so much that the suit just fell off my body. Claire was laughing so hard at me from the shore and was making me beg for her to bring me a towel to conceal myself."

"You two really are bad influences on each other."

"Yeah, we really are."

"What other trouble have the two of you gotten into?"

"She almost had me get my belly button pierced. But apparently tattoo and piercing parlors do not work on drunk customers."

"Well, that's at least reassuring," he mutters, highly amused by this topic of conversation.

"We were definitely stumbling when we entered some shady place near campus after our drinking game went wrong."

He shakes his head at me and takes a long drag from his beer bottle. "I have checked pretty thoroughly, and notice you don't have any piercings," he says with a sexy smirk.

"No. None. Not even my ears. The closest I came to putting a hole into my body was that time with Claire."

"Why the avoidance while sober?" he probes.

"Surprisingly, after the car accident, I developed an irrational fear of pain." I frown and look down at my hands. "Which is weird that I ever resorted to cutting in the first place."

His hands join mine, and he brings them up to kiss each knuckle. "You wanted control when you were feeling out of control. You found it the best way you knew how at the time. You are a survivor, sweetheart. A warrior."

I don't think of myself as either of those things. And definitely not the latter. When I look back at that chapter in my life, it was a time where I felt my weakest. My loneliest. A time when I didn't care if I lived or died.

"Hey."

I look up into Graham's eyes. "Hmm?"

"Quit shutting yourself off to me. I can see you are already putting up some walls. Please stop. I want to be your safe place. You may not see yourself as those things. But that is how I see you. And maybe with time, you'll retrain your brain to see how strong you really are."

I give him a lopsided smile. Doubtful, but whatever.

A worker comes from behind the bar to drop off a slice of twelve-layer chocolate cake in the center of the table along with two cappuccinos. We both dig in to the layers with forks and enjoy the coffees that have beautiful leaf designs created in the foam at the top.

"I love it here," I whisper softly.

Graham's smile is warm and genuine. "I'm glad. It's one of my favorite places to eat and grab a drink. And it's within walking distance of HH."

"When did you start your company?"

"Hoffman Headquarters existed before the jewelry company was born. I was able to secure a loan after college and use the money I saved to purchase it. I utilized HH for office leasing and real estate ventures at the time. But when I became more financially stable, I took back the entire building slowly and then bought the adjacent building as well with the idea of connecting them with the walk bridge."

I can barely afford rent on the townhouse from month to month, so buying up entire buildings is so foreign to me. I just never had the freedom that money brings to understand its power.

"Pretty incredible and ambitious. To know at a young age exactly what you wanted to accomplish. And then have the balls to actually go for it."

"Maybe you should come to work with me on Friday. It's going to be a more relaxed day. Then I can show you around some more. Give you the professional tour."

"Try to convince me to work under you?"

"Hmm…I definitely love you under me."

I eye him speculatively. "Is that all you're going to give me, Mr. Hoffman? Just a look around your domain?"

His grin breaks out on his perfect facial features. "The tour will end with an up close view of my polished desk."

I clear my throat. "I bet," I say, rolling my eyes exaggeratedly—despite being very turned on by his previous promise to lay me across the top and enter me from behind.

"You don't have class on Fridays. So why not come hang out with me?"

"As long as I'm back in time to get ready for Girls' Night with Claire."

He straightens his posture. "Wait, you're ditching me Friday night?"

"Yeah. I thought I told you. I cannot ignore my bestie, and I want to make sure I make time for our friendship. Ethan is spending some one-on-one time with his son, so we are both free."

"Will you still come home to me?"

"I think I'll spend the night at the townhouse, if that's okay? It'll just be easier."

I can tell he wants to say something but resists. "I'm trying my best here, Angie."

I look up into his eyes. "I know. I appreciate your effort."

"I get you the entire rest of the weekend to myself though."

"Deal."

25

Thursday's lab class features the analysis of different lie detector devices, using fellow students in class as test subjects to predict results based solely on body language. Labs are definitely more my speed. I love the hands-on component to the five-credit Human Behavior class. But having Bryce as a partner is stressful when I am worried he is going to get us kicked out based on his laid-back approach to basically everything in life. And his inappropriate humor. Let's not forget about that. There is no reason for all of his questions to be presented as sexual innuendos. No reason at all. Especially when I am kind and ask him questions such as the name of his hometown, his favorite color, and if he is looking forward to life after graduation.

I hang around campus in the computer lab to type up some of my research notes and scan through the private email where I sent some of the pictures. Zander is not working until later in the day, so I know there is minimal chance of running into him. Right now, I think avoiding him is best until he calms down. Then, maybe we will be able to work at building back our friendship. He is still so pissed at me, and I cannot erase his nasty words from my memory.

When I feel like I actually accomplished something, I pack up my belongings and make my way out of the building to my car. It only takes me fifteen minutes to park at the penthouse and find the exit into the street. I am not ready to go up and be by myself while Graham is at the office, so I walk around and explore the area.

I somehow manage to find myself hovering outside a tattoo parlor—named Ink Coat—completely mesmerized by the artwork on the display windows. Maybe it is the reminder from yesterday's dinner that I almost got my belly button pierced. Maybe taking more chances and conquering some fears will help me step forward instead of always falling backward.

I have always had a fascination with detailed graphics and imaginative expressions. The windows contain art etched into the glass and colored with translucent paint. It catches my attention. The intricate designs and details portrayed take my breath away and make me want to see the inside. Surely if the window honors the art, a body part would as well.

I am not sure if I really would ever want to ink my skin. I have seen the teenage tramp stamps around campus, usually underlined with whale tales from dainty thongs. But, I doubt I would ever succumb to the rebellious impulse. It's a bit too cliché for my liking. I mean, I have nothing to prove to anyone now. If I were to mar my pale white skin, it would definitely have to be for me. No one else.

As if hooked and pulled by a fishing line, I am reeled

through the door, completely dazzled by the real photos of body art aligning the wall. I stare at a girl in a spaghetti strap tank with the word "love" spelled out on her pelvic bone in elegant handwriting that curls into the shape of a heart. Some guy has a fingerprint on the back of his neck. While I don't know the stories behind the designs, I just can't help but stare and find appreciation for the uniqueness of the ideas. My favorite image is of the word "forever" spelled out in tiny capital letters, wrapped around each ring finger of a man and woman. It is a beautiful representation of commitment.

"Hey cutie."

My body whips around to find a fiery redhead, with enough facial piercings to piss off any TSA worker at the airport, behind the counter greeting me with wide inviting eyes. I swear that even her eye liner is a permanent stamp.

"Can I help you with anything?" Her accent is English, and just listening to her talk makes it difficult to actually focus on anything but the way she pronounces words.

I glance around the space to find a male artist working on some middle-aged bald man's shoulder art. The artist has blond hair with a dyed-tipped mohawk. The sound of the buzzing equipment absorbed by the sound system's rock music fills the air.

"Oh, I'm just browsing."

"Browsing?" Her eyebrow quirks as her short figure steps around the counter, gesturing with her hand outward. "In a tattoo and piercing parlor? Surely, you're not here by accident?"

Oh. Umm… "I'm sorry," I say, turning my body and making my way toward the exit.

"Hell, do you have to scare all the ladies out of this joint?" The masculine voice booms from the back room scolding the girl, making Mohawk pause and turn toward me with a sexy grin. The man from the back reveals himself, eyeing me with curiosity. He has brown hair and is all smiles, with dangerous roaming eyes. He removes his black latex gloves, snapping them off and rolling them inside out into a ball. He tosses them into the trash can several feet away, making the basket with ease. "Hey there. You don't have to leave on account of her rudeness. I can assist you." He reaches out his hand for me to shake. It seems so old-fashioned, yet comforting. "I'm Logan, by the way. What can I do for you?" He studies my face and lingers on my eyes longer than is socially acceptable without being creepy.

"I asked her the same thing, Log."

"Shut up," Logan and Mohawk say in unison.

I stand in my spot on the tiled floor while the redhead glares at the men and shakes her head in disgust. For all being coworkers, they definitely need help getting along. At least in front of the customers.

"You would look absolutely adorable in my chair," Logan boldly admits. I can hear Mohawk chuckling under his breath, returning his focus to filling in some color for the man's tat. "And why the hell do you look so familiar?"

I look him over. There is no way I have ever seen him before. I would remember his striking looks. This is not the same shop that Claire and I stumbled into while tipsy. No, this shop looks sanitary and safe.

"I don't think we have met before," I say slowly.

"What's your mood? A butterfly? Perhaps some script? Celtic symbols?"

"Oh, umm. I really just saw the sign and thought I would come in and take a look. I have never been in here before. The art on the front windows drew me inside."

Out of sheer politeness, Logan refrains from rolling his eyes at my clueless demeanor. Even I am judging myself; I sound like an idiot. I mean, seriously, who randomly enters a tattoo and piercing parlor?

"Well, then. Let me give you the grand tour, darling. But if you want a Grateful Dead teddy bear, that's a no."

"Anything celestial—that includes the sun, moon, or Star Wars?" Mohawk chimes in.

"Is a *hell* no," Logan finishes.

I can't help but burst out laughing. I know from my gut instinct that he is being one hundred percent real and honest with me. Apparently they have standards.

Logan winks at me. "And unless your lover's name is Logan…"

"And if it is, I'm sure he's a douche!" Mohawk harasses.

"Shut the fuck up, dickwad!"

Logan turns back toward me, throwing his arm around my shoulder, which I politely shrug off. He leans in dangerously close to my ear, whispering, "I sure as hell am not tatting your ass with some boy's name."

I swallow and nod.

"Because that's the sure way to end any relationship, or booty call. That's where I draw the line," he says.

Humor plays across his features, and I can't help but laugh.

"That's only because he's famous for his horrible spelling!" the redhead yells out from behind the body jewelry counter, earning herself a middle finger.

My phone buzzes from the pocket of my jacket. I pull it out and see it is Graham calling. "Please tell me you are not getting a unicorn tattoo."

I laugh into the receiver. "You need to quit spying on me, Graham. You said you would be discreet. This is not being discreet."

"Put Logan on the phone."

"Wait. How? You—"

"We are old high school buddies. We often got together for lunch when I had more of a set schedule at work. He may even recognize you since he has seen your picture on my office desk."

Huh, that is why I look familiar to him.

"Logan?"

"Yes, sweets?"

"My boyfriend, Graham Hoffman, wants to have a word with you." I pass him the phone, biting my lip to hide my smirk.

"You have got to be shitting me," he mutters under his breath. "Well, I'll be damned. What are the freaking chances?" He grabs the phone from my hand and keeps his eyes on me while he talks into the receiver. "I almost had your girl in my chair. Tatting her with some other dude's name." Logan throws his head back and laughs. "You got it so bad. This is going to be such fun now that I know her curiosity is piqued. Yeah, yeah, I'll send her on her way. No, wouldn't dream of it, you possessive asshole."

It is entertaining listening to someone other than me dish attitude back to Grumpy Graham. Logan stays on the phone a minute longer, and I can tell he is listening to Graham rattle on. He hands me the device back, and I can tell Graham is amused.

"Interested in a tattoo or piercing, my rebel girl?" he asks seductively.

I want to reply with something sexual just to make him wonder, but at this moment, all three workers are staring at me. "I may just get my ears pierced. Too bad I am terrified of needles."

"If you want them done, I would love to supply your jewelry to wear. But wait until I'm there with you to support you and hold your hand."

"If I leave now, I won't come back because I'll lose the courage."

"I can be there in five minutes. Just wait."

"Okay," I say, as he disconnects the call.

"Today is the day?" Logan asks eagerly.

"I want a nose ring and an eyebrow one. But we have to hurry before Graham gets here and tries to fill my head with reason."

"Okay, let me wash and glove up."

"I'm teasing!"

"Ah, you got my hopes up. Making Graham lose his shit is what I strive for in life."

"Because you have zero ambitions," Red goads.

"Shut up."

I giggle over their interchange. As promised, Graham only takes five minutes—maybe even less—to get to Ink Coat. He greets me with a hug and a kiss.

"Did I get you out of a meeting?" I ask apologetically.

"It was worth it." He smacks hands with Logan and then turns his attention back to me. "You sure about this?"

"No."

His laugh relaxes me. "We can go to a less shady place," he suggests, a smirk playing on his lips.

"I heard that, asshole," Logan calls over his shoulder while washing his hands. I watch nervously from the sidelines while Logan snaps on a fresh pair of black gloves that he removes from a plastic package. I look up at Graham. "I have wanted my ears pierced since I was a little girl. But by the time I understood what I was asking for, my mom was too sick to take me. Then I just couldn't bring myself to do it on my own."

He nods at me and pushes a stray piece of hair behind my ears. "I'm glad we can do this together. But are you sure? You don't have to get anything done. Or you can wait until another time."

"Today's the day."

Logan points to the leather chair that is in his workstation area. It looks like a reclining chair that would be seen at the dentist's office. Graham helps me to sit down and holds my left hand as Logan rolls his stool over to my right side. I close my eyes and try to forget about the temporary pain I will soon be in.

Graham is at my ear telling me about his day—trying to distract me. Logan plays some rock anthem through the sound speaker that is sectioned off to just this area. The thumping bass coincides with the same rhythm of my heart—only adding to my anticipatory fear. I open one eye and catch Logan peering down at me.

"You okay?"

"I need something fluffier to listen to. This is just adding to my stress."

He looks at me in disbelief. "I don't think I have anything to your liking. Just some heavy death music."

"Then shut it all off," Graham snaps. "You are going to make her freak out before you even get close to her."

Logan hits some button with his elbow, as to not contaminate his latex gloves. Once the music stops, I go back to closing my eyes and focusing on Graham's soothing words and the feel of his hands.

"You better use the numbing gel if you have any available," Graham demands.

"Dude, let me do my job. I got this."

Logan applies some type of liquid to each lobe and runs a cotton swab around both sides. I keep my eyes squeezed shut and try to think good thoughts.

I feel the pinch of my lobe from some type of plier tool and then the blunt prick of the needle. I curse under my breath and try to calm myself down from the cliff I feel like I am about to fall off.

"Perfect," Logan mutters. "Now the next side."

I keep my eyes closed but hear the sound of movement around my head. "I can't believe I am finally doing this. I never do anything this impulsive."

"Sweets, impulsive would be a nipple piercing. Which I can easily do, but this asshole beside me would need to give us some privacy. I can barely work in these conditions right now, with him shooting daggers at me with his eyes."

"If I wasn't worried about you messing up on my girl, I would punch you," Graham growls, but the fierceness behind his tone is lost.

Logan chuckles, "You would miss. We both know how bad your reflexes are when it comes to sports."

I listen to Graham's lighthearted laugh beside me. Other than with Dominic, I have not seen Graham interact with his friends. It's nice to see a different side to him. I cringe as Logan grips my lobe with his device, and then stops my heart with the searing pain.

"Worst is over," he says smoothly. "Now for your after-care instructions."

"You okay?" Graham asks, placing a chaste kiss on my forehead.

I open my eyes and grab the hand mirror that Logan gives to me. I reach up and touch the little stud earrings.

"I'll upgrade them soon," Graham whispers. "Once we know you are in the clear from an infection."

"She isn't going to get one," Logan interjects with a huff. "This isn't a little mall kiosk that uses piercing guns and unsanitary practices." Logan turns his attention to me. "Angie, here is a bag of cleaning supplies for you to use. Please don't let this man of yours make you paranoid. You'll be perfectly fine. Just follow the directions."

"Thank you," I say with a smile. I cannot stop looking at my ears. The pain is gone, and I finally have earrings.

"Graham, you ready for your Prince Albert piercing we talked about?"

Graham sighs beside me, grabs my hand, and pulls me from the leather chair. His credit card gets swiped, then he gets handed a receipt to sign. "Bye, Logan. We won't be back."

"Yeah you will. Now that Angie has a taste of my talents, she'll be back for more."

"You wish," he mutters.

"You just better hope that when she does return, it is your name I am tattooing on her ass and not someone else's."

I get pulled out of the shop and into the refreshing fall air. "Well, that was fun."

"Fun?" he asks with confusion.

"Yes. Exhilarating. Let's go skydiving now."

Graham looks down at me and smiles. "How about next weekend?" he says with a laugh.

"Graham? Is that you?"

The saccharine sweet voice coming from behind us makes the hairs on my arms stand up. Sophia.

We turn and see her puffing her way down the sidewalk in heels and a long wool trench coat.

"I got another text," she says, ignoring my presence entirely.

"When?" Graham snaps, taking her phone from her hand. He glances at the screen and tenses. "Dammit."

"I'm scared," she whines. "I'm being targeted."

I can't tell if she is being sincere or if she is simply trying to get Graham to notice her. "I need you to hang low this weekend," he directs. "I'll try to trace the message. And put out feelers."

"But what happens if my stalker shows up at my apartment?"

"I had the security system installed, remember? You have my cell number and Collins's. You'll be safe."

"You can't guarantee that and you know it."

"Just stay put for one weekend, Soph. Your apartment building is a fortress. Nothing bad will happen to you if you stay there. And why are you just wandering the streets? The office is a mile away. Let me drop you back off at your place."

I stand in silence as if I am invisible. No one looks at me. Sophia doesn't even acknowledge my presence with a passing glance. I follow Graham to his parked car, and Sophia slides into the front seat before I can even say or do anything. And Graham just allows her to claim it. I move into the backseat and stare out the window. I work at keeping my temper at bay. It's a short car trip to her place. We are basically neighbors—despite living in different buildings.

"Want to move up front?" Graham calls back to me once Sophia is safely inside the lobby.

"I'm fine."

He looks back at me through the rearview mirror, and I refuse to make eye contact with him. We are back at our place within minutes. I open my car door and slide out, walking silently beside Graham as we make our way through the parking garage to the elevator.

"You lying to me?"

"Maybe."

He lets out a sigh. "We are friends, Angela. That is it."

"You're blind not to see what is so obvious to anyone watching. How can you be so intuitive on so many other things but miss her infatuation toward you?"

"I have a responsibility toward her. Not only is she my employee, but she has had a string of bad luck happen to her that I feel compelled to fix."

"What kind of bad luck?" I press.

"Her face now appearing in ads for my jewelry line has

opened the door to secret admirers making unwanted advances toward her."

"Has she filed any police reports?"

He runs a hand through his hair. "She's worried that the stalker will just get pissed off and try to harm her."

I frown over this explanation. It doesn't really make sense. What's stopping the stalker from causing her harm now?

"How long has this been going on?"

"A couple of months."

The elevator leaves us off on our floor and we exit. I kick off my shoes and enter the main living area.

"What time do we have to be at the office tomorrow?"

"Typically I'm there around eight. But lately, I have been in closer to nine. I don't have a meeting until ten, so we can sleep in together if you want."

"That sounds great." I stand on my tiptoes and kiss him. "Thanks for being there for me while I got pierced."

"I'm glad I could support you. Want me to make dinner?"

"You don't have to serve me. I'm fine just having a can of soup or something simple."

"I just had groceries delivered. So, I can make us a salad with some grilled chicken if you want."

"That sounds good to me. Thank you."

"How about you go lie on the couch. Flip on the TV. Play with your phone. Just go relax."

I nod and head over to the sofa. I lay my head on the pillow but have to turn a certain way as to not put pressure on my ears. They are sensitive to the touch.

"Here," Graham says, handing me a glass of wine.

"Thank you," I whisper, sitting up to take a big sip. It is a delicious bold red blend. We sampled it at the second winery, and I fell in love with the robust flavors packed into one bottle. "Do I have time to shower?" I call into the kitchen as I hear a pan start to sizzle.

"Yeah, this won't be ready for at least fifteen minutes."

I pad up the stairs and strip down. I start the shower and allow it to warm up. Steam fills the air, and I walk into the powerful jets of water. It feels good to allow the tension to leave my body. I have a lot on my mind, and being able to stand in silence is refreshing.

I wake the next morning before my alarm and before Graham. I roll so I can see his sleeping form and marvel at how peaceful he looks. All of the muscles of his face are relaxed, and he appears to be a new person without the strain of stress broadcasted on all of his features.

I kiss his cheek, then work my way to his nose, while ending with a small peck to his lips. I linger there and then lick a path down his chin, to his neck, and then along his bare chest. I scoot down farther on the bed and lick along his belly button and make a few circles around it before I keep going south. Him being completely nude helps my conquest as I trail my tongue along the soft tuft of hair. I slide his softened cock into my mouth and suck harder to try to breathe life back into it.

Hands are suddenly in my hair, and I know I have woken up both beasts. I hear him mumble a *good morning* and I mumble one back—which turns out to be a slurred *gah morn'n* with my mouth stuffed full.

"I could get used to this type of alarm clock," he says sleepily, massaging my shoulders as I go to work on him.

I get him nice and hard and then pull off and dart off the bed into the closet.

"Oh no you don't!" he yells, rolling from the bed. I can feel his chuckling behind me as I start flipping through hangers of clothes. He pulls me to him. "You going to finish what you started back there?" he asks, pointing down to his massive hard-on.

"Yup."

"Okay. Get on with it."

I look up into his eyes innocently. "Oh, not here. Later."

"Later?" He grips my waist so tight that I know he is going to leave fingerprints if I don't help him with his release.

"Yeah, later," I say, nonchalantly rocking on my heels. "Consider this edge play that you love so much."

He narrows his eyes at me. "I'm not going into the office feeling like I am going to burst. You're going to make me go in angry, and when I'm like this, people lose their jobs."

"Well, you need to work on your tantrums then. And what better time than today. What a wonderful learning experience!"

I go back to pulling clothes from the hangers and meandering about the closet until I find what I need for the day. I settle on a classic cranberry-colored wrap dress. I find black thigh-highs, garters, panties, and a bra that all seem to be part of the same designer line to complete my look.

"You're going to pay for this, sweetheart. And I cannot wait to be the one to do it."

I click my tongue. "Good. I love it when you get restless and fed up and all needy."

"Oh, do you now?"

"Yup," I answer cheerily.

Graham pulls me to him and snarls into my ear.

I stand on my tiptoes and lean up into his to whisper, "And I'll let you in on a little secret."

"What's that?"

"My pussy likes it too." I step back and flip my hair over my shoulder. Man, do I feel empowered.

I walk back into the bedroom and lay my selection on the bed. I sit down on the end and start getting dressed while Graham ogles me from the doorway of the closet. He watches my every move, as I make it my mission to act unfazed. He mutters a string of curse words, and I can't help but glance over. Our eyes connect for a second, and I burst into a fit of giggles, flopping back onto the mattress.

"You're evil, and paybacks are bitches."

I swallow and hoist myself back up. I go back to the task of getting dressed and looking polished enough as to not embarrass Graham. I move into the bathroom and heat up my straightener. I brush through my hair to remove the knots that accumulated from sleeping and then press the iron over sections to smooth out the frizz. The last couple of times I have been at HH, it was full of drama. So, today, I hope to reestablish myself as not being *that girl* who causes a spectacle wherever she goes. Hopefully security will not have to intervene and no blood will be shed. I just need a normal visit.

When I am done in the bathroom, I unplug my iron and glance one more time in the mirror to triple check that my makeup is in place. Graham is dressed in a crisp black suit with a pressed white shirt and black tie. He looks powerful, and I revel in the fact that he is all mine. My toes curl at the thought of what he is going to do to me in his office. It is the anticipation that makes this all the more fun. I can tell by his posture and brooding facial expression that he is on edge—just the way I want him.

"Ready to go?" he barks, looking me up and down. "Don't you think that is too sexy for office attire?"

"First off, you bought this for me. Second, I'm not your employee anymore. So shut it."

He growls and stomps over to me. He pulls me toward him. His mouth swoops in and bites my bottom lip, then kisses it to make it feel better. "You could be wearing a ratty sack, and I would find it too revealing. You have me on a flipping cliff, barely holding on. So if I were you, I'd be careful. Otherwise, you may not make it to the office at all before I jump you."

I swallow at his words. This is the Graham I crave.

He pulls back and exits the room. I follow behind him as we walk down the stairs, into the elevator, and through the building's lobby. When we get outside, Collins is waiting for us at the curb.

"Good morning, Miss McFee."

I smile. It is good to see a friendly face—especially when Graham looks murderous. "Good morning, Collins."

We slide into the backseat, and Graham pulls me to him. "I can't wait to make you beg for release. I'm going to have so much fun making you pay for getting me all hot and bothered this morning just to tease me."

I settle back onto my side and snap my belt into place. Maybe my little stunt this morning wasn't one of my smartest moves.

Oh, but the office sexcapades are going to be so worth it.

26

We arrive at Hoffman Headquarters' main entrance and get out of the car. Graham's hand is at the small of my back, as I am guided through the main doors. Several security guards and employees greet us as we move through the lobby and go straight for the elevator bank. The doors shut and the car seems to grow infinitesimally smaller. We are no longer on neutral ground. This building is entirely Graham's. His turf.

I look down at my shoes but jolt at the feel of his warm hand sliding up the back of my dress. I don't even fight it. There is no use. I want him. He wants me. This is the game we play with each other. The game where we tease and torment until one of us snaps and gives in. It is like a slow dance—but where the end result is sex. This round is short-lived as the car comes to a stop and the bell sounds indicating the floor is reached.

The doors slide open, and Graham reluctantly removes his hand from my ass, after giving it a hard squeeze. I yelp but recover as we exit and come face-to-face with Kylie—

the new personal assistant. Even though I saw her the time I cut my hand, it is like I am seeing her for the first time. She has light brown hair, pulled back in a sleek professional bun. Her eyes are green and her freckles make her look younger than she probably is.

"Good morning, Mr. Hoffman. Miss McFee."

I smile and wave my hello. She has a shyness about her. I don't blame her; working for Graham would be intimidating as hell. In the beginning, if I knew I was actually working for Graham at Entice, I would have been scared as hell with him interviewing me. Dominic is way more of a chill type of boss—despite not actually being the boss.

"Your breakfast was delivered and it is on the table, Mr. Hoffman."

"Thank you, Kylie. If the facility calls, please call my desk phone. I'm expecting a call today and have yet to receive one. Otherwise, do not interrupt us."

"Yes, sir."

I walk hand in hand with Graham down the hallway to his office. When we get inside, he immediately shuts the door and locks it, letting go of my hand. I cross my arms over my chest and watch as he makes his way over to the table near the wall of windows and starts taking out the breakfast items.

"Come eat. So I can then eat you." His voice is gruff.

I swallow hard and cough. Alrighty then. I hesitantly walk over to him and look at the dozen or so items that he removed from the takeout bag. Pastries, breakfast sandwiches, bagels and fresh fruit bowls. Everything looks delicious, but I am not that hungry. I can't eat when I'm a wound up ball of nerves.

"Sit. Eat, Angie."

"I, um, I'm not that hungry. I'll just have some of the coffee and the fruit."

"You seemed to be fine stuffing your mouth with my dick this morning."

I stifle a giggle. It is true. "I just don't think I can eat much."

"It has been over fifteen hours since you last ate something. Please, eat," he says, handing me a partially unwrapped breakfast sandwich.

I look at it. It does look good. I relax my shoulders and take a hesitant bite.

"Baby, why are you so nervous here?"

I look up into his concerned eyes. I swallow my bite. "The past couple of times I've been here, it was a huge spectacle. I just don't want everyone who I pass in the halls today to—" I pause and think.

"To what?" he prompts, growing agitated.

"Judge me? Think I'm some crazy person? Wonder if you're making the worst mistake by being with me."

He moves over to my side and envelops me in a hug. "No one thinks any of those things. And if anyone makes you feel less than the amazing person you are, then they can just walk themselves out. I have no problem firing anyone."

"Why did you fire Hanna? It was obviously because of me."

He breaks eye contact and looks out the window. "She got a nice severance package, despite only being a fill-in for my other assistant."

"Why do you go through so many?"

He rubs his forehead. "I have trust issues."

"Don't we all."

He studies my face and then points down to my sandwich, encouraging me to keep eating. I take another bite. It really is tasty.

"So what is on the agenda today, Mr. Boss Man?"

His smirk is extra sexy or perhaps I am just horny. "Well, in between a couple of meetings, I plan to fuck you all over my building. Starting right there on my desk," he says confidently, pointing over to the polished piece of furniture.

I choke on my bite, reaching for my coffee in a rush. I guess I am getting everything I asked for after my game play this morning by stopping mid-blowjob. I knew he would be hot and bothered and itching for revenge. I just didn't expect him to be this wound up over it. He is edgy and hungry and borderline angry.

"Did you eat enough? I'm going to have Kylie put the extras in the break room for whomever wants it."

"Yeah, I am full."

"Correction, you *will be* full."

Maybe I should just start stripping right now. Get this show on the road and appease him long enough to dull down some of the sexual frustration radiating from him.

He gathers up the leftovers, opens up his office door, and yells down the hall for Kylie. Once she is gone, he slams the door shut and turns the lock into place.

With deftness, he undoes his leather belt and pulls it through the loops of his suit pants so quickly that it snaps against the wall. I jerk at the suddenness, feeling like I am about to be a part of something bigger than myself. He drops the strap unceremoniously, making my head spin with need. Passion courses through my veins, snaking through the dark parts of my body, begging for surrender.

I want him.

I need him.

"Come here."

My heart rate increases, and I feel a little lightheaded over the anticipation of what is to come next. He watches me with precision as I move closer to him inch by inch. He loosens his pants and unbuttons part of his shirt in preparation for what I know will soon come.

When I am within reach, Graham's hands grip my ass, and he hoists me up into his arms. I get carried over to his polished desk. He places me in the center. His monitors have been relocated to the side—in what I assume was wishful preparation. He shoves his pants and boxers to his knees, sits down in his leather chair, and scoots closer to me. His hands pull my knees apart.

"Lean back onto your elbows. I'm going to eat my breakfast now." All humor is gone from his tone. His expression is of determination and fire.

I obey. I made my bed. Now I have to fuck in it too.

I follow his directions, scooching my butt toward the edge. I feel vulnerable and exposed to him. Open and ready.

Graham gently places each of my feet on the armrests of his chair so I can keep from sliding to the floor. He reaches up my dress. His eyes stay locked onto mine as his fingers pull at my panties, ripping them from my body. He fishes them out from under me and places them into an unlocked drawer in his desk, like some kind of collector's item. I pray that this is not the drawer where all office panties go to die.

My garter belt remains intact, keeping my thigh-highs

up and in place. He flips the skirt part of my dress up to my waist and licks my bare skin along the suspender straps, all the way up to my apex. His tongue trails down my other thigh. It is slow. Methodical. Deliberate.

"If you follow my directions, I will let you come."

What?!

"Be a defiant and sassy thing? And I will keep you so on edge that you'll be begging for the chance to finger yourself off in private."

I nod my understanding.

"Spread your legs for me."

I open my thighs a little more, teetering on the desk.

"Hmm," he hums. "You look delicious."

I throw my head back and moan as his mouth connects with my pussy. He sucks onto my clit hard and shoves a finger into me so fast that I shudder with the start of an orgasm. My vision fades to black as the fierce tidal wave washes over me. Before I can come down, he repeats his pattern and another wave hits hard. He licks at my juices and goes back to sucking my clit and fingering me, but now with two fingers. Another orgasm ripples through my body, shaking me and making me throw myself forward from the intense pleasure. He pulls his fingers out just to slide them into my mouth.

"Suck." He pushes them a little farther back. "Gag on them. Taste how your body responds to me. And know that I own you. All of you."

His words piss off the feminist side of me. It is the logical side that says I don't need a man. The other side of me craves and salivates at the dirtiness of his words. But mainly the truth behind them…he does own me. While my brain has resisted for so long, I can no longer deny what my heart has known all along. I am his.

He slides his fingers out of my mouth and then thrusts them back inside of me. He pumps them a few times and then pulls them out swiftly, just to suck them dry with his own mouth. He helps me down off the desk, just to move me to the end of it. He pushes gently on my shoulders to get me to lean over. It is the scene he has described to me. Fucking me across his desk from behind.

Even though I know what he is planning, I am still pulsing from the uncertainty of what Graham is going to do. My right cheek rests on the wooden surface. My ass is exposed, with just my lace garter belt providing any coverage. I hear the sound of a desk drawer and crane my neck to see what is happening.

"Do not move, Angie."

His words startle me, and I return to my position. I hear the sound of rustling, and I feel his hand on my lower back. I can sense his eyes staring at me. I breathe. Inhale. Exhale. Then—

"Ow!"

The slapping sound of his hand landing hard across my ass cheek jerks my head up from the desk.

"Stay still," he warns. "Do not move."

I rest my head back against the desk but am now a bundle of tense muscles. Graham rubs his hands over my bare skin, soothing me—relaxing me. Then, he lands three more slaps to my ass, and I can feel my skin heat. The pain subsides quickly, and I am left with a delicious burning. I can feel the moisture from my apex dripping down my thighs.

"I knew you would be turned on by this," he says with awe. "Draped over my desk, with your ass high in the air. You are such a fucking delight for my eyes." He runs a finger along my cleft, making me rise up on my tiptoes. "I love how responsive you are to me. How in tune your body is to everything I can give it. You are thirsty for it. Starving. Your body needs to relinquish control in order to feel free. We belong together, sweetheart. As if you were made specifically for me."

I feel coldness between my legs and jerk over the sensation, only to get reminded to stay still. *Easier said than done, mister*! The sound of the vibrations registers to my ears before my body can comprehend what is happening between my legs.

"Graham!" I yell, jolting upward, as his hand simultaneously presses me back down. The vibrator buzzes along my entire slit. I fidget wildly on top of his desk. "I can't do this!" It feels too intense. Too good.

"Yes, you can. And you will. Surrender to the pleasure." He shifts the device to press into me harder, and I nearly bolt into the air. "I've been meaning to try out my gift you got me, since I received it. Today seemed like the perfect day to give it a spin."

Oh no. The shiny, neon pink, vibrating dildo cock.

It is like I am getting pleasured and punished at the same time, by the same method. I pull oxygen into my lungs through my closed teeth. I exhale through my nose. My pulse quickens and my inner muscles clench as I climb and climb and…

"Dammit!" I bellow, as Graham pulls the vibrator away suddenly.

"How does it feel?" he asks me.

I push back my hips to him, trying to maintain some form of contact. I need friction. Pressure. Him.

I feel the velvety head of his cock rub against my swollen and slick entrance. I sigh over the relief of not having to wait long. I stand on my tiptoes and try to relax my body so it can accommodate him. All of him. His hands spread me apart and he slides in slowly.

I hear Graham groan behind me, muttering under his breath about how tight I am. How I am gripping him like a vise. His words add to my already aroused state.

Once I have adjusted and reacquainted myself to his size and this angle, he starts to pull back and push into me. My stomach and breasts squish against the desk, and his hands grip my hips for leverage. I submit to him and love what doing so brings. Not being able to see him heightens my other senses. I can smell the wood polish from the desk, feel the cold surface, and hear the staggering sounds of his labored breathing. His fingers push firmly into my waistline. He is close. I can feel his cock growing harder and his thrusts becoming more determined. The friction of my clit rubbing against the desk, coupled with the angle he is able to achieve inside of me, brings me to a roaring orgasm.

I shout his name so hard and so loud that my throat is raw. My back arches up off the desk, and he gathers my long hair around his hand and uses it as leverage. He tugs and brings his other hand underneath my stomach to pull me closer to him as he thrusts one last time and empties himself into me.

I flop forward and feel like my body is made of just Jell-O. I hear the sound of a zipper and the brush of fabric against my backside. Strong arms scoop me up and carry me over to the sofa. Graham plops down on his back, and I go down on top of him. He cradles me to his chest, and I close my eyes in exhaustion. I am spent.

"What do you do to me, woman?"

I moan and cuddle in closer to his warmth. I rest my head against his neck and kiss him softly at his pulse point. I stay still and recover from my high. Graham is like a drug to my system, and I am undoubtedly addicted to his power over me.

It isn't until I can feel him leaking out of me that I make a move to stand up.

"What's wrong?" he asks.

I look down at my legs and get nervous that I am going to have a stain on my dress if I don't do something fast. "You…I'm…leaking." My words come out as a stutter but I can't help it; I am panicking.

Graham kisses me on the forehead and then rolls so I am lying on the cushions. He stands up, tucks his dress shirt into his pants, and finishes straightening himself up. He is back to looking like his dapper self—with minimal effort. I, on the other hand, probably look like I barely survived a tornado.

"Stay put. I'll get a cloth to clean you."

I hear the water running in the private bathroom. Graham returns with a warm washcloth and a clean pair of panties. I eye them like they are the most fascinating thing in the whole world.

"I have a few extra changes of clothes for the both of us here. Just in case—"

"We get covered in…" I point down to my crotch but don't fill in the blank.

"And as much as I would love to have you walking around with my cum dripping down your leg to let everyone know you are mine, I also want you to be comfortable here. So today, I'll let you hold on to a sliver of modesty."

I am wiped clean, and the action is so loving that I melt a little bit more into the couch cushions.

"I think I'll just spend the rest of the day here. Napping. Jilling off when I get the slightest urge. You go forth and earn the money." I shoo him away.

"Oh no, I have more fantasies I want to explore with you."

My eyes are droopy and heavy. "I doubt I'll be able to withstand any more pleasure. I've reached my quota for the day."

He laughs at me and bends down to cage me in. His lips kiss along my jaw and up to my mouth.

"We need to go in the next fifteen minutes if we are going to make the all-hands meeting at ten. It's over in the other building."

"We?"

"You're not leaving my side today, baby. I can't have my security team breaking out in hives over what you will get yourself into if I leave you unaccounted for."

I narrow my eyes at him and sit up. I want to argue, but what's the point of arguing with fact? I do have trouble controlling my snoopy side.

"Let me straighten myself out then." I get up and walk toward the bathroom.

"You're going to need these," Graham says, dangling

the pair of white panties from his index finger. "White to preserve your innocence."

"Ha. Pretty sure you single-handedly destroyed every ounce of my innocence." I snatch the garment out of his hands and saunter into the bathroom. I use the floor-length mirror to readjust my dress. I slip on the clean panties and slide my garter belt into a comfortable position. I brush through my hair with my fingers, but it looks a little ruffled, and there isn't much I can do to tame it, other than sprinkle a little water from the sink into it. I look like I just had amazing sex. Or maybe I am just projecting.

I finish up and exit to find Graham sitting on the edge of his desk.

"Ready to go watch me work?"

I find my bag on the table and pull out my notebook and fancy pen. "Yup. I even came prepared to take notes."

He looks at me with amusement dancing in his eyes. I can tell he is trying to figure out if I am being serious or not. He pulls me to his side and wraps an arm around my shoulders. We walk out his door, through the hallway, and take a few floors down on the elevator. We cross over the walkway and enter into a conference room with rows of long tables and rolling chairs. There are eight rows with about twenty chairs per row. Unlike the conference room where I attacked him, this is arranged to hold six times the amount of people.

"Sit wherever you would like. I am going to be speaking to my staff about a few pressing agenda items. Then directors from various teams will be doing short presentations on the happenings from the previous week. This is our weekly run-down. On Mondays we do a similar all-hands meeting, but with the layout for the week."

I nod and find a seat in the fifth row toward the left side of the room. Several staff employees are already filtering into the room. Many are in clusters from their departments, chatting while they find a seat.

Graham steps out of the room and comes back with two bottled waters. He walks one over to me and winks. I smile back, and my cheeks heat from being shy that some of his staff saw our interchange. I am trying not to stand out and yet here he is drawing attention to me. He walks down to the center podium. There are five there in total. Microphones are secured on poles. Three projectors are set up from the ceiling and three screens are lowered down behind the podiums with the simple touch of a button on a remote control.

I open my water and take a sip. A woman sits down with her colleague to the left of me. They both have a muffin and orange juice that they begin to eat. To my right a man sits down and leans back in his chair to talk to the group that is seated behind us. I recognize no one and am relieved in a way. I try not to think about if anyone recognizes me—especially from when I crashed into the conference room and climbed on the table to attack Graham. Not one of my finest moments, albeit memorable.

Every two rows of tables is on a different level, cascading down to where the podiums and screens are set up. Graham clears his throat and wishes everyone a good morning. The room quiets, and he uses a tiny remote to control the presentation being broadcast behind him on the screen.

"This week marks the 2.5 cycle of production for our Discovery Line of jewelry. Both the production and distribution teams are working at managing the importation for the supply chains for the metals and gems. The second phase will be starting in the next two weeks, where marketing and sales teams will be pitching their ideas to the board of associates. A survey was sent out to each staff member, through the directors, to establish realistic timelines and provide the opportunity to anonymously voice concerns over the workload and functionality of the teams before the next trial release is set to launch. Please keep in mind that casting blame on any staff member is unacceptable—regardless of being anonymous or not. We are one unit here at HH with a lot of moving parts. Keep comments professional, not personal."

I watch in awe as Graham commands the room, flips through slides with a graceful flow, and stands confidently amongst his staff. I don't write much in my notebook except for a few doodles and the words—*hot*, *confident*, and *mine*.

I take a sip of my water, and as I try to reseal my bottle, the cap slips out of my fingers and drops onto the floor under the chair beside me.

"Psst," I whisper over to the guy adjacent to me.

His smile is big as he looks at me. "Have we met?" he whispers softly. "You look new. I would remember those pretty eyes if our paths had crossed."

His words make me smile.

I can hear Graham's authoritative voice introducing some of the directors who are being called up to the podiums to do their portion of the presentation.

"I'm just visiting. But can you please get my cap?" I ask, pointing to it.

"I'm Tim," he says, passing me the cap.

I take it from his hands and seal up my bottle. I turn my attention back to the front of the room and shiver as Graham's eyes stare daggers at Tim. Shit. If looks could kill… I cringe and hope he didn't think Tim was doing anything wrong other than introducing himself. Graham messes with some notes at his desk and then looks up at me. His eyes are smoldering and possessive. I cross and recross my legs.

I dig into my bag and see my phone blinking with a text. I pull open the app and see that Graham just sent me a message.

Graham: Quit flirting.

Oh, the nerve of him. I don't even have words for him, so I just send him the eye roll emoji, because that is exactly how I feel. Then in true bratty form, I pull out a lollipop from my bag and rip off the wrapper before I can even think about the consequences. I shove it into my mouth and savor the artificial taste of wild cherry.

I can hear him clear his throat from the front of the room and see another incoming text.

Graham: I can't stop staring at your mouth. The only thing I want to see in it is my cock disappearing deep down your throat.

Fuck. I take out my lollipop, lick around it absentmindedly and put it back inside to rest against my cheek. Tim mutters something to me, and I look over to see him smiling.

"I love that flavor," he says.

I want to tell him to stop talking to me, but don't know how to do that without it seeming rude. Graham is going to lose his mind any second now.

"Mr. Larson, can you contribute any details to the room about the projected earnings going into the next quarter?" Graham asks an employee.

Tim sits up in his chair and coughs. "I, yeah, of course," he mumbles.

Shit. Graham is calling out Tim—probably for talking to me. I feel like I am in high school all over again. This is getting too awkward. I need some air. I throw my notebook, pen, and bottled water into my bag and walk toward the exit at the top of the room. Once I am in the open hallway, I take a deep breath and look for the restroom. I find the women's and push open the door. I bite the stick of my lollipop and breathe through my nose as I look around. For being one of many in this office complex, the room is very spacious—but sterile. I sit down and pee and then hear the sound of the door and soft footsteps.

I flush and push open my stall door and come face-to-face with a cranky Graham. Actually, no. Cranky is an understatement. More like livid. He pulls the stick out of my mouth and takes a taste of the hard candy.

"Hey, that's mine, candy thief!"

"Not anymore." With a flick of his wrist, the lollipop goes flying across the room and hits right inside the corner trashcan with ease.

"What the hell?" I prop my hands on my hips. "I liked that flavor! Do you have a thing against empty calories, bub? And what are you doing here anyway?"

He takes a step closer, and I am pressed against his stacked body. He captures my lips, grabs my ass, and lifts me up. His tongue delves deeper inside my mouth, and he rips it away only to say, "It's a mighty good flavor."

My legs wrap around his waist. He carries me to the handicap stall and locks the door. He pushes me up against the metal door and runs his tongue over my lips.

"Hmm," I hum.

"My little kitten," he says, while pushing my hair back from my forehead, "who is determined to be a tiger."

I claw at his back and then tug at the hair around the base of his neck.

"I didn't think I could want more after the office desk sex. But I do. I need more."

"I love that you are insatiable." He bites my neck, and I scream out. His mouth covers mine to stifle the yell.

"You are going to leave a mark!" I whisper-shout once he releases my lips.

"Good."

Within seconds, Graham has his belt undone, his zipper down, and my panties pulled to the side. His entire length pumps inside of me. It is fast. Impulsive. And exactly what I need to take the edge off. The more we go at it, the more my body craves his touch.

We both hit our zenith together, clutching onto each other for stability. I slide down his body, enjoying every hard edge I scrape across on the journey.

"You're going to be the death of me," he sighs, straightening my poor dress before fixing his own clothing back into place.

I give him a sly smile. "Then quit attacking me."

He rubs his hand down his face. "I have never lost this much control before—especially while trying to run my damn company."

I give him a sheepish look. "Sorry," I mouth innocently.

"You don't look sorry. You look satisfied."

"Well, that too."

"You may be the reason why I fire all the male staff members and just hire females."

I make a face. "That sounds like a horrible idea. You know how moody we can get," I joke.

"This is true."

Graham leads me to the sink area where we wash hands. When I start to dampen a paper towel to clean myself, he discards of it before I get the chance.

"But—"

"I want your body to have every reminder it can of where I've been. What I own. I want to possess your thoughts, because you consume mine."

I bite my bottom lip and watch his reflection in the mirror. With a smack to my ass and a yelp from me, we leave the restroom.

Graham shows me around the different departments of his building. When we pass through several corridors with huge, framed advertisements displayed on the walls, Graham briefly shows me the different layout ads and magazine features, adding a few comments about the dates behind each. I am surprised Sophia is not lurking around the building; we have yet to run into her. I resist mentioning her name. Maybe it is her day off or maybe she is keeping the low profile Graham told her to do.

"You want to head out and get some lunch?" he asks.

"Sounds good." Now that my nerves have simmered down, my stomach is cramping from hunger.

We leave HH and walk to a little bistro a few blocks away and get delicious Thai food. I enjoy an iced coffee made with condensed milk with my meal. It definitely helps with the burn from the spicy coconut chicken rice soup I ordered.

"Promise me you will be safe tonight when you go out with Claire?"

"I'm always safe."

He eyes me speculatively. "Danger always finds you. And I'll be on the brink of a nervous breakdown all evening until I know you get back to your townhouse safely."

"Just relax. I'll be fine. Plus, I am sure you will have a whole Project Angie squad prepared to slay any hypothetical dragons I encounter."

His eyes flash with an emotion I cannot distinguish. "Don't leave your drink unattended. Definitely do not drink from anyone else. And please don't forget that there are nefarious people out there in the world trying to hurt women for their own sick agendas."

I swallow a sip of my drink and look down at my hands. "I'll be careful," I say sadly. "I hate that you're so worried. But I really need this time with Claire to make sure she knows I can still be a good friend to her and be in a relationship with you. She is family to me."

Graham nods his head as if it makes sense to him as to my strong desire to have this time with her. We finish our meals and walk into the main lobby of the second building of HH. I haven't seen this area yet. Graham has key cards to get through three doors. There are no metal detectors, and the security staff are just sprinkled throughout the area—instead of lined up near the door for the admittance of employees and visitors.

"What's on the afternoon agenda?" I ask.

"I would like to show you some of the new design pieces we are working on. Maybe get your opinion?"

I stop and look up at him. His eyes are a rich shade of blue in the artificial light of the lobby. "My opinion? I don't know anything about jewelry. It took me twenty-three years to get my ears pierced."

His eyes travel to my ears, where my little studs from Ink Coat are situated. He nods his head, while trailing his fingers gently over my earrings.

The residual soreness causes me to flinch. I still cannot believe I went through with the very thing that I feared.

"I would still love to hear your thoughts on a few projects anyway."

I swallow. I am not really sure how to feel. Nervous? Excited? Thankful that Graham respects me enough to value my opinion?

We continue walking until we are in the elevator car. He pushes some buttons on the number pad, and we ascend. Once we stop, we exit into an open floor plan. The layout is modern with massive industrial desks spaced around with huge fixtures coming down from the ceilings to offer ample lighting to each workspace. Several groups of workers are on stools, with sketchbooks and pencils in hand. A few stop and eye up Graham as he walks with me around some of the workstations.

It feels awkward—like we are interrupting some creativity by our mere presence.

I follow Graham hesitantly as he joins a group working on earring sketches. He sits down on a stool and pulls me to his side so I am leaning my bottom against his propped up knee. Even if I wanted a job here—even doing something menial—I would be pegged as the girl who got her job by spreading her legs for the boss. Everyone who witnesses Graham's possessive touch on me would know that I would only be here as a convenience to him. And that is not how I want to feel for the long term.

I cannot allow any man to inhibit me from the things that I want to do in the world. While there was a time I didn't have much to live for, I am starting to have a different outlook, and it is a positive one.

"Let me see the three versions your team has been working on," Graham says to a male worker who quickly retrieves three drawing pads that each feature a different style.

I look at the earring designs and try to imagine the finished product. All look simply stated, but beautiful. One pair are drop downs, another studs, and another set appear to be dangly loops with diamonds attached to the ends.

"Wow," I say, trying to envision what the pairs would look like in 3D. "These all look incredible."

Several male team members look from me to Graham and then smile at my praise. I guess they think that having an "in" with the boss is beneficial to them if I approve. As if my positive opinion will equate to a hefty paycheck bonus.

"Thank you," Graham says with pride but shifts in his seat. "Now, tell me where there may be faults in the designs."

I swallow. What? I have no experience in this. I don't

even wear earrings. Well, I do now, but I just started a day ago.

"Just try," he whispers into my ear. "It's just an opinion or another perspective. You're a designer from all the sewing items you have moved into our place. So, I would love to hear some thoughts about these pieces that we may have overlooked."

I nod and climb up onto one of the tall backless stools, leaning over the drafts. I look at the sketches some more and look up at the team lead for this particular group. "Do you have a 3D model of what the designs would look like?"

"We have a computer simulation of all the pieces," the lead states concisely and confidently.

I nod and then furrow my brow. "Maybe something out of plastic?"

"We never really do a 3D model for earrings. Sometimes for bigger pieces, yes. What's your logic?"

I can feel Graham tense at my side over his worker's curt question. Maybe he didn't mean for it to come across as aggressively as it does. I gently squeeze Graham's hand that is resting on his knee to keep him from steamrolling the situation.

I was asked to give my opinion, and while I was reluctant at first, I am now trying to prove myself to a stranger who cannot stop staring at me. I may not know anything about jewelry, but Graham is right, I do have a love for design. When I would make more complex clothing items, sometimes I would replicate the style using very cheap fabric, just to get an idea for the final product. That is all I am trying to get across to the team lead. Why he cannot be receptive to my ideas is beyond me. Is it because I am female? Or is it because he thinks I am the boss's fucktoy? I am not really sure which thought pattern is worse.

I clear my throat, fix my hair behind my shoulder, and straighten my posture. "If there is access to a 3D printer, then it will be easy and cost pennies for your team to cut them out and print to real-life size." I have no experience with the technology behind all of this. However, when I broke a uniquely shaped button off of my favorite shirt, I had Zander print me a new one while at work to match the rest. It was so helpful to be able to replicate sizes for something very specific. "Perhaps, being able to feel the earrings in actual hands prior to production would help in determining if they are too cumbersome. It would be easier to see if the design needs to be altered in length or size because you would have a solid representation of the product. This is what I would do before I made an actual prototype and wasted valuable resources for something that might need multiple alterations."

He nods his head and glances at Graham, who appears to be deep in thought.

"Can this be done?" Graham asks the team.

"Of course," the team lead says confidently, but I see through his overzealous positivity. I don't think he thinks fondly of my idea. "This would definitely help with managing other design flaws as well."

"Do that then," Graham instructs. A few men jump up from the table and disappear down into the elevator with laptops in hand.

After several long minutes, the team lead seems to have moved from being embarrassed to being introspective. I continue asking several questions about the type of metal used and the different post backings for how the earrings will stay in the ears. As expected, Graham's jewelry line consists of the best precious metals—mainly platinum and gold—that he imports primarily from Canada and South Africa where they are mined.

When the 3D models arrive back, I hold them in my hand and examine them. I am reluctant about saying anything negative in front of this table of men. Who am I to even be qualified to do this?

Graham whispers so only I can hear, "I would love to hear your thoughts, sweetheart. You obviously have some."

I smile up at him. "I love these drop down earrings. I just worry that the heaviness of the diamonds would pull out the ear and cause some unbalance. Maybe the backing could be altered to compensate for the weight distribution?"

"But we—"

"Keep going, Angela," Graham interrupts the team lead, giving him a stern look of disapproval.

I swallow hard. I hate being in the middle of something that is bigger than just sharing my opinion. "The studs seem nice but with the shape not being uniform, I would imagine a bunch of women constantly looking in the mirror to make sure they are *in place* and not turned opposite ways. I guess you could switch out the round stones from the drop down pairs for the pear cut stones for the studs. Then it would look more like tear drops dangling instead. I think that would be more elegant."

"I hope someone is taking written notes," Graham stresses, eyeing each of his workers with an unspoken directive. He runs a hand down my spine, making me shiver. "Go on."

"The dangle pair just needs to be short enough not to touch the shoulder. I think too long would snag clothing. Or tickle the shoulders if strappy clothing is worn."

Graham looks at me with an expression I cannot decipher. Is he mad or pissed off or—

"You guys get all of that? And will you now hire some females for your team to add a different layer of perspective for the gender who will mostly be buying and wearing your creations?"

"Yes sir," the team lead says calmly. If he didn't have his tail between his legs before, he does now. He won't even make eye contact with me.

I slide off my stool and walk with Graham to the elevator. He kisses my forehead as we wait. It feels weird openly advertising our relationship for everyone here to see. Yet I am thankful that he cares enough about me to not give a damn what others think.

"You have a knack for seeing the big picture."

I shake my head. "I just tried to imagine what it would look like wearing the jewelry and then think of anything that may go wrong or not be comfortable." I shrug. It was no big deal. "The point is to wear it without knowing you are wearing it, right?"

"Yeah. But you aren't giving yourself enough credit. You basically walked in there and served them all their balls on a silver platter that they didn't want to eat. In front of their boss. You are very badass."

I scrunch up my face, covering it with both hands. "No. No, please don't say that," I cringe. "I don't need more people here thinking negatively of me."

"Wait, what? Who thinks that?"

"Sophia. And probably your entire security team," I say, using my fingers to keep track of the running count. "Maybe even a few people who were crushing on their boss but then saw me here today. Oh, and perhaps those who saw me freak out when I came to attack you during your meeting." I lose count and shrug. "So, practically everyone in this building."

"No one thinks that way of you, baby. You just have these ideas," he says with a pause, tapping a finger into my hair, "in your head. So, I would advise you to just stop thinking about it. Plus, Sophia isn't even here today, and besides her opinion of you doesn't matter."

Which basically confirms the notion that she thinks negatively of me and has made her feelings known to Graham. Shocker.

We arrive at the floor that hosts the Marketing Department, which is probably one of the largest departments in the company, at least in comparison to the others I have seen so far today. Graham introduces me to his marketing manager—the woman pushing for Graham and Sophia to be seen publicly for the sake of sparking up buzz around the jewelry line. It is not a bad strategy. Except this is not a Hollywood scene where movies are being released. This is Portland.

This department is vastly different from the one we just left. This floor is decorated modernly with bright colorful abstract art on the walls, as well as mockup ads of the jewelry. Computer screens line glass desks, and fun chairs rest behind them in a variety of neon colors. On the far end of the room, a photo area is set up where I assume Sophia—the signature model for Jealousy—is photographed. There is a makeup section, wardrobe section, and a changing area. Everything is neat and organized. The director for this floor must have some major OCD. And I'm not talking about the healthy amount that most humans have. I am afraid to even walk on the perfectly polished marble floors and smudge them up with my heels.

"Come," Graham says, pushing me gently toward a large conference table that is in the middle of the room. "I want you to see some of the layouts for our future ads and give me your thoughts."

Huge poster-sized ads are secured to the table with a glass sheet protector overtop. Written notes made with washable markers accompany each ad. Team members can make comments or list out needed changes to any of the works-in-progress.

"What do you think?" Graham probes again, pulling me to his side.

I have been silent for several minutes as I try to take in the entire scene, and hopefully not have a repeat of what just happened on the design floor.

I look over at more lip advertisements—similar to the one that is in his main office. Everything is overly sexualized, close up, and featuring the jewelry for sale. My mind visualizes Sophia getting her makeup professionally done, and then flirting with the camera as she works. I do have thoughts. I am just not sure I want to voice them and have them backfire on me.

Graham cups my face and leans down to be level with my eyes. "Be honest. I can already tell you are trying to put up your guard."

How does he read me so easily? Am I that obvious?

"You wear your emotions on your face and in the tightness of your shoulders, sweetheart. Like I said the first night I met you at the mansion's pool, you would lose all your money to me at poker."

My bottom lip pouts out. "I lost all my money to you at Monopoly too. And my clothes."

He throws back his head and laughs, causing everyone in the large room to turn and look at him in shock. It is like they have never seen him laugh before. And once the newness of it wears off, the employees turn back to their projects and resume working again.

"Back to business, Angie. If you saw these ads in public, would you want to buy the jewelry?"

"For starters, I wouldn't be able to afford anything you were selling." I shrug. "So, doubtful."

He looks at me deep in thought and rubs his hand down his chin. His skin is smoothly shaven, and I wish he would leave a little scruff because I find it sexy.

"Tell me what is in your head."

"I don't know, Graham. I have zero experience with any of this, and I don't want to have my *nobody* opinion sway you into something that is not financially wise."

He rubs at my back in a casual manner. "Tell me anyway."

"I think you should run two lines. Maybe have a sister company that is an offshoot for what you already have created. One company is higher end and luxurious, catering to those who want one-of-a-kind pieces and don't scoff at the price tag that comes with such items. The other company appeals to those who want more than costume jewelry but at a more reasonable price. I think that both companies can still use similar designs for the products—just use less clear diamonds or less pure metals for the lower line. However, I would make the ads cater to those you are marketing toward. I think the higher end line appeals to those who are in relationships. Make the ads with flair and include couples in them."

He nods his head, and I can tell he is letting my ideas marinate. It feels good being able to voice my thoughts without fear of him berating me or making me feel stupid—even if he may not agree. He is proving to me that I can be an equal in some respects.

"Keep going."

"The ads for the less costly line, I would create them based on the month they are put out. I would make them seasonal and edgy. Maybe for fall, feature vampire teeth in the ad. Keep the colors blood red. Valentine's Day time, incorporate flowers into your ad. Summer, keep the graphics light in tone and airy." I sigh and lean my butt against the table. "I don't know. This is not my thing. I just think that someone who is shopping the less expensive line will probably be single and may want to treat herself to something nice without having to wait for a partner to do so for her. I would also see what movie, book, or entertainment avenue was trending at the time on social media and maybe incorporate aspects of those phenomena into the ads. Ride on the coattails of something already very popular. And if you can predict what will be the latest craze before it actually hits mega stardom, then being slightly ahead of the curve would help as well and possibly send profits skyrocketing exponentially."

Graham taps a finger along his jawline, looking back at

the mockups that are plastered along the table. "What about the male line with watches and cufflinks?"

"I would stick to dark colors and no humans in the ads. Guys want simple. Let the actual product speak for itself. Guys don't buy into fantasy the way that women do. And I bet they don't want to compare themselves to anyone in the ad. Too much ego."

"You are incredibly insightful."

I furrow my brow and let his words marinate. It has been so long since I have expressed myself to someone else like this and it be rewarded. I love sewing my own clothes —but it is primarily for me. I make them the way I want them, without thinking of others. Thus, giving my opinion on ads and marketing projects is so foreign. And maybe knowing that my opinion is just that makes it easier to vocalize my thoughts because there is less of a consequence if I am wrong or off the mark.

Graham hugs me, as I whisper, "Thank you." He kisses me on the forehead and then squeezes me tighter.

"Can I run with some of these ideas, Graham?" the marketing manager asks.

I startle at her voice. I wasn't even sure she was listening to me rattle them off; she seemed to zone out and go about her business while I was sharing them with Graham.

"Yeah, write up a plan and show me a series of mockups for me to give the final review. Email them when your team has them completed."

"Deadline?"

"Two weeks."

"Done."

I follow Graham back to the elevators and kiss him on the lips. "I have to go if I'm going to make it home in time to change and get ready for Girls' Night."

His eyes flinch when I refer to my townhouse as being home. To me, it still is in a way. He recovers and pulls out his phone from his inner breast pocket. "Can you take Angie back to the townhouse? Yeah. Add two more. Make sure they blend. Nonintrusive." He guides me inside the elevator car when it arrives. "Okay, great. Keep me posted. Hourly, nothing less."

I listen to the interchange and watch the tic of his jaw. He is not thrilled with me going out tonight. But life goes on. I especially know that. I watch silently as he ends the call, hits the lobby button, and leans against the metal handrail. "I'll text you while I'm out tonight. Will that ease your worries?"

"No. But do so anyway, because I always love to hear from you."

When we get to the lobby, Collins is waiting for me. I give Graham a longer kiss goodbye.

"Thank you for showing me around your work. I really enjoyed seeing you in action."

"Thank you for a wonderful day. I think we should make every day bring-your-girlfriend-to-work day."

I giggle and then get serious, "Yeah, and watch-your-company-plummet-while-the-boss-boyfriend-fucks-said-girlfriend-all-over-the-damn-place. Your dick would get raw anyway."

He laughs, "Boss Boyfriend, eh? What happened to Teddy Graham?"

I burst out laughing to the point that tears are filling my eyes. "That's the name Claire calls you."

"And why is that, Angie?"

"She thinks you are a big ol' teddy bear who is just a softy under a hard exterior."

"But what do *you* think?"

I make an exaggerated point of looking deep in thought. I then move closer and grind myself discreetly against his groin, causing him to twitch. "I think there is nothing *soft* about you under your exterior."

His groan is only for my ears. I pivot on my heel and walk over to Collins with a little added sway to my hips. I can feel Graham's eyes burn into my retreating backside.

I turn and look over my shoulder at him.

And wave goodbye.

27

"Well, damn," I mutter, staring at the revised sign when we get to the front of the line.

"Shit," Claire commiserates at my side, with a hiss of solidarity.

"I guess it is Ladies' Night *and* Open Mic Night," I sigh. The poster has an add-on strip of paper with the dual night posted with scribbled Sharpie lettering. Very classy.

"Doesn't mean he'll be here."

"Except that he hasn't missed one of these nights in the past four years."

"Ugh. This night was supposed to be relaxing. Now it's going to be a race to get drunk the fastest."

My head moves up and down as the realization hits me. "Yup, pretty much."

We have been waiting outside in the cold for twenty minutes with black dresses on, made of the thinnest material. Despite being more modest than our typical going-out attire, it is only forty degrees, and I regret not sucking it up and wearing a coat. It's too late now. My knees are banging together, and I am bouncing about on my heels just to stay warm. We are just a few people away from entering The Shack. I am sure the volume of people stuffed inside the wooden box will bring on the sweat, so I should savor this moment. But I don't.

Claire and I squeeze through the side entrance and push through the barricade of people to find the bar. Two male bartenders are moving quickly behind the counter, mixing up drinks and swiping cards.

"Half-price night ladies, what'll it be?" one asks us—serving us before a few other customers waiting longer.

"Two Irish car bombs," Claire responds, "but make them doubles."

"Waters too," I add. I stick my tongue out at Claire's disapproving expression. "Your liver will thank me later." One of us needs to be responsible.

Our drinks arrive, and a pang of guilt stabs at me.

"Now's not the time to be health conscious. Now's the time to make stupid decisions. And think about the consequences—"

"Later," I interject.

"Never," she corrects. "Cheers to no regrets."

"Cheers."

A guy around our age plops down on the stool beside me. He has a five o'clock shadow, gray ball cap, and navy hoodie on. He appears single. I hold on to my drink, knowing that bad things can happen if I let down my guard. Claire may be living the carefree life right now, but the drugging and near rape has made me more cautious. More self-aware.

"Can I buy you ladies a drink?"

"No," Claire and I say in unison, then look at each other and burst out laughing. The car bomb takes effect fast, and I already feel lighter than I did five minutes ago. I drink my water and try to make some better choices tonight.

"Come on, not even one drink?" He has a southern drawl to his voice, and while I may have found it sexy at one time in my life, right now I only have one man on my brain.

"No," we say again.

Claire leans over my lap to make eye contact with the stranger. "This is our girls' night. We are not on the prowl. We have men. They are jackasses most of the time. But they are still ours."

He nods his head but handles the rejection well. He takes a long swig of his beer and goes back to playing on his phone.

The opening act makes an announcement about what Open Mic Night is about for those who are here for the first time. Then he jams out to some Papa Roach song with his bandmates.

Claire and I listen to several acts and relax, thinking we are in the clear. And then I see the wavy blond hair and the thrift shop T-shirt from the side of the stage and know it is Zander before ever seeing his face. He turns, pushes his hair back from his forehead, and spots me at the bar. I give him a lopsided smile and a wave. But he just ignores me with a sad frown.

I miss him. I miss my best friend. The guy who would make me laugh, sneak me contraband candy, and tease me for breaking my computer for the umpteenth time. I miss things being easy between us. When I could talk to him about almost anything and never be met with judgment. Who could blame me for wanting to preserve that type of friendship and never let it get damaged?

The current act finishes up, and Zander walks onto the stage solo. He is a bit of a celebrity here on nights like this. He always performs but never by himself. Tonight he is alone. And my heart hurts from the symbolism.

I think back to our duet and how he brought me out of my shell. That's Zander, though. He gives those he cares about the confidence to be themselves and to flourish while still stepping outside comfort zones.

He clears his throat into the mic, and he stares out into the crowd. "This song is dedicated to all the assholes out there who think it's a genius idea to fall in love with their best friend. And the horrific nightmare that follows when she breaks your heart."

The crowd goes wild with boos and hands raised into the air. A bunch of "fuck women" chants echo—despite the majority of the crowd being female for Ladies' Night.

He bends down and retrieves a shot glass a patron delivers to him. He throws back the amber liquid into his throat and wipes his hand over his mouth to dry up any residual drops. "This song is called 'Best Friend.'"

I stare at Zander as he adjusts the mic and starts to play a rhythm on his guitar. The words that follow are meant for me. I am the one who is the heartbreaker. I broke him. All because I belong to someone else.

I used to settle for less, hmm
I would take what I could get, yeah

I did not need those three little words
All I wanted was more

But you never saw me for who I am, no
You had eyes for another cruel joke
That's not how fairytales always go, ohh
Bad guy wins, underdog chokes

Why did no one warn me
Why did no one care
To tell me I was an idiot
To fall in love with my best friend

I let down my armor
You broke down my walls
I fell head over heels
With a beautiful girl

Why did no one warn me
No, no, nooo
Why did no one care
Oh, oh, ohhh
This would have been easier
If we never met

Love is for fools, oh, oh, ohhh
Protect my own heart
Listen to my words, oh, oh, ohhh
Never fall in love with your best friend

When the song ends, he slams back another shot. He

slings his guitar over his shoulder and tracks me again with his eyes. "And in case she is here listening," he slurs, "just know that it's agony knowing that I lost you as my best friend because I was helpless in keeping myself from falling head over fucking heels for you." He stumbles off the stage and is greeted by a mob of girls who now see him as a hero.

"Well, that was intense," Claire mutters beside me.

I can only nod and stare at Z. I feel sick. Like I could throw up from the pain that this whole freaking mess has caused.

He is hurting.

But so am I.

I lost my best friend too. And he can't see past his own pain to even notice mine.

"So much for a relaxing night out for drinks," I mutter sarcastically. "I feel like my heart just got run over by a Mack truck carrying explosives."

"He is going to come around, you'll see."

"I'm not sure how much of this I can take without losing it."

I alternate drinks with water. Claire orders us some appetizers to share, and we listen to the artists on stage entertain the crowd.

I pop in a jalapeño popper and slide down off the stool. "Be right back. Gonna go use the restroom. Save my seat."

I bump and push my way through the crowd and wait in line for the ladies' room. I pull out my cell from my handbag and text Graham like I promised I would.

Angie: Hiya

The moving dots let me know he is typing a response back.

Graham: I miss you baby.

Graham: Hope you are having a fun time with Claire.

Angie: Nope. Sucks ass.

I send the saddest emoji I can find in my preset list to punctuate my words. That is my current mood. Sad and slightly tipsy—but I don't think there is a face to represent that combo. I lean up against the wall and almost stumble into the girl waiting in front of me. My phone vibrates with an incoming call.

"Hi," I say to Graham.

"Why are you sad, sweetheart?" His tone is of genuine concern.

It is so loud with being closer to the stage where the speakers are stacked. "I just am."

"Why don't I send a car or come get you myself? Then you come here, and I'll cheer you up?"

I shake my head no. And then giggle at myself when I realize he can't see me.

"Can you slow down on the alcohol, baby? Please?"

I shake my head no again. Shit. I keep doing that. This time I laugh so hard I drop my phone.

"Angie? Angie, what happened?"

"Just drop me phone. Waiting for the pee station and this damn line is too long. Gonna use the men's side."

"That sounds like a horrible idea. Don't do that."

"But I gotta pee. Really bad." And my head throbs. I really haven't had that much to drink. For once, I have limited myself majorly. Maybe I am stressed from seeing Zander have a public throwdown with my heart. "Gotta go, I'm next in line."

I hit the end button and go into the next stall. I fish out my tin container of pills and pop one into my mouth. It should at least help with the headache. Unfortunately, there is no cure for heartbreak.

When I make my way back to the bar to find Claire, I see her talking with Zander and stop in my tracks. She is animated and yelling and waving her angry finger at him. I don't need her to slay my dragons, but I love her for trying.

I reach into my handbag and pull out another pill—for extra reassurance. I toss it into my mouth and chomp down on it. The taste is so bitter and nasty that I second guess why I do this shit to myself. I need something to wash down the lingering flavor. I roll my shoulders back and force myself to walk into the train wreck that is about to catch on fire.

I reach between Claire and Zander to grab the drink that she ordered for me. I take a big gulp and then wipe my mouth on my bare forearm.

The two of them stop their showdown and stare at me. I feel dizzy and lightheaded but ready to clear the air and defend myself. Enough is enough. Tears fill my eyes, and I pull on Zander's arm to get him to follow me. "We need to talk. Outside."

I plow through the sea of people, tugging Zander behind me—afraid that if I let go, he will run. I push open the side exit and cough at the group of smokers lighting up cigarettes and puffing out a polluted cloud into the cold air.

Yuck. I take the ramp down into the back parking lot and find an area that is not inundated with smoke.

The frigid temperature and Zander's hard expression sober me up enough to say my piece. I stare right into his harsh eyes as mine start to water.

"I'm so sorry I hurt you. But you hurt me too."

He flinches at my words. But it's true, so I continue.

"You put an ultimatum on us. I either date you or you walk out of my life. How is that fair? Not only do you blindside me with your revelation, but you make me feel like shit for not reciprocating your feelings. Maybe I have led you on? And if I have, that was never my intention. I never wanted to hurt you. Ever. So I get you are pissed off at me. Fine. But why do you keep trying to seek revenge by hurting me in return?" Tears pour down my face and leave cold streaks on my skin.

He just stands there. Looking at me as if he doesn't even know me or recognize me. Maybe he never thought I would turn the tables on him. But I feel good for the first time in weeks over this situation. I am not completely at fault, and he deserved to hear it from my own mouth.

I am cold and done standing out here in a barely lit parking lot, while smoke starts to dirty up the air around us from the people ignoring the ten feet away from a building rule. I turn and go back up the ramp inside the building, never looking back. I have said what I needed to say. It is up to Zander on what to do next—if anything.

I scope out the best way to get through the crowd and over to the bar. People are packed in like sardines in a can, and it is nauseatingly warm with everyone breathing the stale air.

"Hey bitch," a masculine voice says from behind me.

It takes my brain a few seconds to register who it belongs to. Ugh.

Russell.

I turn around and look at his beady eyes and smug expression. What did I ever see in him?

"We meet again," he says bitterly. His eyes rake down my body, and I feel violated and dirty.

He looks rugged. Like his life isn't as affluent as it was a few months ago. He didn't look so unkempt when he stopped into the cafe for a smoothie last week. But upon closer look, his eyes appear like the light that was once behind them has been snuffed out.

"What do you want from me?" I ask, hands on my hips. I turn back to see if I can see Claire. Even on tiptoes I can barely see the bartenders. My arm gets jerked, and I whirl myself around. "Do not touch me!"

His eyes glare with a fiery hatred. "Oh, quit being dramatic. It's not like you aren't asking for some fun in this" —his eyes narrow in on my breasts—"skintight outfit."

"You're disgusting. And I'm leaving." So much for being conservative tonight. Even pervs will find some way to objectify you. Asshole. I have zero tolerance for them.

I work my way through the crowd and am a few yards from Claire. I push through a bunch of people who are drunk and swaying to the acoustic song being played by a few people with guitars.

"Wow, what took you so long?" she asks. "Saving your seat nearly cost me an arm."

"Sorry. I wanted to clear the air with Zander. It was a fail." I take a sip of the cocktail that is in my area and enjoy the sweetness. However, I just can't find the desire to keep drinking it. Switching to my water, I take several gulps. Alcohol isn't going to dull any of the pain I am feeling inside. "At least I got to finally vocalize my feelings of how he hurt me too."

She nods and checks her phone. "Ethan keeps sending me texts despite this being a no-contact night. He always breaks the rules. So I'm just ignoring him."

"Oh yeah, I've been meaning to ask how your"—I tap my chin to think of the right word—"*endeavor* went the other night."

"Mission Hershey Hole was a no-go. I couldn't go through with it."

"It's a big commitment," I point out. "Once you give it over, I'm sure that's all he'll want."

Claire lets out a long groan. "Most definitely. I just"—she looks off toward the stage and then back at me—"need more time."

"Do what is right for you. Always."

My phone rings with a call from Graham.

"Go ahead. Answer it. We both know how he gets when you make him worry."

I laugh bitterly. "Yeah, I'm surprised he isn't lurking in the corners here just to make sure I'm not lying in a gutter somewhere." I slide the answer bar.

"Angela."

"Graham."

"Did you get to the restroom safely?"

"Yes. And I'm perfectly safe here as well with Cl—" A loud noise erupts behind me, and I whip around to see a massive fight break out. "Shit."

The singing on stage stops, and the herd of people start rushing toward the exit to avoid being a part of the throw-down that is happening in the center of the venue. I look to Claire. Her eyes are wide.

"Angie! Angie, answer me! What's going on?"

"There's a huge fight and people are fleeing," I yell. My words jumble together, and I try to keep my throat from closing up in fear.

"Fuck! I need you to look for the man with the gray ball cap. He was sitting beside you earlier. Do you see him? His name is Austin. Do not leave his side. I'm coming for you." His voice is calculated. Controlled.

I scan the bar and see the same man. He's the one who offered to buy Claire and me drinks earlier. "I see him."

Austin jumps across the top of the bar to get to me faster. In an instant, I am pulled to him and flipped behind the wall of the bar. The sudden action causes my phone to slip out of my hand. I frantically search for it and see the shiny redness of blood dripping angrily from my right knee.

My eyes close and open. My vision blurs with the sight of glass and James's helpless body. The smell of gasoline penetrates my nostrils and burns the inner lining. My name is being chanted to me in my ear. Over and over and over again…

Angie.

Angie?

ANGIE!

But I am stuck in my nightmare. It is the same night-mare that I can't stop reliving. I can't separate the past memories from my current reality.

I struggle to hold on to the present, my fear paralyzing

me and making me lose track of my surroundings. I squeeze my eyes shut and take a deep breath. When I open them, I am looking into the eyes of Graham's hired security worker, Austin. He instantly looks relieved when I seem to see him.

"Are you hurt?" he asks. "Can you walk?"

I nod my head and then realize that I was talking to Graham. "My phone! My phone! And Claire! I can't leave without Claire!" I shake in Austin's arms as he binds me to his side. He is young. Can't possibly be much older than twenty-one. However, his reflexes and ability to think on his feet make him seem seasoned.

"Calm down, Miss McFee. I'll get you out of here safely. Just stay calm."

"Claire! Where is she? What about Zander?"

"Claire is with my partner who was also assigned to detail for tonight. She'll be safe. Worthington left to go home after you chatted with him outside."

Austin snatches up my phone from the ground, sliding it into his pants pocket. He tucks me close to his side as gun shots sound. A series of them—one after the other.

Oh shit. My heart races, and I feel like I'm going to be sick. I whimper into Austin's body, the sound of my own voice muffled. I am trembling so much that I feel like I am going to pass out.

Austin pushes me farther behind the protection of the bar. He then crouches down, flips up his pants leg, and releases his own gun. Is he even old enough to have a gun? He looks younger than me now that I take another glance. I don't know much about guns but it looks to be a Glock. My eyes fill with tears as I take in the scene. I try to focus on the present and not drift back into the past, which swirls around in my head, waiting to swallow me up. The blast noise is so loud that it feels like I am in the eye of the storm.

"Just breathe," he instructs. "I promise to get you out safely."

I try to concentrate on breathing between my words as I ask, "What is happening?"

He ignores me, places a device into his ear from his jeans pocket, and speaks so fast that I can't even understand what or who he is talking to.

"Stay down," he instructs. Austin cocks his gun and evaluates the situation before sliding back down to the dirty floor with me. His eyes level on me, and he takes a deep breath. "We are getting out of here through the kitchen. I need you to stay low. Do not stop and look. Just keep moving and do not let go of my hand. If for some reason we get separated—"

I let out a small whimper. Austin cups my face and forces me to look at him.

"Listen, Miss McFee. If for some reason we get separated, I want you to stay low. And stay unseen. Hide. Someone will find you."

He pulls out a bracelet from his pocket that is made out of a bendable rubber and has a rectangular plate at the top. He grabs my trembling hand and snaps the device around my left wrist.

The sound of a dozen or so gunshots reverberates across the room. Are they getting closer? The volume of noise inside has not dissipated at all. If anything, it has gotten louder. The exits are probably completely blocked with people trying to get out at the bottleneck.

"We're moving now," Austin says—more so to the

invisible person listening on the other end of the earpiece than to me.

He locks his hand around mine and shields me with his body as he guides me to the door behind the bar. It is locked. He points his gun at the handle and stays back. I hide my face into his back. The gun must have a suppressor because the sound is not nearly as bad as I was expecting.

Austin kicks open the door and then shuts it hard behind him. We move quickly through the prep stations and the oven area. When we make our way into the supply area, we are inundated by a mob of people rushing from the main floor like a herd of elephants. My hand slips out of Austin's, and I am crushed against a metal standing freezer. I scream out in pain, as darkness floods my vision.

Pitch black.

"Austin! Austin, where are you? Austin!"

The roar echoing through the kitchen makes my head hurt. The banging metal sound ricochets through my ears from the pots and pans slamming together. I get bumped to the side, staggering into a shelving unit. Things fall onto my head, as I get shoved forward. On my hands and knees, I crawl into what feels like a corner and curl into a ball. Light flutters into the space, flashing images of panicked faces as people try to escape.

My bracelet lights up with a bright green color, and I scan the area. Dread fills every inch of my body. I feel trapped, like I will never get out of here.

The crowd pushes through, knocking down the weak, like a stampede. In the background, I can hear the pelting of gunshots.

Then I see it. The light. It is the same one that is illuminated on my wrist. Sitting up, I scream at the top of my lungs, "Austin!"

The matching light moves toward me, and strong arms envelop me.

"Thank God I found you," Austin grunts out with relief.

He picks me up from the floor and carries me into an alcove where there's a window. Lights from the parking lot shine through the pane. My eyes try to adjust to the change. With the handle of his gun, Austin busts through the window, clearing the glass. He rips off his jacket and uses it to pad the wooden part of the frame.

"Climb up," he directs. "I'm going to jump down and then I will catch you."

I get hoisted up. Within seconds, Austin descends. I take a deep breath and climb through the glassless frame, taking the leap toward the gravelly parking lot, into Austin's awaiting arms. My scream burns my lungs, and I gasp for the fresh air that I thought I would never breathe again.

Chaos unfolds as the entire building is consumed with first responders and people fleeing the scene. Austin starts to move, toting my limp body with him as I just channel all my focus into gulping up the oxygen that I am starving for.

When we are away from the mob of people and safely on the sidewalk, Austin puts me back on my feet, running his hands over my arms and trying to see if I have been hurt.

"Are you okay, Miss McFee?"

"Claire?" I pant, bending down and placing my hands on my knees.

"Angie!" she yells, running to me and wrapping me in a hug. "I was so worried."

Austin and his security partner pull us away from the

building as the police and SWAT teams have finally arrived to handle the mayhem still happening inside.

"We need to get away from here," Austin announces, pulling me along to a fast-paced run. Claire and the other security guy join us as we run past all of the cars trying to get out of the parking lot. Roads are blocked, and people are running and screaming from the building. It is a disaster.

I hear my name being called up ahead, and I look up to see Graham and Ethan running toward us, in the shadow of the streetlight. Claire and I break free and charge as fast as we can to our men. I jump into Graham's arms, and he lifts me up and cradles me to his chest. He kisses all over my face and wraps his hands into my hair. I sob and wipe my damp nose into his shirt, breathing in his smell.

"I thought I was going to die," I wail. "People were fighting and shooting at each other. And I have no freaking clue what was happening."

"You are safe. I have you."

"I was so scared."

"I was beside myself with worry over you. My life does not exist without you in it."

I lift my head to see Ethan and Claire kissing and embracing each other. I can hear Ethan telling her he is taking her to his place and not to argue with him. I already know where I will be spending the night. And the whole weekend. So, I don't even ask.

Ethan and Graham shake hands and say a few parting words before I get carried down the sidewalk to the waiting car.

"Are you okay?" he asks, his gaze cast down to me.

I shake my head and shiver against his strong chest. I

am just so cold. He opens up the backseat and straps me inside before shutting the door. I kick off my shoes and pull my feet up to the seat and wrap my arms around my knees. I stare out the window as Graham speaks to his men. Collins makes his way to our vehicle and enters the front seat. Graham shakes Austin's hand, and then it transitions into a partial hug. He does the same to the other man, whom I have yet to officially meet.

A dozen marked and unmarked police vehicles race down the road we are on and surround The Shack. Tonight was crazy. And if it weren't for Graham's men keeping an eye on me, I might still be inside—trapped and alone.

The door opposite me opens and Graham slides inside, slamming it.

"Angie," he says breathily. He looks like he has aged a few years just from the wrinkles forming on his forehead.

"I'm sorry," I whisper.

"You didn't do anything wrong, sweetheart. This may have just been a freak occurrence and not something targeted. Nothing that you could have prevented. I'm just glad you were not harmed. You aren't harmed, right?"

He runs his hands up and down my sides and arms. When he spots the dried blood on my knee and the bruises forming on my arm, he slips out of the car, opens the trunk, and comes back with a travel first aid kit. He opens the disposable wipes and cleans my wound and then places a bandage over the cut. Breaking open the ice pack, he places it on my arm.

"Thank you," I whisper. He takes such good care of me that it pulls at my heart.

Graham kisses me gently on the forehead. "There is

nothing in this world I wouldn't give you." Our car starts to pull forward and weave between the influx of first responders entering the lot. He removes my bracelet and places it in his pocket. "You sure you're okay?"

"I'm okay. Just really shaken up. There were so many people fighting and then the gun sh—"

"Shhh," he soothes, wiping the tears that keep flowing down my cheeks. "I'm so sorry you were in the middle of all of that. Plus, all the Zander drama. And then your ex-boyfriend who must have a learning problem because he cannot keep himself from harassing you."

"How did…" I start to ask how he knew about Russell but stop myself. Of course, Graham makes it a point to stay informed, whether it be through his own research or his hired men. What used to bother me in the past with his hindrance to my personal space is exactly what saved me from further trauma tonight. "Thank you."

"You never need to thank me. I'll always protect you, sweetheart." He bends down to kiss my hairline. "I just want to lock you away and shield you from all of this. Keep you hidden away from the nastiness of the world."

"I just want to go back to your place and—"

"Our place, baby. It is just as much yours as it is mine. If changing the name on the deed will help you see it that way, then so be it."

I look up into his burning blue eyes. He is sincere. And I love him for wanting to share his space—but mostly his life—with me.

"What was the bracelet for that Austin put on me?"

"It's a tracking device band. It was reassurance in case you got separated. That way I would be able to find you if you were missing. All of my men carry a set with them when they are in charge of guarding you. It is for a worst-case scenario. I just never thought tonight would be the night that the trackers would need to be utilized."

Collins gets us parked and safely into the building within fifteen minutes. Graham carries me the whole way into the elevator, through the main floor's living space, and upstairs to the bathroom. He draws me a bath and helps me inside.

"Are you not coming in?" I ask, leaning my head back to look at him.

He is resting his body along the tiled steps leading into the spa-sized tub.

"I just want to focus on you right now, baby. Make sure you are alright."

Graham hands me a glass of water, and I take a long sip. So many emotions flood through me, but I just try to focus on the here and now. I am safe.

He takes an empty cup from the supply basket and fills it with water. He dumps a few cups over my head and then pumps almond smelling shampoo into his hands. I relax my shoulders as he runs his fingers through my hair, massaging my scalp. It feels like heaven. He rinses out the soap and then adds some conditioner to the ends. I rest my head back and allow his fingers to rub at my neck and shoulders—turning me into a pile of Jell-O.

"That feels so good," I moan.

I can feel him smiling without even looking. It is like I can sense his mood without seeing his face.

Graham rinses out the conditioner and then takes a wide-toothed comb and brushes through my damp hair, removing tangles and playing with the locks. It feels divine.

"Do I need to go to the police station to write a report or something on the incident?"

"Collins is providing all of your contact information and if any witnesses need to produce a statement, they will be contacted. However, Austin had a clearer view of what went down, so his testimony would most likely trump yours."

I nod. "Everything happened so fast. It was like I wasn't even there."

He kisses my forehead, running his hands down my arms that are buried under the water. "I don't even want to imagine what my life would be without you in it."

Graham dries me off, wraps me into a fluffy robe, and hands me my toothbrush already loaded with paste. When I finish brushing, he carries me to bed. The covers are already pulled back and waiting for me to bury myself inside.

Graham joins me on the other side and settles himself behind me. He wraps his arms around me. "I love you," he whispers into my ear.

"I love you too."

And then we drift off to sleep.

28

The feel of the heat wakes up my senses. I move my head to the left, slowly opening my eyes. I blink hard. Through the moonlit darkness, I see the crimson liquid pour from his hairline at the temple. Suddenly eyes shoot open and stare at me through the blackness. Chocolate brown eyes. Beautifully eerie and mimicking mine. I jerk back and feel the coldness of the blowing air. The pain stemming from my lower back surges, making me groan and double over from the pressure.

No. No. No.

This can't be happening. Not again. I move my attention back to the body. A perfect body—now broken. The tremors start from my core, as my stomach twists from the sight. I find myself on the carpeted floor, crawling to the door in the corner of the room. I need a toilet.

Oh, shit! I make it to my feet. My hands press on the door to open it. A closet! My torso doubles over, my face staring at my knees in the darkness. I straighten myself and find another doorway. The light seeping out from under it helps me find the handle. I turn.

Nooo…

The pool of blood on the floor makes me crumble into a heap. I can feel the moisture saturating my skin. I blindly wipe it off, feeling it spreading instead. I squeeze my eyes shut, but the only thing I can see are the brown ones staring back—the whites filling with a vibrant crimson red. All the beauty gone…lifeless.

James!

My body lurches up in bed, the feeling of sweat dripping off my brow. Another nightmare. It was just a nightmare. I pat my hand to the other side of the bed, finding it empty. A door flies open, and a dark figure rushes to my side, fumbling with something on the nightstand.

"Fuck."

The light switches on, illuminating my shaking body. I pull my knees up to my chest, my head resting on top, rocking back and forth. I am naked, except for the blanket covering my lower half.

"Sweetheart, what happened? You alright? You had a bad dream about last night?"

"Not from last night." From the accident that took James away from me—the source of most of my nightmares.

Tears fly angrily out of my eyes as I remember the color of blood. My stomach dry heaves, warning me of what is next. I dart out of bed, searching the room for the bathroom, finding a series of doors, all closed. I shudder at the déjà vu feeling, still unsure of what is real or not. I have been in this bedroom many times, and I am struggling to find the bathroom. It is like my brain is having connectivity issues.

Graham's body shadows mine as he sees my dilemma and confusion over my surroundings. He pushes around me, taking me by the arm, opening the middle door in the back of the bedroom with ample speed. I hear a blur of soothing words—followed by a series of unintelligible curse words—none of them registering as being coherent. I fall over the open porcelain bowl, feeling my hair being pulled back from my sweaty neck. I retch the acid and bile from my system, grimacing and crying over the vinegar aftertaste. I grip the seat, my body lunging forward with each heave. Tears streak down my face, dripping into the water. I push away from the toilet, closing the lid and hitting the handle to flush. I slide to the floor, pressing my heated face to the cold tiles.

"No, please, leave me here to die," I whine, feeling my naked body being tugged upward. "Please…I need to die alone."

I hear a rustle and then padding and the creak of the door. I curl up in a naked ball and welcome the shivers penetrating through me, calming down the flaming heat. Seconds later, Graham is back—going against my wishes, of course—and has me lifted into a soft blanket and transported out the door. I catch a glimpse of my face in the mirror in passing, cringing at my blotchy skin and swollen eyes. He carries me downstairs and into the living room, placing me on the sofa and handing me a mug of hot cider.

I whisper a "thank you," barely recognizing the scratchiness of my own voice.

The TV is on with the local news channel covering the scene at The Shack. I listen as several reporters talk about the fireworks going off inside—causing the mass chaos as patrons tried to escape.

My forehead wrinkles over this discovery. “Fireworks?”

“Yes."

“There was not a shootout?”

“Apparently not.”

I can sense his reluctance to share information with me, as he grabs the remote and shuts off the power.

“Why would someone set off fireworks into a crowd? Was someone trying to cause fear and make everyone flee?”

“I don’t want you to worry about this. I have my men looking into it. I want you to tell me about your nightmare instead.”

He rubs the wrinkles from the fleece blanket over my back, silently coaxing me to open up to him. His eyes search mine for answers or at least some sort of explanation as to why I was screaming in the night and emptying the contents of my stomach into his perfectly pristine porcelain bowl.

The sun is barely visible over the mountains, indicating the start of a new day. But I feel like there is nothing about today that hints at a fresh start. I have so many unanswered questions about last night, and I am still having the same issues as I was months ago with nightmares. If I can’t get over my past, how will I ever be able to move forward with my future? It’s like I am always being held back—by the memories and by the guilt that I am living and James is dead.

“I’m going to get dressed and go back to my townhouse.”

“What?” He shakes his head back and forth as if trying to understand my words.

"I just need some space."

"No," he answers suddenly. "Why?"

"I…just…I…can't do this…"

"Do what, Angie?" He can't keep the anger out of his tone. "Tell me."

I slump back into the plush cushions of the sofa, wanting to be swallowed up inside them.

"Okay, you don't have to talk. That's alright. Just don't leave. Please stay," he implores.

I sip the cider, using the mug to warm my now frigid body. I find my handbag on an end table and unzip it to pull out my cell phone. Two messages flash over the screen and three missed calls. It is seven a.m., and the streetlights of the city are starting to disappear like dying stars as dawn breaks. I play with my phone, remaining silent, looking for the simplest of distractions. I give Graham an affirmative nod in regard to his request. I unlock the phone and read through my messages. He gets up from the sofa and paces a trench near the windows, running his hands through his hair in a nervous gesture. Great, I am driving him just as crazy.

The first one—sent last night from Zander—catches me off guard.

Zander: Text me that you are alright. Please. I heard about the riot. It is all over every news station. I left before it all went down.

He was also the one who called me three times. I stare at the screen and type out a quick message that I am okay and was physically unharmed. Mentally? Still up for evaluation.

I open the second message, smiling at a silly picture of

Ethan and Claire both wearing face masks and cucumbers with the caption—*Self Care*. She knows exactly what to do to make me laugh.

I snap open my pill case when Graham seems distracted and toss back the little white pill before he can notice. It will help with my migraine. The bitter taste explodes with my saliva as I force it down my throat with a scratchy swallow.

Graham's expletives shake my core; he's pissed. "What did you just put into your mouth?"

"Calm down; it was just a Tylenol," I lie. "I have a headache."

"You need to drink water." He walks over to the kitchen, grabs a glass out of the cupboard, and fills it up through the fridge's filtration system. "Here," he says, handing me the huge glass. "Drink it all."

"So bossy."

"Don't pretend not to like it."

I smirk at his words. "True. You are mighty sexy when you get all authoritative."

He narrows his eyes at me. "I need you to talk to me. But I'll wait until you are ready. I want you to trust me enough to talk about these nightmares."

I sniffle and slurp down the water from the glass. "Why even bother with me? Surely there are easier women?" I stare up at his bloodshot eyes—an obvious sign that he too needs more sleep.

"I'm in too deep now to quit. You make it near impossible for me not to want you, despite my better judgment. You should have never joined Entice, but if it wasn't for you joining, I might have never met you. So maybe Claire isn't so bad."

I suppose this is progress. "I'm glad you guys are starting to see eye to eye. She is my only best friend." I swallow hard. I used to have Zander too. But he is so emotionally driven at seeing me as *more* that he is willing to lose me from his life entirely.

"His loss," Graham mutters, reading my thoughts.

I watch as he sits on the ottoman opposite of me, resting his upper body on his elbows. My eyes lock onto his, making me almost embarrassed of the hold that his have on mine. Why does this man still have the capacity to make me blush—despite all the sexual encounters we have had?

I can't turn away from his gaze. I would only be fooling myself if I thought that giving up now is something that I want. I swallow my pride—tasting grudgingly more bitter than any chemically processed pill ever could. Despite the nightmares, which I'm starting to realize are in direct correlation to my feelings of happiness, I can at least try to see where this goes. When the pills run out—and they will soon—I can try to keep supplementing my supply.

All of the hot and cold liquids filtering through my stomach give me the sudden urge. "I need to use the bathroom," I mumble, rising with the blanket wrapped around my body. I stumble to the master bath and relieve myself, wash my face, and throw on a lounge outfit folded perfectly in the closet. I stare at the designer label and grimace that even casual wear has to be exorbitantly expensive in Graham's standards. The purple pants and long-sleeved velour ensemble fit like a painted-on glove—as well as all the articles that go underneath.

When I shuffle into the bedroom, I find Graham lying under the covers with an arm outstretched to me. He has the drapes closed, and the only light is cast from the lamp on the nightstand. “We both need more rest,” he says through a yawn.

I nod and crawl into bed with him. Graham’s hands pull me into his side, and I rest my cheek against his bare shoulder. My legs bump into his, and I find that he is still wearing pajama bottoms.

“You are going to have sex with me sometime this weekend, right?” I blurt out, my mind completely elsewhere.

His light chuckles vibrate the mattress as he clicks off the light, brushing the hair out of my face in the dark.

“Why would you think I wouldn’t?”

“I don’t know. Maybe being afraid to break me after last night’s events? Maybe you are more into edge play than you originally let on? Regardless, I’m glad you appear receptive.”

I can feel his smile even in the darkness. His fingers slide up over the bottom hem of my shirt, pulling up the fabric to feel bare skin on the ascent. Every place the pads of his fingers touch, my skin chills and then warms instantly.

“Rest first and then get ravished later.”

“Deal.”

I relax my muscles and try my best not to fear drifting off—knowing that my brain can conjure up images and memories to scare me without warning.

Graham’s soft hums and steady breaths must have lulled me into a sleep, because it’s the sound of his phone vibrating on his nightstand that wakes me. I stir. The warmth of his bare chest produces a great contrast to the cool air surrounding the cocoon I am nestled in. I reach for my phone to check the time. It is now noon.

Graham hugs me tighter to him as he yawns and stretches his lower half. "Go back to sleep," he whispers in my ear.

"It's noon."

"Point?"

"The point is, if we keep sleeping, then we'll be off schedule for wanting to go to bed tonight."

He rolls me over and kisses me. "I'll make sure you get worn out and exhausted again."

I exaggerate my exhale. "Finally."

Graham and I spend every moment of the weekend together —mostly in bed and mostly naked. So, going our separate ways on Monday is difficult on my heart.

"I miss you already and you haven't even left," I say softly, watching him lay out his designer suit on the bed. He needs to be at the office early today, while my class doesn't start until late morning.

He crawls back onto the bed and cages me in with his long arms. "I miss you too, baby. What are your plans after your work shift?"

"Probably work on my research paper."

"What is it on?"

I swallow. I want to tell him, but I know it will cause conflict. Everything Graham deems as dangerous causes an argument—one I do not need this morning. "Corporate corruption." It's the first thing that comes to my mind.

"How are you getting your data?"

"An anonymous email address I set up. And a few posts on a fake social media account." Lies. And I hate myself for it. I am a hypocrite.

He nods his head and then stands. I whistle at him as he starts to pull on his dress pants.

His eyes smolder. "Quit looking at me like that."

I decide to have a little fun with him and pull down the blanket that I have wrapped around my naked body. I spread my legs and run my hand down my chest. Down my stomach. And then I rub my fingers into my folds.

"Can you go slower and turn forty-five degrees clockwise so I can get a better view?" I ask, playing with myself —but really playing with him.

He kicks off his pants, picks up his cell, and punches a few buttons.

"Reschedule my nine o'clock."

I yelp as Graham pounces on me so hard and so fast that the headboard hits against the wall. He pulls my hand away, licks my fingers off, and then pushes his hard cock into me with a force that ignites every nerve ending from the friction alone. I am rolled so I am on top. Riding him. His hands dig into my hips as he controls the movement of my body. Up and down.

"Did you get what you wanted, my little tiger?"

"Mm hmm."

After class ends, I head over to the Campus Smoothie Cafe for my first real shift of work. I enter the shop a few minutes early and head to the private bathroom to slip on my work shirt, pull back my hair, and use the toilet.

When I head out, Paul is behind the counter making a drink. I place my bag and phone in the cubby area behind the bar, right beside his belongings. I wash my hands and catch his attention.

"Hey, didn't see you come in," he says, deep in thought as he adds a bunch of ingredients to the blender.

"I was in the restroom getting changed."

He nods. "Pretty slow afternoon so far."

I wipe down tables and counters while I wait for the crowd to pick up. And it does. I wash my hands again and move to the cash register as a group of wrestlers walk in and start ordering health shakes. The team captain charges it on one card, which makes it a lot easier on the growing line that begins to form. I make sixteen protein smoothies and line them up on the bar for the team. Luckily, they were all made the same way, so I just tripled recipes to speed up the process.

I move around Paul, only bumping into him by accident a few times.

"Why don't you take your break?" he suggests.

"You sure? There's still a decent line."

"Yeah, it's fine. You have been on your feet for a couple of hours. And we just got a few new blenders, so I can work on several drinks at once."

I nod and smile. He really seems like a nice guy—except with big secrets to hide. I walk over to my storage cubby and glance back at the register to make sure he is occupied. I then slip my hand into his book bag and see if I can see anything out of the norm. I find zero books inside his bag, which is pretty weird for someone who is attending school here. His phone buzzes inside but it's locked. I can only see partial text messages coming through. Several are from MT. Mark Tanner? I read what I am able to see.

Another shipment ready for test…

Meet at Hideaway tmw @ 4 to…

I quickly finish my snooping session and stand up with my lip gloss and phone in hand. I go into the restroom and freshen up.

When I exit, I find a corner booth to rest in, while I pretend to fiddle with my phone. Opening up my search engine, I type in "Hideaway" and discover it's a bar in the suburbs of Portland—on the west side of the city. I text Claire.

Angie: I need a favor.

Claire: It'll cost you one kidney.

Angie: Good thing I have a spare.

I can tell she is typing out another message from the dots blinking across my screen. I glance around the room and try to look casual in my demeanor. The last thing I need is to act suspicious.

Claire: What's up buttercup?

I take a deep breath and type out my plan. I haven't really thought it through, given that I have to act fast or I will miss a potential opportunity. However, something tells me this meeting is going to be a key component in figuring out Paul and hopefully in catching Mark in a criminal act.

Angie: I need you to dress up in disguise, go to the Hideaway bar tomorrow at 4 PM and see if you can spy on Mark and this guy named Paul.

Claire: Is this going to piss the Teddy Graham off?

Angie: Only if he finds out.

Claire: I'm game. I love playing dress-up.

I shake my head at her response. I knew she would find this whole adventure fun. I lock my phone and slip it into my pants pocket. When my break time is over, I wash up to get ready for the new customers entering.

"You can take your break now, if you want," I suggest to Paul, who nods and moves off to the side to grab his phone. He then takes a rest on a stool at the bar. In my periphery, I try to watch his reaction over his messages from whom I assume is Mark Tanner. Paul might be the messenger and connection on campus to help with the administering of the drugs. Mark obviously would know which girls should be drugged since he has access to the Entice database.

When I can't spy any longer without it being obvious, I move over to the register and greet the next customer. I ring up the order and go to the prep station to make the drink.

The girl drops a dollar into the tip jar. “Thank you,” I respond with a smile. “Have a good day.”

“You too,” she says, moving off to the side to open her straw.

“Hey Angie.”

I look up from the cash register to see Resa’s boyfriend waiting in line. “Oh hi, I’ve been meaning to reach out to you to ask about Resa.” A wave of guilt washes over me for not trying harder to contact her. She made it clear she wanted to be left alone and was spending a chunk of time at her home with her parents. We text on occasion but that’s about it.

“You tried with her. I tried. But she really was looking for a way to get out of going to college. The whole night she was chased did her in and gave her a way to drop out and go home.”

“That’s a shame. Hope you got some closure for your relationship.”

He shrugs. “Not really. But it’s okay.” He looks over the menu. “I’ll have the strawberry banana with oat milk.”

“Coming right up.”

I fall into the rhythm of serving customers, enjoying the routine and mindlessness of the task. There is something refreshing about not having to overanalyze a recipe. I just follow it and am done.

“Hi.”

I look up into sapphire blues and my lips curl into a smile. “Hey! What are you doing here?”

“I heard that this place has the best smoothies in town.” He places his hands on the counter and leans in closer to me. “And the hottest girl on the planet making them.”

"Hush," I hiss, looking around to make sure no one heard his comment.

"I can start this drink," Paul says, sneaking up behind me to look over my shoulder at the screen, "if you type in the order."

Graham looks over and behind me to glare at an innocent Paul. Despite whatever shady business he is doing on the side, he has been nothing but kind to me since I first started interviewing for this position. So, the last thing I need is for an unnecessary testosterone showdown to make my daily work-life stressful.

"I got this one," I tell Paul. "I know this guy."

"Oh yeah?" he asks.

"Yes," Graham interjects. "I'm the *boyfriend.*"

I roll my eyes at how he says the word. Could he be any more transparent in his possessive feelings toward me?

"What would you like to drink, boyfriend?" I ask sweetly, relaxing a bit once Paul stands a few feet away from me.

Graham's megawatt smile makes me stifle a giggle. He is so sure of himself. "Surprise me. But make it big enough so I can share it with the girlfriend."

"What happens if your girlfriend is on a strict diet?" I tease.

His eyes narrow and then get angry. "Tell her that her body is my perfect playground and to add some extra calories to the beverage so I have more to hold on to when I fu—"

"Graham!" I shriek. My eyes dart around and grow big as I wonder who is within earshot. "I work here. Please stop."

"Fine. Go make me my drink, woman."

"Ugh, you're the most difficult customer of the day."

"Good."

I scrunch up my nose. I am really starting to hate that word. I hit the button for "Build Your Own" and select medium—which should be plenty big even if I take a few sips. I move over to the prep station and start building the base for the drink. I add some yogurt, milk, and a variety of frozen berries. I add just enough agave nectar to sweeten it up. I blend it, dump it into a cup, and garnish it with whipped cream and a dusting of pink-hued sprinkles. It looks delicious but not something that I would expect a powerful businessman to drink. I giggle as I hand him the girliest looking drink. He looks at it with hesitation, and I just laugh harder.

"Pretty like a princess," I coo.

"Might be the worst drink I ever bought."

"Just try it," I encourage.

I take his credit card and charge the five dollars and thirty-five cents.

Graham then puts his card back into his wallet and pulls out a one-hundred-dollar bill. He sips his drink and then stuffs the bill into the tip jar.

My eyes watch him speculatively. "That seems excessive."

"So does your flirting."

"Flirting?" I prop my hands on my hips. "With whom?"

"Smoothie King behind you."

"I was being friendly."

"Too friendly."

"You are comical sometimes. I'm working. Let me work."

"When's your next break?"

"Tomorrow on my next shift."

"You're being overworked then to not have another break. Are you part of a union?"

"I'm being treated fairly, and I'd like that to continue while I'm here. Don't ruin this for me. Please."

Graham frowns. "I want to share this with you. When do you get off work?"

"In an hour."

"Awesome." He glances at his watch, while he takes another sip of his drink. "I have an hour to kill."

Of course he does. He moves over to the bar area and sets up his laptop from the bag I didn't even realize he was carrying.

I take a little card from behind the register and slap it down on the counter beside him. "There's the Wi-Fi password."

His smile grows at my unease. "Thanks, baby." He acts like nothing is at all weird about this situation. Ugh.

I do my best to ignore Graham and remain focused on waiting on customers and making drinks. It helps that Mondays are busy days at the shop and staying busy helps the time go by faster. When my shift ends, I use the restroom and change back into my normal shirt. I wrap my arms around Graham's stomach and rest my head along his back.

"I'm all done."

He shuts his laptop and turns in his seat to look at me. "Want to go for a walk down by the river?"

I nod my head yes. It is a surprisingly nice day for the end of November. And dry for once. He grabs his smoothie and holds the straw up to my lips. I take a sip. It really is good. I love the tart and sweetness of the berries.

"What do you think of your drink?"

"It's really good, baby."

I wave goodbye to Paul, but he stops me with a raised hand and a "hold up."

He walks over to me with an envelope labeled "tips."

"Oh thanks!" I say with a smile.

"We made out well today," he says with a smirk. "Best day for tips since I started working here."

"I bet," I mutter, looking up at the man who deserves the praise.

Once we get to the car, I hop into the passenger's side and lean my head back against the headrest as Graham searches for the best place to park along the waterfront. It wasn't long ago I was here with Zander the night he decided to put terms on our friendship. Yet, everything right now—with this man—feels different.

We walk hand in hand along the smooth paved walkway that follows the path of the river. We talk about our day and make plans for dinner.

And just like that, we have fallen into a beautiful rhythm. One that I hope lasts forever.

29

On Tuesday, I arrive at the townhouse after my shift ends at three p.m. to catch Claire in her obnoxious disguise.

"Really? This is what you think is going to keep you from standing out in the crowd?" I ask, looking at her drag outfit. I'm not even sure it can be called drag, since she is dressing like a female still. It is just over-the-top and loud. "No. No, no, no, Claire. This will not do. You look hideous enough for the circus. You are supposed to blend in—not stand out."

She pouts her bottom lip out. "Awww, you're no fun."

"True. But this is important. I need to know what Paul and Mark are doing. And if you can eavesdrop, that would really help me out. You'll be in a public place, so dress as you would if you were simply going there to dine."

"Okay."

"I'm getting to the desperate stage for my article that'll get submitted to several news outlets offering internships. Not to mention, it will also be for a grade for my last class before graduation. I'm still holding out hope that I can convince Dr. Williams that this is worthy of writing about."

"Fine," she says, fluttering her fake eyelashes that are an inch in length. They look cartoonish and unnatural. "I'll dial it back. But can I still wear a wig? I found a bunch I forgot about in the bottom of my Doomsday bin."

I look at her with disbelief. "Why would you need them if the world was ending?"

"Because what happens if it's a slow, drawn out end to the world? And they close access to all nonessential businesses…and my hair gets all wackadoodle, and I need it to look cute again, just so I can forfeit my body over to the highest bidder." She pauses and then bursts into fits of tears and laughter. "Wait, that's what I've been doing for the past six months. Shit. Anyhoo, at least I have that skill set already in place."

"Silver lining," I deadpan. How did we even get on this topic of conversation? I watch as she puts on a curly blond wig, makes a face into her phone for a selfie, and then puts another one on. Oh yeah, the disguise. "Dial it back at least by eighty percent. And post none of these on social media. You are supposed to keep a low profile and not stand out. This isn't a fashion show or a photo op moment."

"Okay. So not the pink wig."

"How about no wig?"

"Killjoy."

"Whatever."

"Have some faith."

"I have to go. Graham is coming home around five, and I want to make sure I have my things all packed for tomorrow when we leave for Hillsboro. What are Ethan's Thanksgiving traditions?"

"Well, he is forcing me to spend time with his ex-wife for the sake of their son. So we are going to carve the turkey together and play nicey-nice for a few hours. And then I'll probably stay at his place and spend all his money online shopping for Black Friday gift buying. I saw a ton of things that I want for myself—from him."

I laugh and then give her a hug. "Thanks for doing this for me. If you can take any pics or video anything, that would be great. Just do not get caught."

"I got this."

"I sure hope so."

It is quarter to five when my phone rings with a call from Claire playing "Girls Just Want to Have Fun" as the ringtone. I have been nervous for the past hour over her being at the Hideaway. I am lying on the king bed, rummaging through my previous email I sent to myself about Mark and consolidating the information into one document.

I take a deep breath and answer. "Hey."

"Angie," she whispers.

"Yeah? What's wrong? Where are you?"

"In the parking lot at the Hideaway. It was too risky going inside since Mark has met me before, so I'm camped out in the backseat of this taxi."

"Don't get caught."

"I won't. The windows are tinted."

"What's happening?"

"More people just showed up. They are all talking outside."

"Okay..."

"You know I'm not typically a paranoid person, Angie. But something seems really off about this. Like someone or something is going to hit an iceberg without any knowledge of its size or magnitude. Do you want to be the freaking Titanic? Have all the warning signs but still never see it coming? I think it would be best to cut your losses. Find a different topic. Anything but continue this."

"I'll be fine. What do you see now?"

"Packages being exchanged."

"To whom?"

"To Paul and to some other guy who just showed up."

"Can you tell who he is? What he looks like?"

"No. He has on sunglasses and a ball cap. Appears young. Shorter than Paul."

"Do you think these men are the deliverers? The middlemen?"

"I have no idea. But I've watched enough crime shows to know when to bail ass home. So, taxi man," she says, moving the receiver from her mouth, "take me home, please."

"Snap a picture before you leave. I need to see if I can recognize the last arrival."

"That sounds like a horrible idea," she sighs.

"Why?"

"Because that idea sounds like you're still going to pursue this shit. Do I need to go to Graham and squeal on you? Should I completely out you in order to protect you?"

Like the sinking of the Titanic, the warning signs are

visible. However, when you think you are unsinkable, you make rash decisions that easily can put your life in danger. This whole thing is bigger than me. But I am too far involved. I am so close to figuring it all out.

"Only if you want to be responsible for my failure with my future career."

"Fuck, Angie, you're in a horrible position between the chance of landing an amazing internship and possibly dying because you know too much."

"Those shows you watch…they are dramatized. Not real."

"Pretty sure *Cops* is real."

"Yeah, for petty theft crap," I respond.

"Whatever. You're too damn stubborn to see reason right now. And I swear you're like a walking, breathing after-school special. You know, the ones they air on Lifetime and the defenseless girl always winds up in trouble with the bad guy?"

"I'm not defenseless," I correct her.

"Sure, minor variable change, but the rest is still the same."

I humor her. "And what happens to the girl?"

"Everyone dies."

I huff. "No really, what happens?" I really have no idea what she is talking about. But I rarely do.

"She ends up pregnant, has to go into the witness protection program, or learns the true meaning of Christmas."

"Wow, Claire."

"Or she becomes a prostitute."

I ignore her comment. When she gets on these kicks, the best thing is to ignore her but still let her rant.

"I have to go. I think I hear Graham downstairs. Enjoy your holiday. I'll stay in touch."

I log out of my email accounts, roll off the bed, and come face-to-face with Graham in the doorway of the bedroom. It looks like the blood has drained from his face. Something is wrong. A chill runs up my spine at his weary eyes and messy hair.

"Hey you. What's wrong?" I ask. My voice is shaky.

"Change of plans. We're going to Hillsboro tonight."

"Okay." I draw out the word, expecting him to give me an explanation for the rush to get there a day early. But I don't ask. He would tell me if he wanted me to know. I am slowly learning when to push versus when to pause and accept. This looks like a pause and accept moment. "My bag is already packed."

He nods and grabs his luggage from the closet and starts throwing in some folded shirts and pants from his drawers. "Good." He seems to be operating with an invisible check-list—going from room to room to gather what he needs. His calm, quiet demeanor unnerves me. What is going on? Are we in danger? What has changed?

He walks over to me as I stand staring at him from the center of our bedroom. *Ours*. The one I am starting to visu-alize as being for the two of us… And here we are, about to leave its comfort.

He pulls me close to him and kisses me so hard and with so much passion that I pull back from the force of it.

"Is everything okay?" I ask softly.

"It will be."

"Are you hiding something from me?"

"Only temporarily. I thought sheltering you from all this

would be best for you. Now, I'm starting to think that telling you the truth from the start would've saved you from this hailstorm that is about to occur."

"Graham…you're really scaring me."

"Good."

I pull back and push at his chest. "Stop it with the fucking *good*! If you say that word one more time, I'm going to go ballistic. I need to know what you're hiding. I need to know what I'm up against!"

"*Me* hiding? Me? What about you?! I've been working my ass off at keeping you safe and you go and literally walk into fucking danger every chance you get."

"I don't know what you're talking about." I didn't do anything dangerous today at all. Why is he so visibly upset?

He shakes his head and grabs our bags. "Let's go. We don't have time."

Why the rush? I follow him downstairs and see Collins sitting on the couch watching us enter the room. Why do we need a driver to go to his family's house?

"Ready to go?" Collins asks, standing up and rubbing his hand on his chin. He seems stressed and is wearing a similarly pained expression as Graham has been sporting since he came home. I've never seen him rattled before —until now.

I look up at Graham and back at Collins in confusion. "What the hell is going on? Tell me."

"No," he snaps. "I have a whole list of other more important things on my mind, dammit, and hashing this out with you right now is not one of them. We need to go. Now. Let's go. Before—" Graham snaps his mouth shut.

"Before what?" I prop my hands on my hips. "Before I

find out what you're hiding and run? Is that what you both are scared of? That I'll find out more lies that you spew and then run for the fucking mountains to get away?"

"Let's go," Graham says, pulling me toward the elevator and then smashing the button that will take us to the garage with his fist. It seems to take us twice as long to descend. As if every moment from the time Graham arrived home until now is moving in slow motion. My mind searches for clues as to what is happening. What has these two men so frazzled?

Collins opens the backseat door for me of a car that is idling at the curb. He places our bags in the trunk and then slides into the driver's seat. This vehicle is one I have not been inside before, with very tinted windows and a sound-proof privacy screen that takes a button to press for the speaker.

Graham slips into his side and pulls me close to him. He snaps the center seatbelt into place around me. He kisses my forehead and mumbles into my hair how much he loves me. His phone buzzes, and he answers it with an abrupt, "Hoffman."

I look up at his bloodshot eyes as he growls to the person on the other end. "This changes everything. You know that, right? All the promises I made to you are now gone." His eyes lose focus for a few seconds, taking him somewhere else that is not here. "I don't give a damn what consequences I have to endure. But she is my priority." He squeezes me with the arm he has wrapped around me. Collins has us out of the parking garage and already heading west through the city. "Then let's work out another deal. Renegotiate. I can't keep doing this."

I feel my phone vibrate in my pocket and slip it out to see that it's Claire sending me photos. I open the text and look down at the images while Graham is busy chatting to whomever is on the other end of his call. I see Paul and Mark in the picture. I also see Mark's "business" associates, Benjamin, Samson, and Edward—which is not surprising since they have been meeting with Mark since our first date. But the new person in the photo—the one with the sunglasses and ball cap—is someone I don't recognize. Not surprisingly, since he is trying to remain concealed. I email myself the pictures using my secret account and make a mental note to cross reference them when I get a private moment to myself. I delete the text chain.

"What has you so distracted?" Graham asks, looking down at me as I close down my windows.

I startle at the sound of his voice. "Just catching up on email."

He nods and then glances out the window behind me. "My mom and dad are so excited to meet you."

"Yeah?" I ask, looking up at him. None of the stress is washed off his face. If anything, there is more of it visible in his forehead wrinkles and the redness in his eyes.

"Yes. I never bring girls home. Ever. So they're probably excited that one even exists in my life."

He says the words so seriously, but I laugh at the meaning behind them. I guess I should feel special. And if it wasn't for this cloud of mistrust hovering over us, then I probably would.

"I used to love Thanksgiving."

He looks down at me and frowns. "Not anymore?"

I shrug. "Holidays don't really mean much to me

without a home or a family to share them with. The months before my mom passed, we rushed all of the holidays for the entire year and celebrated one a week starting with New Years and ending with Christmas. We would decorate her room that had the hospital bed and play music. James and I would make pictures for the windows that would represent the season of that particular holiday. It was our way of coping with the uncertainty of when we would lose her. And with losing her came losing all of the traditions associated with those holidays. The day my mom died was the death of so many other things that I could not even comprehend as a twelve-year-old girl. She was the glue that made everything in life better. Without the glue? Life just crumbled."

Graham hugs me closer to him, and his warmth is comforting. "What about all the years since losing her? You and James would have been still living at home with your dad…"

"It just wasn't the same. My dad had his own issues that just seemed to grow worse with time. So we basically stopped celebrating anything that used to make my mom happy. It seemed weird making a turkey or putting up a Christmas tree when those were the things that would make her excited."

"Don't you think she would have wanted you to keep on living? That she would want you and James and your dad to remember her through the things she once enjoyed?"

I frown. "Maybe. But we were all grieving and never really got over it entirely to truly move forward."

"So how did you get to this place in your life then? Because you *are* moving forward. You are trying to live."

I give him a half smile. "It took a lot of work to get me

to this place. I leaned on James a lot during our teenage years. We would involve ourselves in school and were inseparable. We never dated anyone in high school, so we just spent our days doing schoolwork together or riding bikes or joining clubs. After he died, I went through several months where I had no purpose. No will to live. Then I started to—" I stop. I can't even say the word.

"Cut?" Graham fills in the blank.

"Yeah. It was a shameful time in my life and not something I am proud of by any means."

Even though I shared a lot of this with him at the lake house, it oddly feels good to talk about it again and tell him a bit more. Maybe if we keep doing these sessions, he will know everything that there is to know.

"How long did that last?"

I can barely hear his voice, it is so soft.

"I don't know. Not long. I didn't do it very often…just when I was very lonely and felt like I couldn't find any control in my life. So, a month? Maybe two?"

"Then what made you stop?"

"I had an incident." I look out the window. It is a memory I'd rather not remember.

"Tell me," Graham coaxes. "Let me in, please."

"I accidentally nicked myself a little too much, nearly hitting my femoral artery."

Graham hisses out a curse word but I continue before I lose the courage.

"My dad found the trail of blood all throughout the house as I searched for a bandage."

"Did he get you some help?"

I shake my head no. "I never told him I was cutting. I

lied to him and told him it was a wound still trying to heal from the accident. But from that day, I vowed that I wouldn't cut again. And I didn't. Instead, I became obsessed with finding out who killed James and fled the scene. I lost a lot of my memories—maybe it was my mind's way of coping with the tragedy. Or maybe it was that I never had any of the memories from the crash in the first place and just fabricated what I thought I remembered in my own mind's space. But I needed a focus to survive without James. So I tried my best to find out who could do something so appalling. Hit us and then just leave."

Graham nods, understanding passing over his face. "I understand the need for revenge."

"With Penny?"

"Yeah. But I may have to let it all go."

"Why? What has changed?"

He swallows hard and looks down at me with sympathy. "My biggest fear since I met you is happening."

"What is that?"

"You're being targeted."

I flinch at his words. "How do you know that?" I ask in a rush.

"That'll have to wait; we are here already," he sighs, as we pull up the cobblestone driveway that is showcased by a beautifully manicured lawn. The house sits at the top of the lot with an intricate stone exterior and huge windows. The house is very geometric with sharp angles and rectangular windows. Balconies are featured at the sides of the house overlooking the majestic landscaping. It's as if the house was transplanted in the middle of a private garden. The structure is modern despite being the home Graham grew up in—so at least twenty-some years old. Maybe his family did a lot of renovations recently.

"Wow, this looks amazing. I love all of the windows and all the stone. Looks earthy yet contemporary."

"My dad is an architect and runs his own business. My mom is an interior designer."

I laugh at this information. "I can see why they would be attracted to one another."

"They are more in love now than they were when I was growing up. It's obnoxious at times." He scrunches up his face and looks boyish in a way.

I giggle at his fake disgust. No one wants to think of their parents ever being intimate with each other. But yet, it is refreshing that I am about to meet a couple who is happily married after decades together.

Graham pulls me out of the car and drags me up the front stone steps with excitement. He knocks a couple of times and rocks on his heels in anticipation. My heart feels like it is stuck in my chest as the sound of the door unlocking jolts it awake.

"Honey, our Graham's finally home!" a woman greets, hugging Graham into her body. "C'mon in, both of you. Oh, how I missed having my family all home." She is a friendly looking woman about my height, with beautiful blue eyes and shoulder-length auburn hair.

A taller man, around the age of sixty, with salt-and-pepper hair, crystal-blue eyes, a clean-shaven face, and broad shoulders peeks around his wife, shaking hands with Graham and then patting him on the back. "Good to see you, son."

"You must be sweet Angie?" his mom says, pulling me

into a hug. It catches me off guard, and tears instantly fill my eyes at how warm and safe she feels. Like my momma's arms used to feel like.

"Yes, this is my Angela. Sweetheart," he says to me, "these are my folks—Donna and Germain Hoffman."

Donna releases me from her hold, and I step back to Graham's side. "Nice to meet you both."

"Graham, where's your brother? Is he not coming? I told that boy that enough is enough, and this is a holiday to celebrate the togetherness of being a fam—"

The door creaks. "Don't worry, I came. Wouldn't miss your home-cooked turkey, Ma," the voice behind me says.

And I know that voice. I am certain. My heart plummets to my stomach as I put the pieces together without confirming my conclusion with actual visual proof.

Graham squeezes my hand and looks down at me.

"I can't believe you never told me," I whisper.

"I'm telling you now."

30

I turn slowly and eye the man walking into the house. It's as if I am seeing him for the first time. As if the blue eyes staring back at me are not the same as the ones I have come to love so much. Holy shit. How did I not notice before? Why has Graham only talked about having a sister but never a brother?

"Oh, Nic!" Donna exclaims, throwing her arms around him. "I was worried you wouldn't be able to get off work."

Nic?

I look at Dominic with so many questions. I am bursting at the seams to beg for him—*anyone*—to fill me in on the big secret.

What is going on? Is this the secret that Graham doesn't want me to know? And why is it such a big secret? Why am I just finding this all out now?

My mind scrambles to try to understand why I didn't put the pieces together sooner. Surely there was some sign that I chose to ignore.

I look up at Graham, and I can feel the blood washing out of my face, settling at my feet. I feel like they are molded in cement.

"I, um," I clear my throat. "You guys are related?" I ask stupidly. Why am I constantly feeling dumb at the worst times possible?

"Oh, Graham, have some manners and introduce Angie to your brother," Donna urges.

"Yeah, Graham," I state blankly, "introduce me."

"They met before, Mom." His tone is even, and the fact that he is not adding any detail to this grand charade is what is unnerving me the most.

"When? How? And why does Nic get to meet your lady before we do, son?" Donna asks, obviously hurt.

"I'm on a temporary leave," Dominic—or Nic—says. "And I met Angie while I was undercover."

Undercover? Undercover for what? My head hurts.

"Can I please use your bathroom?" I ask softly. I am going to be sick. What the hell is going on right now?

"Of course, dear. Just go past the kitchen and there is a door that is labeled with a public man and woman decor sign."

I excuse myself from this mental overload and go in search of the bathroom. My head starts to throb, and I feel my hands getting twitchy. I grab at a tissue on the vanity to wipe at my eyes. I look in the mirror and frown at the image looking back at me. I look weak and worn out. I pull open my purse and find my handy Altoids container. I am running dangerously low, and with my headaches—that are moving from a rare occurrence to a daily one—I am going to be out of my stock before I hit the end of the week. I toss a pill onto my tongue and cup my hands under the cold running water. I slurp it up out of my palm, wipe the residue off into the tissue, then toss it into the trash can.

I make my way out to the group gathered in the foyer to hear Donna chatting with her sons.

"Well, sorry to sound selfish, but I'm glad both my boys are home, no matter what the circumstances. Now, to get Penny here tomorrow. Then we'll all be complete again. Dad took your advice, Graham, and is going to fly up to Seattle in the morning to sign her release papers for the day."

"That's wonderful," Nic says with a relieved smile.

"I'm looking forward to seeing her," Graham interjects. "The last time I tried, it wasn't a good visit. But the daily reports for the past week look promising and the first sign of a positive progression."

"Well," Germain interjects, "I think the new therapist you hired has been life changing for her. She is finally able to vocalize her fears, which in and of itself is a break-through."

"Was the hypnotizing a no-go?" Nic asks, standing on the sidelines.

"It went horribly, and they had to stop the session immediately," Donna chimes in.

"It was a setback," Germain says softly. "One Penny will move forward from. We just all have to have faith in her."

Graham catches my movement from the corner of his eye and side steps toward me, wrapping an arm around my waist. I don't find it comforting. I want to push him away but do not need to add any more stress to this awkward first meeting with his family.

"Is the place in Victoria still a consideration?" Nic asks.

I feel Graham tense up. He has had his focus on Penny since I met him. I can tell he carries the weight of her recovery on his shoulders.

"I really don't want her out of the country," Germain chimes in, "but if it's best for her recovery and her psychiatrist recommends the facility, then we'll definitely consider it."

"I've been having the facility checked out," Graham reassures, "but I'm not convinced it's a good fit. I think having her closer to family is what she needs right now."

"Well, I for one am thrilled it's going to be a full house," Donna says with a warm smile. "Anyway, come on in, everyone, and make yourselves at home. Angie, can I offer you some wine?"

"Absolutely," I say with an awkward laugh.

"It's our pleasure to have you here," Germain says with a half hug to me.

Donna returns and puts an arm around his waist and hands me my goblet of a rich red wine. The aroma is strong. I take a sip and savor the delicious semisweet blend.

It has been so long since I have been around a family for a holiday that I don't even know how to act. And the desire to be part of something—anything—has me sticking around rather than running out of the house and away from the liar who cannot stop with the lies.

I turn to Graham who has yet to relax his shoulders. "Can I have a word with you outside?"

He gives me a hesitant nod. He guides me through the

beautifully decorated house to the back patio that is lit with uplighting. There is a serene pool and hot tub, along with a rock structure and waterfall. It is an enchanting backyard oasis. It looks very similar in design to the lake house, and I wonder if Germain helped with the construction of both properties.

"Why did you lie to me?" I whisper. "Again?"

He stares up at the sky. It is approaching nighttime, and some of the stars are visible even though the house is lit up with artificial light filtering out through all of the windows. "I didn't have a choice."

"I call bullshit. There's always a choice."

His eyes soften. "Please don't leave me. Just promise me you won't leave me before I can fix all of this. Promise me."

I turn to glare at him. "Haven't we learned anything from the sins of our past? Haven't we learned that lying to each other pulls us apart?"

"What about all that you are hiding? I have been working overtime trying to keep you safe and have been going about this unobtainable task completely blind."

"How can I hide anything when you always have a team watching me? Huh? It is wearing on me, Graham. I have my life to live, goals to accomplish, and a future to secure. How can I even do anything anymore without you finding out and sabotaging all of my efforts?"

"Why can't you trust me to take care of you? You put up walls faster than I can ever tear them down."

"Because I cannot put trust in people. People die. People leave. People screw me over. People aren't permanent."

His eyes water, and for a second I think he may cry. It

breaks my heart with each passing second he doesn't say something. He just stands and stares at me. "I'm never going to be enough for you."

His words cut me, because they seem plucked from my own thoughts. I feel the same way, and here I am making him experience the same doubt that I have cumulatively put on myself over the course of many years.

"I am sorry."

"Sorry for what? For involving your best friend in your affairs? For putting her at risk?"

"You knew about—"

"Yes, Angela." He runs a hand through his hair, while his eyes never waver from mine. "Just tell me. Was it worth it? Because I'm running out of patience over this whole ordeal. This isn't a fucking game."

Tears fall into my hair that is draped over the front of my shoulders. I turn away from him and stare out at the water in the pool. Maybe the truth hurts more than the lies I tell myself to justify all of my actions.

"How did you even find out she was involved?"

His hands fly up in front of him, his anger sizzling through him. "I always find out, Angie. But that should not be the point. You have no room to talk about me holding back the truth. You have yet to tell me why you're so compelled to involve yourself with Tanner. Between accepting dates with him, meeting up with him privately that ends with you in a hotel room, and now sending your roommate out to gather information for you. Why? Why are you so driven to push every single one of my buttons?"

I look down at my feet and then pivot toward him. He runs his fingers through his hair.

"I, um…" I hesitate. I know revealing the truth will make it even harder to gather the information I need to be able to write a compelling story. But being at a standstill is hurting our relationship.

"Tell me!" he snaps. "Why are you so involved?"

"Because I'm striving to be an investigative journalist." There. I said it. And as much as people say the truth sets you free, I do not feel free at all. I feel like the truth is actually going to hinder everything about my freedom. This truth is going to get me bound with protective shackles to the man who cannot stop himself from trying to keep me safe.

Oil and vinegar. That's what we are. Two people with goals in life that contradict each other.

Incompatible.

I watch him closely as his expression changes from shock, to disbelief, and then to understanding. I can tell he is trying to analyze my words and then go back in time to evaluate all the events leading up to this very moment. He opens his mouth and then closes it again. I can tell he is confused. I guess he only focused on my current class schedule and not what I have been pursuing the past four years. And for once I have rendered him speechless.

"Well, this is all finally starting to make sense," he exhales. "All this time I thought you were walking into danger. And here I find out that you are not simply walking, but instead *running* toward it. I thought you were an English major. You have it on your profile for Entice that you are studying English. You aren't even taking journalism classes right now. And I took what you were saying at face value. Because why would anyone lie about their degree? Fuck! How did I miss this key piece of information?"

"You aren't the only one who can lie, Graham."

"Dammit, Angela!"

"You have these double standards. You act like you have some kind of monopoly on lying or caring about issues like girls getting drugged. But you are wrong. I care too. This affects me too. My entire future is riding on figuring this all out and then being the one to report on it before anyone else has that chance. I failed last semester with a story falling right through my fingertips. I've been given a second chance. So, I need you to step aside while I do it. Otherwise, this entire repeat semester is for nothing. I'll have wasted my money and my time trying to reach for something that was never there to grasp."

He throws his head back and curses up at the sky. "You're not continuing on with this!" He stares right into my eyes, and for a second, I think he penetrates my soul. "You get that, right? Find something else to write about. Anything else. You're in way over your head. This is going to end horribly for you if you continue on. You won't keep this up. This ends tonight."

"No, it doesn't. Telling you about it changes nothing about what I plan to do. I'm only being up front because I'm tired of hiding it from you. But I've already failed a semester last spring due to some asshole reporter hijacking my discovery and beating me to the printshop." Why do I have to keep explaining myself? Why is he not understanding? "This is my one chance at a do-over. My *only* chance. I'm on the verge of figuring everything out. Which helps you too, because—"

"Helps me?" His words are cold. Harsh.

"Yeah," I say with a frown. "This might help you figure out what happened to your sister. A win-win."

"That's where you're wrong. This revelation does not help me out at all."

"Why not?" What am I missing here?

"Because you're going to get us all killed," he sneers.

My breath gets stuck in my throat. "Wait, what? How—"

The sound of a throat clearing lets us know we are no longer alone out here. "Sorry to interrupt," Dominic says, "but mom wants us all inside for dinner. She made chicken pot pie."

Graham and I turn to glare at Dominic, who at least has the decency to look apologetic. His eyes avoid mine, as if he is afraid to see the pain reflected back at him. He deceived me too.

"I have a bone to pick with you as well, Dominic or Nic or Nicholas? But really, who the hell are you?"

"Angela," Graham warns. "He didn't have much choice."

"Are you guys even brothers? Or is that some made-up lie or half-truth as well?"

Graham sighs in defeat. "We are brothers."

"My name is Nic Xavier Hoffman. To everyone who is not family or privy to certain information, I am Dominic Crawford—CEO of Entice Escort Agency. As you already know, Graham is the real owner, operator, and decision maker for that company. He also runs and manages Hoffman Headquarters which houses his jewelry company, Jealousy. All of that is true."

"Then why all the secr—" I start to say and get cut off by Donna yelling for us to get inside before everything gets cold. Ugh! I am afraid to move. As if delaying this conversation will somehow prevent me from learning more about the Hoffman brothers and all the lies they seem to tell.

"Let's go. My mom can get pretty fiery if we ruin her dinners," Nic says with a smirk. "And considering I haven't been home much in the past year due to work, I can't disappoint the woman."

Despite the name change, he still represents the laid-back one of the brothers. I want to be mad at him. I want to scream and hit something—or him. But I am still holding out for an explanation that will make this all be okay. That somehow everything I am confused about will be worth it—with just some simple reasoning.

I walk between the men as we make our way into the house. Donna is adding the finishing touches to a beautiful table-scape. Every seat has a sophisticated gold placemat, a charger plate, and then a dinner plate. Little folded place cards are set on top of each plate, with names written in the most elegant calligraphy. A white fabric runner spans end to end of a long rectangular dark wood table. White pumpkins and huge lit candles fancy up the center with their gold painted tops.

"This looks wonderful, Mrs. Hoffman," I say, looking at all the details that she added to make this dinner special.

She leans into me and lowers her voice. "Mrs. Hoffman was my mother-in-law and that bitch hated me. God rest her soul. So please, call me Donna."

I laugh over her serious face that breaks out into a big smile. She is so prim and proper in her tailored ivory pantsuit that it makes it even funnier that she is breaking through the box I tried to put her in to let down her guard with me.

"Well, *Donna*," I say again with a smile, "I love how you kept the decor of your table classy but still part of the theme."

"Thank you, my dear. Come, have a seat right here," she says, helping to pull out my chair. I already misplaced my previous wine glass or maybe I never got one. I can't even remember. But a new one is placed in front of me and filled up high with a sparkling pink champagne.

"Graham, sometime tomorrow morning, can you look at the oven on this floor and see if you can fix it? I have to resort to using the basement kitchen because I think something is wrong with the one up here."

"Yeah, I can see what I can do," he answers.

"Oh, and the security system. Can you see that the outdoor cameras are working properly? I miss having you and Nic home when you guys would just be a room away to help me fix everything."

"Sure. I can look at it in the morning."

"Thank you."

Germain clears his throat and holds up his glass to us. "I would like to make a toast. Thank you all for coming, especially you, Angela, and thank you to my lovely wife for making this wonderful meal. To happiness and to good health. Cheers, you all."

We clink glasses, and Graham pulls me to his side to kiss me sweetly on the lips. "Cheers," he says against my lips.

My own response gets stuck in my throat, as a whirlwind of emotions encompasses me. I am just so confused.

"So, tell us, Graham," Donna says, passing out the individual mini pot pies to each of our dinner plates, "how did you and Angie meet?" They are beautifully designed on top to represent a heart shape—with the little air holes oozing out gravy and steam.

"She showed up at a social mixer that Nic and I were hosting and was the only woman there who wasn't fawning over the elaborateness of the event. She stood out from the crowd because she was—"

"Basic."

Graham shakes his head at me. "Beautiful."

"That she is," Donna agrees with a loving smile.

"In fact, I found her outside by herself, hanging out by the pool eating candy. From that moment, I knew my life would never be the same. And it hasn't, that's for sure."

My eyes flicker to Graham's, and I can see the awe he has for the moment in our past. It was the moment that changed everything. He warned me then, and I didn't listen. We were souls just waiting to find each other—and once we did, there was no denying the magnetic force.

Donna claps her hands together and turns to her husband with a look of love in her eyes. Germain grabs her hand, kisses her wedding ring, and then places her palm over his heart.

"I love these types of chance meetings," she says breathily. "Just meant to be."

"But nothing is ever easy," Graham says sternly.

"Never is, son," Germain agrees. He smiles over at me, and I feel the warmth of a blush hit my cheeks.

I sit and eat quietly, enjoying my food and the peaceful table dynamics of watching Graham interact with his family.

"So how long can you stay?" Donna asks, turning her attention to Graham.

"Just a night. Maybe two," he says sadly. "We'll have to come back another time. Soon."

They live less than half an hour away and yet Donna acts like she rarely sees her kids. That has to change. Do they not realize that tomorrow is not a promise?

"Did you drive yourself?" she continues.

"Collins brought us."

"Where is he? Tell him to come in and eat. I always make extra. Tell him he can have the guest room. Where are the manners I have instilled in you, Graham Xavier Hoffman?"

Xavier. Interesting. He and Nic both share the same middle name. "Mom," Graham sighs, "Collins is working right now. After his shift is over, he'll switch with my other man."

Donna is one of those moms who doesn't seem to put up with any fuss—especially from her son. "Well, can you at least bring him a container of food? I realize that you live by a different set of rules—or at least think you do—but when you're in my house, you take care of those who take care of you. Respect, Graham. Keep it mutual."

"Okay," he says, shaking his head for added emphasis, "I'll pack him up some pot pie. I'm sure he'll love something homemade."

Her smile goes back to being sweet again. She may be calm, but her flame is mighty. I instantly feel connected to her. And that alone helps lessen the anger I feel toward Graham. If someone as amazing as she seems raised him, then he can't be all that bad.

"Nic," Germain says quietly, "are you able to have this week off work?"

"Dad," he sighs, "I'm never really off." His passiveness makes me turn to look at him. "Basically just living my life as if I'm always on call or always working. Can never shut off my brain."

"This lifestyle is going to catch up with you, son. You may need to start saying no."

"I'm in too deep right now, Dad. There's no turning back," Nic explains.

"We always have free will. If you need help with anything, please let us know and we can try to support you."

He nods and coughs into his cloth napkin. He glances at Graham, and a sympathetic look passes between them. Nic plays with the ring on his finger and lifts his head with a half smile. "Thank you, Dad. I just need to finish this one out. And who knows, maybe the whole project will open up doors to something a bit more exciting?"

I watch the interchange between the men at the table and try to pick up all the clues being dropped. It's like they are speaking in code and talking around a secret subject.

After dinner, Graham walks out a container of food to Collins and then helps his mom clear the table with me. Donna shoos the guys away as she cleans and resets the table back to a lovely display for Thanksgiving, all while talking nonchalantly with me. I try to assist where I can, but let her flitter through her dining room as if on autopilot—placing all the decor back to its exact location. She mimics an artist, more than an interior designer. Her eye is for pretty things, and she nails it with such understated beauty in her choices. But I know she is shopping at the boutiques and not the Home Decor Warehouse that would meet my type of budget.

"So, that boy of mine…is he as demanding in his personal life as he is in his professional life?" she asks, rolling her eyes.

"Pretty much," I laugh. "And intense." Apparently both boys of hers are.

"Always has been, my dear. Did you know that when I carried him, he would get his foot stuck in my ribcage almost daily? And he was a month early but still over nine pounds. That is Graham. Always doing things his way—on his own timeline."

I laugh over this information. It really humanizes him and makes him more than just a control freak. The more his mom talks about him, the more layers get added to him. And I have already peeled back so many.

"But what makes him who he is at the core?" I ask, knowing that honesty is what I have been yearning for all along. Something real. Not some fabricated half-truth.

Donna stops washing pot pie ramekins, dries her hands on the towel hanging from the oven door handle, and leans her back against the island.

She frowns and then looks up into my eyes. "Graham is not perfect. He may give the illusion that he is—but it's all a facade. Deep down, that boy of mine is just looking for someone to accept him and his lifestyle. He's fiercely protective of those he loves. That is probably why he keeps Germain and me hidden from a lot of his life."

My brow furrows over her words. He will lose me if he cannot come clean on all of his agendas. I am tired of the secrets. I am tired of always wondering when the next shoe will drop on our life we are trying to create together. And then asking myself, is it worth it? Is it worth risking my heart at a chance to get to know someone who may never let me inside enough to see the real him? The answer is not easy. Especially when I am a hypocrite who wants to keep my own cards close to my chest.

I cannot accept any more lies. And I am equally tired of trying to preserve the level of secrecy needed to further my own agenda.

Being lonely, and broken, and an empty shell is comforting, but only because there are no expectations. There is nothing to dream for and then have it slip away.

That was how I used to live my life. That is my past. Everything changed with Graham. It's like he put a magnifying glass up to my heart to show it what it can feel like—if I can just let go and take that chance.

"I don't want to lose him," I whisper to Donna. "But relationships can't be built on dishonesty."

"Oh dear," she says, wrapping her arms around me.

Dampness hits my cheeks before I can register the source. I wipe it away with my shirt sleeve.

"What have you ladies been talking about?" Graham asks from the corner of the room. He says each word slowly and with hesitation. He leans against the wall and places his hands into his pockets.

I pull back from his mom and look at his sad eyes. He looks like he has been through a war. He moves over to me with caution and reaches his arms out for me to walk into them. And I do. He is my safe place. He hugs me to his chest and rubs my back.

"We were just chatting, Graham," Donna answers him, without really answering him at all.

"I see that. About me?"

"Surprisingly, son, this world doesn't revolve around you. Maybe we were chatting about butterflies and rainbows," she says sarcastically. And I instantly like her a bit more than I did a few seconds ago.

I laugh at his fake disgust expression, earning a tickle to my sides. I twist out of his arms.

"Seriously though," Donna says, "I like this girl. So do not jack this up. Understand?"

"Okay, okay," he sighs, obviously a bit embarrassed that his mom is being so blatant with her unsolicited opinion. I look up to examine his face. The slightest pink has reached his cheeks. Not for a second would I have ever predicted that Graham Hoffman would ever be able to feel that emotion.

I like it.

31

I smile up at Graham sweetly—too sweetly. He shakes his head at me and whispers "let's go" to me. He pulls me toward the stairway and takes me on a tour of the house that he grew up in—showing me all of the new changes his parents have done to update the interior. When we get to the bedroom that is almost entirely black and white, I know that this one is his. A huge potted fiddle-leaf fig tree is in the corner of the room—which adds the one pop of earth color that the room desperately needs to not feel claustrophobic.

"What remodeling did your parents do to this one?" I ask, looking around at the simplistic decor. If it wasn't for the abundant amount of recess lighting and lamps, it would look like a cave. But somehow it is cozy and inviting—despite the extreme color contrast.

"Not much. This is pretty much the place I spent my teenage years. The only thing that has changed," he says, opening his closet door and pointing to the boxes on the floor, "is that the teenage mementos are no longer shelved above my bed."

I turn back to the huge king-size bed that is in the center of the main wall. It is way too big for someone still living at home. "How many girls have been in this room?"

"I lost count. After a bunch of drunken nights I would come home with two—maybe three—at once."

"Ew! Really?"

"No, Angie. I'm not a whore," he fake scoffs.

I hit him on his arm. "You are attractive enough to be one."

His lips curl into the biggest smile. "You find me attractive?"

"You know you are, and you know I do."

"To answer your question, no one has been in this room other than family and some friends growing up. And the bed got upgraded a week ago when I knew you would be visiting for the holiday, and hopefully more holidays hereafter. A gamble I made on hope."

"Oh." Why this is meaningful to me, I'm not quite sure. Maybe it's his subtle planning for the future. Maybe it's that this future will include me. I am falling so hard for him, and I fear that I am allowing myself to accept his lies because I have already accepted his heart.

I kneel down on the floor and pull out the trophies and ribbons and award certificates. Some items date back to over a decade ago, while other items appear to be from his college days. Graham moves over to his bed and lies back on it while I snoop around.

"See anything interesting?" he asks.

"Wow, you were pretty nerdy," I say passively, scanning

through all of the robotics ribbons and the Junior Engineer certificates. "This is awesome how you seemed really inventive as a young boy."

I look over to Graham and find him with his eyes closed. He rubs his fingers over the upper bridge of his nose —perhaps to ease a headache. I look back through the box of items and it's like I am looking into a window of his childhood. But it's as if I have a bunch of clues that belong to entirely different puzzles, and nothing really fits together as a whole.

I turn a trophy in my hand, looking at the bronze athlete at the top—crouched and ready to pounce.

"I didn't know you were an All-American wrestler." It is not surprising that he is good at sports with a stacked body like he has. I just never pegged him for a wrestler. "Is this how you met Dr. Saber?"

He confirms with a nod. "Wrestling was just a high school thing. I didn't want to continue on in college. I wanted to focus on my studies." He gives me a smirk, and it makes my core tingle. "I was a bit of a nerd."

I smile. That makes sense, given how accomplished he is now at such a young age. Some people spend decades making what he has built. I guess if he didn't have to rely on an athletic scholarship, then he could be more selective with how he spent his time. "What was your major?" I remember reading an article about him, but it lacked any real juicy details.

"I ended up at North Pacific University in Seattle and double majored in computer science and electrical engineering, with a minor in business management."

"Could you be any more of an overachiever?"

He chuckles. "I've always been up for a challenge."

"I figured with a jewelry company you would have had a degree in design or something more artsy and creative." I make a scrunchy face. "And less math. Yuck." I stick out my tongue.

His eyes flash to me, and I can tell he is pondering over my comment. "You're beyond insightful."

"Just tell me the truth, please."

"I never planned on having a jewelry company when I graduated from college. But I knew I wanted to do something hands-on. My last semester in college was the game changer for how I would secure enough money to even be able to buy up companies or start my own."

"What happened that last semester?"

"At NPU there is an electronics lab that is typically used by students working in the graduate research programs, but I was allowed to utilize it because I had a work-study job and the professor who ran the lab gave me free access to it. I used to tinker with electronics all throughout my childhood. Take things apart. Put them back together again. But what separated me from most other kids was that I would try to find a way to make the device better before I would piece it back to its original formation. It became a little hobby of mine, but you would refer to it as an obsession."

"Probably," I agree. "You do like to take things a little too far."

"Ha. Well, I would start with computers. Take them apart and rebuild them to be faster, have more memory, etcetera. Well, during that last semester, I had access to many different tracking devices. Probably twenty different models and styles. Most had GPS capabilities and were bulky, and none were tinier than a memory card for a camera. I spent months messing around with the ones that were in the lab. Taking them apart and putting them back together again. I did that until I could produce one that was small. Smaller than any others on the market. I held on to my idea after graduation. There was no need for me to try to replicate it in a factory setting without a steady income to back my project."

"What did you do with your idea then? Just forget about it?"

"I waited until I graduated and worked for a couple of years with my dad on commercial building structures handling the electrical issues and some of the system engineering stuff. But I was really waiting for Nic to finish his degrees and move back to the West Coast. He was skilled and had talents beyond his computer science degree, with a specialty in privacy and security."

"What does that mean?"

"He became an expert, really. And several government agencies sought him out. He just wasn't interested in the private sectors. He had other dreams."

"Okay…"

"Nic was young and ambitious and able to see outside of the box on solutions. While I was more physical with my skill set, Nic was more behind the scenes, but put us together and we could be a force. However, he fell in love with a girl named Tara. He was going to marry her and it changed his outlook for the future. No longer was being a hacker as thrilling as it was to having a family of his own."

"Love can change everything," I say softly.

"Or ruin you," Graham points out with a frown. "And

that's what it did to Nic. He would have stayed east but he broke off the engagement to Tara."

"Oh no, why?"

"He suspected she was cheating on him."

"How did he find out?" I ask. And then it dawns on me. "Oh no, did you put a tracking device on her?"

"No. I didn't. But I gave Nic the resources so he could. He wanted concrete evidence before he called everything off."

"Pretty sure that is illegal in most states."

"Yeah, and neither of us cared. He needed to know where she was going and wanted proof. He got it. And thankfully avoided a train wreck later on."

"Why not just place one on her car?"

"Because she would use a taxi. Knew all the tricks. Except the one where she led Nic straight to the other man's bedroom."

"Wow. That just sucks."

"Yeah, but it helped him find closure and move on with his life—despite being jaded toward women and refusing to date or get involved with any girl who even breathed the word 'commitment.'"

"Sheesh." I stretch out my legs to avoid them getting the pins and needles feeling from falling asleep. "Has to be pretty lonely shutting yourself off from women."

Graham snickers. "Oh, he definitely has his fill of them. Don't let the boyish looks fool you. It is all a facade. Pretty sure his tastes exceed my own. And you know first-hand how demanding of a bastard I am."

I nod eagerly, making him laugh. I think about Nic now

that I know his background. "That is still lonely. Never connecting beyond a physical standpoint."

"Finally you see how life changing you were for me. Before you, everyone I—" He taps a finger against his jawline, making me cringe over where this storyline is going.

"Banged."

"*Encountered*."

"On an intimate level…"

He sighs. "Surface level, sweetheart. Don't you get it?" He shifts his weight, adjusting to get comfortable. "You have changed my entire view of what I want out of this life. Flipped my world completely upside down. No one has gotten under my skin like you have—and no one ever will."

"I hate every single bitch that you ever touched before me." It makes me crazy to think about all of those women who have been lucky enough to have had Graham. I want to preserve how he makes me feel for only myself.

"I may have touched them, Angie. But they never touched me like you have."

I know he is speaking in a figurative sense, and in a way, I feel better at his confirmation. However, it is still something I need to continue working through if we are going to move forward.

"Okay." I nod. "Keep going with the story."

"The silver lining for helping Nic catch Tara was that it gave me confidence that my prototype worked and could be concealed. He moved back to the Portland area looking for a fresh start and to hopefully erase the memory of Tara from his mind. He wasn't interested in a desk job or something formal. He was never that type of conventional person. He needed to jump into something exhilarating and meaningful. He was still healing from the pain of a failed future life with someone he thought he loved. So he yearned for a distraction while he had time to put his life back together."

"That's so sad." I cross my legs on the floor and lean back on my palms. I am waiting. Waiting to hear some kicker. Something that lets me know about the current situation.

"So we started a business together running a secret company that would catch people cheating. Nic kept his name out of the company—although we were equal partners off-paper. He still had his eyes set on a government security job—the ones that did not require sitting in a cubicle and doing mundane tasks—and didn't want to fail any lie detector tests if he were to need clearances. So, I made sure he was not on any documents. I kept his name clean and tried my damnedest not to dirty up my own. We did everything online through the use of an encrypted website using fake IP addresses to keep ourselves hidden from any potential fallout. Nic felt inspired over his ex and wanted to channel his energy toward something productive."

"And help other people find revenge?"

Graham shrugs. "Perhaps? He knew the ins and outs about cyber privacy and security. I was able to create my tracking devices to help facilitate us in letting customers know if their significant other was being unfaithful. But a lot of the evidence was found through hacking texts and email. Believe it or not, there are a lot of people who cheat who like to take candid pictures of their new partner."

"Gross."

"We were a team to be reckoned with and yet no one

knew we were pulling all the puppet strings. It was thrilling and exhilarating. It was the exact type of rush Nic needed to pick up the pieces of his own life and channel his hatred."

"How were you able to run a company doing illegal activity with the tracking devices?"

His eyes grow dark. "I told you I wasn't a good man, Angela. I convinced myself that the useful results justified the shady method to retrieve them."

I nod. That seems to be a motto for how he lives his life too. But if I felt like someone was cheating on me, I would want to know—regardless of how.

"And I was helping out my brother," he adds. "And to me, that drove the desire. We did everything behind the scenes using fake names and never meeting with clients face-to-face. We had a ninety percent success rate in proving cheating. The other ten percent we would say the sourced information was inconclusive. There was no way to prove someone was not cheating. I perfected my devices and was even able to remotely shut them off when each job was done. We told ourselves what we wanted to hear so we could sleep at night peacefully."

"Did you ever plant video cameras?"

I watch Graham swallow, his Adam's apple moving in his throat. He glances away, and I know the answer.

"You made a lot of money from this?" I ask.

"A ridiculous amount. But then we had a family emergency."

"Penny?"

"Yeah. And it changed everything in one moment."

I know exactly what he is talking about. The accident

changed my life forever. One moment. Just one. And I am still feeling the ripple effects that could last a lifetime.

"Penny was hospitalized for possible assault from a drugging incident. Some stranger had to call 9-1-1 and get her help. She could have died in her own vomit from whatever she was slipped. She had to deal with it all alone until we were notified. It devastated our family to the core."

"That must have been horrible."

"She is my baby sister and so young and impressionable. How could something like this happen? We all wanted answers. Would stop at nothing to get them. Nic and I were able to get Penny to admit that she was an escort and was lured into it by a photographer claiming to help her further her modeling career and put her on the map. She was young and inexperienced. And we all sheltered her in a way. Her going to college was her way of breaking free."

"Which college?"

"Same one you go to—River Valley U. You two are very close in age, actually. She had a jump start on classes from taking a bunch of credit eligible ones during high school. But she started later than most kids, so she was a bit older. Your paths may have even crossed and not realized it. But she is extremely naive, with the same attraction to danger as you seem to have."

My eyes twitch at his description of me.

"She was so upset at the hospital that she made me and Nic promise not to tell my parents about the escort service."

"Was she having sexual relationships with the men?"

"I think so. She won't talk about it. But the night of the drugging—no one knows. There was no—"

"Physical evidence?"

"Exactly. She can't even remember. That is what is causing her relapses for her therapies—not knowing. She won't even open up much to anyone about what she does remember."

"Not even to the police?"

"Huh," he scoffs, "the police are useless. Penny wouldn't even have a leg to stand on because being in the escort service immediately discredits any truth you want to share. No one will believe a word if you were ever to go to trial. Even with a heartfelt testimony over the drugging, it would still seem less impactful due to the lack of credibility. Society still believes that women 'ask for it' based on how they dress or act or what they do in their spare time."

He's right. There are double standards on sexuality when it comes to men and women. Even recent high-publicity cases where girls were raped, the predators were still able to get community service or be put on light probation. As a result, the victims were worse off because of having to relive their stories during the trials and then see their abusers basically protected. The law definitely does not favor the victim of assault—especially in a society that puts men at the top of the gender list.

"Yeah, I can see that," I agree. "It sucks though." And irks every feminist cell in my body. Until men hold themselves accountable for their actions and not try to justify them based on how a female acts, nothing will change. It starts at birth. This whole "boys will be boys" mentality is destructive and inexcusable. How about boys will be good humans? Why can that not be the message parents imbed into their babies' heads?

"Nic and I spent several months gaining insight on the

company she worked for called Illusion Escorts Services. It was a company that catered to the rich. Those who could afford to blow money on easy-access girls loved having the freedom of choice to peruse a database full of flirty pictures and profiles. Nic and I put all of our energy into trying to figure out the logistics of how the company worked."

"What did you find out?" I ask.

"Illusion Escorts Services was underground and full of corruption—with roots spread up and down the West Coast. I had a suspicion that Penny's drugging incident was not isolated, but I needed to have more control of the company to gain more information."

"Okay…"

"Right as I was about to buy up the company, Nic and I were tricked into attending a meeting in regard to a traffic incident. I should have known something was up when we both received different letters in the mail. We were contacted by a division of the FBI doing internal investigations on some underground happenings that we were also personally interested in because of Penny. They had watched us for half a year, gathering up enough information so they could hold it over our heads and get us to do what they wanted. They wanted puppets to control. How someone tipped them off to our data collection means, we're not sure. But the threat of doing jail time for illegally tampering with security systems, putting tracking devices on humans, and acquiring information without consent through video footage had us both nervous over our wrong-doings. Stalking is a serious crime, and they had a whole file of evidence on what I was doing with my inventions.

So, Nic and I didn't have a choice. We had to sell our souls over to the bureau."

"What does that mean?"

"We became confidential informants in exchange for our freedom and the guarantee we would not be tried."

"You work for the FBI?"

"I used to. Not anymore."

"Does Nic still work for them?"

"Yes. And if you tell anyone, we could all be killed."

"Why?" This is what I don't understand. He alluded to this before dinner when we were cut off and had to go inside.

"Snitches are always looked down upon. Bringing down a crime ring has horrible consequences. And I don't want to live in fear. Not for myself…but for those I love."

"So you have fake IDs?"

"Yes. And that is why you need to refer to Nic as Dominic Crawford—or you are putting him at risk."

I nod. Holy shit. My head hurts from all of this.

"We were all in this situation to find out what was happening in the underground world. The FBI was interested—and also could turn their backs on me using illegal measures to gather information—for their own purposes. Nic and I just wanted to find out who hurt Penny. Informants never testify in court, so we would be able to stay anonymous. Since we were undercover, we could do what we wanted and not get penalized for it in the name of the law."

"Wow."

"Then another incident happened with Illusion Escorts. Three of the girls who were active escorts died within a week's time. The company folded and dissolved before I could buy it. A huge investigation was done on the local level. All while the FBI was using Nic and me to pass back information to them."

Fuck. "What did the girls die from?"

"Overdoses."

"Damn. That could have been Penny."

"Exactly. She was spared and was able to get out. And I was so thankful. The FBI wanted to lure out all of the key players, so we brainstormed and came up with a plan. Our company that caught cheaters got shut down, for obvious reasons. However, we avoided being fined or having to pay a huge amount of back taxes. It was like they turned a blind eye just to use us for the chance to gather information. And it seemed like a fair trade at the time. Avoid prison time and become informants."

"Seems so surreal. Like a TV show."

"Except it's real. And now I have more to lose than ever." His eyes darken as he looks at me.

"What happened next?"

"I used the money we profited from that adventure to set up an alternative escort service with hopes to gain a database list of men who were wanting their fun but could flaunt it in a public setting—and through a legitimate business model. And that is how Entice was born."

"Everyone who works there has no idea that you are calling the shots?"

"The higher up positions know I am a key investor. The details are not important to the business or to them."

"So, let me get this straight. You are running Entice behind the scenes and Dominic is working undercover as an informant—using an alias name and pretending to be the CEO? How do you even get information to pass back?"

"Men with money get cocky. But doing the background checks alone helped us turn all of the disqualified names over to the FBI and gave us a chance to continue trying to lure out those who never had any criminal record. Those people are the most valuable because they are on no one's radars. Obviously that is all about to change."

"But Entice does not have a sexual encounter requirement."

"Correct, none that could be charged for money. People do what people do. But the agency would not be taking a cut in those side dealings."

So much information is running through my head all at once. "How are you able to keep girls safe who work for you?"

"The FBI planted some informants inside the agency… at least we think they did. Nic and I have no clue who they are though. And who knows, we could be completely wrong. It is really just a theory."

"Wow."

"We thought you were one at the beginning."

"Interesting…"

"But I knew you weren't one within a few meetings."

"How so?"

"You're the worst liar on the planet," he says with a smirk.

"And you basically told me that when we met outside the mansion at the pool." I remember that night so well.

"You wear your emotions in your eyes. I knew there was something so pure and innocent about you. Therefore there was no way you could be one. But Nic was convinced otherwise. So no matter how much I tried to get him not to interview you and allow you to join, he thought he needed to just for the extra backup."

"Why would you have been worried if I was one?"

"Because I am so infatuated with you that it would, for one, make working extremely difficult, and two, make it so hard to sit back and watch you put yourself at risk. Which oddly enough, has been what you've been doing from the start. Anyway, informants could get caught and then the consequences could be horrifying. Ironically, you are doing something worse than being an informant. You are a fucking aspiring investigative journalist. Is this some cruel joke?"

"I'm being careful."

"You're being downright reckless. You are diving head-first into a situation that is dangerous and trying to uncover the mystery, but with little knowledge of how bad this could get if you get caught."

"Are you using these trackers on girls at the agency? On me?" I glance down at my body as paranoia rushes over me. "Where's it at?" I ask, pulling at my clothes and running my hand all over the fabric. "Am I wearing something now? You said you put them on bodies. Where is mine?"

Graham sits up and slides to the floor to join me. "Calm down."

"Calm down? Calm down? That is what you have to say? Calm down? That is like the worst thing to say to a woman, Graham!"

"I see that now," he sighs. "You're not wearing one."

"But I did? At some point, right?"

He nods slowly, hesitant to set me off.

"Shit, Graham. Really? Is the FBI telling you to put them on me?"

He shakes his head no. "But I had to keep you safe. And I couldn't trust you to stay away from Tanner."

"How does Mark even fit in?" I remember what he told me in the hotel room, but I really want to know more details. Something isn't adding up.

"Mark used to use Penny as an escort when she worked in the previous company."

"This is like a soap opera."

"And it gets worse."

"I don't know how much worse this could get," I breathe out.

"He was the owner of said company."

"Do you think he is at fault for what happened to Penny?"

"How could he not be—even if just partially? The way he flaunts her name to me every chance he gets may suggest that."

"On our first date, when you picked me up instead of Nic"—I cringe over the name change, still scolding myself for not seeing it sooner—"I remember Mark mentioning Penny to you. That was the first time I heard her name. But I had no idea who she was."

"I tried to convince you that night that there were more suitable jobs. I tried to stay away from you afterwards. I swear I did. I tried everything I could to get you to either quit the agency or to exclusively date me. And it was all because I was desperate to protect you the only way I knew how. I tried to lock you into only dating me and then tried to hack your account to force you to reject Tanner. But you would still find a way to meet up with him. I even resorted to blackmail. Nothing seemed to work. You just kept pursuing him—relentlessly."

"Well, now you know my motive behind why I couldn't stop. Mark is hiding something. He has connections with other men, and I think he is just a puppet to someone making all the orders."

"If he's responsible for the drug overdoses that killed three of his previous employees, he could go to prison for a very long time. His shady underground club got Penny in trouble. And who knows if she will ever be the same girl I grew up with. And now my own agency's girls are moving down that path. Whoever is doing the drugging is getting more aggressive with it. And it terrifies me. Nic is working at finding the connections, but he is limited in what he can do."

"This explains why you hate Mark. But why does he hate you so much?"

"Because before you, I had nothing to lose. And every time he had a business venture, I would outbid him or sabotage him."

"And now?"

His intense stare at me causes goose bumps to form on my arms. "I have everything to lose now," he snarls. "And Tanner knows it."

"Tell me more about the tracking devices. Where are you hiding them?"

"Having two very creative parents helped to drive me toward doing something hands-on. So I created HH and used it to house a jewelry company. But in one of the divisions that is extremely private—hence all the security features I have in place—we analyze and test body trackers. And having Jealousy established helped me to be able to place the trackers undetected in jewelry. I was able to make them small enough to fit on the identity bracelets that are given to girls at Entice."

I think to all the times I've been out with Mark that I haven't been wearing my bracelet. "I don't wear mine all the time."

"I know." His words come out as a growl. "And you not wearing one when you were coerced into going to the Maylord almost caused me to lose my mind."

"I wasn't on an agency date," I say in defense, realizing after the fact that Graham is getting angrier.

"When Tanner took you to the hotel room, I wouldn't have been able to know which floor you were on anyway—with or without the tracker. I had to rely on someone getting paid off to share the room number. But I would have torn through the entire building to find you."

"How are you able to get away with the bracelets? Isn't even placing trackers on vehicles now illegal in the entire state of Oregon? As in having to serve a year of prison time for the felony offense?"

He sighs. "That's correct. California has similar strict laws—mostly to prevent stalking from occurring. But nonetheless, I would be in violation if there was not written consent. But in the fine print of the fifty-page document that you signed upon getting hired, there is a brief mention of the bracelets and the usage of a tracking device on them. You wear them voluntarily and can take them off whenever you want. Nothing is mandated. Signing the documents implies consent. Thus, I can get away with including them in my product. I built the company Jealousy from the ground up and hired a team of people to work at making it a successful company. However, there are huge areas at HH that are for the development of tracking devices and how we can insert them and keep them undetected in other products. The FBI gets what they want from me. And I get what I want."

"So you are tracking the agency girls to see if anything looks off?"

His eyes twitch.

"Are we all just pawns in this game?"

He glances away. "You aren't. At least anymore."

"But I have friends. My *best friend.*"

"And I promise to keep her as safe as I can."

"No one is safe, Graham. No one."

"Dammit, I know, Angie. I know."

"You shared that you were a confidential informant. But then stated that you aren't anymore. Why? What happened?"

"You happened."

"Oh."

"I was working as an informant for months. Just going with the flow. And dating through the database so I could look like a participant—rather than the owner."

"Sophia."

"Yes. But she knew I was never serious about her."

"Pretty sure she never received that message, Graham."

He sighs but ignores my comment. "The mixer events at the mansion were extremely beneficial because I would have access to sound and video footage. Plus, everyone congregated at one location. It is easier to gather information when everyone is together. But during the last social event at the end of summer, you were there. Out by the pool. I knew as soon as I saw you that I wouldn't be able to keep myself from pursuing you. I wanted you that night. Wanted to take you into a room and fuck my memory into your body."

I swallow hard and let out a moan.

"I was pissed off at the world. Peeved that I made a deal with the devil for my own selfish reasons to stay out of prison and of course to find justice for Penny. I was irritated that Claire involved you when you were so innocent. I was mad at Nic for allowing you to walk into the office I technically owned and join the agency that was simply a cover for luring out criminals. I wanted to scream. I have never felt that helpless and out of control in my life."

"I'm sorry," I whisper. "I just thought you didn't like me."

"I liked everything about you. I became obsessed. I strived to have some type of control over you because your actions seemed so volatile. So I went to my FBI supervisor and told him I needed out. I promised him I would get you out of the agency and keep you from interfering in the internal investigation. I showed him footage of you seeking out Tanner. I proved that you were a threat to the safety of the investigation and promised that I could assist by getting you to back off."

"I was working toward my own personal goals."

"And that is why I have to make my next move. Because up until now, all of my efforts have not gotten you to give up."

"Graham…"

"You have literally left me no choice."

"What are you going to do?"

"Stop you from getting us all discovered and killed."

"Why do you keep saying that? Before tonight you didn't even know I was working toward a coveted internship."

"You are investigating a drug ring that the FBI is also investigating for a potential criminal case that may go to trial. If you get caught, you are jeopardizing everyone involved—including myself and Nic—just by mere association. We could all go down like dominoes."

"But you aren't an informant anymore."

"Nic is though. You don't have to be tied to the FBI to be in danger. These drug dealers are out for blood if it impacts their cash flow."

I frown over his words. I am so close to figuring out the truth behind Entice girls getting drugged. But is risking my own life worth it? Can I set aside an ambition that sparked inside me when I lost James and find happiness in another career path?

"It ends tonight, Angie. All of this nonsense is over when you wake up in the morning."

I shake my head. "Why tonight?"

"Because you are being targeted."

"Is that why we came here a day early?"

"Yes."

"Graham, I'll be extra cautious."

"Come up with a backup plan, Angie. Because you're done seeing Tanner. You're done sending your roommate out to do your spying. It all ends. Find another topic to write about. Or switch majors again. I don't give a flying fuck what you do. But this research pet project you think will lock you into an internship? It's over."

I glare at him with pent-up anger. "Oh how dare you, Graham Hoffman!" I get up from the floor and pace in front of him. "You can't control everything. I'm not a pawn in your game."

"That's correct. But you are becoming one in their game." He joins me in pacing. "I cannot sit back and allow someone else I love to get hurt by this craziness. I just can't. When I tell Nic all of this new information, you'll have to get through his firewall too. Because he cares about you too. You have that effect on people."

"So you both would sabotage me?"

"I'm prepared to put my entire security staff on you. I don't even care about being discreet about it anymore."

My mouth opens like a fish. *Well, damn.* "You wouldn't."

"I already have."

32

The sun peeking through the slivered opening in the drapes wakes me. I roll on my side and feel around on the mattress. The only thing my hand finds is cold sheets. Graham and I stayed up way too late last night baring our souls and removing the skeletons from our closets. My body is exhausted despite getting some sleep. But mostly, it is my mind that needs to recharge.

I stretch and pull the comforter aside to get out of bed. I look at my cell phone and see it is almost seven. I throw on my two-sizes-too-big hoodie for warmth and sneak quietly out of the bedroom. The smell of freshly brewed coffee awakens my senses, and I walk down the stairs to find its source.

When I get into the kitchen, Germain, Nic, and Graham are standing around the island having what appears to be a family discussion. I turn on my heel and start to walk away when I hear, "Angela, please join us."

I stop and exhale. Caught. I pivot and give Germain a lopsided smile. "Sorry, I smelled the coffee."

"My wife's Colombian friend brings it back for us from her country every few months when she visits family. It is delicious," he explains. "It would be plain insulting for you not to have a mug full."

I smile shyly. This morning feels much different being around the men than it did the night before. Now I know so much more about them, and it makes me feel vulnerable to the fact that they may know things about me in return.

Graham walks over to me and hands me his already prepared mug. I take a sip of the warm liquid. It is smooth and rich—with the slightest hints of chocolate and cinnamon. "Wow, this is amazing coffee."

He kisses me on the forehead and goes to the cupboard to pull out another mug. He pours me some fresh and fixes it the way I love—which is how he fixes his own but with bigger measurements. "How did you sleep?" he asks softly.

I shrug. "Okay, I guess." It was one of the few times we were in bed together and just slept. But it was not what I would call *restful*.

"Well, I better head out to the airport and go get Penny," Germain says. "I appreciate the gesture, son."

Graham glances at the clock. "Glad I could help."

"Boys, please help your mother to not be so stressed today with this whole holiday meal. You know how much of a perfectionist she becomes on these types of holidays. She's probably really nervous about Penny being home after being gone for so long. Bear some of the weight with her."

"Okay, Dad. We're on it," Nic promises. "Where is Mom anyway?"

"Downstairs double-checking roasters and temperature settings in the other kitchen. She always worries about getting this one too dirty when there's company. Plus, I think she is having a few issues up here that need to be looked at."

Germain heads out the front door, and I am left alone with the brothers.

"I hope she is not anxious over me. Does she need help? I can go down and offer," I suggest.

"We already know that she'll refuse help," Nic says calmly.

I nod. I get it. It is sometimes easier to refuse help instead of admitting that it is needed.

"Angie," Nic says with hesitation, "can we chat?"

I swallow my mouthful of coffee and mouth a barely audible "yes."

Graham's eyes dart over to Nic's, and I can tell he doesn't want to leave my side. "I'll go take a look at the oven and security system."

Nic and I move into the living room, and I curl my feet up under me on the sofa. He settles on a chair.

"Did Graham fill you in on everything?"

"Maybe," I say hesitantly. "But I would love to hear what you have to say so that I can see if your stories match."

He narrows his eyes at me. "Are you serious?"

"Yes," I deadpan.

"How about you tell me what you know?"

I sigh. "Graham was an FBI informant. You still are one. Graham owns Entice after Mark Tanner's Illusion Escorts left three women dead and was to blame for Penny getting drugged. Penny was getting involved in modeling and then got sucked into that agency, while Mark would take her out on dates. You're running the Entice company under the name Dominic Crawford, and it's all confidential and should stay that way. Mark probably thinks, because of Penny's drugging, that Graham helped to dismantle his company secretly, despite having three girls overdosing. Maybe he thinks there is a connection between getting caught and Graham itching for revenge. Mark joins Entice, while avoiding prison time for the tragedies that occurred while he was the employer of Illusion. So, now there's a huge rivalry, not to mention major testosterone-induced public taunting sessions. But no one knows you're related to Graham or Penny. And I'm pretty sure your parents have zero clue as to what you and Graham have gotten yourselves into and you both want them out of this situation, so you barely visit them. How am I doing so far?"

"Great," he says, turning his ring around and around again, "except for the part where you're going to promise to back off and stay out of this open investigation. Let me do my job. Give Graham a chance to focus on something other than trying to get you out of trouble at every turn. You're being targeted, Angie. And to think all along, Graham was worried that having any connection to him would be enough to put you at risk. You didn't need him at all to do that. You're doing a fine job all by yourself."

I frown over his words. "I'll be careful."

"Seriously, though"—he shakes his head in disbelief—"an investigative journalist? What are the flipping chances?"

"You're aware that the FBI has no control over media publication and that we as Americans have a right to free speech?"

I watch as Nic's eyes twitch and he sits up farther in his chair. "You're aware that you're putting your nose into a situation that's riddled with crime lords and toxic drugs? That you're going to get discovered while going on with your ridiculous antics and get us all killed for even being connected to you? Is that something you're willing to ignore and continue on with your quest?"

"I've been careful all this—"

"Bullshit, Angie," he snaps, making me jolt back from the force of his tone. "Have you not heard anything I just said? They have been on to you almost from the start. All of our intel has basically suggested it. The whole hotel scene was a setup to prove to Tanner that you're the most valuable bargaining chip in Graham's life. While we are trying to out him and his ring, he's trying to out us and all those connected with trying to bring him down."

"I'm not some kind of token."

"No," he says, shaking his head, "but you basically allowed Tanner to exploit Graham's only weakness—you. Graham's so freaking in love with you that he can't see straight. Now the underground world knows."

"Why does this matter? I have a crap ton of guards watching me, right?"

"With good reason. Because as soon as Tanner sees an opportunity, he's going to try to take you away from Graham."

I swallow hard. Shit. Would things really go that far?

"But don't worry. Graham's working on an alternate plan to keep you safe. And for once, I actually approve."

"What does he have planned?" And when will I be privy to this type of information concerning my life?

"The only thing I can do to keep you out of harm's way," Graham says, entering the room with a scowl on his face. He joins me on the couch and fixes a piece of hair behind my ear. A gentle kiss to my forehead doesn't lessen the sting of the words I know I am about to hear. "And I'm doing it, Angie. So enjoy this time before it all comes crashing down."

My eyes fill with tears over these cryptic hints at a big change that apparently I have no say in. *Shocker*.

We stay like this. Motionless. Just sitting here.

No one has anything to say. And no one has energy to make the first move.

Several times Donna comes up from the basement to get ingredients or add something to the table decor. And we just sit here.

"Are you up for playing some football?" Nic suggests, completely breaking the silence. "Fresh air and exercise will help all of our moods."

"Sure," Graham says, "let me throw on some clothes."

He tugs me up from the couch, and we make our way into his childhood bedroom. I yelp as he pushes me onto the bed and follows beside me.

"Hey! What are you doing?"

"Everything your body craves." His voice is gruff and raspy.

Before I can even utter a syllable, he is pulling my

hoodie over my head and stripping me down to nothing. "Hmm," I moan. "It feels like forever."

He warms me up with his mouth on my nipples and a hand on my mound. His leg drapes over me lazily, and I can feel his cock hardening on my thigh. When I am twitching with need, Graham rolls on top of me and slides in from tip to base. I wiggle to adjust and love the pressure of his body holding mine down to the comforter. I relax my mind and submit to the desire that has accumulated over the past few days and let go of control.

He slides in and out in a slow burning rhythm, while I clench my inner walls to milk him.

"You feel so good, baby. I could stay buried in you the entire day and still want more."

I bite at his neck and try to get him to pick up the pace. "Ahh!" I start to yell but get silenced by his mouth suctioning onto my lips.

Graham lifts my ass up from the mattress, angles his hips, and pushes into me to hit my sweet spot. When I start to yell again, his hand muffles the sound. I can't even think past the next second and the growing need to get closer to the edge of the cliff. I feel so exhilarated at the thought of getting caught that it sends me over, and I arch my back and push my chest up into him. His deep growl echoes in my ear, and I feel him tense and gush inside me.

"You drive me so mad outside the bedroom that it makes me want to fuck some sense into you inside the bedroom," he explains, wiping some beads of sweat from my forehead. He rolls me on top of him, smacks each of my ass cheeks, and tickles my sides. "Go get dressed. We can't celebrate Thanksgiving without playing some football."

I scurry off of him and find my bag on the dresser. I unzip and dig through to find a pair of cranberry leggings, my obnoxious cartoonish turkey socks, and a sweatshirt that says "Feminist and Proud" in puffy letters.

Graham eyes my shirt as soon as I am still enough for him to read the words.

"Got a problem?" I ask, cocking a hip.

He opens his mouth to speak but then shakes his head and stays silent.

"What?"

"Nothing," he says slowly, pulling a sweatshirt over his head to pair with his jeans. "I just love how you call yourself a feminist but then you relinquish control to me in bed. Should change the words to 'Feminist and Fucked.'"

I giggle at his observation. It is not false. "Ready to lose to me in football?"

He chuckles. "It's just tossing the ball around. Nothing to win or lose. Plus, you will be watching from the sidelines."

"What? Like some"—my eyebrows rise—"cheerleader?"

He purses his lips. "Hmm, that does sound like the making for an epic fantasy."

"We'll see," I say, sauntering out of the room with him hot on my tail. I turn around to glance at him. "I'm playing."

The sound of the front door opening causes everyone to stop what they are doing and go greet Germain and Penny. I stand in the background and watch silently as Donna holds back tears and gives her only daughter a huge hug. Germain wraps an arm around his wife in support. I do not know the last time Penny was around her family or back home, but the twisting of her hands and rocking on her heels suggests it has been some time.

"All my babies are home," Donna says softly, smiling through the tears. "What a holiday to celebrate—even if we're a day early."

Penny walks over quietly to Graham and they embrace. I can tell he is afraid to touch her. Maybe worried to set her off? His hands tremble as he pats her gently on her back. It melts my heart to see the relief in his eyes—probably for the fact that the therapy center is making progress with her. Nic joins as well, ruffles her hair, and gives her a lopsided smile. When her eyes catch mine, she looks to the men with confusion.

"Penny, this is Angie McFee. My girlfriend," Graham answers her unspoken question.

"Wow, girlfriend? Why didn't you tell me that you had a girlfriend when you visited a few weeks ago?"

"Probably because at the time our relationship was working out some kinks," he says, looking over at me to give me a flirty wink. "It took Angie some time to learn not to resist my charm."

I glare at him. *Behave in front of your family, Graham!*

"She's just lovely, isn't she?" Donna says cheerfully, making my cheeks heat. "Penny, Angie is studying English at River Valley."

At the mention of *English*, Graham growls so deep into his throat that if I wasn't standing right beside him, I would have missed it.

“Are you guys all going to play football?” Penny asks. I see the glimmer of hope flash in her eyes at the thought of doing something that must be a tradition in the Hoffman household.

“You can watch,” Graham says sternly. “Angie can keep you company.”

Hey! I press my foot onto his when no one is looking.

Penny puts her hands on her hips and taps her foot. “Why just watch?”

Penny is slightly taller than Donna and has beautiful long auburn hair, much lighter than her oldest brother’s. She is stunning with piercing blue eyes and barely visible freckles on a backdrop of the purest porcelain skin.

Graham’s forehead wrinkles, and I can tell he is wanting to give in. But how can he call the shots—all the damn time?

“Come on, Penny,” I say, “I have an outfit you can borrow that is fine if you get dirty.”

For the first time since meeting her, I see a genuine smile spread across her face. Even her eyes light up.

“That sounds great,” she says, sticking her tongue out at Graham, who cannot decide whether to congratulate or strangle me.

Penny follows me up the stairs into Graham’s room, and I rummage through my belongings until I find a similar outfit to what I have on. This time the sweatshirt says “Girls Do It Better.”

“These sweatshirts are awesome. Are they custom?”

“I ordered them online; however, as soon as I collect enough money in my savings account, I’m going to buy one of those heat presses so I can make my own shirts and jazz up mugs and water bottles."

"Oh, that sounds like fun. If you open one of those sales shops online, I'll be your first customer."

"Thank you," I say with a smile.

"I should be thanking you."

"For what?"

"Ever since I was,"—she pauses—"you know, my entire family has been treating me like a dying flower that just needs to be drowned in water. I am fragile now to them, and I just want to forget sometimes and have things go back to the way they were. So thank you for lending me the clothes and not treating me like I'm broken."

A sadness washes over her, and I can't help but see the similarities between us. Her dull and lifeless eyes are reflected back to me and once were my own. After the car accident, I lingered in the dark place for a while. When I finally climbed up in search of the light, it was an adjustment to get myself assimilated back into normal life. Moving away helped to separate myself from those who had preconceived expectations on how I was supposed to act posttrauma.

"Do you ever wish that your mind would shut up for a few minutes and let you vacation to another place where everything is functioning in harmony?" I ask.

Penny sits on the end of the bed, looks down at her hands, and then back up at me. "All the damn time."

"It's okay to stay in that place longer than a few minutes. It's about survival. And knowing that you're stronger than you realize."

"I hope Graham deserves you," she says sadly.

I furrow my brow at her statement.

She sighs. "He's an amazing brother. But sometimes his good intentions get overshadowed by his need to have things his way."

"Wow, you have him pegged." I laugh.

"I would never believe it, unless I was witnessing it with my own eyes, that he was able to secure a girlfriend who would put up with the crazy shit that man pulls. I can only imagine what overprotective, idealistic protocols he has implemented for your relationship with him. He basically has my entire therapy staff scared every time he visits. I think they all think he's the supervisor or something."

I smile. I love her authentic personality. "He definitely takes *controlling* to a new level, doesn't he?"

"I'm pretty sure seeing me in the hospital sent him deeper into the darkness that he sometimes hovers in. So, if that trickles down to how he walks through life with you, I'm sorry."

"He just wants to make sure what happened to you does not happen to anyone else," I explain. "Me included."

Penny looks up at me with a sad smile. "I don't even know what happened to me. That's what is creating my mental roadblock. I spent months not wanting to talk to anyone, and then I finally woke up one day and decided that I can't keep living like this. I have these"—tears well up in her eyes—"episodes."

I can relate. The ambiguity of the car accident that killed James eats me alive some nights when I go to bed thinking about it and wake up covered in sweat. "Sometimes moving forward means letting go of the notion that in order to completely heal, you have to know all of the answers. Putting a stipulation on what needs to happen to move on might prevent it from ever happening."

Penny seems to mull over my words inside her head. "How did you get so wise?"

"I had to grow up fast. Too fast." I don't want to talk about the details—I never do—but something inside urges me to share. Maybe by opening up about my journey through trauma, Penny can see that recovery can start, and maybe I can move forward in my own journey as well. "I lost my mom when I was twelve to cancer. It was a horrible time watching her suffer. Then when I was a freshman in college back in Baker City, my twin brother and I were in a car accident. He didn't survive. It was a hit and run. To this day, I am haunted by the what-ifs and the unknowns surrounding the entire thing. It eats at me. But I have to come to terms with the idea of never knowing what happened that night. If I keep living in the past, I will miss my future."

Penny bites her bottom lip that wants to keep quivering. I can tell she is holding back her emotions as best she can. For meeting each other for the first time, these topics are weighty. I can only hope that I've helped her and not actually hindered her progression.

"But hey," I say, forcing myself to sound cheery, "let's go show your brothers that girls can play football too."

Penny eyes me suspiciously over my change in subject but gets up from the bed and follows me out.

"At the very least, it'll be entertaining watching them

buzz around the field making sure we don't hurt ourselves," she says with a smirk.

We are both good at masking our emotions. I'm just not so sure that is an admirable quality to have.

"Good point," I agree. The last thing Graham needs for his nerves is for us girls to join forces. But Penny is hard not to like, so he will just have to deal with it.

On my way down the stairs, I remove the hairband from my wrist and twist my hair into a messy bun and secure it with the tie. We put on sneakers and head out back in search of the guys.

"There's a field over that hill," Penny says pointing. "Let's go."

When we get to the destination, I am surprised to find Collins and Austin gathered with Graham and Nic. I walk over to Graham, and he wraps an arm around my waist, pulling me close to his side. I love how safe I feel when he has me close to him—like nothing could hurt me.

I look around the field and see the play area boundary that is marked with cones and dots of orange spray paint. "I haven't really played before," I say hesitantly, looking up at Graham. "Thought we were just tossing a football around."

"That's what the men are going to do. You and Penny can watch."

"Oh no. That's not how this is going to work."

"You can be cheerleaders," Nic suggests, but I know he is simply trying to get a rise out of us.

Penny laughs so hard that she doubles over, with her hands bracing her knees. Everyone stops and looks at her, as if they are seeing her for the first time. She must know Nic is just messing with us. Graham, however, is dead serious about excluding us. Ugh.

"Relax a bit," I tell him. "It'll be fun and good for the soul."

"Fine," he grinds out.

"I want to be on opposite teams though," I say with finality.

"Why?" he asks suddenly.

"So when my team beats yours, the victory is sweeter." I bat my eyelashes at him. "And then I can rub it in the rest of the day."

He narrows his eyes at me. We both love competition and thrive on winning against each other. Graham definitely brings out this side of me—one I really didn't think existed prior to meeting him.

Penny and I each pick back and forth until our teams—identified by colored mesh shirts—are settled. I choose Nic and Austin to join me on the red team, while Graham, Collins, and Penny are on the blue. The game is adapted based on the number of people we have available to play. Points are earned like normal football—except anyone can score, throw the ball, or pull yellow flags from waistbands. There are no set positions.

"Remember, no tackling," Nic says, eyeing me and Penny.

"Worried we'll cheat?" Penny scoffs.

"No," Graham says sternly. "Worried you guys will hurt yourselves."

Penny throws her hands up in the air. "Oh, for the love of God!"

I can't stop giggling. She and I are basically the reason

for all Graham's current anxiety. Neither of us give a damn what he says. And in this moment, a friendship is born.

The game starts with a coin toss, and the blue team has the ball first. Graham catches the snap from Penny and tosses it halfway across the field to Collins, who loses a flag by Nic. Penny catches the snap this time, and Graham charges down the field but misses the catch by a foot, so we start back where the original down last occurred. Next, I chase after Collins who is running toward the end zone with the ball, and as I throw myself forward in pursuit of the flag, I fall hard onto the ground on my stomach.

"Omphf," I choke out, as my lungs try to recover from the sudden shock.

"Oh no, Miss McFee," Collins says, picking me up and setting me on my feet. He pulls the yellow tag from his pants. "Here, you had one of my flags."

I look up at him in confusion and shake my head. "No. No, I didn't. I missed."

"But you would have had it."

I frown. "That is not fair and you know it."

"You okay, sweetheart?" Graham asks, dusting off some grass from my sweatshirt.

"I think I broke a rib, my middle left toe, and I may even have a concussion," I deadpan. I hear him curse and I start to giggle. "Graham? I tripped. Let the game proceed. Your team would have scored a point because Collins had a clear path to the end zone."

"Yeah, seriously, Graham," Penny huffs, "not all women are fragile flowers."

The game starts again, and I snap the ball to Austin and then take off down the field, weaving between Graham and

Penny as the ball comes barreling through the sky. I jump and reach my hands out as the ball hits against my chest. I clutch it under my arm and dart down the field, with Graham stalking me. I get to where the cones are and jump for joy at my scored touchdown, whooping and throwing my hands into the air.

"Nice!" Penny shouts. "Girl power!"

"Hey! Cheer for your own team!" Graham fake scolds.

The next play involves Collins snapping back to Penny, and Penny throwing it across the field to Graham. He then throws it over to Collins, nearly having it intercepted by Nic. I make my way over to Graham as Collins launches it back to him. I lose my focus and just leap onto Graham's back and try to get the ball out of his arms.

His chuckle makes me smile as he runs down the field with me perched on his back like a bear cub.

"Pretty sure this is against the rules," he says, laughing, spinning me in his arms as he scores a touchdown for his team. He squeezes my butt cheeks and growls into my ears. "But I like it."

We play for an hour with the score being close the entire time. Donna's group text to her kids with a picture of the beautiful carved turkey is what officially ends the game with my team barely in the lead.

"Better get inside before Mom blows a gasket," Penny says with a big grin. I can tell that seeing his sister happy and functioning has a positive impact on Graham's mood.

"Take Angie back to the house, Pen," he says softly. "I want to talk to my men in private."

"Okay," she says, drawing out the word.

I look up into Graham's eyes and can tell he is back in

serious mode again. Carefree mode lasted all of sixty minutes.

I follow Penny inside and quickly run up to the room to wash up and put on something less grungy. I settle on a long-sleeved mustard-yellow wrap dress with tiny maroon and white flowers. I brush my hair and add a chunky headband. I rush downstairs and join the family in the kitchen. Graham is the last to come inside, but he only needs a few minutes to change and be ready.

"This looks picture perfect," I say to Donna, who beams with pride.

"Thank you, my dear. I love all things holidays. So this is fun for me to do."

The table looks very similar to last night's display—just more over-the-top with elegance. She really has an eye for it.

Everyone sits at the place setting that has their name written on a golden card shaped like a leaf. Graham pulls out my chair and slides me into the table. He sweeps my hair over my shoulder and bends down to kiss the side of my neck before taking his own seat. I reach underneath the table and squeeze his hand.

"Thank you," he whispers into my ear, "for being so good with Penny. This is the liveliest I've seen her since the whole incident happened."

I give his hand another squeeze and smile up at him with watery eyes. I look away and blink a few times. Germain clears his throat and stands at the head of the table while Donna places the turkey platter on a side table adjacent to him.

"I would like to make a toast," he says with confidence.

Everyone holds up their goblets of wine as he continues, except Penny who just has sparkling water. "To my beautiful children, my incomparable wife, and Angela, thank you for gathering here today to celebrate the holiday of thankfulness and togetherness. Let our bounty be that of good health, good food, and good conversation. For now and for the year to come. Cheers."

"Cheers," everyone says, clinking glasses and taking sips.

Food is passed around, and Donna gathers huge forkfuls of turkey and walks portions around to everyone based on their preference for white or dark meat. Mashed potatoes, green bean casserole, yams, corn, macaroni and cheese, and cornbread stuffing fill my plate. Conversation is light due to everyone chowing down. It is delicious.

I help with clearing the table, and Donna passes out individual pumpkin cheesecakes with a dollop of homemade cinnamon whipped cream. It takes me back to working at the bakery where the place smelled like fall the entire months of October and November.

"I may need this recipe, Donna," I say after shoveling another spoonful into my mouth. "It's divine."

"Oh, thank you. So glad you like it."

"It's great, Mom," Graham agrees, followed by his siblings.

"Is everyone up for some minute-to-win-it games before I have to drive Penny back to Seattle?" Germain asks, a twinkle in his eye. He gets out of his seat and reaches behind the china cabinet to pull out a big poster board that is transformed into a grid with teams down the side and game titles across the top. "Donna and I will be on one team. Graham and Angie. And then Nic and Penny."

Donna throws her hands up into the air. "Winning team gets bragging rights."

"And the losing teams?" Nic asks with hesitation.

"Get a pie in the face," his mom chants with excitement.

Wow. The Hoffmans really get into this. But a pie in the face? Nope. Graham and I better win this. We all move into the living room that has the coffee table and ottomans moved off to the side so that there is plenty of room.

"The first game," Germain explains, "is human Hungry Hungry Hippos. There will be two rounds with alternating hippo eaters and a chance to earn double the points if your team wins both times. The rules are simple. The first team member will lie on their belly on the moving roller board and act as the hippo while the alternate member grips their legs and pushes them forward where the apples will be gathered. The team that retrieves the most apples and has them in their basket by the time the buzzer sounds will gain a victory point."

"You eat first," Graham says, helping me onto the cushioned roller board.

He arranges my dress so that I don't feel exposed and grabs my ankles. Once Germain announces "go," Penny, Donna, and I get jolted forward and our mouths chomp down on apples. Graham pulls me back, and I drop off the apple into our team's assigned bin. I laugh as I get catapulted forward again and bump my nose on an apple, causing it to roll.

"To the left," I call back, craning my neck to reach the

Granny Smith. Got it! "Baaa!" I yell, hoping he heard me to pull me back to the basket before I lose my grip.

It feels like just seconds since we started when the buzzer blares through the room. Apples are counted, with Donna and Germain locking in the first point. Members switch positions and the timer gets set again.

"Go!"

I laugh so hard at Graham's overachiever-ness as he manages to gather two small apples with one massive bite. I push him forward so hard that he rolls off the board and has to get back on, wasting some time. I pull him back and he drops an apple as he falls off again. I flop to the floor as the buzzer sounds and cannot stop laughing at our shit show.

Graham sits up and stares at me with mirth in his eyes. "If we weren't on the same team, I would think you were trying to deliberately sabotage me."

"I am so sorry," I cry out, trying to contain my laughter. "At this rate, the only hope I have is that the pie will taste yummy."

"The winners are Nic and Penny!" Donna cheers.

Nic picks up Penny and swings her around in the air while she yelps for him to put her down.

"The next game is the frozen T-shirt contest," Donna announces, handing each team one bag that contains a block of ice.

"Um, what is this, Mom?" Graham asks, shaking his head at his parents. "You two have way too much time on your hands."

Donna shushes her son and starts her demonstration of the rules. "Each bag contains a T-shirt that has been soaked in water, put in this Ziploc bag, and then tossed into the freezer. Each team needs to melt and unravel the shirt and put it on one team member's body. There will not be a time limit for this one. Fastest team secures the win," she says proudly.

"Where do you even come up with this stuff?" Nic asks, looking between the bag and his mom.

"Well, son, there is this thing called Google," she says sarcastically, making us all burst out into laughter.

I have not laughed this hard or this much in a really long time. It is exactly what I needed, without knowing I needed it. My world is a chaotic mess right now, but these moments here in Hillsboro give me hope that everything will be right again.

"Collect yourselves, family," Germain says, stifling a laugh. "Get ready, get set, go!"

I grab the bag in a hurry and start tearing the plastic apart to remove the balled up shirt of ice.

"You could have just used the zipper," Graham slowly says.

"Hurry and breathe on this thing," I say, exhaling with the shirt ball close to my mouth. "Use your heat and your mouth."

Graham holds one end of the deformed fabric and tries his darnedest to pull it apart, but it doesn't budge. "Sit on it," he says.

"No. You sit on it."

He hugs it close to his body, and little ice chips fall off like snow to the floor and collect on the towels that are spread out to catch any drippings. I roll up the sleeves on my dress and rest my forearms on the frozen mound. So cold! Graham tugs and tugs until the crackling sound echoes in the room. I glance over at Nic and Penny and see that they almost have theirs unraveled.

"Hurry," I squeal. "Your brother and sister are going to beat us!" I pull at the fabric with all of my might and stretch it out the full length. The only problem is that we have to separate the layers so it can go over one of our heads. "Oh, I have an idea," I whisper yell so the other teams can't hear.

"It better be a good one this time," he hisses.

"Take off your shirt."

"Why?" he asks dumbly.

I start tugging at his shirt before he has a chance to say no. Then I take the frozen pancake shirt and press it against his bare chest, making him jump into the air at the sudden shock from the cold.

"Quit being a baby about it," I snap. "You have a greater surface area of body heat. We need to win this one!"

The shirt melts enough so I can yank the layers apart and pull it over Graham's head. He pushes ice crystals out of the sleeves as his hands plow through the arm holes.

"We win!" he chants, picking me up and swinging me around.

"Cold!" I howl. "Put me down!"

"Good job, Angie and Graham. We are all tied up now," Germain says, marking my team with a point.

"The next game is called Bam Bam Bowl," Donna explains, passing us each a one-legged nylon stocking that has a baseball encased in the footie part. "Put these nylons over your face. No hands are allowed during this game or you will be disqualified. Each team has ten bottles of water set up. Your goal is to knock down all ten bottles by swinging your head and hitting them with the ball. The timer will be set to one minute and the team with the most pins knocked down wins. Ready, set, bowl!"

While the concept seems easy, Graham and I struggle to keep our balls from tangling with each other's stocking. I work on the right side of the lined up pins and get three down almost instantly. Yes! Graham gets two down, and I focus on the others but end up just hitting myself with the ball.

The buzzer buzzes and Donna announces that she and Germain are the winners. We play a few more rounds of games until the clear winners are decided—Nic and Penny.

"Good job, you guys," I say in congratulations.

"Thank you," Penny says happily. "But I can't wait until I watch you all get pied."

Nic retreats into the kitchen and comes back with four disposable tin pie shells filled with whipped cream. Penny pies me and Graham, while Nic takes care of his parents.

"Ugh!" I yip as Penny rubs the shell farther into my face for added emphasis. I lick my lips and gather cream on my fingers to eat. "Delicious." My words come out a mumbled slur, making everyone chuckle. Pictures are snapped of our messy faces and more laughter erupts over the silliness.

Graham pulls me to him and swipes his tongue down the side of my face to eat more whipped cream. "You taste," he says, making his eyebrows wiggle, "almost as amazing as—"

"Stop!" I hiss, smacking him on the arm.

He looks so bizarre with cream stuck in his eyelashes and some smeared on his shirt. I glance over at his parents and laugh as Germain helps his wife clean up with a wash-cloth and towel.

"Well, Penny, it's time to get you back to the facility for the evening rounds and your group session," Germain says sadly. "We need to be on the tarmac within the hour." Turning to Graham, he gives his son a smile. "Thanks again for chartering the jet for us. It's a way easier commute compared to the eight-hour trip I've taken in the past."

Graham nods. "It's never a problem."

Penny turns to me and gives me a hug. "Nice meeting you, Angie." I squeeze her back and feel the pang of sadness in my chest. "Take care of my brother, please," she whispers so only I can hear. "He is a softy underneath his rough exterior."

"Of course," I say. And I agree with her. "I hope our paths cross again soon."

Graham and Nic say goodbye to their baby sister and walk out with Donna and Germain. I pad upstairs and get a head start on a much-needed shower. It only takes a few minutes for Graham to enter the bathroom and start undressing.

"Did you have fun today?" he asks, sliding the glass door to join me under the steamy spray of the water.

I wrap my arms around his back and lean my body into his. "I had the best day. Your family is terrific and fun."

"They really like you," he admits. I barely hear his words, and I wonder if they were meant for me or just himself.

I smile anyway. "I'm glad."

Graham washes my body tenderly and thoroughly before taking care of his own needs. He shuts off the water and wraps me in a giant towel. I brush my hair and wrap it up into a smaller towel to dry some more before I mess with it.

"We need to leave early in the morning," he says. His mind is elsewhere. Like he is here physically but mentally in a different place.

"Is everything okay?" I ask, even though I know it's not. Not at all. I slip on a comfortable pajama set and look at him for a reaction, searching for any indication of his plan.

"It will be."

"You have no intention of telling me what is going on?"

"No."

I don't argue. What is the point? His mind is already made up. With choosing to be his girlfriend, I have to learn when to fight and when to let things be. And right now, I know I cannot win.

When I get back into the bedroom, I see Graham's retreating back out the door. "Where are you going?" I call out.

"I need to check in with my men outside."

"Have they been out there the entire time?"

"Yes," he says flatly.

"What about Thanksgiving?"

He turns to look at me, propping his hand up on the door frame. "What about it?"

"I know we celebrated it a day early, but what about tomorrow? Don't they want to spend time with their own families?"

"Angela, they're getting paid well to do their jobs. And sometimes their jobs fall over a holiday." He shrugs. "So be it."

I frown over his words. Why do they need to be out

there anyway? Is he really worried that Mark is going to jump out from behind a tree and scare us? Surely we are safe here, of all places.

"Go lie down," he says passively. "Take a nap. Relax. I'll be back soon."

I nod and climb up into bed, pulling the comforter over me for warmth.

My eyes grow heavy from the activity of the day, and I close them just for a second until Graham comes back.

33

I wake up the next morning naked, with the sun beaming rays of warmth over the bed. I roll to my side and feel hands wrap around my midsection.

"Good morning." His voice is full of need. "How did you sleep?"

I stretch and let out an exaggerated yawn. "Really well. Despite you waking me up three separate times." My eyes meet his, and the slightest bit of sadness is visible through his filter of happiness. It is subtle, but I have been able to pick up on this pattern with him.

"Good. Because I want you worn out and wanting me for the rest of the day."

I swallow hard. Pretty sure my body is already worn out from last night, but I am not one to complain. He shimmies down my body, trailing his mouth along for the ride. He licks my core in long laps, spreading his tongue out as far as he can to increase the surface area. I attempt to push my legs closed at the extreme sensations, but his hands hold me wide open for him.

"Hmm, so pretty and pink," he coos, sucking at my most sensitive spots, before inserting his tongue inside my opening.

If pussies can blush, I think mine just did under his attention.

I moan as he fucks me with his tongue. My hands squeeze fistfuls of sheets, as I grind my teeth and submit to the pleasure. He uses just his mouth on me, and it is divine. I thrust my hips upward to match his rhythm, and when I can't take anymore, I arch my back and grind myself onto his mouth as an orgasm overtakes me.

"Delicious," he says, crawling back up my body. "Here, taste." He kisses my lips long and hard, biting a bit at my flesh. "I'm going to miss this."

What is he talking about? I push him back so I can look into his eyes. "Miss it?"

He studies my face and then turns away so he can nuzzle my neck, completely ignoring my question.

I want to ask for clarification, but he is distracting me with his cock, rubbing up and down my wet slit. I want him. He knows it. The sexual need I have for him outweighs my curiosity. I reach down between us and grab his shaft. He feels so huge in my hand. I can almost get my thumb and middle finger to connect as they curl around him. Almost. I pump him a few times and then roll us over so I can be on top. Graham lets me do what I want, and I take this moment of control as a small victory. I roll my shoulders back and lift my hips up off him so that I can slide down to the base of him. I wiggle my butt and adjust to his size.

"Temptress," he says between his teeth.

"You feel so good."

When I am not cringing from the fullness and have stretched out a bit, I begin to move. Up and down, up and down…

Graham's hands dig into my waist and he helps to facilitate my movements, thrusting his own hips upward as I slide downward. My breasts bounce with the rhythm, and I feel feminine and free. It is a powerful combination.

I toss my hair over my shoulders and circle my hips, as I grind my bottom down on his groin. The only sound in the room is that of his fleeting curse words. Graham removes a hand from my hip and toys with my clit with the pad of his thumb. It's like he sets off my detonator.

I throw my head back and scre—

"Mumpff!"

Graham's hand flies over my mouth, cupping it and muffling my noise. He thrusts up one last time for his own release, his face distorted with pleasure. I flop forward and regret allowing him to slip out by my sudden move. He waits until I am done with my high before releasing my mouth.

"You're going to let everyone in this house know you belong to me. Do you want that?"

"They already know."

"You want to be experiencing the walk of shame while we say our goodbyes today?"

I giggle into his neck. "Pretty sure they know we are together after they saw how enchanted you are by my mad skill in family style games."

Graham breaks out into a half laugh. "It was hard carrying the team."

"Yeah, carried us straight to the losers' couch."

We lie beside each other and giggle over the rehash of yesterday's games. I loved seeing Graham in a different light. Watching him with his family and really relaxing has given me another puzzle piece to add to my collection; slowly, I am learning more about the man who has me so enchanted.

I look down between our entangled legs and feel the moisture leaking from me. He rolls out of bed and scoops me up into his arms like a baby.

"Let's take a quick shower and then we have to go."

"Are you going to tell me where we're going?" I pry. "For how long?"

His body stiffens under mine. "No."

"How do you know that I even want to go wherever we are going? You know I have class, right?"

He ignores my questions. It annoys me more than just a one-word answer. What the hell is going on? Is he taking us on a vacation? A trip someplace to rejuvenate?

When the water is heated, Graham places me on my feet.

"Get started without me, I need to make a phone call."

He turns and walks out of the bathroom. I stand under the steady flow and close my eyes as the water pelts off my face. I must be daydreaming, because I don't even notice the sound of Graham joining me until shampoo is squirted into my hair and massaged into my scalp.

"You are so freaking beautiful," he mutters softly, kissing down my spine.

I turn to look up at him and can see the heaviness in his eyes.

"Graham?"

He holds my hands and studies my face—like he is trying to memorize all my features. "Hmm?"

"You're really scaring me," I whisper.

"I'm working at fixing all of the mess that is trying to pull us apart. Trust me. Please."

I nod my head slowly. "I do trust you." Which is foolish considering how many lies and half-truths he has told. But, deep down, I know he will not hurt me.

Fact is, I don't really have set plans until classes are back in person. The university gives students a long fall break, and for a lot of the seniors, an even longer break—with the assumption that students will be working on their final projects independently. I don't have to technically return until after next week. It also helps that I have a decreased workload this time around. However, if I don't have ample progress made on Dr. Williams's research article, I might as well say goodbye to my dream of being an investigative journalist. The stress over this final paper is making me a bit desperate.

We finish up in the shower, dry off, and get dressed. It is officially Thanksgiving day but Graham is on a mission to leave—why the rush, I have no idea.

I slip on a simple charcoal sweater dress and pair it with black tights and ballet flats. Graham slips on jeans and a gray-and-black striped sweater. When we make our way downstairs, bags and luggage in hand, Donna and Germain are in the kitchen packing food into containers with lids.

"I'm sending you back with some leftovers. No need to worry about returning the containers. I have plenty."

"Thank you," I say with a forced smile.

"Thanks, Mom."

"Now, when will I see you guys again?" she asks, giving Graham a serious look. "Will you be able to come back for Christmas? No more trips to Europe, I hope."

"I'll let you know soon," Graham appeases. "Promise."

She seems to accept his noncommittal answer and walks over to give him a huge hug and kiss on the cheek. Then she moves to me and embraces me in her warm arms. It feels more than just a hug. There is so much emotion and understanding transpiring between us.

"It was really nice spending the past couple of days here," I say softly, trying to keep my voice from cracking with tears. "Thank you for welcoming me and allowing me to stay."

Donna pulls back to look at me. "My dear, it was a pleasure to meet the woman who has my son so smitten." She then moves her attention to Graham. "Son, do *not* mess this up. I like her. Don't ruin this for me."

I laugh over her bluntness. She is a spitfire.

He sighs and nods. "I'll try not to." Then he looks at me and mouths, "awkward," which causes me to smirk.

"We mean it," Germain chimes in. "Do not jack this up, son. We already consider Angie family."

I smile as my eyes water. It feels amazing to be wanted, just as I am. We give another round of hugs and exit out the front door into the chilly morning air. A group of ten men is standing around four black SUVs—all with tinted windows.

I look up at Graham in confusion. "Why so many?"

"For safety purposes."

"What do you think is going to happen from your parents' house to the penthouse?"

His eyes darken to navy steel. "I'm done taking any chances when it comes to protecting you from this mess that we are both wrapped up in."

"Where is Nic?" I scan the group of men to see if I can find him in the crowd.

"He left earlier this morning. Something came up. He wanted to say goodbye to you and touch base, but it just wasn't possible."

I watch as Graham places the paper bag of leftovers into the trunk of the third SUV in the lineup. He then puts our belongings inside and opens the back passenger door for me. I look out the window as I sit by myself in the empty backseat. Graham talks with his men, and based on the amount of nods they give back to him, I assume he is rattling off a bunch of orders.

Graham may have been a nerd when he was in high school and college, but there is nothing nerdy about him now. He is authoritative. Direct. He fits the role of a powerful businessman like he was born into the position. He makes decisions with unwavering confidence, and anyone stupid enough to go against his demands probably doesn't understand the magnitude of his wrath.

And he is mine.

Took me long enough to realize it. Took me even longer to accept it. And here I sit in the back of his SUV awaiting my fate.

The sound of the back door opening startles me from my thoughts.

"Come here," he says softly, widening his arm so I can join him on his side. He straps me into the center seat and kisses my forehead. Then he reaches into the back flap of the seat in front of him and pulls out a gold box with the word "Jealousy" embossed across the top. "I love you so much. You know that, right? No matter what happens after today, just know that I love you."

I look up into his pained eyes. What the hell is going on? It's like he is saying goodbye and I love you all in one breath, wrapped into this single moment in time. He removes the lid on the box and reveals a beautiful platinum and diamond bracelet that is shaped like a ribbon tied into a beautiful bow. He gently picks up my hand and massages his thumbs along my wrist.

"It is engraved on the inside with the date and exact time we met. It was that moment by the pool that I realized life would never be the same. You have completely turned my world upside down. You make me dizzy, sweetheart."

I give him a sheepish look. "Sorry."

"It is worth every struggle and every wrinkle you have given me the past three months."

I give him a weak smile. There is such sadness and finality in his words. Like he is expressing his love for me but also breaking up with me.

"I love you too."

It always feels sad saying those words. Mainly because the last person I said them to has left my life too soon. I haven't even said them to my dad since the accident. I was too afraid of the curse that those three words bring to my life. But that is the thing about Graham. He is the wrecking ball my life needed. He breaks down all my walls—even ones that I have reinforced with years of shutting people out.

"You are a gift to me, Angela McFee," he says softly. "One of the rarest and purest things in my life."

"Graham…"

The car starts to move, and I don't even recall anyone entering the driver's seat. I glance up ahead and see the side profile of a man I don't even recognize. I turn my attention back to Graham as he secures the elegant band onto my wrist. It is so unique and pretty. The perfect fit to a wrist that is not accustomed to wearing much jewelry.

"I also got you these," he says, pulling out another box from the backseat panel. "But you'll have to save them."

"I, umm…"

"What's the benefit of having a boyfriend who owns a jewelry company if not to let him spoil you with custom-made jewelry? Seems silly to not at least allow him to have some fun too."

He opens a similar looking box, but one that is much smaller, to reveal a stunning pair of dangle heart earrings that sparkle even in the dark backseat of the SUV. The style matches that of the bracelet, and they make the perfect set.

"These are so beautiful," I say, touching the piercing studs that I have in my ears from when Logan pierced me. They are a definite upgrade to my current assembly line creations.

"They are one of a kind, just like you are. However, I want you to follow Logan's protocol to avoid any risk of infection and save these for when it's safe to change them out."

"Okay…" But why is he giving them to me now, when he could have just waited for another time to show them to me?

"I even took your advice on the creation of them and followed through with the 3D printing—which is now being implemented into our standard protocol."

A sense of pride beams from the smile I can't keep contained. He listens. Despite having daily power struggles when it comes to my safety, Graham respects my opinion and never makes me feel inferior.

He kisses me gently on the lips. "I need you to know that everything I do over the next twenty-four to forty-eight hours is to protect you."

"I deserve some type of explanation, don't you think?"

I wait for Graham to say something—some type of answer. But that's all I do; I wait. Feeling my anxiety spike, I pull back from him and look out the window for the first time since departing from his parents' house. I lost track of time and of my surroundings. Have we been driving for twenty minutes? Forty?

"What is happening? What are you going to do?" I ask again, this time my tone infused with frustration.

The car comes to a stop in front of a metal gate that requires a code to gain access. The driver punches in the numbers on the keypad and then drives through the opened gate up a winding driveway. He parks in front of a house that looks more like a fortress than someone's residence.

"I'm going to do the one thing you will hate me for."

My forehead gets a chaste kiss, as tears roll down my cheeks. Every emotion is bundled into this very moment.

"What will I hate you for, Graham?"

"For taking away your freedom."

Follow Angie and Graham's story in *Taste of Addiction*, as their journey continues.

ACKNOWLEDGMENTS

To the bookstagram and online community: Thank you for all of the likes/shares/comments/saves for my material. Finding the bookish community online has been life-changing. I met so many amazing people along the way. Through the laughs and the struggles, you all have encouraged me to keep pushing forward to following my dreams. Thank you.

To my beta readers: Thank you for enthusiastically showing interest in this series. So many of you have rooted for me since the beginning and your support has been amazing. I am so excited that you fell in love with Angie and Graham!

To my husband and children: Thank you for always cheering me on, helping me to not obsess, and listening to me during my monologues over this series. I struggled with confidence at times, and you all managed to help me rebuild it.

To my friends and family: Thank you for being the sounding board I needed, when I needed it the most. Your support means so much to me, and this journey has been made better because of all of you. Thank you for listening to me ramble on about book covers and marketing strategies. Your advice and opinions have been influential for me getting these books launched, and I am forever grateful.

To Andrea R., Jenni R., Kristen L., Jen B.: Thank you for going above and beyond in helping me get these books ready for publishing. I appreciate your honesty and your suggestions. I am so excited to see you holding my book babies in your hands!

To Ann S. and Ann R. (Happily Editing Anns): Thank you for helping me to grow as an author. I never feel like I am bothering you with questions over my books. I just want to soak up all of your knowledge and to continue to improve my writing. You both have exceeded my expectations with your attention to detail—something I really respect. Your kind guidance has helped me to feel proud over my work. For that I truly thank you.

ABOUT THE AUTHOR

Victoria Dawson is the creator of books with fiery heroines and possessive heroes. She thrives on writing stories that transcend the minds of readers, allowing them to get lost in the journey to love—and all the drama that entails. Prior to delving heart first into the romance writing world, she taught middle and high school students mathematics for ten years.

Victoria is a unique combination of hopeful realist and hopeless romantic. She is an iced coffee connoisseur, a reality TV enthusiast, and a habitual wearer of stretchy pants. If she is not chasing after her three active children, she is often found scouring social media for her next book boyfriend.

Having grown up in an itty-bitty town in Pennsylvania, Victoria is a little bit country. She currently resides in Maryland with her family.